"YOU'VE BEEN STUDYING ME, NARI?"

She met his gaze without flinching. "Of course."

He didn't like that. Not at all. She wasn't even trying to be coy or discreet. "I'm sure your HDD handlers appreciate that."

She rolled her eyes. "They're your handlers, too. I've never hidden the fact that I would've disbanded the team if you had gone off the deep end, and you've been right on the edge several times. But you can't say I haven't helped, or even been loyal."

True. Most shrinks would've shut down the team the first time they saw the dog drunk or Wolfe with a kitten sleeping in his jacket pocket.

"Enough," he barked, the sound echoing around the room as he fought her stubbornness and his raw desire. "For once, tell me the truth, Zhang. Why the hell are you with this sad little group of agents nobody else wants? We really can't be that large a threat to the HDD."

She drew back. "It doesn't really matter, does it? We're both here and have a job to do, unless you go off the deep end again. Then it'll be over for us all."

DRIVEN

REBECCA ZANETTI

ZEBRA BOOKS
KENSINGTON PUBLISHING CORP.
www.kensingtonbooks.com

First Printing: February 2021
ISBN-13: 978-1-4201-5301-9
ISBN-10: 1-4201-5301-3

ISBN-13: 978-1-4201-5302-6 (eBook)
ISBN-10: 1-4201-5302-1 (eBook)

10 9 8 7 6 5 4 3 2 1

Printed in the United States of America

This one's for Tori Younker, who has provided endless hours of entertainment and pride for all of us watching her play basketball. She's an inspiration, and I can't wait to see what the future holds for her. (She also can't read this book until she's twenty-one.)

Acknowledgments

A heartfelt thank you to Tony Zanetti, Gabe Zanetti, and Karlina Zanetti—you're the best family in the world, and I love you all;

Thank you to Jim Dorohovich, who came up with the perfect name for this series;

Thank you to my hardworking editor, Alicia Condon;

Thank you to the rest of the Kensington gang: Alexandra Nicolajsen, Steven Zacharias, Adam Zacharias, Ross Plotkin, Lynn Cully, Vida Engstrand, Jane Nutter, Lauren Vasallo, Lauren Jernigan, Kimberly Richardson, and Rebecca Cremonese;

Thank you to my wonderful agent, Caitlin Blasdell, and to Liza Dawson and the entire Dawson group, who work so very hard for me;

Thank you to Jillian Stein for the absolutely fantastic work and for being such an amazing friend;

Thanks to my fantastic street team, Rebecca's Rebels, and their creative and hardworking leader, Anissa Beatty;

Thanks also to my constant support system: Gail and Jim English, Debbie Smith, Stephanie and Don West, Jessica and Jonah Namson, Kathy and Herb Zanetti, and Liz and Steve Berry.

Prologue

Thunder bellowed a distant warning while the wind rustled dried leaves along the lake path. Angus Force stumbled over an exposed tree root and somehow righted himself before falling on his ass. Again. The mud on his jeans proved he'd slipped at least once.

Roscoe snorted and kept scouting ahead, his furry nose close to the rocky trail. His snort held derision.

"Shut up," Angus said, surprised his voice didn't slur. He'd started the morning with his fishing pole and two bottles of Jack. Several hours later, it was getting dark, he had no fish, and the bottles were empty. The forest swirled around him, the trees dark and silent. He glared at his German shepherd. "Be nice or I won't feed you."

The dog didn't pause in his explorations. His ears didn't even twitch.

Angus sighed. "I should've left you with the FBI." Of course, the dog had a slight problem with authority and would've been put down at some point. Angus brightened. They had that in common. "All right. I guess I'll feed you."

Roscoe stopped suddenly.

Angus nearly ran into him, pausing at the last second and slipping on the leaves. "What the hell?"

The fur on Roscoe's back ruffled, and he stared straight ahead down the trail. He went deadly silent, his focus absolute.

Angus dropped his pole and the sack containing the bottles. Damn it. He hadn't brought a gun this morning. He'd been more concerned with having enough alcohol to get through the day.

He gave a hand signal to the dog and veered off the trail, winding through a part of the forest he could navigate blindfolded. The scents of fresh pine and dead leaves commingled around him, centering his focus. He approached his solitary cabin from the side, where he could see front and back.

Roscoe kept at his side, his ears perked, fur still raised.

The woods around them had gone silent, and a hint of anticipation threaded the breeze. Roscoe sat and stared at the cabin.

Yeah. Angus remained still. There was definitely somebody inside. He angled his head to study a black Range Rover parked on the south side of the cabin. They weren't trying to stay hidden.

His shoulders relaxed and he waited.

Waiting was what he excelled at. Well, waiting and drinking. He'd become a master at downing a bottle of whiskey. Or several.

Ten minutes passed. Something rustled inside the cabin. Now he was just getting bored. So he gave Roscoe a hand signal.

Roscoe immediately barked three times.

The front door of the cabin opened, and two men strode out. Government men. Black suits, pressed shirts, polished shoes. The older one had a beard sprinkled with gray and the worn eyes of a guy who'd already seen too much.

The younger guy was a climber. One who stood like he was on his way to the top and had no problem stepping on bodies to get there. The shoes were expensive, the blue silk tie even more so.

Angus crossed his arms. "You're trespassing, assholes." Was it a bad sign he could sound and feel sober after the amount he'd imbibed all day? Yeah. Probably.

The older man watched the dog. The younger man kept his gaze on Angus.

The older guy was obviously the smarter of the two.

The younger guy smoothly reached into his jacket pocket, withdrew his wallet, and flipped it open. "Special Agent Thomas Rutherford of the HDD." His voice was low and cultured. Confident. He was probably about Angus's age—in his early thirties.

"You're lost," Angus returned evenly.

"No. We're looking for you, FBI Special Agent Angus Force," Rutherford said, his blue eyes cutting through the space between them.

"I'm retired." A true statement, which had made nosing around lately a little difficult. However, obviously he'd shaken something loose, considering these guys were now standing on his front porch.

The older guy cocked his head. "That's a tactical Czech German shepherd," he said thoughtfully.

Angus lifted an eyebrow. "Nope. He's a mutt. Found him last week in a gully." Was he drunk, or did Roscoe send him an irritated canine look? Angus jerked his head at the older man. "You are?"

The guy also took out a wallet to flash an HDD badge. "HDD Special Agent Kurt Fields." Rough, with an edge of the street—no culture there.

Angus crossed his arms. "There is nothing the Homeland Defense Department could possibly want with me." The agency was an offshoot of Homeland Security; one of the offshoots the public didn't really know about. The name alone made it easy to divert funds. "Go away."

Agent Rutherford set his hands in his expensive pockets in an obvious effort to appear harmless. "We'd like a few minutes of your time."

"Too bad." Angus would like another drink. They stood between him and his bottles. That was a bad place to be.

Agent Fields had a hangdog expression. He finally looked away from Roscoe and focused on Angus. "We know you've been contacting witnesses from the Henry Wayne Lassiter cases."

Heat flushed down Angus's spine. "The last person who said that name to me got a fist in the face and a broken nose."

"We're aware of that fact," Rutherford said. "FBI Special Agent in Charge Denby still has a bump on that nose."

Yeah, well, his former boss had known better. Angus shrugged.

Agent Fields tried again, his gruff voice matching his weary eyes. "We just want to talk."

"No," Angus said softly. "You're here to warn me off a case I was just playing around with." If they hadn't shown up, he would've probably chalked up the scenario of Lassiter still being alive to a ghost theory, but now that they were here, he was inspired. Finally. "I know something is up and I'm not going to stop until I know what." He'd been a good tracker for the Behavioral Science Unit until that case, and then he'd fucking lost everything. Maybe even his mind. "A source reached out and told me Lassiter isn't really dead." Yeah, he'd shot the lunatic, and blood had sprayed. But he'd been shot as well, and he'd passed out before being able to check the body for a pulse. Apparently his recent nosing around had ruffled some feathers.

Rutherford smiled, showing perfectly straight white teeth. The guy probably had them bleached. "We understand that an old file clerk contacted you, but you have to understand that the FBI had just forced Miles Brown into retirement and he was trying to make trouble by reaching out to you and drumming all of this up. He apparently succeeded. Lassiter is dead and you killed him."

Apparently the HDD still wanted to keep secret the fact that one of the most prolific serial killers in history had been a low-level computer tech for the agency. Why? Who the hell cared?

Miles Brown had been a great recordkeeper, and the only thing his message had said was that there was a problem with the Lassiter file and for Force to call him immediately. "Fine. Then let me talk to Miles." His phone number had been disconnected and, so far, Angus had been unable to find the old guy.

Agent Fields winced, his salt-and-pepper eyebrows drawing down. "Miles Brown suffered a stroke and is in St. Juliet's on the east side of DC. He has no family, so we put him up."

That would explain why Force couldn't get to him. "I'd like to see his office and all of his records."

"His office was cleared out," Fields said, clasping his gnarled hands together. "Per procedure. Nothing out of the ordinary there."

Right. Except that Miles had called, and there had been a sense of urgency in his voice. "Yet you're here," Angus murmured.

Agent Rutherford sighed, looking as if a bartender had served him too many olives in his martini. "We know you've been through an ordeal, but—"

"Ordeal?" Angus growled. "Are you kidding me?" He'd give anything for his gun.

Fields held up an age-spotted hand. "We're very sorry for your loss, but this is important."

Loss? Had he really just said the word "loss" to him? Angus took two steps toward the agents, and Roscoe kept pace with him, low growls emerging from his gut. "Leave. Now." Angus still hadn't dealt with the fact that a serial killer had murdered his sister . . . and it was Angus's fault. Loss didn't cover it. Not by a long shot.

Rutherford eyed the dog warily. "We want you to stop pursuing the issue. Lassiter is dead. Let him lie."

Angus snorted. Roscoe remained at attention but stopped growling. "Why are you here, then? If the case was really closed, you wouldn't bother." Homeland Security had barely been able to shut down news of Lassiter's former employment before it became public. Of course the agency wanted this dropped.

Fields shuffled his feet, his gaze descending to his scuffed shoes.

Angus straightened. His gut churned and his instincts flared to life. "Say what you need to say."

Rutherford swallowed and looked toward the older Fields.

Fields sighed and glanced up again, experience stamped hard on his square-shaped face. "Let it go. We're not going to give you a choice."

Ah, shit. Lassiter really was alive. No way would two HDD agents have sought him out if he wasn't getting close to something. Or maybe they were really afraid he'd let the public know about Lassiter's former employment. Governmental agencies had definitely taken a beating lately in the press, and Homeland Security wanted to keep HDD under wraps.

Angus stood perfectly still, his mind focusing despite the booze. "Well, then. We all know you don't want me talking to the press. I guess, for now, that gives me leverage." Just how much? How worried were they?

Their silence gave him even more confidence. It also urged him to pursue that nagging feeling at the back of his neck that had never really left. The Lassiter case had never felt . . . finished. Sometimes his instincts were all he had. Well, his instincts and his dog. What else did a burned-out, obsessive, drunk of an ex-FBI agent really need?

He rubbed his jaw and let whiskers scrape his palm. "Let's see. Either I work on this myself, along with a couple of really good investigative journalists I befriended during my years with the FBI, or you give me the resources to do a little investigating and I keep everything to myself. That seems fair."

The wind tousled Rutherford's blond hair, and he scoffed. "Not a chance."

"Bull," Angus returned instantly, reading the men. Oh, they were seasoned and pretty good, but he hadn't lost all his abilities. "Try again."

Fields shot a hand through his thick hair, making the gray stand up through the brown. "You know we can't have you at HDD looking into a closed FBI case."

Fair enough. "You could have me at HDD working on other cases while simultaneously pursuing this one." Before either agent could deny him, Angus sweetened the pot. "I'll compile a team, stay under the radar, and do what I need to do. Come on. You two look like tough negotiators. I'm sure we can come to an agreement without my having to call the media."

"Lassiter is dead," Rutherford gritted out between perfect teeth.

Angus shrugged. "Then you have nothing to lose. You do, however, have everything to gain, and I'll do my best to toe the line." There was no doubt the HDD would try to get rid of him the second he set foot in an HDD office. Even so, he couldn't give this up. He looked down at the dog. "Wanna go back to work, boy?"

Chapter One

One year later

The swirl of red and blue lights exposed the taut crime scene tape in a back alley outside of DC. Rain blasted down, pinging off battered metal garbage bins at the rear of businesses long since closed for the night. The bastard had dumped the victim near a pile of litter the rain had mangled into a sopping mess of paper and take-out cartons.

Angus kept his face stoic as he ducked under the tape and flashed his badge to the uniformed officer blocking access. It felt good to show the badge, even though he worked better without it, apparently.

It would be the only good feeling of the night, without question.

HDD Special Agent Kurt Fields was the first one to reach him, skirting several numbered yellow evidence markers placed on the wet asphalt. The guy was pale and had grown even grizzlier in the year they'd worked together. Kind of worked together. "I heard the call go out, got the details, and figured you'd be here on this fine Monday night." His T-shirt was wrinkled and his brown shoes scuffed. He grimaced. As an HDD handler, he wasn't bad. "The locals don't want us at the scene, just so you know."

"The FBI will take over soon enough." Unless there was a way HDD could force itself in, which didn't seem possible. Federal agencies rarely played well together, regardless of the party line. Force straightened, acutely aware of his men at his back. West and Wolfe had both seen some rough shit in their time, but this was something new. He needed West's mind clear to run the office for now, but when he turned his head to issue an order, West was already shaking his head at him, his gaze direct. No way would he be left behind.

The guy would make a good profiler. Angus had never known an undercover operative who could inhabit another identity as completely as West.

Angus turned back around and started to focus, speaking as much to himself as to his team. "Everything is relevant. Anything out of place on a piece of garbage, any scratch on a building, any glint of something shiny."

Agent Fields shook his head, sliding to the side and putting his barrel of a body between Angus and the scene. "You're not understanding me. This is not your case. Hell, it isn't even *our* case. Never will be."

Fire ripped through Angus so quickly, his ears burned like he'd been touched with a poker. "Lassiter killed this woman, which makes this my case. Period." He had to get to the body to make sure, but his gut never lied.

Special Agent Tom Rutherford, his blond hair mussed for the first time, reached them next. For once Force's partner was not impeccably put together, although his too-blue eyes were as pissy as ever. "You're not supposed to be here. Neither are we."

"I still have some sources in law enforcement and was contacted immediately about the crime," Angus muttered, his hands itching for his gun. "Now get out of my way."

Rutherford had light stubble at his chin—a very rare sight. "Don't make me track down your source and fire them."

Angus turned his focus to the HDD agent. He'd look good with two black eyes again. "I'm working this scene—this is Lassiter. He's finally making a move."

"You're wrong. This scene isn't the same as all the others," Rutherford said, his eyes bloodshot.

Wolfe rocked back on massive boots. "What do you mean?"

Rutherford slid a manicured hand into the pocket of his perfectly creased dress pants. Who dressed up for a crime scene at midnight? "I've studied your old case files on Henry Wayne Lassiter. His MO was unique. This crime scene is different."

Angus swallowed. "Where's the note?" The psychopath had always left him a note.

"No note," Fields said as the local techs moved around efficiently.

"Look again," Angus said evenly, his gut aching so bad he wanted to bend over and puke.

Rutherford planted a broad hand on his shoulder. His law school class ring dug into Angus's skin through his T-shirt. "Please leave before I have you escorted away."

Wolfe shoved Rutherford's hand off before Angus could grab it and break a finger or two.

Angus probably owed Wolfe for that. "There are two

options here. Either you get the hell out of our way so we can examine the scene, or we get in a fight, beat the shit out of the two of you, and then we go and examine the scene." His voice had lowered to a hoarse threat. Once the FBI showed up, he was definitely going to be thrown out of the alley. His exit from the agency hadn't been cordial.

Wolfe tensed next to him, while West drew up abreast, his shoulders back.

They were ready to fight with him if necessary. Angus would reflect on how much that warmed him later. His team was good. Better than good.

Rutherford smiled, no doubt wanting payback for when Raider, another team member, had broken his nose a few months ago. "I'm ready. You hit one of us, just breathe wrong on us, and I'll plant your ass in a jail cell. You're done, Force."

West cleared his throat, his green eyes piercing through the dark. "If you're so sure Lassiter didn't do this, give us a minute with the scene. Force will know the truth."

Rutherford began to shake his head.

"Okay," Fields said, stepping aside. He shrugged at his younger partner. "Why not? Lassiter is dead, right?"

"Right," Rutherford gritted, his gaze promising retribution.

The stench of puke, garbage, and worse filled Angus's nostrils as he stepped past the agents to venture deeper into the alley. "Lassiter kidnapped women and tortured them for days. We'll need an autopsy on this one, but we probably won't know much about her heart."

"Why not?" West stopped short as the body came into view.

"That's why," Angus said, consciously switching from feeling human to something else. Something that would allow him to analyze the crime and not lose his soul any more than he already had.

West's breath caught. "Oh."

Yeah. Oh. A tarp had been erected above the body to protect it from the elements. The woman lay naked on the pavement, her eyes open and staring straight up. She had long dark hair, milky brown eyes, a petite form. Her arms were spread wide, hands open and facing up. Her legs were crossed and tied at the ankles with a common clothesline rope. Worst yet, her chest gaped open, the ribs and breastbone spread, leaving a hole. The crime signature was similar to Lassiter's, but not exactly the same. What did that mean?

West coughed. "Her heart is gone."

Angus went even colder. Rain dripped off his hair and down his face. The scene was . . . off. "He eats it. Says it keeps the victim with him forever." Nausea tried to roll up his belly and he shoved it down.

Wolfe came up on his other side, his movements silent. He didn't gasp, stall, or go tense. He just stared at the body, his jaw hard. He pointed to the victim's arms. "Burn marks?"

"Affirmative," Angus said crisply. "There will be both cigarette and electrical burns." Outside and inside the woman. "As well as whip marks, ligature marks around the neck, and knife wounds. Shallow and painful. Not enough to let her bleed out." Angus noticed that the cuts for the heart were rough—not smooth, the way Lassiter liked to do—which was why the press had dubbed him "the Surgeon."

Yet the heart was gone.

West coughed. "Raped?"

"Probably," Angus said.

Agent Rutherford approached from the far end, carefully stepping over water-filled potholes with his shiny loafers. "There's no note, and she's not blond. In addition, the cigarette marks are too large—almost like a cigar was used." He looked around, as if worried they'd be caught working outside their jurisdiction. The Homeland Defense Department didn't deal with serial killers. Well, not usually.

Angus breathed in and out before responding. He much preferred Fields to this guy. "Lassiter is very choosy about his cigarettes and would never use a cigar. Too common." Angus dropped into a crouch, closer to the woman. Lassiter had also loved blondes. This close, the victim's skin looked dusky, not pale. Was she Asian? Lassiter had liked them pale, the whiter the better. "Are you sure there isn't a note?"

"No note," Rutherford snapped. "Told you it wasn't him."

Everything inside Angus insisted it was Lassiter. But was it a certainty born of necessity? Because he needed to be on the case and hunting the evil psycho down—finally? He looked around, noting the alley had been cordoned off, blocking the view of any nosy neighbors or the press. In a different situation he'd be fighting with Rutherford right now about the news media. It probably killed the guy that he couldn't chase the cameras. "Once you get an ID, track down her medical records."

"No ID," Rutherford said, glancing down at his shiny phone. "Her prints came up negative, and this isn't our case. Time to go, gentlemen."

Wolfe scouted the alley, his gaze sharp. "You think Lassiter did this?"

Yes. "I don't know. The MO is close, but not perfect, and he was a perfectionist." Frustration tasted like metal in Angus's mouth. "If it isn't Lassiter, it's a copycat. That I'm sure of, and I was the best profiler the FBI had."

"Until you drank the entire wagon," Fields said, his bushy eyebrows rising. "You no longer work for the FBI, remember?"

Something on the victim's hand caught Angus's attention. "Glove?" He gestured toward a couple of techs.

One tossed him a blue glove and he slid it on, gently turning over the woman's right hand.

"Shit," West said, leaning down. "Is that what I think it is?"

Angus swallowed. "Yeah." A perfect tattoo of a German shepherd had been placed right beneath the knuckles on the back of her hand.

Wolfe swallowed. "Looks like Roscoe."

"Could be a coincidence," West said, his lips turning down.

"Probably is." Angus stood. Oh, that was his dog; the markings were distinctive. "Fields? I want this case. Lassiter or not. FBI or not."

West gripped his arm and pulled him to the side. He leaned in to speak quietly. "Even if the FBI and HDD both allow it, are you sure you want this? Serial killers don't just change their MOs, right? Especially ones like Lassiter."

Angus nodded. "You're right."

"You're obsessive and you're just getting your drinking under control. If this isn't Lassiter, and that tattoo is a coincidence, why take on HDD, the FBI, and the local DC police force right now?" West released him, his gaze again straying to the poor woman on the ground.

Right now they were the best chance for justice the woman had.

Fields slid his phone back into his pocket. "The HDD higher-ups say no way to you taking on this case. Sorry. It's a no-go."

Angus turned on his heel and shoved his hands in his jeans pockets, striding down the alley. The rain increased in force, a cold, angry prelude to the dark, oncoming winter.

His team members flanked him.

Wolfe stepped over a puddle. "We're not letting this go, are we?"

"Not a chance in hell," Angus said. "Call everyone in. We have a new case." He ducked under the crime scene tape, walking away from death.

This time.

Chapter Two

Nari Zhang zipped her leather jacket as she stepped out of the Porsche, forcing a smile onto her face and leaning down. The crisp fall breeze lifted her hair. At least it had stopped raining after midnight. "Thanks for dinner, Ronald."

He angled to the side in the driver's seat, a lock of blond hair falling over his strong forehead. "Why don't you let me follow you home? Maybe come in for coffee?" His blue eyes were earnest in the dim light from the car.

Nari kept the smile in place, looking around the nearly deserted parking area of the seventies-style office building. Her new VW Bug waited for her beneath the one streetlight, which showed there were no predators close to her vehicle. "That's all right." She purposely didn't look at the large truck parked in the darkness closer to the building. Did Angus Force ever go home any longer?

Ronald reached for her hand. "I had a good time tonight. How about we meet up for another late dinner tomorrow? The senator's intelligence briefing should be done by ten, and I could pick you up around eleven. Okay? Very late dinner? Maybe dessert?" His voice lowered into a suggestive tone that was probably beyond sexy to most women on Capitol Hill, and his hand was large and warm around hers. In his dark sports jacket and red power tie, he looked as powerful as she knew the chief of staff for the Senate majority leader to be.

"Work is heating up, but I'll call you." She pulled her hand free and stepped away to shut the door. Ronald was intelligent and mature, and he'd bored her into glancing at her watch before the appetizers had been served. What was wrong with her?

His jaw tightened and he sped off, leaving her alone in the parking lot. Most women probably didn't turn him down.

Nari sighed, her gaze going to the darkened doorway of the old office building. Shadows danced across its face and over to the adjacent, desolate park. Thunder rolled in the distance, promising another late fall storm. Her bed called to her; it'd only take twenty minutes to drive home. And if she couldn't sleep, it was time she rearranged her kitchen, anyway. She needed things to be color coded.

The wind rustled the barren trees and leaves crackled. She shivered.

Yet she steeled her shoulders and strode across the wet, cracked concrete to the front door, which she unlocked with a scratched key. At some point she needed to learn not to beat her head against brick walls, but apparently this wasn't the night for that. Her boots clip-clopped across the dusty wooden floor of the deserted hallway to the rickety elevator. She said a quick prayer and stepped inside, hoping this wasn't the night it decided to just break free and crash to the basement.

It hitched and jerked, but finally the door opened to a

quiet, dark office. She fumbled for the switch and flipped on the yellow fluorescent lights in the vestibule, illuminating the bullpen with its empty desks.

Male muttering across the bullpen in Case Room One pulled her like a magnet. This was a mistake, but it was time somebody made it. Apparently she was the only one on the Deep Ops team willing to cross Angus Force right now.

Enough was enough.

The smell of whiskey caught her attention as she drew abreast of the doorway. Wonderful. He was drunk again.

She stepped inside to find Angus sitting with his boots on the conference table, staring at a whiteboard of mutilation and death. Papers were scattered across the table in no apparent order, as if he'd flung them across to see where they'd land. A half-empty bottle of Jack Daniel's rested on several manila file folders, no cup in sight.

Roscoe snored quietly over in the corner on a new blue bed she'd bought for him the week before.

"Angus. You have to stop this," she whispered.

He didn't flinch, no doubt having heard the elevator arrive. "Go home, Nari."

She wanted to go home, but she had a duty to the team, and it was time she finally did it. "I had the power to take you out of this position for the last year," she murmured, leaning against the doorjamb. "I haven't exercised it because I think the team works. But you're killing yourself, and I can't let that happen."

His chair swung around and his boots hit the floor as he turned to face her. The force of his gaze almost had her stepping back. His eyes were a clear green, deep and tortured. Her body took the hit from that look with a slow roll and shiver that had nothing to do with fear, and she could only study him in return, her nipples peaking like little traitors. Thick, dark hair curled around his ears and matched the scruff covering his stubborn jawline. In his ripped jeans and faded black T-shirt, he all but bellowed wounded bad boy who needed saving.

She snorted. "You're a cliché at this point." That didn't mean she couldn't save him. Yeah, she was as dumb as the rest of the women who were drawn to Angus Force, wanting to ease his pain. Oh, most of the team didn't know about the women who flocked to him, but she'd been watching him for months. Long, torturous months during which she'd tried to figure out the right thing to do for everyone while dealing with dreams nearly every night starring his hard body and firm mouth.

His lips turned down. "You're back early tonight. Another bad date?"

"No. It was lovely," she said, straightening.

He rolled those desperate green eyes. "Right. Either you're choosing the wrong guys to go out with or there's a demon from your past still chasing you."

Sometimes she forgot that he'd been one of the FBI's best profilers before his life had disintegrated—yet another intriguing facet to him. "Maybe both," she acknowledged, willing to give him that much. "At least I haven't stopped trying to live."

"Neither have I." He turned back to his murder board in a clear act of dismissal. "You ever wonder why we don't like each other?"

The continuation of conversation surprised her more than the pang in her heart at the words. "Because you're an asshole?" she burst out.

His chuckle was low and dark. "That's only part of it.

The other part, my pretty shrink, is that we see right through each other. To the soul."

She cocked her head, rising instantly to the unspoken challenge only she could hear while ignoring the possessive tone with nice compliment. "You don't like what you see? Somehow I don't think that's your problem with me."

"That's irrelevant," he murmured, the atmosphere relaxing slightly as he turned his focus from her to his obsession. "You're gonna want to stay off my radar and out of the way for now. Trust me."

Awareness ticked down her spine. She'd tried that tactic, and it hadn't worked. "No."

He stiffened, and the atmosphere in the room changed. Slowly, deliberately, he swiveled his chair once again. "Nari."

Her body went on full alert and she lowered her chin. "Such a reaction from a simple no. Don't tell me the entire team is so scared of you that they never defy you." Her voice emerged breathy and she cleared her throat.

He snorted, his expression not relenting in the least. "Are you nuts? Our team is full of hotheads who do nothing but defy me. Sometimes Wolfe defies the laws of physics."

True. The team was both ragtag and dangerous. She narrowed her focus to his clear eyes. "You haven't been drinking."

"No." He sat back, watching her.

This was new. He was using the bottle as a paper weight. "Why not?"

One of his dark eyebrows rose, the look oddly threatening. "I'd take offense at that, but I have been in a bottle lately. I stopped drinking an hour ago—at least for a while."

"Why?"

He sighed. "Because we just found the first body."

Angus Force had been around dangerous people his entire life and nobody compared to the woman reading him with midnight-dark eyes. For yet another failed date, she'd worn black slacks, shiny boots, a pink, silky-looking shirt, and a leather jacket that probably cost more than his apartment. Yet the clothing was nothing compared to the beauty of the woman herself. Long black hair, delicate features, compact body that was trained to fight. Her intelligence was enhanced by an almost mystical empathy for others.

It was too bad she was a complete pain in the ass, terrible at choosing men, and stubborn to the point that it was a huge character flaw. Worse yet, she was a fucking shrink.

He hated shrinks.

Worst of all, he didn't trust HDD operatives, and she worked for the agency, not for him. A fact he repeatedly forced himself to remember. If everything went to shit, and it always did, her loyalty wasn't to him, or even to the team. She could pull the plug on his one and only mission, and he couldn't let that happen.

Lassiter had to die this time. For certain.

She moved toward him, and the scent of cinnamon wafted his way. How in the world did she smell like cinnamon all the time? His mouth watered and his cock hardened.

"What do you mean, a body?" she asked, leaning over to study the notes scattered across the table.

He flipped open the nearest file folder to show a picture he'd shot with his phone earlier, banishing all thoughts of bending her over the table and taking what they both wanted. "New body, and I think Lassiter is the killer." His voice was confident, not revealing any doubt.

She swung her gaze to him. "You're not certain?"

He hated insightful shrinks. They always got too deep and screwed things up. "There are differences this time."

She pulled out a chair and sat, reaching for the manila file folder. Her scent surrounded him, and as her gaze focused on the notes, intelligence shone in them that was as sexy as her tight body. "I'm surprised you didn't call the whole team in."

He shrugged. "I did, but then we decided to meet first thing in the morning. I wanted some time with this first."

She stared at the picture of the victim. "Lassiter was obsessive and driven—he had his routine, never varied from it. He's dead, Angus. Stop chasing ghosts."

Angus sat straighter, his heart rate elevating. "That's not what I'm doing." Or was it? If Lassiter really was dead, he'd lose his team, and then he'd be alone again. After their recent successes, it was hard to believe the HDD would really shut them down.

She pushed the picture to the side to read his hastily scrawled notes. "Yes, it is, and we both know it."

Angus inhaled quickly and then smoothed out his expression. "Wrong."

"Right," she murmured, reaching for the photograph. "In a whole year you have found no evidence that Lassiter is alive because he is not. Even the clue that had you rushing across the country a couple of weeks ago turned out to be nothing." Her eyes softened as she studied the crime scene photo.

"I'm not wrong."

"This victim is different. She has dark hair and is petite. He liked blondes before, and they were often curvy and tall. I think the smallest victim was just under six feet tall, and she put up a good fight," she said.

Angus turned toward her. "You've studied the files."

She let the photograph of the brutalized victim slide out of her fingers. "Of course I've studied the files. I know as much about your case as you do, except I've concluded that Lassiter really is dead. There's no mystery or cover-up here. I've learned everything I can about your cases."

"As much about me?" His jaw hurt, so he tried to loosen it. Heat coated down his throat as he held on to control with both hands. The woman really had no idea who he was and what he wanted to do with her. To her. "You've been studying me, Nari?"

She met his gaze without flinching. "Of course."

He didn't like that. Not at all. She wasn't even trying to be coy or discreet. "I'm sure your HDD handlers appreciate that."

She rolled her eyes. "They're your handlers, too. I've never hidden the fact that I would've disbanded the team if you had gone off the deep end, and you've been right on the edge several times. But you can't say I haven't helped or even been loyal."

True. Most shrinks would've shut down the team the first time they saw the dog drunk or Wolfe with a kitten sleeping in his jacket pocket. "Why are you here? You're a first-rate shrink, whatever that means, and you're wasted here, just keeping an eye on me and the team. It's too low-level. Why take this on?" The question had kept him up at night, but he'd never really asked her.

For the first time she faltered. "The team needed me."

"Enough," he barked, the sound echoing around the room as he fought her stubbornness and his raw desire for the woman. Roscoe lifted his furry head, his German shepherd markings dark in the fluorescent lights. He blinked, must've decided all was well, and went back to sleep. "For once, tell me the truth, Zhang. Why the hell are you with this sad little group of agents nobody else wants? We really can't be that large a threat to the HDD."

She drew back. "It doesn't really matter, does it? We're both here and have a job to do, unless you go off the deep end again. Then it'll be over for us all."

Chapter Three

Nari scratched Roscoe's ears in her minuscule office as Adele crooned from the speakers of her computer. After a sleepless night she'd just given up the idea of resting and headed back to work, wearing her black jeans and a mint-green silk shirt. Dressing up had been too much effort, although her opal jewelry and tall boots made her feel put together.

Roscoe set his jaw gently on her thigh, closing his soulful brown eyes and sighing. His markings were dark across the lighter fur on his face, making him probably the most handsome German shepherd alive, in her opinion. At least he wasn't hung over.

"Did Angus drink that bottle last night after I left?" she whispered.

Roscoe opened one eye, looked at her, and then shut it again.

Oh, she didn't think the dog really understood her question, but sometimes Roscoe seemed almost human.

The whole team had gathered in the office this morning. Angus remained in the case room, obsessing over his obsession. At least he'd made it home to shower before showing up in yet another pair of ripped jeans and a dark tee that stretched across his wide chest. He'd given her one of those looks earlier that had made her want to both kiss him and punch him. How did he affect her like that?

Brigid Banaghan worked away in her computer room, no doubt running searches for Angus that would lead nowhere, while their new member, ex-journalist Dana Mulberry, conducted research on one of the free computers. Well, maybe not ex-journalist. There was no doubt Dana would take a story and freelance it, if an interesting one came up and was okayed by Angus.

In the middle of the office, testosterone reigned supreme. Malcolm West, Raider Tanaka, and Clarence Wolfe sat at their desks in the center hub, going through busy-work case files sent by the HDD brass. They were all dressed in jeans and dark, long-sleeved shirts, their normal uniform for the office.

Agent Millie Frost, their new Q, had disappeared into the storage room turned vault with her mysterious equipment. The blue streaks in her blond hair had faded to a light aqua and her face had finally lost its pinched look. Nari had given Millie time to get settled in and now she needed to set up a schedule with her for weekly counseling appointments, as she had with the rest of the team.

Except Angus Force. He wouldn't set foot in her office—a fact she appreciated. While she wanted to help him, the attraction between them wouldn't dissipate.

The elevator dinged, high and tinny. Roscoe stepped away and turned his head toward the door, while Nari straightened in her chair. "It's probably Jethro," she whispered. The British professor consulted with Angus; he'd just finished rehab on his leg after injuring it during an Op.

"What the fuck are you doing here?" Wolfe snapped loudly.

Nari sighed. All right. It wasn't Jethro.

Roscoe bounded out of the office and she stood to follow him, anxiety rippling through her with just enough of a bite to hasten her steps. She stopped short in her office doorway. Oh, crap.

HDD Special Agents Fields and Rutherford stood in the vestibule in front of the rickety elevator, while techs holding boxes sidled in behind them, quickly scouting the room. The techs were dressed in dust-resistant gray jump-suits, and one guy held a stack of more folded boxes.

"What's going on?" Nari asked.

Fields shrugged, chewing loudly on what sounded like hard candy. "We have orders."

Rutherford, for the first time, didn't smile at their mis-fortune. "I'm sorry to inform you that the Deep Ops team is hereby disbanded. Please hand over your badges and weapons. We'll box up the records, so no need to worry about that."

Angus stepped out of the case room, his expression frighteningly calm. "No."

Wolfe kicked back in his chair and plunked his overlarge boots on the desk in a relaxed pose that was anything but relaxed. Malcolm just stared at Rutherford, while Raider sighed, shaking his head.

Fresh rain dotted Rutherford's blond hair and his Armani suit. "You don't follow the rules, Force. Never have, and you never will. That gets people killed. I'm sorry about this."

The guy actually did sound sorry. Nari focused on him. Man, she'd like to get into his head. "I don't understand. What's happening?"

Everyone turned in one fashion or another to look at Angus.

His jaw hardened.

Fields sighed. "The deal was for one year for Force to find evidence that Henry Wayne Lassiter was alive, and that year was up last week. Your team is disbanded."

Raider leaned forward. "Are you nuts?"

"The team is a liability," Rutherford countered. "HDD is celebrating right now."

This was crazy. Why hadn't Force said anything? Hurt slithered through her, but she pushed emotion aside to deal with the situation. "On the contrary," Nari said, "we've saved a lot of lives with our cases. Shutting this team down is a bad idea."

Brigid emerged from the computer room, her red hair piled high on her head and irritation in her green eyes. Dana stepped up behind her, at least five inches taller than the Irish computer hacker. Dana's blond hair was in a ponytail and the flannel shirt she wore matched her pretty blue eyes.

Brigid's pale face flushed. "We're in the middle of several cases right now that were assigned by you. Where are we going to finish them?"

Agent Fields's hangdog brown eyes softened. "Nowhere, Agent Banaghan. The team is disbanded. You and Raider have new assignments."

The air went out of the room.

Rutherford turned toward Nari. "Same with you, Dr. Zhang. You've been reassigned."

All eyes focused on her.

"Wonderful," she snapped. How the heck was she going to keep this team together and employed? They really had done good. A lot of it. She scrambled to find a solution. "How long do we have a lease for this, um, office?" The place was depressing, but they had managed to spruce it up a little.

Rutherford shrugged. "Doesn't matter. We'll use it for something else."

Wolfe snorted, his bourbon-colored eyes piercing. "Right. Like you could talk anybody else into working in this crappy dump."

A tech with a box moved toward the hub, and Wolfe stiffened, lowering his chin. The guy stopped cold and looked toward Rutherford for help.

Nari cleared her throat. There had to be a way to get through this without anybody being punched in the face. "Everyone relax." What the heck were they thinking, just showing up in the midst of a volatile bunch of armed alpha males?

Her phone buzzed, and she looked down to scan an email telling her to report to headquarters in an hour. Her stomach dropped.

Fields cleared his throat, his gaze on Roscoe. "It's done, Agent Zhang. The deal was for a year." He turned and faced Angus across the bullpen. "In one year you haven't found one iota of proof to show that Henry Wayne Lassiter is alive, because he isn't. It's a fact, and it's time to move on."

"A body was found last night," Angus retorted, his thick,

dark hair mussed and his deep, green eyes glittering. "Most of the scene was a flashback to Lassiter's work."

Finally, Rutherford let a small smile lift the corner of his lip. "The Metro police have a guy in custody for last night's crime. Ex-boyfriend of the victim who thought that copying a serial killer would lead police in the wrong direction."

"I want to talk to him," Angus said, pushing away from the doorframe.

"You no longer work for the HDD," Rutherford returned. "Or the FBI. Or anybody, to be honest. Go back to your cabin in the Kentucky woods with your mentally challenged canine."

The temperature in the entire bullpen rose. Fast and hot.

Nari stepped closer to Roscoe and patted his head. He dropped his butt and sat, staring intently at the agents. "Insulting the dog is a big mistake, Agent," she murmured. Oh, the dog didn't understand, but Angus was two seconds from going for Rutherford's throat, and he could probably get across the room in a heartbeat.

Roscoe snarled.

Maybe he did understand. Nari dug her fingers into his fur to calm him. He was probably picking up on the high tension level in the room.

Fields motioned for the techs to get to work. "We should be done within a couple of hours."

"No." Angus's chin had the look of solid rock, and he strode toward the bullpen. "If you're kicking us out, that's fine. We'll go through our files and personal items and box everything up on our own."

Rutherford shook his head. "You know that's not how this works. Everything here is owned by the HDD and we'll break it down."

"I. Said. No." Angus stepped up to within a foot of the agents and crossed his arms.

In a movement that was as uniform as a choreographed dance, Wolfe, Malcolm, and Raider pushed away from their desks and fanned out behind Angus, big and strong. A solid wall of muscle and determination, all masking the surprise they must be feeling.

Brigid and Dana quietly disappeared back into the computer room, no doubt to start transferring files while they had the chance.

Nari stood in her doorway, her hand on the dog's head, watching the showdown. She could fight as well, if not better, than most agents, but which of them would she fight? The HDD had the law on their side, but the Deep Ops team had rights as well. In their own minds anyway.

The elevator hitched and burped, opening again with an even higher pitch. Dr. Jethro Hanson strode out, limping only slightly. He paused and took in the scene, his gaze landing on Angus. "Got your message, mate. Lassiter is alive?"

"No," Agent Rutherford bit out. "Not alive." He didn't turn to look at Jethro, but instead kept his gaze directed at Angus. "This department of the HDD is shut down, Professor. You can go back to your ivory tower and your new life away from danger. Godspeed."

One of Jethro's brown eyebrows lifted. "I see." The professor was in black slacks and a button-down shirt, with his dark blond hair ruffled by the rain. "Why do I feel like I've been pulled into *West Side Story*?"

Nari bit back a laugh. Why did sarcasm sound so much better in a British accent? "The Sharks and the Jets are about to stand down. All of them." If she didn't take control of the situation, blows would soon be thrown. "I don't have bail money for anybody, so here's what's going to happen."

She waited for everyone's attention to turn to her before continuing. "Agents Rutherford and Fields, you will take your workers back to headquarters while leaving the boxes. We will box up anything that belongs to HDD and just take our personal items home. In the meantime, because I've been ordered to headquarters today, I'm going to meet with my superiors and try to get an extension on that year. Or perhaps find another deal."

Angus's chin lifted. "Deal?"

She swallowed. "The Lassiter case is finished, Angus. He's dead. However, this team has prevented bombings, taken down part of the Mob, solved murders, and destroyed a heroin pipeline. We might be unconventional, but we've done our jobs, and the team should be able to continue its good work."

"'Unconventional' is an understatement," Fields said, reaching in his pocket for another cough drop. He slowly unwrapped it, taking in the situation. "You do understand that we could have SWAT teams here in a second to clear you out?"

Raider cocked his head, his black eyes confident. "Sure. We could also have every news outlet in the DC area here just as fast. Think of the footage they'd get."

"I'd rather just hit somebody," Wolfe drawled, his broad hands at his sides. "Whoever's still standing after the fight wins?"

"That gets my vote," Angus said grimly.

Malcolm tugged on his dark gray shirt. "Pippa hates it when I come home bloody. I vote for Nari's plan."

"That's two to two," Wolfe said helpfully. "British dude? Jet? What sayeth you?"

Jethro scratched his head. "I could go a round or two."

Nari's mouth gaped open. She'd expected the opposite answer. "Wait a minute."

Wolfe cracked his knuckles. "Raider? You wanna fight and give Rutherford another black eye?"

"Nope," Raider said easily. "Nari's idea is better."

"Wait," Dana called from the back of the office. "I vote no violence."

Wolfe sighed. "Brigid? Get your Irish tush out here. We're outnumbered right now."

Brigid poked out her head, her red hair escaping its clip. "Go for it. You guys could seriously burn off some energy."

Nari's nostrils flared as she pulled in air. "You people are all crazy."

Wolfe scratched his head. "We're tied. Somebody get Millie Frost."

"She went to a meeting," Raider said. "An hour ago."

Dana stepped out. "Well, then. Nari's plan wins because I'm voting for two."

Nari nodded. "Good point." The woman was about three months pregnant, although she wasn't showing yet. She did throw up a lot, though.

Wolfe's shoulders went down. "Shoot. I guess that's fair."

Angus rubbed his hands together. "I suggest everyone not on my team get the hell out." He gestured to the elevator, looking sad that he didn't get to hit anybody. "Now."

Chapter Four

Angus waited until the HDD techs had left before speaking. The silence was heavy enough to make his shoulders ache from the tension.

Wolfe tilted his head. "I guess you forgot to tell us about the year?"

Angus kept his gaze stoic, while his team faced him, as usual masking their expressions. "I'm sorry." It was the truth and the only thing he could think to say. "The year went fast and I figured Lassiter would make a move before now."

Raider's eyebrows rose. "It's quite the coincidence, right? He reengages with you one week *after* your deadline?"

True. Very true. Angus would have to mull that one over. Did Lassiter have a mole in the HDD or DHS? For now, he had a volatile team to handle. "So." Guilt ached through him and he fought it, looking for anger but finding none. Had he let everyone down?

Wolfe looked around. "Well, we're gonna need lattes to figure this out. I'll make sure those HDD jackasses are gone and go get supplies."

Angus stiffened. He'd figured Wolfe would at least throw something at him.

Raider nodded. "Yeah. We should secure everything we have, just in case they show back up with SWAT."

"Good plan," West said.

Angus couldn't breathe. They were sticking with him? Rallying around him? "I could be wrong about Lassiter," he said slowly.

Malcolm shrugged. "Maybe, but the team is good, and we have work to do. If nothing else, there's a dead woman who needs justice, and you said we took the case last night. We're with you, Force."

The moment hit Angus square center. With him. His team. Okay. They trusted him and were willing to continue working with him. It meant something. Hell, it meant everything. They had to get to work and fast. "Wolfe, please get lattes. Nari, head to your meeting and see what you can do."

The two moved toward the elevator.

Angus zeroed in on the most immediate necessities. "Brigid? Get everything onto USB drives and scrub any personal information about the team. Dana, same thing with your records." He nodded at Malcolm West and Raider Tanaka. "Wrap up any case files you can and leave the open cases with any notes we've compiled." He gestured to Jethro. "Let's take a look at this crime scene, while you're here." Without waiting for an answer, he skirted the bank of desks and headed back into the case room, nearly overcome by the loyalty of his team.

"Where's Kat?" Jethro asked Raider before following Angus.

"The kitten is hanging out with Pippa at West's place," Raider said.

Angus pulled out a chair at the large conference table and dropped into it, facing the board of death.

Jethro entered the room and drew the nearest chair, whistling at the scene on the board. "I take it that's our victim from last night?" He glanced at the papers and manila files spread across the table.

Angus nodded. "Yep."

"No note?" Jethro asked.

"Haven't found one." Angus steepled his fingers beneath his chin. There wasn't a note. The victim wasn't blond. Yet he couldn't shake the feeling that Lassiter was just fucking with him. He pushed papers out of the way to reveal one of the photos that he'd taken on his phone the previous night. "This tattoo was placed on the back of her hand."

Jethro slid the picture closer with one finger. "Looks like Roscoe."

"Yep." Didn't mean it was Roscoe, though.

Jethro leaned back in his chair. "Was the tattoo recent?"

"Looked like it, but I don't have access to the lab to ask," Angus said, his skin crawling with irritation.

Jethro cleared his throat. "Well, that's not the only interesting connection, right?"

Angus's chest heated. "I'm aware."

"Is she?"

"I don't know." Angus ground the palm of his hand into his left eye, where a migraine was rapidly approaching. "The victim looks Chinese, and she's petite, like Nari. It's hard to miss that fact, especially with the German shepherd tattoo on the woman's hand."

"Could be a coincidence," Jethro said.

Which Angus didn't believe in, unfortunately. "Perhaps."

"Are you shagging the psychiatrist?" Jethro asked.

Angus coughed, his ears heating. "Of course not. She's a shrink, for crap's sake. You know how I feel about shrinks."

"Uh-huh."

"I wouldn't even think of getting close to somebody with Lassiter on the loose. If he is on the loose, that is." Bile swirled in Angus's gut at the thought.

Jethro rocked back on his heels. "There's enough tension between you and Nari that I can feel it across a room. Anybody watching you would see it, too. Although I'm still of a mind that Lassiter is deceased and rotting in hell."

Enough of that conversation. Angus turned to face his old friend. "There's a suspect in custody. Don't you have connections with Metro?"

Jethro leaned over to read Angus's notes. "I consulted on a case a year ago and I'd like to think I was supremely helpful. What do you want?"

"I want to interview the guy they have in custody," Angus said instantly. "Just a quick in and out. Think you can make that happen?"

Jethro sighed. "I'll call in the favor, if it's possible, on one condition."

Angus held up a hand, his heart thundering. "If the suspect did kill the woman in the alley, I'll drop the case. I'll never ask you to consult again, and you can go back to your college and pretend that you're a normal professor studying philosophy and all that shit." Although he knew better than anybody that Jethro would never be able to outrun the past. None of them would.

"I do appreciate that," Jethro said dryly, pulling his phone out of his pocket to send a quick text. "What's your plan if your team is disbanded and it turns out this horrible murder wasn't committed by Lassiter?"

That was quite the question. Returning to solitary life in his cabin didn't hold as much appeal as Angus would've thought. He was saved from answering when Jethro's phone buzzed.

"My friend isn't on the case, but he's sending over the file. Give me a sec." Jethro pushed a few buttons on his phone.

It did help to have connections, now didn't it? Angus twirled a pen between his fingers.

"Ah. All right." Jethro read quickly. "The victim was called Lori Chen and she was a twenty-four-year-old graduate student in business administration at Georgetown." He scanned down on the phone. "Suspect is her ex, Levi Mackelson. They lived together briefly and there were two domestic calls. According to the file, they broke up two months ago."

Angus set down the pen. "Any priors on Mackelson besides the domestics?"

"No." Jethro looked up. "No alibi, at least from the little bit in this file. He only spoke for a few minutes before demanding an attorney."

Angus needed to talk to this man. It'd been a while since he'd profiled anybody, but he couldn't have lost his edge that much. "Anything else?"

Jethro read the face of his phone and then whistled. "The lawyer was big-time, there wasn't enough to hold Mackelson, so he was let go." Jet winced. "I have a name and an address. I suppose you want to go and have a little visit?"

Of course he wanted to go. Angus stood and fetched his leather jacket from the far chair. "You're welcome to join me."

"I have to join you, if for no other reason than to keep you from hitting this jackass. That would get me in trouble with the authorities." Jethro stretched as he stood and took a moment to put weight on his healed leg.

Angus paused. "How's the leg anyway?"

"Aches, which means it's raining," Jethro said shortly. He'd been shot while helping Wolfe on an Op. "Let's get this over with, shall we?"

Angus faltered and pulled his badge out of his jacket, then put it on the table. His HDD-issued Glock was next.

Jethro straightened. "Force?"

Angus lifted a shoulder. "If I'm with HDD, I can't talk to him without a lawyer." He strode out of the room before Jethro could stop him.

Nari rode the fancy elevator up to the top floor of HDD headquarters and slipped her identification back into her handbag. Soft music played from the speakers, and the spacious lift smelled like orange-infused cleanser. Oddly enough, she missed the rickety deathtrap of the team's office. She held her breath as she ascended, hoping nobody else entered the elevator on the way up. The last thing she needed right now was to run into her asshole of an ex.

She reached the top floor and forced her shoulders

down where they belonged. She'd been summoned and that was never a good thing.

The door swished open with barely a whisper, and she stepped out onto the thick, navy-blue carpet of a reception area that led in several directions, depending upon which part of the organization one wanted to visit. A bright spray of orchids sat on a credenza beneath a stunning oil painting of an Arizona sunset; the waiting area was vacant.

The receptionist looked up from behind her rounded mahogany desk, sliding a professional smile into place. What was her name? Nari had never really paid attention. The woman was in her early thirties with blond hair perfectly twisted into a professional bun. "Dr. Zhang. Do you have an appointment?"

"No." Nari matched the smile perfectly. "However, I have a matter of urgency. Would you mind seeing if the deputy administrator has a few minutes to spare?"

"Not at all," the woman said. She lifted a phone to her ear.

"Thank you." Nari turned and strode to the reception area to remove her wet raincoat and hang it up on the polished coat-tree. Had that been catlike glee in the woman's eyes, or had Nari imagined it? Man, she hated this office. If she couldn't save the team, maybe she'd finally go into private practice and give up this quest with the HDD.

"Dr. Zhang? The deputy administrator can fit you in right now. Please go back to his office." She hung up the phone and returned to the notes on her desk.

"Thank you." Nari strode to the right and down the long hallway to knock on the imposing wooden door of the corner office.

"Enter," came from inside.

Nari took a deep breath and opened the door to a spacious office with a spectacular view of the Potomac River. The sprawling desk in front of her was vacant, so she turned to the conference area with its gleaming table, where her biological father usually worked. She stopped short when she found him there with his boss, the administrator of the HDD. "I didn't mean to interrupt."

He gestured her to an empty chair at the table. "Not at all. You said it was urgent, and Administrator Clemonte and I have a few minutes right now."

Nari swallowed and moved forward, taking the administrator's hand in a brisk shake. "It's good to see you, Administrator."

Opal Clemonte had a firm handshake and a tight jaw. The woman was in her early sixties but looked fifty, tops. Her blue suit was Chanel, her shoes Louboutin, and her eyes intelligent. Very. "It's nice to see you, Nari. I hope things are going better for you this year."

Nari forced another smile. "That's kind of you." She thought of the man before her as Quan, rather than Father; she had hoped to change that while they were working together. She took the seat he had motioned her toward, while hiding any bit of irritation. Now wasn't the time to get into it with Quan's boss. Just being in that office meant she'd bull frogged over her own boss, their handlers, their boss, and another boss. Yet another situation that would get her in trouble. "I'm sure it's not a surprise that I'd like you to reconsider the disbanding of Force's team."

Quan's dark eyes darkened even more. He was a couple of inches taller than her five-five, but he seemed much taller. Black hair, peppered with gray, framed his face. No emotion showed in his expression. "That seems unwise."

Administrator Clemonte sat back slightly, as if giving Quan the lead in the conversation.

Nari kept her focus on Quan, who was sitting rather close to the other woman. Her instincts started to murmur, but she shut them down for now. Her folks had been divorced for eons, and her mother had remarried when Nari was a young teenager. Her mom and stepdad lived in LA, and she missed them every day. If Quan was dating his boss, that shouldn't matter to her. But how freaking hypocritical.

She cleared her throat. "The team saved countless lives by preventing the bombings at the marathon last year, and we took down the Boston Mob. It's a team that gets results, which is vitally important to the HDD." Surviving as a secret branch of Homeland Security required results. A lot of them.

"Nari, your judgment is of concern to me." Quan frowned, which was as damaging as a yell from another man. "You were temporarily assigned to Force's team to give you distance and time away from headquarters, not to form attachments there. The year has concluded and it's time to advance your career, which might be possible now."

"It should've been possible in the first place," Nari returned before she could stop herself.

The administrator stood gracefully, her hazel eyes direct. "I believe this is a personal discussion. Quan, we can continue the budget planning after the meeting with the secretary of defense this afternoon. Nari, I hope your new assignment goes well." She gathered several of the dark-blue file folders off the table and turned on her three-inch heels, striding out of the office with a sense of impressive power.

Nari barely kept from crossing her arms.

Quan tossed a gold-and-burgundy Montblanc pen onto the table, where it rolled to a stop against a pad of paper. "Do you or do you not like working for the HDD?"

She knew better than to delve into the question with any sort of depth. "I do."

"Good." He pushed yet another blue file folder near her. "If you want to salvage your career, this is the team the administrator requires you to work with right now. The team is engaged in a high-stress case and requires counseling and monitoring."

Sounded perfect for her. Except she didn't want to leave her current team. "Force's team is a good one."

"That team doesn't exist any longer. Either you want this assignment or you don't." He sat back, looking at his watch.

Her stomach dropped. So much for doing Angus and the team any good. "I'll read through the file."

"Good." The tone of dismissal was hard to miss. "I should warn you, though. The team leader is Vaughn Ealy."

Her mouth dropped open. "Are you kidding?"

"No. The team needs you, and this is a good opportunity to show the administrator that the two of you have put the past behind you." He lowered his chin, his gaze piercing. "Vaughn has agreed, so there's no reason for you to act like an injured female."

Heat flashed down her back so quickly, she nearly yanked off her jacket. "An injured female?"

Quan would never stoop to rolling his eyes, but he came close. "Please. You created a PR nightmare and nearly derailed both of your careers."

"I was doing my job," she snapped, in one second going from a tough HDD agent to a little girl wanting her father's support. "Agent Lisa Barksow was at serious risk of a mental breakdown and needed treatment. It wasn't my fault that the media got hold of the story and blew it out of proportion." The young agent had been with their team and had been on the edge, but Vaughn had disagreed, so she'd had no choice but to go over his head to force Barksow into treatment.

Quan waved his hand in the air as if batting away a fly. "Enough. You each have your own versions of what happened, and the truth is probably in the middle. Vaughn was your team leader and you should never have gone over his head."

She drew in a breath. "You know I took an oath and have to reveal if anybody is a danger to themselves or others. I was trying to help her."

"Well, she's no longer with the agency, and both you and Vaughn were demoted. Let's get past it, shall we? Show you're a team player, do your job, and do not embarrass me again."

"I wouldn't think of it, Quan," she said, realizing she would never call him "Father." She stood and nodded, wanting more than anything to argue with him, but it wouldn't do any good. So she left, having failed to save Angus's team. What was going to happen to everybody?

Also, the "what if" of her attraction to Angus swirled around in her mind and landed in her body. While they'd worked together, seen each other every day, there had always been a "what if" or a "maybe" between them, even though they argued most of the time.

It hurt to say goodbye to that "what if."

Chapter Five

Angus finished off a burger from the fast-food joint as he drove his truck through an established neighborhood in the Georgetown area, with town houses lining both sides of the street. "Which one is it?"

Jethro craned his neck to peer through the rain splattering the windshield. "It's the blue one between the brick house with green shutters and the white one with the purple flowerpots. I'm thinking your suspect has either a decent job or family money; the small amount of info my friend was able to send didn't specify which. With our luck, the bloke will be a lawyer who just had to call in a partner to get him sprung. Aren't these places all around a million dollars each?"

"Probably." Angus found a spot at the curb and quickly parked. He looked into the back seat. "You want to come in or just stay in the truck?"

Roscoe sprawled across the entire seat, his nose on his paws and his eyes closed. He didn't move.

Angus rolled his eyes. "Stop pouting. One burger was enough and probably isn't even good for you. I'll give you dog food when we get home." Roscoe didn't twitch.

What a drama queen. "Fine. Stay here." He opened his door and jumped out, letting the rain have its way with him. Once Jethro had exited the vehicle, Angus locked it up tight. Last thing he needed was his dog going to look for another burger. Or for a bar.

"What's your plan?" Jethro asked, shoving his hands into his jacket pockets as rain plastered his hair to his head.

Angus jogged around the truck to the sidewalk. "I feel like the direct approach will be best. Let's just ring the bell."

"Interesting." Jethro strode along the sidewalk next to the connected townhomes, ducking his head against the rain. "Should we talk about your team being fired?"

"No." The cold of autumn had started killing the pots of plants and flowers in front of several of the town houses, giving the pretty neighborhood the sense of change. Of winter coming. Angus scouted the quiet neighborhood before walking up the steps to the dark-blue door and knocking.

A shuffling could be heard inside, and then the door opened. "Yes?" Caucasian male, brown hair, blue eyes, about six-feet tall and 225 pounds with decent muscle mass. He wore expensive black sweats and a green tank top.

Angus read him in a minute. "Are you Levi Mackelson?"

Levi started to shut the door. "I have a lawyer, asshole. Call him, not me. You can't be here."

Angus plunked his boot in the door. "I'm Angus Force and I'm the foremost expert in the world on the guy I think killed your ex-girlfriend. Do you have a minute to talk?"

Levi paused. "I can't talk to you without my lawyer."

"I'm not a cop." When Levi just stared at him, Angus shrugged. "Any longer. I was, but now I'm not. Just don't say anything that could incriminate you and it won't matter anyway. You're smart enough to do that." Yeah, manipulation. He was good at it and didn't give a shit.

Levi straightened. "You know who killed her?"

"I think I might, but I need to talk to you." Angus put on his most disarming smile. "The sooner I catch him, the sooner the cops will stop trying to build a case against you. You do know that the boyfriend or ex, especially if there are a couple of domestic violence calls in the past, is the guy they're going after, right? You're smart enough to get out of it in the end, but let's be honest. Do you have time for this crap?" Yep. More ego stroke.

Levi turned toward Jethro. "Who are you?"

"Professor of philosophy," Jet said easily, his British accent all charm. "I'm just along for the ride."

Levi's gaze narrowed. "You're a cop."

"Ha," Jet said. "Not even close, mate. I was in M16, but that was a long time ago, and now I teach philosophy, with emphases on ethics, moral theory, decision, game, and rational choice theories."

A slow and not entirely nice smile tilted Levi's mouth. "Running from some bad shit, are you? Good luck with that." He opened the door and gestured them inside. "Come on in."

This guy wasn't a moron. Angus walked across the polished wooden floor of the threshold, which was a short hallway leading to a narrow staircase leading to the second floor. A silver bike rested against the right wall beneath a mirror, and to the left was an opening to what looked like a living room. He moved that way, with Jethro right behind him.

A gas fire flickered in a hammered steel fireplace, and he moved past it to sit in one of two chairs facing a blue sofa. The dining area, kitchen, and a small backyard showed through another doorway by the fireplace, the rooms laid out in a narrow, shotgun formation.

It was classy and expensive.

Jet sat next to him, while Levi took the sofa. Pastel watercolors decorated the walls. The coffee table and end tables were antiques.

"Who decorated your place?" Angus asked, clicking facts through his brain.

"My mom," Levi said easily. "My parents own the town house. I just rent from them." He pushed a stack of outdoor magazines to the side of the table. "What do you know about Lori's murder?"

Guy went right for the issue, showing he wasn't going to avoid it. Or maybe he just thought he was that much smarter than everyone else. Angus sat back in the surprisingly comfortable chair. "Not nearly as much as we want. It'd help me figure out what to ask if we started generally. How long did you two date?"

Levi lifted his chin and looked to the right. "I think about eight months? She moved in after three and we lived together for five."

So far, indicators of truth. Angus nodded. "Why'd she move out? Any chance she was seeing somebody else?" Could lead to a suspect.

"By the end we hardly saw each other." A barely perceptible whine elevated Levi's tone. "She was so busy with her studies that she wasn't any fun any longer." He picked a thread from his sweats. "I also got busy at work and started hanging out with friends from the office, and she didn't like that."

In other words, he hung out with women from work. "I couldn't care less if you cheated on her," Angus stated quietly. "If anybody you were seeing had cause to harm Lori, I need those names."

Levi rolled his eyes. "Nobody. I slept with a couple of chicks, but I didn't share feelings or anything."

Yeah. Douchebag. All right. "Where do you work?" Angus asked.

"I manage a series of apartment buildings and single-story residences," Levi said.

Ah. So he worked for Mommy and Daddy. "Where did you and Lori meet?" Angus asked.

"At a bar. You know The Cottonwood over on Third Street? It was karaoke night, and that girl could sing." Levi sighed, his chest sinking. "I can't believe somebody killed her like that. Who would do that?"

Great question. "Tell me about the domestic violence calls," Angus said evenly, keeping emotion at bay and trying to sound like a buddy just shooting the breeze.

Levi shrugged. "It was nothing. Really. We got into a couple of bad fights toward the end and there was shouting. Both of us yelled. The asshole neighbor to the right called the police, and both times the cops showed up and asked me to go somewhere else for the night. There was no violence, and nobody was arrested. It was all stupid, to be honest."

That sounded like the truth, but sometimes sociopaths were good at sounding honest. They usually were. Angus didn't get a bad vibe from the guy, but he was out of practice. "Where were you the other night? When Lori was slashed open and had her heart ripped out?"

Levi turned pale. Then he coughed. Okay. Honest emotions. "I was here asleep. Stayed in, ate some casserole my mom left, and went to bed early. Didn't think I'd need an alibi."

"When was the last time you saw or talked to Lori?" Jethro asked.

Levi jumped at the Brit's interjection. "I don't know. Maybe a couple of weeks ago? I ran into her at the farmers market and we were nice to each other. Cordial, I guess. It was the last market of the year and the place was packed, so we didn't talk long."

"Did you see anything suspicious? Like anybody hanging around or following her?" Angus sat up.

"No," Levi said. "I didn't notice anything like that." His blue eyes softened. "I wish I had. Maybe I could've done something. Nobody deserves to die like that."

Jethro tapped his fingers on his knee. "Do you have any idea of anyone who'd want to hurt her?"

"No. I already told the police that everyone loved Lori. Nobody would want her dead." Levi shook his head. "It just doesn't make sense. You said that you know who killed her. Who was it?"

Angus scratched the whiskers on his chin. "There was a serial killer who hurt people in the same way, but this scene was a little different, so I'm not absolutely sure. You've been a lot of help." Not really, but what the hell. He stood. "Thank you, and I'm sorry for your loss."

Jethro followed suit. "If you think of anything else, please call Angus."

Angus grabbed a business card from his back pocket and scrawled his cell phone number on the back, considering he might not have an office any longer. "Yeah. Anything. You never know what might hit you. She could've said something, or maybe there's something in the back of your head that will spark a memory. Just call me."

Levi stood and took the card. "Okay. Thanks."

Angus turned toward the open archway. "Oh. I almost forgot. Did Lori like dogs?"

Levi nodded. "She loved dogs. She grew up north on a bunch of land and had several animals as a kid. Big dogs, especially."

"German shepherds?" Jethro asked.

"Probably. I don't know," Levi said.

That wasn't much help. "Did she have a tattoo of a German shepherd on the back of her hand?" Angus asked, his skin prickling.

"Not when we were together, but we broke up a couple of months ago, so I wouldn't know." Levi tossed the business card on top of the magazines, his brows drawing together. "Now that you mention it, there might've been something weird. I didn't think it was strange at the time, but . . . " He turned and hustled into the kitchen, returning with a small stack of mail.

Angus barely kept from snatching the stack away. "What do you have?"

"A few letters sent here for Lori." Levi handed over three unopened envelopes. "From the Dog Society of Poseidon. Probably junk mail, but I thought maybe I could call her and take them to her. She's pretty great, or at least she was, and I guess maybe I wanted another chance. Even if it was just as friends." He threw the other envelopes onto the coffee table and shoved his hands in his pockets, his expression turning even more sober. "The stamps on all three are of German shepherds."

Angus frowned. "Didn't she have her mail forwarded when she left?"

"Yeah, but those came here anyway." Levi glanced at the envelopes. "Does that mean something? Should I hand them over to the cops?"

"We'll hand them over," Angus said, turning and heading for the doorway. "I doubt it means anything, Levi. It's just junk mail." Right. The envelopes hadn't gone through the mail system. They'd been left here on purpose as another clue for him to find. "Thanks for your help."

Jethro followed him out into the rain and down the sidewalk. "What are you thinking?"

"Nothing yet," Angus said, his jaw so tight his head ached. "Let's just get out of here before he calls the cops and they confiscate these. The dog angle is just the way Lassiter would play cat and mouse."

"If that's really his game, the fact that he killed a Chinese woman is significant, Angus. He'll be coming after your team, and it looks like Nari is top of the list." Jethro reached the truck. "Is there any way she'll let you lock her down or send her on vacation for a while?"

Angus pressed the button, determination flowing through him. "She doesn't have a choice. She has to go, and now."

Chapter Six

Nari shook out her sopping-wet umbrella and rode down the ancient elevator, almost wishing for the first time that the darn thing would just crash to the ground. After a lonely dinner, she'd decided to return to the office and finish up whatever she'd missed. The elevator groaned, jolted, and halted at the basement offices. The doors remained closed long enough to increase her heart rate. Finally, they opened with the scratch of metal scraping against metal.

She leapt out before the doors could close, gasping in the small vestibule. The smell of whiskey hit her first. Then surprise. She moved hesitantly into the main room of the suite.

Wolfe, Jethro, and Angus sat to one side of the room, leaning against the wall, their long legs extended toward the empty bullpen. The *very empty* bullpen. Dust outlined the spot where the pod of desks had been.

"They even took those old desks?" she asked.

Wolfe nodded, his brown eyes more mellow than usual. "Yep. Three armed teams showed up and cleared us out. Who'd want that scarred furniture?" He gestured, and his broad hand impacted an empty Jack Daniel's bottle that fell onto its side and clattered away.

Nari narrowed her gaze. "You're all drunk?"

"We had to say goodbye. We're touchy types of folks," Wolfe said.

Jethro snorted in a very un-British way and looked at Angus. "Drunk? Are we?" He slurred only a little.

Angus lifted one powerful shoulder. "Could be." Another bottle—this one half full—sat by his hand. There was no mellowness in his gaze, unlike Wolfe's. No. Angus looked at her, his eyes glittering with something she couldn't name but made her body flush with a heat that was as annoying as it was intriguing. He cocked his head. "How'd it go at headquarters?" His sarcastic drawl helped her gain her equilibrium.

"Obviously not good." She swept her hand around the empty and rather dusty room. The HDD had even taken the painting she'd plastered on one wall for some color. Annoyance ticked right up to anger, and she let it reign. "You three are grown men, for goodness' sake. Stop acting like college freshmen who just lost their first love. Buck up." Drinking never helped anything.

Roscoe padded out of Angus's office and sat at the far end of the bullpen, his nose slightly in the air.

Nari's eyes widened. "Tell me you didn't let him have any alcohol." The dog had a problem.

Angus rolled his eyes. "Of course not. That's why he's acting all pissy."

Wolfe's phone dinged and he tugged it free of his back pocket before glancing at the face and quickly reading the text. He smiled. "Dana's here. I don't want her in that elevator, so I told her to wait in the truck. Let's go."

Nari softened. Wolfe in full protective mode was kind of cute, so long as she wasn't on the other end of it. "How's Dana feeling?"

"Good. Finally stopped puking all day. That boy inside her is going to be a handful." Wolfe leaned down and hauled Jethro up. "We'll give you a ride."

"Could be a girl," Angus said, not moving.

Wolfe shook his head. "God wouldn't do that to me." He glanced down. "You and Roscoe want a ride?"

Angus hadn't looked away from Nari, his glittering green eyes holding her captive with just a look. "No. Roscoe and I will be fine."

Awareness prickled over Nari's skin in a spiral of heat. Why her body reacted that way to jerks was something she should figure out; after all, she was a psychologist.

Wolfe looked from Angus to Nari and then back. A mental debate obviously went on in his head and then he shrugged. "If anybody needs me, call." He clapped Jethro on the back and the Brit stumbled toward the elevator. "You think I could get a job teaching at your college? I know a lot of shit."

"No." Jethro tripped into the elevator.

Wolfe followed him, and the door closed with him arguing his case.

Angus patted the hard concrete next to him. "Do you *ever* let your hair down, Zhang?"

"My hair is down." The temptation to sit next to him for just a brief moment was almost more than she could resist. Plus, she felt like an idiot just standing there in an empty room, looking down at him. "I really did try, Angus," she said softly.

"Jesus. Just sit down." He reached for the bottle again. "Do you ever fucking relax?"

"Of course." Knowing she was being manipulated didn't stop her from playing along. Her boot heels clip-clopped as she walked toward him and sat where Wolfe had been. At least the concrete was warm there.

Just the two of them in the office, once again. She'd become used to sharing this time with him and surprise filled her at how much she was going to miss it, even though her skin felt too tight and her body too restless. Too needy. "Do you ever feel like we're the two grown-ups in this place?"

Angus chuckled. "On occasion, definitely." He extended the bottle. "One last drink before we close this office?"

"I have to drive home." After the day she'd endured, she would love to lose herself in a bottle. But somebody had to keep a clear head.

"Raider and Brigid are coming by, and they'll give us a ride home. Come on, Nari. This is the last night we'll see each other; we might as well say goodbye with a drink." Without waiting for her to answer, he raised the bottle to his mouth and took several deep drinks.

She shook her head. "I would hate to see your liver, Angus."

He chuckled and set the bottle back on the ground.

Roscoe whined across the room.

"No," Nari said firmly. "You are not drinking, Roscoe."

The dog wagged his tail, yipped, and flipped around to disappear in the office.

She laughed. "He is so dramatic." And adorable. The humor deserted her faster than a contact high. "I'm really going to miss him." Her chest ached and she eyed the bottle. No. Getting tipsy with Angus was a huge mistake, and one she'd likely not recover from. At least for a while. She sighed and rested her head back on the wall, closing her eyes.

"Rough day?" Angus rumbled.

"You have no idea," she muttered. "Get this. I've been reassigned to a team led by my ex-boss, who was also my boyfriend, and last time we worked together we almost destroyed our careers because he's an ass."

Angus patted her leg, shooting jolts of electricity through her body. "Sorry about that. How did that happen?"

His touch warmed her, and she settled in to a comfort she hadn't realized they'd developed. "There was another member of our team who kept jumping into danger after she lost her partner. I also thought she was doing drugs to cope."

Angus winced. "She wouldn't be the first agent to do so."

Nari nodded. "I know, and I couldn't get her to seek help. Vaughn wouldn't force her to seek assistance, saying she just wanted disability, or that women shouldn't be in the agency anyway. I had no choice but to go over his head. The press found out and HDD was almost exposed." Remembered anxiety pinged up her chest and she breathed through it.

"That sucks," Angus said, his voice thoughtful. "Were you correct?"

"Yeah. The agent did end up in counseling, and she quit the agency to open a gardening supply store with her cousin. She's much happier now." Nari opened her eyes to see his intent ones focused on her. Green and shining with that undeniable light only he had. If she could paint, she'd try to capture that look.

One of his dark eyebrows rose. "This is why you were demoted to our team?"

"Yes," she said softly, unable to stop her gaze from running over his impossibly rugged face. Strong angles and stubborn shadows matched the strength, cunning, and pain in the depths of his fierce eyes. As a psychologist, she wanted to get into his head and provide some assistance. As a woman, she craved to dive into his heart and provide comfort. During her time in his unit, he hadn't allowed her to do either.

Of course, the first was a risk to him and the second one to her. Definitely. At some point, she needed to learn she couldn't save bad boys who didn't want to be saved. She sighed.

His lips twitched into a smirk. "Yeah. I know."

At least they could laugh at themselves together. Or at least smirk. She finally let her body relax and absorb the fact that it was over. Her time with Angus's team had come to an end. The idea hurt. "I wish I could've saved the team," she murmured.

"We're not done yet," he said, his shoulder touching hers in a way that provided comfort despite the turmoil around them. "Although I do have to ask you a question. You were willing to lose your job to force a teammate into counseling and yet you've never tried to push me into getting help."

She sighed. "You aren't weak or at risk, Angus. Oh, you're obsessed and on the edge, but I've never thought you were a true danger to yourself or anybody else. Plus, you're excellent at this job."

He blinked. His smile was almost boyish, and the brief glimpse of the sweetness inside him warmed her from head to toe, giving her that gooey feeling she didn't know what to do with.

The moment stretched on, and finally he broke eye contact. "Want me to beat the crap out of your ex and tell him to be nice to you on your new job? I've already been fired, so I don't have anything to lose. I wouldn't mind hitting somebody, actually." Angus took another deep gulp of the whiskey.

She grinned. "No, but that's a kind offer. We were a bad match from the start, and he wasn't the nicest guy."

Angus stiffened, the bottle still at his lips. Slowly, deliberately, he set it down next to him before facing her fully. "That's a large statement from you. How bad did things get with him? I believe you said his name was Vaughn." Intensity swirled around him with an intimidating flash of warmth.

She blinked. "Angus, I—"

"What, Nari?" He grasped her arm, his hold gentle but firm, conveying an insistence she felt to her toes. "What did he do?"

She couldn't breathe. Angus in full-on, protective alpha mode should be a turnoff, but her breath quickened and her abdomen turned over. Where was the easy camaraderie they'd just enjoyed? She tried to diffuse him. "Nothing for you to get irritated about," she croaked. Jeez. She needed to get herself under control before she just jumped the guy. "He was angry and called me a bad shrink and an emotional bitch."

"I'd very much like to punch him now," Angus drawled, his eyes a sharp emerald. "What's his full name?"

"Why?" she asked.

He paused, his chin lifting. "So I can beat him until he begs."

The idea perversely warmed her heart—as well as several other places on her body. "Oh yeah? Why?" she challenged, unable to think of another response. This was going somewhere she needed to avoid, but she couldn't help herself. Didn't really want to.

He paused. His jaw tensed.

She held her breath. Was he finally going to go there?

His nostrils flared the slightest amount. "We might have been disbanded, but until a few hours ago you worked for me. We were on the same team. I'll take care of this guy."

Her lungs deflated. "God, you're a coward." She pushed to her feet, shocked when he stood twice as fast.

"Think so?" He angled his body, putting her back to the wall. One of his hands flattened against the chipped paint right next to her face. Heat from his hard body washed over her, and the scent of whiskey filtered through her senses. "I'm doing the smart thing and you know it. We're not good for each other."

That was an understatement. With him standing so close, towering over her, bracketing her with his body, her mind struggled to stay in control. "You can't hate everybody who knows psychology, Angus," she murmured. "You have to stop pushing everyone away."

He leaned in even closer, ducking his head to trap her gaze. "Baby, the last thing I want to do is push you away."

Nobody in her entire life had called her "baby." She should be insulted. Yet her knees wobbled and desire ripped through her system with a force that stole her voice.

He was so much bigger than she, and even that thought spun hunger through her. What would it be like to unleash all that male strength and fire? Angus Force concealed his fire with sarcasm, dogged determination, and intense control. But it was there. Fire, anger, pain, humor, hope. The emotions were visible now in his eyes, fighting one another. Fighting him.

"Angus," she whispered, feeling for him. Wanting to somehow ease him.

"Stop me, Nari." He leaned closer, his lips almost on hers. Slow and deliberate. "Please. Stop me."

She couldn't. Instead, she closed her eyes and leaned toward him. The second his mouth touched hers, she realized her mistake.

Her body jolted and her mind went blank. Electricity zapped down her torso, landing at her core and spreading outward.

He growled, actually growled, and clamped his hand on the back of her head, kissing her so deeply she could only hold on for the desperate ride. His taste flooded her senses. Whiskey, male, and *danger*. She'd known. The danger wasn't all around him; it was *in* him.

She could taste it. Feel it. Drown in it.

Opening her mouth to take more of him, she grasped his waist to keep her balance. She dug her nails into his flanks, her mind spinning, moaning as his tongue swept along hers.

Angus devoured her like a drowning man seeking air.

His phone buzzed and he jerked. He drew air in through his nose, gentled the kiss, and ended it with a soft nip to her bottom lip.

He straightened, his eyes the color of a dark-green forest. Haunted and dangerous.

She blinked, rapidly trying to fill her lungs. What had just happened? Her lips tingled and her body ached. Heat spiraled into her face, but she still couldn't move.

He drew the phone from his back pocket and glanced down to read the screen.

In a second he went cold. Ice cold. He stepped away from her.

She exhaled. "What? What's happened?"

When he looked up his eyes were expressionless. Completely. "We have another body."

Chapter Seven

Lanterns set every few yards marked the muddy trail from the dark parking area at Soapstone Valley Park outside of DC, their light, small beacons leading to hell. Dead leaves smashed beneath his boots as Angus ducked his head against the punishing rain pelting through bare tree branches to attack his head. "You should go back to your car, Nari," he said. Again.

"No." She stepped lightly behind him, unsuccessfully attempting to share her umbrella as they walked through the night.

He didn't want to be dry. Didn't want to find any comfort right now. Most of all, he didn't want her to see what no doubt lay ahead. "Go back to the car and wait with Roscoe. You shouldn't be here," he muttered.

"Neither should you," she countered, slipping on the mud and quickly regaining her balance. "I'm surprised the cop at the trailhead let either of us pass."

A lot of bluster had helped, as had Nari's HDD badge. "Listen. I appreciate the ride, but trust me, you don't want to be here." He wiped rain from his face to see better.

Movement sounded up ahead, and brighter lights flickered through the wet underbrush and desolate trees.

"But I enjoyed our talk on the long ride here," she said dryly.

They hadn't said a word. Either one of them. He'd been consumed with thoughts of another body and she'd been uncharacteristically silent. Yet another thing to irritate him about her. The woman knew when to give him space. Plus, he'd had time to sober up while she'd driven. He scowled into the night.

A small creek lay nearly still and dark to their right and he followed its path.

She kept close to him. "If this is the same killer, he's killed one night apart. If he's copying Lassiter, that's not part of the MO. Right?"

"Right."

She cleared her throat. "One night apart is crazy. I mean, there's no cooling down time."

"We'll see." Angus finally turned a corner and the scene came into view. "Jesus," he breathed.

Nari drew abreast of him, stopping silently.

Angus took in the entire area. Yellow crime scene tape cordoned off a large area, wrapped around thin trees and bushes to protect the area. Bright spotlights shone from four directions, two on either side of the creek toward the center. Darkness encroached outside the circle of lights. A thick tree—old, with rough bark—had fallen across the creek and provided a bridge to the other side. The victim lay on the log, tied to it, with one rope around her neck and the other around her feet. Both arms hung uselessly toward the water and she stared up into the rain.

Techs hustled around, trying to find evidence in the

storm. Two figures in white struggled to somehow fix a tarp from one side of the creek to the other to protect the victim from the elements.

Angus caught the eye of a homicide cop standing to the side and then hustled toward him, ducking under the crime scene tape. "Thanks for calling me." He waited until Nari had reached him. "HDD Special Agent Nari Zhang, please meet MPD Homicide Detective Tate Bianchi."

Nari held out a slim hand and they shook, her dusky coloring a contrast to his deep black skin. "It's nice to meet you."

"Ditto," Tate said, with rain sliding down his strong face. He stood eye to eye with Angus at six-four and still looked as fit as he'd been years ago, when Angus had last worked with him. "You have to be quick, Force." Tate released Nari's hand. "The MPD's Homeland Security Bureau received word that you're no longer with HDD or FBI, and I got a special little note from the chief of police about you."

"So you called Angus in anyway?" Nari asked softly.

Tate flashed a rare smile. "Of course. We also want to keep the feds away and keep this case ourselves, so I can only fight on so many fronts right now." His deep brown eyes sobered. "No kidding. I can give you about five minutes and I'm going to get yelled at, regardless. This way."

Angus followed him toward the tree and the victim, dropping to a crouch at the edge of the log. The woman appeared to be in her twenties, with pale skin marred by bruises and burns. Her chest gaped open, the ribs broken and the heart removed. The cuts looked smoother than on the previous victim. This woman's long hair was wrapped over one side of the log, the rain having darkened it.

"She's blond?" Angus squinted to make out the color in the dark.

"Redhead," Tate said. "Compared her hair to a white sheet of paper when we got here, but then it got wet, too. The body's been here for at least a day, maybe more, and it's rained the whole time."

"You won't find DNA from the killer anyway," Angus said, standing. His heart raced. "When did she die?"

"At least a week ago," Tate said. "I'll compare her to the body last night. Makes me worry about tomorrow night, you know?"

Angus nodded. "This guy is definitely messing with us. Lassiter did like to play games."

Tate's shoulders straightened. "She's not blond or particularly tall, Force. The MO is different. Before you ask, we've scoured the area, and no note. There's no note for you. I think we have a copycat."

Angus stood. "Did you see any tattoos on her?"

"No, but we haven't turned her over yet." Tate shook his head. "You need to get out of here. I'll send you the lab report when we get one, but then I'm done. As much as I like you, I don't want to lose my job over this, especially because this isn't Lassiter."

Angus stared at the victim. He shook his head. "I don't like the coincidence."

Tate frowned. "What coincidence?"

Nari hadn't spoken, but she'd turned pale beneath her smooth skin. "The redhead. First a Chinese woman and now a redhead. I'm Chinese, and another member of our team is Irish with red hair. Could be a coincidence, but it could also be some psycho playing with our team, Angus. Or what used to be our team. You did get a lot of press when Lassiter died, and a new crazy bastard might want to take up where Lassiter finished."

It was possible, but every instinct Angus had told him that Lassiter was playing with him. "If I lose my mind, he wins," he muttered.

Tate glanced his way. "Then don't lose your mind. I saw the closed file on Lassiter. He died, Angus."

"I saw it, too," Angus said grimly. "There was a picture of him in the morgue, a record of his cremation, and a note that the ashes were given to the nanny who raised him. She signed for the ashes, spread them somewhere, and then died two years later." He'd questioned everyone that woman had known, but she'd been a recluse. "Every 'I' is dotted."

Tate sighed and wiped rain off his smooth head. "We have a killer, but it's not yours. Yours is dead. Stop letting his ghost haunt you."

Angus nodded, his head aching. "All right. Let me know when you want to interview me."

Tate started. "Why would I do that?"

"The coincidence, Tate. It never really is one." Angus took Nari's arm and turned back down the dark trail, his gut churning and his temper slowly awakening. By coming out of seclusion, and by forming a team, he'd created targets for a killer. One was the stunning woman walking silently next to him. The HDD had just given him the perfect opportunity to protect everybody. He had to disband his team and put them in his rearview mirror for good.

Now.

* * *

Most of the drive was made in silence as the heat dried their muddy clothing. Nari turned off the interstate while the dog snored from the back seat and Angus sat quietly, his head back and his eyes closed. He hadn't spoken a word since leaving the crime scene and she couldn't think of anything to say. It had been terrible, and her insides felt hollow. How did he live with what he'd seen over the years?

She pulled into the parking area of Angus's apartment building, which was just a few miles from their former office. The building was an eighties-style stucco with a clay tile roof, as out of place outside DC as it could be. The complex was massive and always felt empty. Most of its residents were DC and Virginia workers who spent little time there after work. No doubt Angus had settled for the first thing he'd found and then had never tried to find a real home. Would he ever create one?

He opened his eyes and stared at his building.

She stopped the car. "What's your plan? Is the team going to meet here?"

"No." His voice sounded off. "It's not Lassiter, Nari. It might be somebody messing with the team, or the two victims and their appearances might just be a coincidence. But there are other people to investigate this case. I was involved only if it was Lassiter." He sounded weary. Lost.

She swallowed and turned to face him, rain battering the windshield of her car. "Why the change of mind?"

He ran a hand through his still-damp hair. "Lassiter was obsessed with his victim type. No way would he alter that, even to mess with me. His mother was a long-legged blonde, and he hated her. His victims were all long-legged blondes and he'd never be able to tweak that."

She nodded. "Agreed." Maybe there was hope that Angus could find peace now. It was all she'd ever wanted for him.

"So, we're out. Somebody else can find this psycho. I'll agree to an interview just in case it's a copycat trying to mess with me because I took down Lassiter, but then Roscoe and I are going home. Away from this damn city."

At his name, Roscoe snorted and stretched in the back seat.

A pang hit Nari right in the chest. They were really leaving? She bit her lip. All this was too real. "I'll miss the two of you."

He turned then, his green eyes a laser in the stormy night. "Yeah. We'll miss you, too. Do you want to come in tonight?"

She stopped breathing and her body short-circuited. Even her ears felt like they'd been singed. "Huh?"

He didn't smile. Didn't even smirk. His eyes burned with a predatory green fire. "I'm out of here, Nari. For good. I'm asking you if you want to come in for the night. One night. You and me. Just that."

The temptation sparked her entire body to full attention. Just one night to deal with whatever this was between them. It hurt to think of him leaving, but it also hurt to consider that there was only one night. One chance for closeness with him. The words wouldn't come, so she let her reactions take over. "I'm not a one-night stand type of gal," she murmured, almost to herself.

"It's not a one-night stand," he returned, his gaze no

less intense. "You know that. Even if it's just one night, it's you and me. It's more than that, and I don't understand it any more than you do, but you feel it. I know you feel it, too."

She drank in her fill of him, trying to memorize his features. Never in her life had she met a person like Angus Force, anyone so darkly *male*. Anybody so pursued by demons and yet so strong and stubborn.

Also, it figured he'd finally make his move when they were both sober and raw after the terrible scene in the park. There was no handy excuse for her to grab onto in desperation. She hadn't been drinking and they hadn't spent a fun day goofing off together. If she agreed, it was all on her—no excuses to comfort herself with after he left. And he was leaving. She could see acceptance of the end in his eyes and the settled stance of his shoulders. "You don't even like me." Was she protesting too much?

"Yes or no, Nari." He didn't disagree with her statement.

She didn't like him sometimes either. But he drew her in a way she couldn't pin down. If she left right now, she'd do so with her head held high. But she'd always wonder. *Always*. "Yes," she whispered.

Chapter Eight

He had lost his mind. Angus waited until Nari had locked her car before taking her hand for the first and only time in the year they'd known each other. Her skin was soft and her hand fit inside his perfectly. Figured. The rain drilled them, springing up from the asphalt, so he ducked his head and loped into a jog as Roscoe took care of business in the weeds off the parking lot.

The need for her had nearly driven him insane. Every time he smelled her cinnamon scent, every time her brown eyes softened, every time he heard the clip-clop of her sexy shoes, it was all he could do not to grab her shoulders and press her up against a wall and let his body have free reign.

Now she'd said yes.

For miles he'd scrutinized every vehicle behind them, knew they hadn't been followed. He tuned in his instincts. The area was vacant. Right now, at least, nobody was watching him.

Nari kept to his side, having abandoned her umbrella in the car.

Now wasn't the time for caution. They were way past

that point. Roscoe ran up, shaking his fur wildly by the door. Angus swiped his card across the reader at the main door and drew her inside to the elevator, which was already open.

Roscoe padded inside behind them, his ears perked as if something was happening but he didn't know what. Angus pressed the button for the third floor, keeping her hand. What if she changed her mind? He'd say goodbye and wish her well.

"I've never been to your apartment." She kept her focus straight ahead at the closed door and her voice trembled slightly.

The woman should be wary. "It's not much." He'd slept at the office as often as he had the apartment, and he kept dog food at both places. They ascended to the third floor, and Roscoe bounded out, running to the right. Angus led Nari in the same direction, quickly unlocking his door and pulling her inside, then locking it behind her. "Stay here, please." Finally he released her hand, and his felt empty. Bereft. He switched on lights in the spartan living room and kitchen, briefly dodging into the bedroom and one bathroom to make sure all was clear. Then he returned. "We're good."

She leaned against his door, her eyes a soft topaz and her shoulders back. "You always search your apartment when you get home?"

"Yeah. Don't you?" he asked, not stopping until he reached her.

"No," she whispered, her gaze running over his face. "I'm not that paranoid."

He brushed wet hair from the shoulder of her leather jacket, finally giving himself permission to touch her.

"It's not paranoia if they're really out to get you." He knew the line was a joke, but in his case it was true. Slowly, keeping her attention, he drew down her jacket zipper.

Her breath whooshed out, and the sound barreled through him to land in his groin. He'd wanted her from the first second she'd walked into the office and demanded a space of her own. She was always so put together and sure of herself, the temptation to muss her up had made his hands ache on more than one occasion. More than that, he wanted her safe. "I won't hurt you, Nari." The words came from someplace inside him he'd long forgotten.

She didn't answer, no doubt understanding a hell of a lot more about pretty much everything than he did. Instead, she reached up and tunneled both hands through his hair, sending water droplets scattering to the fake wood floor. Pleasure bloomed a light peach across her face, as if she'd been granted a treat she hadn't expected.

Lightning ripped through the darkness outside, flashing behind the blinds covering each small window. The faintest scent of ozone permeated the air.

"That was close," she whispered, her alluring mouth opening slightly.

He ducked his head and took that mouth. Sweetness exploded on his tongue, through his body. She was sweet and soft and everything he didn't deserve in this world. He groaned into her mouth and slid his hand through the wet strands of her thick hair. It was even silkier than he'd imagined, and the idea of the mass drying later and spreading over his chest propelled him to kiss her harder.

She stretched up on her toes and kissed him back, the

scent of cinnamon spurring his desire higher. Her fingers dug into his scalp, adding even more pleasure to every sensation attacking him.

He shoved her jacket to the ground and pushed her against the door, his body trying to get as flush with her as possible. She was small and delicate, so he plastered both hands on the smooth metal to keep from grabbing her and taking her down to the floor. If she was giving him one night, he was going to take care of her. She deserved no less. Hell, she deserved a lot better than him, but for now she was his. That mattered.

She jerked her head free and panted, sucking in air. "Fast. I want fast, Angus."

He heard the words, but his body revolted. Ah. He tugged his phone from his pocket and turned it off, tossing it over his shoulder to land where he knew the lone sofa sat. "We're not going to be interrupted."

Her lips formed a perfect O.

Yeah, he knew what she'd been thinking. They'd skirted each other for a year like cautious animals, and now that they'd finally made a decision, Murphy's Law dictated they'd be interrupted. Not a chance in hell. "I may not control much in this world, little shrink, but I promised you one night." And she'd said yes. Shockingly. "Nothing is going to keep me from you tonight." His words came out with an edge and, by the widening of her eyes, she caught it.

Good.

Nari couldn't breathe. Her knees weakened and her clothes were suddenly too confining. She'd never felt like this, and that was insane. Her body was foreign for a moment.

Angus shrugged out of his jacket, dropping the heavy leather to the floor. His smell washed over her. Minty and whiskey and man. A scent she'd wanted to dive into for almost a year now. She reached for the hem of his T-shirt, and he grasped her hand, drawing it to his mouth.

Gently, with an intensity that rendered her speechless, he kissed each knuckle. He moved to her then, settling her hand on the door and covering it with his own. His other hand went to her silk shirt, deftly releasing each button and tugging the remainder out of her slacks.

She'd known he'd be like this. Naturally trying to control the moment, even when he was visibly struggling to stay gentle. The pads of his fingertips brushed her bare abdomen, and she sucked in air at the jolt of fire that spread through her torso. Gently, he drew his hands up her ribs to her shoulders and slid the shirt down her arms. He had to release her hand to discard the material, and once he had, he took both of her hands and flattened them to the door.

"Now you're right where I want you," he rumbled, dipping his head to lick and nip her neck.

She knew at least ten ways to knock him on his butt, but her body took over and she tilted her head to give him better access. "Maybe you're right where I want you," she murmured.

"Maybe." He gently bit the shell of her ear and then kissed her again, going deep and holding nothing back.

She returned his kiss, having to stretch up to meet his mouth. When he released her to let them both breathe, she pulled one of her hands loose. "My turn. Mmm." She reached for his hem and pulled the thin material up and over his head to reveal his chest. "Angus." She gentled, her hand flattening over the two healed bullet wounds right beneath his heart, disturbed by how close he'd come to death.

"I was the better shot," he said, flicking open her front bra clasp with one finger.

This must've been when Lassiter shot him, but she wouldn't say that killer's name right now. Not when the muscled expanse of Angus's chest was finally hers to touch. Firm and broad, scarred and strong. Yeah. She leaned in and kissed his pec, a sense of urgency catching her by surprise.

Angus grasped her hips and lifted her against him.

She gasped and then grabbed on to his neck, her breasts bare against his skin. His very warm skin. He turned and started walking—she didn't care where. She pulled him closer, wrapping her legs around his waist and capturing him in her hold.

His stride didn't alter.

He took over the kiss, a low growl rumbling from his chest into her mouth to zing around her body. He laid her down on a soft down comforter, nimbly releasing the clasp of her pants and sliding them partway down her legs.

He crouched and pulled off her boots, running strong thumbs along the arches of her feet.

When had her feet become erogenous zones?

He stood then, looking down at her, taking his fill. The lights from the living room softly lit the room from behind him, leaving his handsome face in shadow.

A place Angus Force was accustomed to inhabiting.

"I wondered." The green of his eyes glowed as he

hooked his thumbs in the sides of her black lace panties. "This is what I hoped."

She swallowed, almost bare to him. He pulled them all the way off and caressed her legs from the ankles up to her thighs, touching her everywhere. It was as if there wasn't an inch of her he didn't want to touch at least once this night.

"God, you're beautiful," he whispered, his hands going to the clasp of his belt.

So was he. How hard did he work out to have a rippled six-pack of an abdomen even though he drank so much? She reached for him.

He hurriedly kicked off his boots and the rest of his clothes, kissing his way across her ribs and over her breasts, finally taking one nipple into his heated mouth.

She gasped and arched against him, surprised by the warmth of his skin. Heat spiraled off him. He played, kissing and licking, while she explored the hard planes of his shoulders and back, finding more wounds and healed scars. And muscle. Tight, dangerous, raw muscle.

He nipped her breast while finally reaching down between her legs, where she was more than ready for him.

He groaned. "I definitely want a taste."

"Later." She dug her nails into his arms to pull him up. "Definitely later. We have all night." For now, she needed him.

"Foreplay," he muttered, scarlet flashing across his rugged cheekbones.

"We've been foreplaying for a year," she gasped. "I'm ready. You're more than ready." And he was. Against her, he felt hard and long. Very. There was a lot to Angus, and it didn't surprise her in the least. She'd been peeking at his jeans for months.

He flattened his hand over her abdomen. "You're not in charge here, sweetheart." Keeping her flat against the bed, he moved down her and sucked her clit into his mouth. Full on, hot, with a slight scrape of his teeth.

She bowed, crying out, orgasming instantly. He didn't stop—maybe didn't even notice. He went at her, tongue and lips and teeth as if he couldn't get enough. She writhed against him, wild and crazy, unable to halt the second orgasm from rolling through her, stealing her breath.

He still didn't stop.

She pulled his thick hair. "Angus. Please, you have to quit."

He paused and looked up, his eyes burning. "I've waited a year for this."

Oh, God. She swallowed. "I can't again."

Wrong thing to say. Definitely the wrong thing. His chin lowered, and his facial scruff stretched across her clit.

The sound she made should've embarrassed her, but she was too far gone. Keeping her gaze, he lowered his mouth and nipped with enough power that she spiraled away again, shutting her eyes and riding out the waves.

"All night," he said to himself. "That's a start." With that, moved up her, flattened himself over her and reached for the nightstand.

She grabbed his tight butt. "You're crushing me."

"Never." He levered himself up on an elbow and ripped open a condom wrapper with his teeth. "You sure about this?"

"Yes." She didn't care what he was asking about. "I'm sure. About everything. The whole night, waiting for more foreplay, doing this now. Finally." Being coy or pretending wasn't her style, and she wanted him. Plus, it was obvious he was in the same state.

Hunger, raw and real, sizzled in his eyes.

She took the condom, reached down, and rolled it onto him. He jerked against her palm, feeling bigger even than she'd expected.

He licked her nipple, and fire arced to her still firing clit. She gasped and settled back on the pillow, her gaze trapped once again by his.

A lock of his hair fell toward his forehead and a droplet of rain landed on her temple.

Slowly, he pushed inside her, big and full. She held her breath, opening her thighs wider, trying to adjust to his size. Not once did he release her gaze as he controlled his body . . . and hers.

Finally he paused, deep inside her.

"Now," she whispered.

His grin was too predatory to be boyish. "Yeah. Now. At last." Even so, he started slow, driving into her with hard thrusts and brushing a spot inside her that had her seeing stars.

"More, Angus. More." She lifted her thighs and clasped her feet at his back, pressing in with her heels as hard as she could. How was this possible? She wanted more of him. All of him.

He let go then, pounding into her, fast and hard and full. Deeper, wilder, keeping her on an edge so sharp she had to shut her eyes.

She reached higher, holding on, her body opening to take all of him. The pressure finally exploded and she cried out, arching into him as another orgasm roared through her and shattered everything she knew. Pleasure swamped her, followed by a feeling of vulnerability she'd never experienced.

He kissed her hard, his powerful body shuddering violently with his own climax. He ground into her again, his kiss gentling as he finally released her mouth. His grin was wicked when he leaned up. "That was a good start for the night."

Chapter Nine

Angus remained on his side, his eyes shut as Nari quietly found her clothing and escaped to the other room to get dressed. Morning light streamed into the room beneath the cheap blinds, while her cinnamon scent hovered all around. His body began to awaken again. He'd learned every inch of her the night before, and now he only wanted her more. A part of him, one he didn't much like, wanted to let her sneak away quietly.

Instead, he rolled from the bed and yanked on a pair of jeans from the floor. He padded barefoot to the doorway and stopped as he heard her speaking softly.

"I'm going to miss you so much." Her voice was muffled.

He sighed and walked into his barren living room to see her somewhat dressed, sitting on the floor with her face buried in Roscoe's furry neck.

The dog looked up at him, his ears perked and his eyes intelligent.

Was he judging Angus? Angus frowned at the mutt and Roscoe's tongue rolled out.

Nari leaned back and scratched his neck with both hands. "It's okay, boy." Then she stiffened and looked over her shoulder. "Oh. Um, hi."

It wasn't fair that she should look so damn appealing in wrinkled clothes with no makeup on her face. She looked edible, despite the obvious whisker burn down her neck and over part of her jaw. "Hi," he rumbled.

Her gaze ran down his bare chest to his unbuttoned jeans and she blushed a light peach. "I was just leaving."

"I can see that." He held out a hand to help her up, fighting every instinct he had to keep from tossing her over his shoulder and returning to the bed.

The dog whined.

"Knock it off," Angus muttered. It looked like Nari was already having a tough time saying goodbye to the mutt. She turned and edged away from him, plastering a fake smile on her face. He sighed. "I'd offer to make you breakfast, but I don't have anything but dog food here. Should we talk about last night?"

She lifted her chin. "What is there to talk about?"

Good question. They'd set the perimeters the night before, and he had to let her go. This was the last time she could be seen with him, because he was going after whoever had killed those two women, Lassiter or not. "I guess this is goodbye." The idea hurt more than he would've expected. Even if the circumstances were different, he wasn't relationship material. Not even close. "I'm sorry."

She ducked for her jacket on the floor, quickly donning it and covering her wrinkled silk shirt. "There's nothing to be sorry about. Last night was our one night." Her smile came more naturally this time. "I enjoyed myself and so did you."

Yeah, he had. "You deserve more." The words were out before he could stop himself.

"I know." She patted Roscoe's head again. "So do you, even though you don't believe that. I hope you find peace back at your cabin with your dog."

There would be no peace. "Thanks." He kept his expression neutral.

With her hair all mussed, she looked adorable—and sexy as hell. "Are you really heading out of here?"

"Definitely," he lied. If a killer was after him, or messing with him, cutting ties to everyone he knew was necessary. He'd been so obsessed with hunting Lassiter that he hadn't protected his own sister from the monster. She'd died at Lassiter's hands, because Lassiter had drawn Angus into his game, and Angus still hadn't recovered from that fact. "One thing. A favor for me."

Her lips twitched. "I did enough favors for you last night."

Humor belted him out of nowhere. "True. Very true. And you're going to give me one more." He tried to make it sound like a request, but he didn't come close. So be it.

She tilted her head, her eyes a clear brown, even though he hadn't let her sleep for long. "What is it?"

"Be safe. Take extra precautions, just until this new killer is caught. I'll be gone, so it stands to reason that he'll move on to another target if he is messing with our team. The appearances of the two victims could just be a coincidence. However, I need to know you'll be safe."

That was as much of his feelings as he could or would admit.

"No problem. Do you think there'll be another body tonight?"

He shook his head as he relaxed at her easy acceptance. "No. I think we weren't supposed to find last night's victim for a while. No serial killer is that prolific."

"Good." She faltered, as if not sure how to say goodbye.

He reached her and enfolded her in a hug, holding tighter than was necessary. Her scent, fresh and spicy, filled him, and she hugged him back, pressing her cheek into his chest. Then he stepped away and forced his body to go cold and his mind to go blank. Releasing her physically hurt. What the hell was wrong with him? "'Bye, Nari."

"'Bye." She turned and left his apartment without looking back. He stared at the closed door for several moments before looking down at his dog, who had on his cranky expression. "Shut up." Then he hustled to the window and lifted the blinds, scouting the entire parking lot to make sure nobody was around. Nari soon exited the building and climbed into her car, driving away and out of his life.

Nobody followed her.

"Okay." He let the blinds fall back into place, scattering dust, his world suddenly empty. "You ready for it to be just you and me again?"

The dog sneezed.

"Me too. Let's pack up." Angus turned to gather his meager possessions. "This won't take long."

* * *

She was sore. In all sorts of interesting places. Her body ached after a full night with Angus Force. Nari sighed, freshly dressed in a light blue suit with coral kitten heels. How awkward had it been that morning with Angus?

Her soft groan echoed around the elevator.

She tried to forget the feel of Angus's hands on her— on all of her—as she rode the elevator to the fifth floor and her new office. It seemed weird to be joining a team on a Wednesday. Shouldn't they at least give her until the following week to wrap things up with her previous assignment?

She felt a pang in her heart. She was going to miss that group of misfits. Somehow she'd felt as if she'd finally fit in somewhere.

The elevator opened and she stepped out into an un-manned vestibule, turning left and walking on thick tile. Slight bruises on her hips from his strong grip rubbed against her skirt, making her ache. Reminding her that he'd all but marked her in a dozen ways the night before. His hands, his mouth, his incredible body. She strode past bustling offices and various conference rooms to another vestibule, where she stopped and opened a thick set of doors to a suite, where the tile floor turned to dark wood.

She walked directly into a conference room with a large, square table holding telephones, notepads, and pens. Nobody was around. Windows in front of her showed a parking lot, while hallways in each direction no doubt led to offices.

"Hello?" she called.

Footsteps sounded, and Vaughn Ealy strode into the room.

Nari swallowed. Her anxiety ratcheted up. Fast.

It had been more than a year since they'd seen each other, but he looked the same. Tall, broad, tousled brown hair and intelligent brown eyes. Today he wore a dark gray suit with a matching tie over a white-and-blue-striped shirt.

"Nari." He strode forward and took her hand, his gaze expressionless. "It's good to see you."

"You too." She shook and then removed her hand as his expensive cologne subtly wafted toward her. "I was surprised to end up on your team."

He gestured her down the way he'd come, all business. "I'm sure, and I thought we could discuss it before you meet the rest of the team. I have them all out on assignment, so I'll introduce them to you on Friday morning. Tomorrow you'll spend all day at HR getting transferred and watching the videos and all that procedural stuff."

She'd take the day of reprieve before starting with new people. Her stomach ached. She walked down the hallway, noting the clean lines and pleasant colors. How different it was from the dingy basement where she'd worked during the past year. How different this man was from the one who'd kissed every inch of her the night before. She swallowed.

Vaughn halted her by the arm at an office toward the end. "This will be yours."

It was a medium-size office with wide windows overlooking what looked like a park. It'd be nice to have windows again. The carpet was dark and she had several watercolors that would look perfect in the room. She could even put a bed for Roscoe in—

She shook her head. Roscoe didn't work with her any longer. Loneliness descended onto her shoulders with a surprising chill.

"This way." Vaughn released her and moved toward the next office, which he opened. "My office."

She followed him in and sank into a guest chair, while he walked around his desk and sat, facing her. A position of power. Framed awards and photos of him with political figures lined the bookshelf next to him, while diplomas covered the opposite wall. Behind him was a wide window.

"So," she said. "Care to explain how I ended up on your team?"

"Ask your daddy."

Ah. There was the asshat she remembered. Oh, he'd hidden that aspect of himself for the first four months they'd dated, but the truth inevitably emerged. She studied him. It was odd that while he was probably the same age as Angus, he looked ambitious and kind of fresh, where Angus, well, didn't. Angus was more wounded, angry, and sexy. Both handsome, but in a totally different way. A fight between them would be interesting.

She started. Where in the world had that thought come from?

Even so, it would be. They were both tough and well trained. Vaughn would be calculating and Angus would be fierce. Yeah. Her money was on Angus Force.

Her abdomen did a slow roll, heating her tender sex.

"Nari?" Vaughn asked. "I lost you for a minute."

He'd lost her for all time.

She smiled. "Well, I suppose my daddy, as you called him, wanted us to get the gossip behind us so we could move on." Quan had liked Vaughn and probably still did. They were similar men. Interesting. She hadn't noticed that before either. Wasn't she chock full of insights today? "Our working together and seeming to get along will quiet any rumblings. Plus, it sounds like your team might need me."

Vaughn sat back and studied her with a look that would've intrigued her before she'd gotten to know him. "I've looked beneath your façade. You're high-strung, irrational, and violent."

She forced a smile, her heart rate speeding up. "That's not fair." A guy with an ego like his would definitely not like the fact that she'd gone over his head—a fact that had, unfortunately, gone public. But she wouldn't apologize for trying to save a fellow agent.

"It might not be fair, but it's true." He flattened his hands on his neatly organized desk.

"Actually, I believe I was calm, collected, and measured in doing my job and protecting Lisa as well as the entire agency." She lowered her chin. Why did jackasses always say a woman was high-strung or irrational when she reacted appropriately? "Get over it, Vaughn." Not the tone she wanted to take with him, but he wasn't giving her a choice.

"I don't want you on my team." Anger shone in his eyes, but he managed to keep his tone level.

"I don't want to be on your team," she agreed. "So you

should request a transfer. You know as well as I do that my father won't help if I ask to be moved."

Vaughn sighed. "I guess he knows you better than I did. You don't belong in this agency."

Maybe not. Sometimes she doubted she did. She crossed her legs, reminded instantly of a slight bite mark on her thigh from Angus. He'd marked her. She felt all warm and mushy for the slightest of moments.

"Come on, Nari. You're only here to prove something to your absentee father. Why don't you quit and open a practice and make tons of money?" he asked.

The words were a direct hit—the truth usually was. She banished thoughts of Angus and what might've been. It was over, and now she had to deal with real life. How had she found herself involved with this jerk again? She had belonged with Angus Force's team and she had made a difference there. She was good at her job. "What's the case you're working on, Vaughn?" They were getting nowhere with this conversation.

He opened a desk drawer and retrieved a deep-blue file folder to slide across the desk. "We're investigating a fairly new transnational gang that originated in El Salvador and has set up here in DC. They're primarily into drug running right now."

She lifted her eyebrows. "They're in competition with MS-13 and the 18th Street Gang?"

"They're trying to be."

She reached for the file folder. "They haven't been taken out by either gang yet?"

"No. They're surprisingly well funded and trained. I'm trying to avoid a drug war in the middle of the Capitol.

In the file you'll find all the research so far. I need you to develop profiles on the top gang members, and then I'd like you to meet the team. No doubt you'll want to set up weekly meetings with everyone, as per new regulations. Except for me because we were in a relationship."

"I'll get started, then." She stood, wanting to get out of there. Now.

"I won't make this assignment easy on you, Nari. If I were you, I'd try to get transferred as soon as possible," he said.

She shut the door on the last of his words.

Chapter Ten

After an extra-long shower and a search for clean clothes in his apartment, Angus had finally packed up his meager belongings. He still smelled Nari on him. The spicy scent of her shampoo somehow clung to his skin, even after his shower. What was that smell? It was light and female, but with a bite. Maybe a combination of cinnamon and chai. He'd had a chai latte once, and that intoxicating smell reminded him of Nari.

He drove for over an hour, retracing his steps, going in odd directions, making sure he lost any tail that might be on him. Nobody caught his eye. The rain had finally let up, leaving the world barren and waiting with silent breath for the first storm of winter.

Finally he reached a diner in Virginia in the middle of nowhere that only had two battered trucks by the entrance. He drove to the far end of the lot near a forested area, where Agent Millie Frost waited in her light green VW Bug. He pulled in next to her.

His former employee, one he'd known only a short while, got out of her car. Today the streaks in her hair were gone, and the blond tresses on her shoulders made her look more like the girl next door. She reached into the back seat for a duffel bag and set it on the hood.

"Hi." He let Roscoe out, and the dog bounded over to the woman for some love.

Millie dropped to her haunches, not having far to go. She snuggled up to Roscoe and scratched his fur. "Howdy, buddy." Then she stood, wiping her hands down dark jeans that matched a T-shirt with the *Firefly* cast on it. "This is weird."

"I'm okay with that. Did you bring it?" Angus asked.

"Yep." She drew the sweeper out of the duffel and came toward his truck, running the box down the first tire. "Did you already conduct a visual search for a passive tracker?"

He signaled for Roscoe to sit. "Yes. There's no passive tracker, and I doubt there's an active one, but I wanted to make sure."

She continued toward the front of his truck. "I thought you said goodbye to everybody last night. Heard you boys got a little drunk."

"Yeah, we did. I just want to check the vehicle before I head back home." He leaned against her car, watching her work. The woman was meticulous; in fact, the only time he'd seen her truly serious was when she was dealing with gadgets. "Thanks for skipping work today. Where did you get reassigned anyway?"

She reached the other side, ducking down and disappearing from sight. "I didn't. I quit."

He launched himself around his truck, his ears ringing. "What do you mean, you quit? You can't just quit."

"You did." She didn't look up from the blinking lights on the scanner.

He crossed his arms. While she'd only been on the team a few months, he was responsible for her. Besides, with her blond hair free of the colorful streaks, she looked a little bit like his sister. Was a smart-ass like her, too. "I didn't quit. I was fired, and that doesn't reflect on you."

She stood and stretched her back. "I need to inspect the undercarriage."

He frowned, a look that had made more than one junior agent take a step back during his FBI days.

Millie lifted one light eyebrow. "What?"

He glowered at her. "You know what."

She sighed, her blue eyes an odd, light-cerulean color. "I quit, Angus. I'm allowed. In fact, I've gotten offers from several top tech companies as well as more governmental agencies than I can count. I can write my own ticket if I want."

"Why did you quit?"

"I wanted to." Without giving him another chance to question her, she dropped and rolled beneath the vehicle as if she'd done so a million times before.

Maybe he didn't have a right to question her. It wasn't as if the woman lacked options. He ducked down to watch her. "When are you going back to work?"

"Haven't decided. I may put more streaks in my hair and travel a little bit first." She scanned the undercarriage. "I could use a walkabout."

That'd be perfect. "The sooner you get out of town, the better. Just in case, I mean." He kept his voice casual and stood to make sure Roscoe hadn't gotten into any trouble. The dog was scouting around the trees, his tail wagging, his body relaxed.

Millie finished her inspection, rolled to the other side,

and checked out the interior of the truck. Finally she jumped down. "You're fine. No trackers. When you drive away I'll scan you just in case there's a tracker that works only when you're moving." She tossed the device in the air and caught it easily in her small hands. "You sure there's somebody after you?"

"No." He wasn't sure if Lassiter was alive and he had no clue whether the new killer was really targeting his team. "I don't know crap, Millie. To be on the safe side, I'd just like for you to get away from here." Until he found the killer.

She pressed her hands on her hips. "If you're worried, there's a bad guy out there. In that case, you're not the type to head back to your cabin."

God needed to spare him from intelligent and insightful women, damn it. "You've read me wrong. I'm gone," he said.

Roscoe bounded over, and she ducked to hug the dog one more time. "We could've done a lot of good if the team had stayed together," she mumbled before standing.

Yeah, and he might've seen another pretty blonde in the morgue. The image of his sister would never leave him, and the last thing he wanted was to see Millie that way. He had to figure out who was behind the latest killings. "'Bye, Millie." He patted her shoulder, whistled at his dog, and then jumped into his truck.

It'd be him against this guy. Period.

Nari stepped out of her car in Pippa's driveway with her mom's Waldorf salad in her hands. She needed a girls' night now more than ever, and she was probably early, but she didn't care. After her disastrous meeting with Vaughn she'd spent the day getting caught up on the El Salvadoran gang. By the end of the day she was as shaky as a new colt. Would Vaughn's attitude toward her be matched by the rest of the team?

While Angus hadn't liked her working with his operatives, he had still been polite. Well, usually. Even when he was cranky, he had a kindness in him toward the team that had made her feel welcome. Or at least safe.

There was only one other finished house in the cul-de-sac where Wolfe and Dana lived. Another house was under construction across the circle, where Raider and Brigid were building. The whole team seemed to be taking over the cul-de-sac, and a pang hit her heart dead center.

She'd never be part of that team again.

Shaking it off, she walked across the porch and knocked on the door of Pippa and Malcolm's charming cottage.

Pippa threw open the door, and the scent of cookies wafted out. "Nari." The taller woman enfolded her in a hug. "I'm so glad you came." She drew Nari inside, looking at ease in a light yellow sweater, blue jeans, and brown leather boots.

"Me too." Nari glanced past the living room toward the kitchen. While Pippa often baked, she somehow smelled like cookies even if there weren't any around.

"I have a new chicken dish in the oven and I took out an apple pie about an hour ago." Pippa took the salad from Nari and gestured her toward the sofa, where Brigid had already settled back with a glass of white wine. "You want red or white? I have both open."

"Red, then." Nari smiled at Brigid and walked toward her, flopping onto the adjacent seat.

Brigid's red hair curled around her soft face. "Rough day?"

"You have no idea." What was Nari going to do without seeing her friends every day? "The leader of my new team doesn't like me." She smiled when Pippa returned and handed over a full glass of red. "It could be because we dated and I nearly destroyed his career, but I'm just guessing."

Pippa stopped in midstride to the kitchen and flipped around. "What?" Her blue eyes widened.

Nari took a healthy sip of the drink. Ah, Cabernet. So good. "This is delicious."

Pippa hustled around the table and sat next to Brigid. "Oh, you're telling all. Right now. The chicken is still cooking."

Nari told them the entire story while enjoying her wine. "So, there you go."

Stunned silence met her tale.

Brigid spoke first. "Your da is the deputy administrator of the HDD?" Her Irish brogue came out full force, while her emerald-colored eyes sparkled.

Nari blinked. Oops. "Didn't I tell you that before?"

Pippa chuckled. "You know you didn't."

Nari winced, her neck heating. "Well, he's just my sperm donor, to be honest. My mom remarried when I was around twelve and I love my stepdad. I call him Dad.

He lives in California with my mom and he's the one I love."

"Does Angus know you're related to our boss?" Brigid asked.

Pippa laughed full-out this time. "Oh, that's going to be a fun discussion." She sobered. "I mean, if we see him again. I can't believe he actually said goodbye last night."

Well, for Nari it had been that morning, but she wasn't ready to share that much. Not yet anyway. "I was surprised he left with a serial killer on the loose. Even if we know the killer isn't Lassiter, when Angus gets his teeth in a case, he doesn't let go," Nari murmured. Maybe he'd just had enough. It wasn't like one night with her would change his mind.

She crossed her legs, and a bite mark on her thigh twinged.

A soft knock sounded and then Millie Frost bounced in. "I come bearing rolls." She held up a basket. "I bought them." The tech wore jeans with a little bit of dirt around the hems and a sweater. Her hair was all blond this time. "Serena called me on the way—she got stuck in some faculty meeting at the college. Says to start dinner without her, but she'll still try to make it."

Nari sighed. Serena was a creative genius and always made the evening fun. Hopefully she'd come at least for dessert.

Pippa stood and took the basket. "You took out your streaks."

Millie grinned. "Yeah. I'll put some back in eventually, but I was tired of the colors. We'll see." She looked around. "I turn twenty-eight next week and I'm no longer under-cover as a computer tech, so maybe it's time to forget the streaks. I kept them partly to tick off HDD, but nobody really seems to care."

The woman did not look twenty-eight. Nari sipped her wine more slowly, her mind spinning.

The door opened and Dana swept in, a small, white kitten in her hands. "Kat wanted to come. I hope that's okay."

Wolfe hovered right behind her, his body braced, as if to catch her. The man was huge compared to the blond journalist, who wasn't exactly short.

Dana's angled face flushed. "I made it here safely, Wolfe. Go back to playing poker with your friends. *Now*."

Nari coughed to cover her laugh.

Wolfe gently, oh so gently, took Dana's elbow and tried to help her sit.

Dana's eyes sparked and she jerked her hand free. "I'm only three months pregnant, buddy. I'm fine. I can walk, I can talk, and I can even spar. Go. Please, Wolfe."

Wolfe's powerful chest filled. "All right, but call me before you walk home."

Brigid pressed her lips together. "Yeah. The several feet between houses can be treacherous."

Wolfe nodded, approval lifting his lips. "Exactly, Bridge. You get it." He leaned down and kissed Dana before turning to the door. "Dana thinks I'm obsessed, but I'm not. I'm just doing what needs to be done."

What needs to be done. Like Angus always did. Wait a minute. Nari's head jerked. Realization struck her. "There is no way Angus Force just left town with a serial killer on the loose. Especially when one victim had a Roscoe tattoo and the other looked Irish."

Wolfe frowned. "He said he was done, and he looked like it. In fact, he acted like it."

Well, that was true. He wouldn't have propositioned Nari if he hadn't intended to leave. Nari sighed. Maybe she just wanted him to still be in town. "Yeah, he really did," she said softly.

"It is what it is. For now, I'm going to go win all the money I can because we're currently unemployed." Wolfe shrugged.

Nari settled more comfortably on the sofa. "Nobody has been reassigned?"

Brigid picked at a string on her jeans. "Raider was reassigned to the main Homeland Security and I'm supposed to report to a new computer center at Homeland Defense on Monday. It'll suck not working together."

Nari bit her lip. Maybe she could figure out a way to have Brigid work with her team. "Anybody else?"

Wolfe shook his head. "It's doubtful that Mal, Dana, or I still have jobs. Thus, my plan for poker tonight. Have a nice dinner. For now, lock the door." He didn't wait for Pippa to follow his instructions but locked the door and then shut it, his bootsteps heavy outside.

Brigid turned toward her. "I'm with you, Nari. Something feels off about Angus leaving. What should we do?"

Chapter Eleven

Angus groaned and unzipped the sleeping bag laid out on the hard bed. The way-too-hard bed. "Where the hell did Wolfe get this thing?" he muttered, an old bullet wound in his side aching.

Roscoe looked up from the end of the bed and glared at him.

Angus rolled his eyes. "I'm so sorry, Your Highness. Most dogs sleep on the damn floor, you know." He looked around the rugged cabin. Wolfe had purchased it about six months before for an Op but hadn't needed it. During that time, Brigid had created a chain of ownership for the place that didn't lead to anybody. Wolfe had finally sold it a month ago, and Angus had bought it through a set of dummy corporations. Even back then, he'd had an inkling he'd have to separate from his team to finish this case.

Man, Wolfe would be pissed if he found out Angus had purchased the cabin in the middle of the woods. Of course, this bed was decent revenge. Angus's entire body ached.

His gaze focused on the murder board he'd stretched across the entire north wall. It was the only wall without windows in the small cabin, and Lassiter's face was right in the middle, next to a blank sheet with a question mark. The new killer, if there was one. Pictures of victims lined the left, while other cops and his contacts to the right.

In the corner a fire crackled in the stone fireplace, next to the sliding door that led to the front porch. His kitchen, if it could be called that, was on the opposite side, and the lone bathroom was next to that. Only a sofa and one chair resided in front of the fireplace.

It was kind of homey, and the electricity worked; that was all he needed.

His phone buzzed. Was it Nari? He grabbed it off the floor, quickly reading the text. "Damn." He sat up and called Tate. "You can't have another body."

"We do, and you're gonna want to see her. I can get you in and out of the scene, but we have to be quick. My balls are on the line here," his friend said, giving him directions.

Angus jerked. "Say that again. The address."

Tate paused and then gave it. "I take it you know the place?"

"I just moved out of that complex," Angus growled. "She's in the laundry room?"

"Affirmative. Laundry room in complex B. That's where you used to live?" Tate asked, his voice lowering.

Heat smashed through Angus's muscles. "Yeah. That's my complex." So much for any of this being a coincidence.

"Hell. Okay. You're officially a witness at this point, so we're going to have to be even more careful if I let you study the scene. Get here as quick as you can. I'll tell the uniform guarding the front to let you in." He paused, and there was a muffled sound behind him. "This is a bad one, Force." Then he clicked off.

His heart pounding, Angus swung his legs over the edge of the bed and lowered his head into his hands. He took several deep breaths, forcing himself to remain calm and rational. Three bodies in three days—and now one near his home. This was a game that seemed carefully planned out by the killer.

He jerked on jeans and a somewhat clean T-shirt, hit the bathroom, and was in his truck within minutes. Roscoe took care of business outside and jumped into the front seat, oddly sober. "I'm sorry, buddy. I know you already miss the team." Angus reached out and scratched the dog's ears.

Then he pulled out of the small clearing by the cabin and drove down the dirt road flanked on each side by forest and a lot of underbrush, all covered with morning dew. At least it wasn't raining.

The substantial ache in his gut increased with each mile until he reached his former apartment complex, where police cars and crime tech vans angled in from every direction. Crime scene tape secured the front of the building. He jumped out of his truck and walked through the vehicles as if he had every right to do so, then gave his name to the first uniform by the front door.

He was nodded through.

So far, so good. He headed straight for the laundry room on the basement level that he'd used many times, passing crime techs and other police officers.

Tate waited for him by the door, standing a head taller than most of the people around them. He was built like a linebacker, but he'd once told Angus that he'd attended college on a tennis scholarship. The guy did move gracefully. Today his dark-brown eyes burned with a fire close to fury.

Angus reached him. "What do you know?"

Tate rubbed the dark skin across his forehead. "Victim looks to be in her midtwenties, but we don't have an ID yet. We don't have the fancy gadgets of the federal agencies, and so far her prints haven't brought anything back. The medical examiner puts time of death at a few days ago. We don't know yet how long she was with the killer or where he had her." Tate stepped aside.

Angus allowed no emotion to show in his expression as he turned and entered the long room with its collection of older washers and dryers.

The body lay on a table used to fold clothes, her body naked, her eyes open. Burn marks showed down both arms and bruises marred her neck as if she'd been strangled repeatedly. Rope tied her ankles together, and her hands rested, palms up, at her sides. Her chest gaped open, one broken rib sticking out. The cuts looked more uniform this time. Her heart was gone.

She had long blond hair and green eyes that were murky in death.

"No note?" Angus asked, the room swirling around him.

"Haven't found one yet." Tate flipped out his notebook, which looked ridiculously small in his glove-covered hand. "Does this victim look like anybody from your team?"

Angus blew out air. "I have two blond females on my team—or former team—and one has green eyes." Dana. Wolfe would lose his fucking mind if his pregnant fiancée was in this kind of danger. "But there are millions of blond women in the world."

"Yes." Tate gestured him toward the body and then gently lifted her stiff arm, turning it over. "Does this ring a bell?"

A tattoo of the *Washington Times* logo was freshly inked on her skin, as evidenced by the reddening around it.

Angus sucked in air as if he'd been punched. "Yeah. Dana Mulberry has written articles for the *Times*."

Tate released the woman. "I guess the killer wants you to be sure now."

"Apparently."

Tate's phone rang and he lifted it to his ear. "Tate Bianchi." He listened, looked at Angus, and then nodded. "Yes, sir. I think it's connected. All right." He clicked off. "I'm supposed to bring you in for questioning."

Angus shoved his hands in his pockets. "Good thing I'm here, then. Let's go."

After the fourth hour of being questioned by two Metropolitan Police detectives in a box of an interrogation room, Angus was suddenly having sympathy for all those folks he'd interviewed through the years. Of course, most of them were guilty. It made sense that Tate wasn't the one to question him, considering they were friends. At least the cops had let Roscoe come in to the interrogation room, where he was snoring quietly in the corner.

Finally the two detectives left, asking him to stay put and seeming cranky about it.

He looked at the sleeping dog. He and Roscoe could leave, but why? He didn't mind helping, and hopefully the cops would let some facts slip. There was no doubt Tate couldn't keep including him now, so his access to information would be limited.

The door opened and HDD Special Agents Rutherford and Fields walked inside, looking like federal agents with their suits and air of irritation.

"Ah, shit. What are you two doing here?" Angus muttered.

They drew out chairs across the metal table from him and sat. "You would not believe the favors we had to call in to get here," Fields said, reaching for a cough drop from his pocket. "Apparently Metro PD doesn't want to share you. They're pissed we're here."

Good to know. Angus could use that to his advantage for the duration of this case.

Rutherford set a leather briefcase on the floor. His blond hair was slightly damp and he crossed his arms over his red power tie. When had it started raining? "I thought you were going to leave town."

"I was on my way out when I heard the news about the body," Angus lied.

Roscoe opened one eye to watch the proceedings from his position in the corner.

Rutherford set his phone on the table, pushing the Record button. "This is Special Agent Rutherford with HDD Special Agent Fields, interviewing former Agent Angus Force." Rutherford finished with the date and time before straightening. "Have you been read your rights?"

"Nope. Want to run me through those?" Angus drawled. Might as well make the jackwad jump through hoops.

Rutherford did so without blinking. "Do you understand the rights as they've been read to you?"

"Yeppers," Angus said. "Is this going to take long? If so, we're gonna need dinner. I'm getting peckish."

"Yes, it's going to take a while, whether Metro or you like it," Rutherford said, his smooth-shaven face darkening. "Let's start with the most recent body. The woman was found in the laundry facility of your apartment complex, right?"

"Yes," Angus answered, his throat parched.

Rutherford reached for a yellow file folder. "Where were you between the hours of three and six a.m. this morning?"

Angus grew still. "Excuse me?"

Rutherford smiled, showing perfectly even white teeth. "Based on our investigation, the body was dumped during that time frame. Where were you?"

Irritation heated through Angus, so he let his lip curl in a smile. "You can't seriously be telling me I'm a suspect."

Agent Fields finished chewing his cough drop, and the smell of menthol wafted around. "Of course you're a suspect. Think about it, Force."

Huh. Interesting. He truly hadn't thought that one out. Angus rubbed his chin. "I've never been a suspect before." Did he know any lawyers who didn't dislike him? The list of people who actually *did* like him was pretty short, and even those he wasn't sure about.

Roscoe, as if sensing a change in the atmosphere of the room, lumbered to his feet and padded over to Angus's side. He sat, at attention, his ears up and his brown eyes facing the agents.

Fields shook his head. "That dog is something else." Admiration glowed in his eyes.

Rutherford slid the phone closer to Angus. "You've

been obsessed with Henry Wayne Lassiter for at least six years, and once you'd killed him, you still didn't think he was dead. The victims this week have all shown markers of the Lassiter case, and they all resemble the female agents from your ragtag HDD team. You need to account for your time, and you need to do so right now."

Angus's phone buzzed and he pulled it free of his jeans to read a text from Tate. Everything inside him went cold. They'd found a note. He looked up, smiled, and then stood. "I have to go."

Rutherford slid back in his chair. "The hell you do. This is an interview."

Angus moved toward the door. "I'm here voluntarily and I can leave. Either arrest me or get the hell out of my way."

Rutherford's nostrils flared and he kicked over his chair when he stood.

Fields stood more slowly. "Okay. Let's compromise. If you agree to come in to our HDD office tomorrow for an official interview, we won't cause a ruckus now."

They didn't have cause for a ruckus and they knew it. But Angus needed information on this case, and they'd be bound to give some while interviewing him. "I'll be there at eight a.m." With that, he hustled out of the room, Roscoe on his heels.

He turned left down a quiet hallway toward the bullpen, but Tate was already heading his way.

"Took a picture. Get out of here and we'll talk later," Tate said, smoothly handing over a printout. "My boss is working on a warrant for your house."

"I consent to a search of my apartment," Angus said, pocketing the paper and turning to head for the exit in the other direction. "I'll text that to you so you have something in writing." He paused, looking over his shoulder. "You don't think I'm a suspect?"

"Oh, you're a suspect," Tate said quietly, "but no way in hell did you murder those women. I'll clear you as soon as I can, but HDD is on the case now, and they're being pushy. Fancy jackasses."

Angus nodded. "You're a good guy, Bianchi." He hurried out of the building in the dribble of rain and jumped into his truck. There were cameras mounted in several spots, so he got Roscoe settled before sending a quick text to Wolfe:

> New victim—looks like Dana and had a tattoo
> logo of one of the papers she worked for. Lock
> her down and keep yourself safe. I'll call you later
> when I know more—Force

Then he ignited the engine and pulled sedately out of the lot. He'd look at the picture once he was out of view.

He drove for a while, the paper in his pocket scalding hot. He tugged it out. Lassiter had always addressed the letter to Angus and then written a quote or combination of quotes from other people. This letter didn't have a salutation, only a quote in italics.

Slivers of time make up each moment, and only the pale horse and his master prevail in the most crucial of breathy gasps.

"Jesus," he muttered. "Not this shit again." Finally he exited the interstate. It was past dinnertime, but he wasn't hungry. Although he should find a burger or something for Roscoe.

A ping echoed, and his back window shattered.

He swerved as more bullets impacted his truck. "Duck, Roscoe." He shoved the dog onto the floor just as a bullet whizzed by his head, smashing his front window.

Chapter Twelve

Nari kicked her door open while juggling her briefcase in one hand and a bag of takeout in the other. What a mind-dulling day she'd spent at the HR department of the HDD. Maybe she should just start her own practice. She stepped inside her peaceful apartment and dropped her keys and purse on the table by the door before shutting it. Silence—blissful silence—surrounded her.

The exclusive, two-story apartments in her gated community were more like town houses. They were rented by urban professionals who commuted from Virginia into DC, or by retired people who still liked to be involved in the DC whirlwind. The quietness of the area was one of the reasons for the exorbitant price tag.

She kicked off her heels and padded in her stockinged feet beyond the peaceful living room to the adjacent kitchen to set the food on the bar. The muted colors she'd chosen for the first floor provided some comfort, but a big old German shepherd on the white sofa would be better. Where was Roscoe? Did he miss her?

Did Angus?

She rolled her eyes and dumped her briefcase on the floor. Of course he didn't. Just because they were attracted to each other didn't mean he actually liked her. Although their night together had been the best of her life and she still had his teeth marks on her lower left buttock. At the thought, her body tingled.

Man, she had to get a grip. It wasn't like she didn't enjoy eating dinner by herself. Alone on her sofa watching the news. Yeah, right. Maybe she should get a pet.

A noise from the home office adjacent to the kitchen caught her attention. Had she left the darn window open? It had rained earlier and the sill would be wet again.

Another sound. The atmosphere changed. Somebody was in her apartment and she reacted instantly, turning and rushing toward the front door. Her heart sped up and panic nearly tripped her. Hard arms tackled her from behind, propelling them both into the solid metal of the door. Her forehead hit and stars blew up behind her eyes. Crying out, she went down, instinctively pulling up her right knee toward her chest to balance herself and not go flat beneath the attacker.

From behind, he reached around her head and roughly shoved a rag against her nose and mouth.

She yelled for help, her movements faltering as blood thundered loudly in her ears. There was no time to think. She plunged her elbow back into his gut and twisted her head away, sucking in clean air and using her knee as a fulcrum to toss him to the side. He grunted, going over and pulling her with him, his hands rough on her arms.

Her temple hit the side of her entryway table and she fell flat onto her back. Pain lanced down her entire body and her muscles started to freeze. He took advantage and pulled her away from the door, levering himself up and straddling her. He wore all black, including a face mask that covered his entire head. Gloves shielded his large hands and he scrambled for the rag that had fallen on the carpet.

Training kicked in and her mind went blank. Her temples throbbed and her vision blurred, but she pushed the pain away for now. She lifted her knees and planted her feet on the ground, her head ringing. Tears filled her eyes and she blinked them away. He was over six feet tall and probably around one-eighty. The eyes looked like a fake shade of brown, and they were blank. He found the rag and punched her shoulder, holding her to the ground. Then he brought the rag toward her mouth.

She pressed down with her heels and lifted her torso, twisting to the side and grunting loudly. He tottered on top of her and she reared up, punching him square in the eye in a rapid set of hits that had him howling and trying to avoid her fist. Grunting, sobbing, she scooted her butt back and tried to get out from under him, punching down toward his groin as fast and as hard as she could.

Her back hit the door and she screamed, high and loud.

Surely someone would hear her.

He swore and jumped to his feet, kicking her in the thigh.

Agony ripped up to her hip, but she shoved the table at him. He jumped back and she surged to her feet, dropping into a fighting stance. He rushed her, and she side-kicked his knee, eliciting a pain-filled grunt. He pivoted in a decent move and didn't go down.

"Nari? Are you okay?" called Mrs. Flannagan, her neighbor, from the front porch area.

The attacker yanked a gun from the back of his waist, his chest heaving. "Say yes." His voice emerged muffled from the mask.

"Call the police and run," Nari yelled, the room swirling around her. Bile rose in her stomach. Her vision blurred.

"Damn it. We're not done, bitch." The attacker turned and ran through the kitchen and out the back sliding door.

The taste of metal filled her mouth. She turned and tried to open the front door. Her hands slipped off the handle and she tried again, pulling it open. Gasping, she stumbled out and into the arms of Mrs. Flannagan. The elderly woman tried to help her, but the last thing Nari remembered before the world went dark was calling for Angus Force.

More bullets impacted his truck. Angus gunned the engine and careened down the exit ramp, taking the turn too fast and speeding along the quiet road. Thank goodness he'd chosen a road far away from the DC traffic to find Roscoe a burger. He looked in his rearview mirror while reaching for the gun in his glove box, seeing a navy-blue truck with darkly shaded windows. It looked like two figures were in the vehicle, but he couldn't be sure.

Roscoe tried to jump up, but Angus pushed him back down and away from the glass littering the seat. "Stay down," he ordered again, grabbing the gun and looking for the right place to stop.

Mom-and-pop stores lined one side of the road, still quietly busy. A long field lined the other side, but he hadn't seen a road or even a trail yet. He passed a diner, a tire shop, a pawn shop, and kept going when he saw folks milling around at the businesses. He wouldn't be responsible for getting anybody else shot.

Apparently the guy behind him agreed because the shooting had stopped. For now.

He glared into the mirror, trying to catch a license plate as he headed deeper into Virginia, twisting and turning on the road. The last thing he wanted was to put himself on the radar of the police, but he'd been with the FBI and the HDD, and that meant something. He flipped over his phone and dialed 911.

A barrel poked out of the passenger side of the truck behind him. He ducked down as far as he could in his seat and sped up even more, stiffening when the operator asked what his emergency was.

"This is Angus Force—" A bullet impacted his back tire, causing the truck to skid. He gripped the steering wheel, trying to keep control of the vehicle. Roscoe barked from his perch.

"Down. All the way down," Angus commanded, just in case they collided. The dog scrunched down all the way, his nose no longer visible. At least he knew when to obey.

"Sir? What is happening, sir?" the operator asked, her voice still calm.

"I'm former FBI and HDD and I'm being engaged by two people in a navy-blue Ford truck, no license plate in front." He reached a semistraight part of the road and grabbed the steering wheel with his left hand, turning to fire out his window with his right. He gave the operator his location.

The truck swerved behind him.

"We have units close," the woman said. Less than a heartbeat later, sirens trilled from the direction in which he was heading.

The passenger behind him shot again, hitting his other tire. The truck jerked, and he tried to pull over, but the vehicle wouldn't cooperate and he plowed into a tree. The airbag exploded into his face and he fought it, kicking his door open. He fell to the ground and leaned against his hissing car, trying to make the world stop spinning.

Digging deep, he edged to the back of the truck and spotted the taillights of the blue truck in the distance. He dropped his arm. "Roscoe?" His face felt as if it was on fire.

Roscoe jumped out of the truck, scattering more glass.

Angus slid down to his butt on the wet grass. "You okay?"

Roscoe moved toward him gracefully, his eyes clear; there was no blood on him. He licked the side of Angus's face, and pain flared. Angus patted his head. "Sit for a minute, buddy." Blood dripped into his eye and he wiped it away.

The sirens grew louder.

A Virginia State Police car skidded to a stop and a uniformed police officer jumped out, gun ready.

Angus lifted his hands and left his gun on the ground.

"The bad guys went that way," he said warily, putting his head back on the demolished truck.

The cop spoke into his radio and then scouted the area before approaching. "Do you require medical assistance?"

"No," Angus said wearily.

"Kick your gun this way, sir. Now." The kid had to be about twenty and was built like a farm boy. Blond hair, thick shoulders, serious eyes.

Angus reached for the barrel with two fingers. "How about I toss it?" The cop stiffened, and Angus flipped the gun close to the officer's feet, so he could kick it behind himself.

"Thanks. Do you have any other weapons?" the cop asked.

"No," Angus lied. He had a gun in his boot and a knife in his back pocket.

"Thanks. Now an ID?" The cop was good.

Angus twisted to reach for the wallet in his back pocket, and pain lashed down his side. He groaned and pulled out the worn leather, then threw it to the cop. He gingerly felt along his rib cage. Bruised but not broken.

The cop opened his wallet, took out his ID, and called it in. "Again, do you want me to request an ambulance?"

"No," Angus said.

An unmarked tan car, sirens twirling, zipped to a stop. Two detectives, one male and one female, exited the vehicle. Did the cops in this town have nothing else going on?

Angus tossed his phone next to his knee. "I just need to call—" He stopped, staring at the innocuous device. Who did he need to call? He no longer had a team, and they all thought he'd left town. He couldn't call Wolfe. Nari? No. She wasn't his girlfriend, and she also thought he'd skipped town. He'd have to deal with HDD tomorrow. He sure as shit didn't want to tonight. Tate was a possibility, but Angus had already messed up his life enough.

"Sir?" the cop asked, shielding his weapon.

"I don't have anybody to call," Angus said, his chest hurting more than his face. He snorted. Then he chuckled. "Not a damn person."

Roscoe whimpered and put his jaw on Angus's thigh.

Angus ignored the pain and petted the dog's head, offering some comfort. "I could call Jethro," he murmured. But no. He'd sent Jet back to the ivory tower of academia, and he really needed to let his friend find some peace. "Nope. Guess it's just you and me, boy." He rested his hand on the thick fur, his body feeling hollow.

The female detective took the lead. She was about fifty, with curly black hair and sharp blue eyes. "Your ID came back, and we'll have to notify HDD. Let's go to the station so you can make a statement."

Angus sighed. It was procedure, but he'd had enough with interview rooms today. His phone buzzed, and he accepted the call on speaker. "Force."

"Um, hello. Is this Angus Force?" a female voice asked.

He stiffened. "Yes. Who is this?"

"This is Sally Weston from North Valley Hospital. You're listed as her boss and an emergency contact for Nari Zhang."

Angus went cold. "Is Nari okay?" He pushed to his feet and the world spun.

"She's injured and is here after an attack, so I'm notifying you."

Angus limped toward the detectives, heat now flashing down his arms and then up his neck to burn his ears. "I'm on my way." He clicked off. "You can interview me en route to North Valley Hospital—which is where I need to go. I'll tell you everything, but I need a ride now."

Chapter Thirteen

Nari sat on the examination table as the doctor finished stitching up the wound along her hairline. The myriad of HDD agents who had descended on the hospital had finally dispersed, reassured that one of their own was okay. At times like this she remembered why she liked working for the agency.

Vaughn stood in the corner and finished typing on his tablet. "I'll have agents rotate security for your apartment until we find this guy."

In that second she remembered why she'd originally liked him.

He looked up, his gaze veiled. "Special Agents Fields and Rutherford have checked in and volunteered for rotation. I take it you made friends?"

Not exactly. "Rutherford offered, too?" she asked, her head still ringing.

"Yes."

Well, maybe the straitlaced agent wasn't so bad.

"We'll need to go through all your cases to see who might've wanted to attack you," Vaughn said, setting his tablet aside.

"I already told you. There's a copycat serial killer, and it looks like he's targeted my former team. We need Angus Force on this." Just saying his name made her body hurt worse. She actually had no clue where Angus was, darn it. His cabin was somewhere in the Kentucky wilderness, and he probably wasn't even home yet. Maybe he'd gone to Vegas for a weekend of debauchery to forget his problems. It was shocking how badly she wanted him to come charging in and taking over in that way he had.

The doctor finished. "You have a minor concussion, but so long as you don't get dizzy or vomit, you should be okay in a couple of days." The woman turned and walked out of the room, taking off her gloves as she did so.

Quan strode in at that moment and she barely concealed a groan. That was all she needed.

He looked her over, his dark eyes sharp. Tonight he wore gray slacks with a light-green shirt, and the scent of aftershave reached her. Had he been on a date? "You are all right?"

Nari nodded. His concern almost warmed her. "Yes. I've made a report and agents are canvassing my apartment complex."

Quan turned toward Vaughn. "I'm sorry you had to be called in on this. Weren't you at the fundraiser for Senator Jones?"

Vaughn nodded. "My date is handling things, and I'll return when I'm finished here." He was the perfect agent, wasn't he? "I think this is a problem left over from that subpar team Nari was on." Was that a smirk? Yep.

That was a smirk. Oh, yeah. That's why she'd broken up with him.

Quan sighed. "Yes. I figured." He glanced at his watch, no longer paying attention to Nari. So much for parental concern. Her shoulders sagged. "Why don't you return to the fundraiser? I'll handle things here," he said.

"This thing can handle herself," Nari said before she could bite back the words.

Both men turned to look at her.

Vaughn straightened. "It was a good fight. You taught her well, sir."

"My mom and my dad taught me to fight. Mom's family owns a series of martial arts gyms, and she's amazing," Nari said, keeping her gaze on Quan. It wasn't as if he'd been all that involved in her life. "My dad is an ex-marine and he's a tough guy. Hopefully you can meet him someday, Vaughn. He won't like you."

Vaughn apparently caught the tension because he edged toward the door. "All right. I should get back. Nari, take tomorrow off. If you're feeling up to it, report to work on Monday." He exited the room.

Quan shook his head when they were alone. "Must you be so emotional?"

Emotional? She'd just been attacked by a psycho in her own home. Her head hurt, her body ached, and she just wanted to crawl into bed and stay there for the next three days. "Please, Quan. You're smothering me with your concern and kindness," she drawled.

His chin lifted and irritation crossed his face. "This wouldn't have happened if I hadn't had to reassign you to that team for a brief time."

"You're blaming me for this?" she snapped, rearing up

and then instantly regretting it as her left hip vehemently protested.

"Nari?" Angus ran into the room, blood covering half his face.

Nari froze. He came. For her. She focused on him. "What happened to you?" His shirt was torn, and it looked as if glass was stuck in the thigh of his jeans.

Roscoe ran in next and jumped from the door to the examination table, landing at the edge and sliding toward her.

"Roscoe," she cried happily, grabbing him for a hug and burying her face in his thick fur. Tears finally filled her eyes, but she hid them, clinging to the dog like a little girl with a stuffed animal. She breathed in as he panted against her. She blinked away the tears before looking at the men again.

"Sir? You can't have that dog in here." A harried-looking nurse with wildly curly white hair hustled in. "No pets."

Angus stared at Nari as if taking inventory of her hurts. "He's a service animal and he's a member of Homeland Security." He didn't look away from Nari, and his eyes burned an unholy green. "She's Homeland Security; I was, but I don't know who the guy against the counter is." It didn't much sound like he cared, but even in the moment, he remembered to hide the existence of the HDD.

The nurse faltered, and then noise came from the hall-way. She threw up her hands and turned on her white tennis shoe to disappear out the door.

Angus limped toward Nari and reached for her chin, lifting it. "How bad are you hurt, sweetheart?"

The kindness almost undid her. If Quan hadn't been standing in the room, she would've burst into tears. "Not as bad as the other guy," she tried to quip, but considering she had a death grip on the dog, it probably fell flat. "What happened to you?"

Quan cleared his voice. "Excuse me?"

Angus didn't even look his way. "Tell me everything about the attacker and what happened."

Nari gaped. Nobody ignored Quan. She bit her lip. "Um, Angus Force, please meet my, um father, Quan Zhang."

Angus started. "I thought your father lived in Los Angeles."

"He does." Nari pushed hair away from her face. "This is my biological father. It's a long story."

Angus's eyebrows rose. "Oh." He turned and held out a bruised hand. "Hello. It's nice to meet you."

Quan ignored the outstretched hand. "I know all about you, Angus Force. You've been let go, and I suggest you be on your way."

Angus's left eyebrow rose in a look Nari knew well. Anxiety rippled through her. "Um—" she started.

"I think I'll stay here," Angus said. "How do you know about me?"

"Until the other day, I was your boss. Unfortunately," Quan said, his voice filled with authority. "I'm the deputy administrator of the HDD."

Angus straightened. "Is that a fact?" he drawled, turning again to focus on Nari. "You forgot to mention that little detail, now didn't you?"

* * *

Angus's ears rang. Yet another smash in the face. Nari's father was the fucking second in command of the HDD? Why hadn't she said anything? Well, he kind of understood that. More importantly, why had she ended up with his team in that dismal basement?

The woman just stared at him, her eyes deep pools of hurt.

He sighed. Now wasn't the time to be mad at her, even if he had the right to be. The idea that a serial killer had touched her nearly made him lose his mind. "You know, Deputy Administrator, you'd think your identity wouldn't be a secret to the folks working under you. Maybe it's time the HDD came out of the darkness and into the light." Something that would never happen in a secret government agency, but it was still nice to mess with the higher-ups once in a while.

"Is that a threat?" Zhang asked, his voice vibrating.

Angus chuckled, so far from real laughter he couldn't even imagine being amused. Nari had been in danger. Serious danger. "Of course not. It was merely a statement." He turned to study this man who'd created Nari, instinctively edging closer to her and putting his body slightly between them. "I find it odd you sent your daughter to my team." Just who was this man?

"She sent herself there," Zhang said, glancing at his wristwatch. He was about five-foot-nine, compactly muscled, with black hair peppered with gray and an annoying air of superiority. "I have a meeting with the administrator in half an hour and she's going to want a full accounting." He looked at Angus's disheveled appearance. "What happened to you, and did it involve the HDD?"

It seemed the man had moved on from his daughter,

who was looking bruised and hurt on the examination table and probably needed more comfort than slobbering from a dog. Irritation grabbed Angus around the throat and dug in. He had to rein in his temper with two hands, and it wasn't easy. "I don't know, but it seems likely. We've successfully concluded several cases and put some bad people away. It's not impossible that we've made enemies."

"Enemies you've now exposed my daughter to," Zhang retorted.

Angus lowered his chin. "Well now, I guess that's up for interpretation. You're the one who sent your daughter to work with a dangerous band of PTSD-riddled ex-soldiers and cops. One has to wonder why you allowed that."

Zhang's features flushed a dark red. No doubt the man wasn't used to anybody challenging his authority. "You had better watch yourself."

"Angus—" Nari started.

"I don't work for you any longer," Angus said, letting the predator inside himself show. It had been a shitshow of a day, and he was done. Just fucking done. "I don't like how you've treated your own daughter, and I really don't like how useless you've been in protecting her as an HDD agent."

Nari gasped.

Instead of resorting to threats, as expected, Zhang narrowed his eyes. "You're sounding rather possessive." He swung his gaze to his daughter. "Please tell me you haven't made yet another mistake with a coworker." The derision in his tone was going to get him punched square in the nose.

Angus growled and his hand clenched into a fist. His temper rose from the abyss to front and center.

Heels clipped down the hallway and a woman entered the room. "Quan? I heard Nari was attacked."

Everyone in the room stood taller, including Angus. It was the administrator of the HDD. Though Angus had never met Zhang, he'd met Opal Clemonte a couple of times.

The woman took in the room, her gaze landing on Nari. "Are you all right?"

Nari nodded, holding the dog closer.

Clemonte then turned toward Angus. "What happened to you?"

Angus studied her. She wore a shiny matching top and skirt in a silver argyle pattern and her gray hair was up in a fancy twist. Obviously she'd been out for the evening.

Roscoe growled.

Angus started. "Roscoe—"

It was too late. The dog leapt for the woman, his teeth sinking into the neckline of her top. Gravity took over and he dropped, taking the material with him. The shimmery shirt ripped right off and Roscoe jumped into the corner, tearing at it. Maybe eating a lot of it.

"Roscoe!" Nari snapped.

The administrator gasped and backed away, her light-pink bra clearly revealed. She watched the dog go to town on her top and tilted her head.

"Shit." Zhang ripped off his jacket and hurriedly pressed it around the woman's torso. "Opal? Honey? Are you okay?"

Honey? Angus studied the woman, who slipped her hands in the coat sleeves but didn't seem overly bothered with covering herself. He had to give it to her. She definitely had presence and confidence.

"I'm fine. He didn't even scratch my skin," she said. "Why is that dog eating my tunic?"

Roscoe finished with the material, which was now a mangled mess. Then he turned and eyed her skirt.

"Oh, no." Angus intercepted the dog, grabbing him by the scruff of his neck. "Sit. Now!" He put enough bite into his command that the dog's butt instantly hit the ground. Then Roscoe whined.

The administrator looked down at her skirt. "He doesn't like silver?" She sounded more perplexed than angry.

"He has issues," Nari hastened to say. "He was involved in a bombing a long time ago, and somebody nearby probably wore a vest with some sort of argyle pattern like your clothing. He still goes a little crazy when he sees that pattern."

Roscoe whined again, his muscles straining as he fought to obey Angus's command and stay in place.

Zhang put an arm around the administrator's shoulders. "Let's get you out of here and away from that attack dog. He should be put down. I can make it happen if you wish."

"Try it," Angus said, letting the threat hang heavy in the air.

The administrator shook her head. "I'm fine. Agent Force, I'm assuming there has been a report filed on why you're bleeding and obviously injured?"

He nodded. "I gave an interview to the local cops and am meeting HDD agents tomorrow. Everything is covered." So far, Angus liked her a hell of a lot more than he did Nari's dad.

"Good." The administrator paused and nodded at Nari, her gaze softening even while her shoulders went back. "I've been caught up on your case, and you did a good job defending yourself. I just received word that the techs have finished with your apartment. The assailant entered through a window in the office. There were no discernible fingerprints. I had them clean up the place after finishing, so you should be okay to return home. The HDD will assist in any way it can and you'll have security in place until we catch this guy. We'll get our best people on the case."

"Thank you," Nari said.

The administrator patted Zhang's hand on her shoulder. "I can see myself home. If you need to stay with your daughter, Quan, we can reschedule tomorrow."

Zhang shook his head. "The security in place is enough. Nari, I will see you on Monday when you report to work. Force? Rumor has it you were leaving town. After your interviews tomorrow, be sure you leave reliable contact information in case we need more details. However, you're cleared to go. In fact, I suggest you do so." He escorted the other woman out.

Angus turned toward Nari, who looked delicate and hurt on the table. A sense of possessiveness, primal to the point of feeling brutal, swept through him. "Your biological dad is an asshole."

Chapter Fourteen

Nari slipped from the examination table, her body feeling as if she'd thrown it down the side of a mountain. Could this be any more awkward? She still had a hickey on her inner thigh from him. Plus, her eyes were all starry because he'd taken command of the room and protected her. Stood between her and Quan. "Do you need stitches, Angus?" she whispered.

"No." He grabbed a couple of napkins from the nearby counter and wiped off his face. "I'm cut, but it's not deep."

"Okay." She tried to keep her tone casual, but she drank him in as if she hadn't seen him in years. The entire world had settled when he'd walked into the room, even though Quan had already been there. "I probably owe you an apology for not telling you about Quan being my father. I mean, our boss being my biological father."

"I wouldn't claim that jerk either." Angus released his hold on Roscoe. "We will discuss that later. First I want all the details of what happened tonight. Everything about the attacker. You know that was a kidnapping attempt by the copycat killer, right?"

She held up a hand, her ears hot. "We don't know that. We have to look at every angle." The last thing she wanted to do was to be so focused in one direction that she missed the threat from another. "But it's definitely something to consider."

"Let's get out of here, find some food, and then go over everything." Concern glowed in his eyes along with a barely banked fury. "How badly are you hurt?"

She shook her head and instantly regretted it. Lights sparked behind her eyes. "Don't be nice to me. I can't take it."

Both of his eyebrows rose. "Fine. Get your ass out of here and let's find this guy."

She chuckled, as he no doubt wanted her to. She warmed around him, to him, just like always. "What happened to you?"

"I was shot at from a truck and that's all I know." He wiped more blood from his neck. "The front license plate was missing and I didn't see the back. Didn't see the shooter either."

Wonderful. They'd both been attacked and couldn't identify anybody. "Do you think it was related to my attack?"

"Maybe, but who knows? Let's find dinner and go through it all slowly." He patted Roscoe's head, his hand broad and so strong-looking.

She had to get away from him before she just jumped into his arms and buried her face in his neck. "I'll call a cab or an Uber. We can meet tomorrow after your interviews with HDD and go over everything." Without waiting for an answer, she limped toward the door, noting a new pain in her right ankle. How had she injured her ankle?

"You're kidding." He grasped her arm, his hold infinitely gentle.

She paused, turning to look at his battered face. A darkening bruise on his jaw was visible this close. "You don't want to go over everything before you leave town?" That didn't make any sense, but she was having a hard time concentrating on facts. Man, her head hurt. Concussions sucked.

"Yes, but you're not going home alone."

Oh. She nodded. "If you want to give me a ride home, that's fine."

"Good." He escorted her outside, where he motioned for a taxi.

She stumbled. "Where's your truck?"

"I crashed it into a tree." He opened the taxi door for her, and once she scooted in, he sat. "There's an extra fifty if we can bring the dog."

The taxi driver, a blond in his sixties, nodded. "You bet."

Roscoe bounded in and settled between them on the seat. Nari rested her head back and tried to concentrate. "Thanks for dropping me off on your way, guys." It was nice to rely on Angus and Roscoe again, even if it was only for another night or so. "We can meet anywhere tomorrow." She shut her eyes and took inventory of her body, not having the energy to talk.

When they reached her apartment complex she leaned out her window to type in the gate code and then grimaced at the ache in her shoulder.

Finally she wearily opened the car door and stepped

out, unable to stop Roscoe before he jumped out and ran over to an empty flower bed.

Angus exited and paid the driver, who sped away.

Nari's mouth dropped open. "What are you doing?"

"Helping you pack your stuff." Angus looked around and started walking toward the nearest door. "I take it this is you?"

She nodded, her body numb. "My car is around the left in the lot. I'm not packing." Why couldn't she form a full thought? The combination of a concussion and the proximity of sexy Angus Force was too much for her. "Go away, Angus."

"No." He opened her door and stepped inside, looking around at her pristine apartment. "The cleanup crew did a good job. Usually there's fingerprint dust everywhere, even after a good mopping."

She didn't care. At the moment all she needed was her bed, so she followed him inside. "All right. Thanks. 'Night."

Roscoe ran inside, twirled in a circle, and leapt onto the sofa. He yipped, the sound somehow happy.

Nari grinned, even though her head hurt. "Looks like he's pleased to visit." Would it be wimpy to ask Angus to let Roscoe stay the night? She didn't think the intruder would be back and the security from HDD watching the place would be good, but it'd be nice to have company. "You know, he could stay. I'll bring him to you tomorrow when we meet."

Angus turned to face her fully, the impact of his gaze almost physical. His left eye was swelling and a bruise showed on his collarbone above his ripped shirt. "I haven't been clear. Sorry about that. You are going to pack enough clothing for a week and then you're coming home with me. I have a cabin, and it's secure. Also, you might want to bring some sheets and a pillow or two, because I don't have any. Oh, and we're taking your car."

She blinked. Her injured body perked right up with interest and a hint of lust. What was *wrong* with her? "I most certainly am not going home with you."

He lifted a shoulder. "Come with your clothes or not. Either way, Nari Zhang, you're coming with me."

Angus drove the car away from the grocery store fully stocked for a week. Nari remained quiet in the passenger seat, pretty much adorable in her pout. Oh, there was no doubt she would do a lot more than pout if at full strength, but right now her lip was out and her arms crossed. She'd refused to go into the store with him, so he'd taken the keys and left the dog to keep an eye on her, hoping they'd eat some of the fast food he'd already acquired.

The bandage above her eyelid stood out against her smooth skin and bruises had formed around her neck in the shape of a man's hand. Only the fact that she was hurt and worn down had caused her to agree to stay with him. Well, and maybe the dog. She wanted to spend time with Roscoe. She rubbed a bruise on her chin.

Angus tried to expel his anger at the sight, but his hands tightened on the steering wheel anyway. Roscoe cheerfully dug into his second burger in the back seat. "You need to eat, Nari."

She turned to look out the window.

Amusement stirred through his anger. "It'll be easier to work on these cases if we're together." Now he was trying to cajole her? He really had lost his mind.

She huffed. Actually huffed.

He coughed to hide his chuckle and sped up, keeping an eye on his rearview mirror to make sure they weren't being followed. The rain started to fall again. The autumn had been wetter and cooler than usual, and he was almost ready for snow. At least then there'd be some blue sky in between storms. Now the entire world was just gray.

He flipped on the wipers and turned up the heat, driving toward the secluded forest and away from civilization. Nari Zhang at his crappy cabin—the two of them all alone. His body tightened, and not with pain this time. They were both injured, but the sofa wasn't big enough for him. Hopefully he could talk her into sharing the bed if he promised not to touch her.

His groin hardened.

Oh, he really wanted to touch her again. One night together hadn't been enough. Not even close. The idea that a killer, maybe even Lassiter, had been inside her apartment waiting for her clawed through him, leaving a sense of desperate possessiveness he needed to banish. He had to think and stay clear for this fight.

Angus cleared his throat. He couldn't wait any longer to get the details. "We have a long drive, so tell me what happened. I have to know if it was Lassiter who attacked you."

"I don't know," she whispered. "He wore a mask and was in good shape. It's possible his height was the same as Lassiter's, and his eyes were brown."

"Lassiter's eyes are blue," Angus murmured, his chest lightening.

"He might've been wearing colored contacts," Nari admitted. "I couldn't really tell with the mask covering most of his face and even part of his eyes. They looked kind of dead. He was strong."

Angus reached out and took her hand. "Sounds like you were stronger." Thank God the woman knew how to fight and how to keep her head in a crisis. "You're impressive."

She snorted. "I was lucky. My training kicked in, and he was surprised."

"No. You were good and stronger than he expected. Now, tell me slowly, from the beginning. Everything you saw, heard, smelled. Close your eyes and remember." He tightened his hold on her hand to provide comfort if she needed it.

She leaned back her head and closed her eyes, telling him step-by-step what had transpired.

He had to force himself to keep his hold gentle when all he wanted to do was punch out the window. The guy had been on top of her with probable chloroform? God. If he'd managed to press it against her nose long enough, she would've been unconscious, easy to carry anywhere. Right now she'd be in the hands of a sociopath who tortured women and cut out their hearts. Lassiter or not, she'd be dead.

Fury edged through Angus, cutting with precision. He had to stop this guy, whoever it was. While the killer had left a note the day before, even that was slightly different from the others left years ago. If it was Lassiter, he was doing a great job messing with Angus's mind. If it was somebody new, he had a good grasp on the members of Angus's team and now had apparently started going for the real thing instead of look-alikes.

Nari wound down, and he asked a series of questions, keeping his voice calm.

She turned toward him as darkness began to blanket the rain. "Tell me about your day."

His was easier to deal with, and he gave her the entire story.

She perked up as they drove down the deserted dirt road through the forest. "It can't be a coincidence that we were both attacked the same day?"

"Hell if I know," he admitted, drawing up next to the rugged cabin. "The MOs are different, but we'll have to look at the situation from every angle."

She studied the structure outside the car. "You said it was a nice cabin in the woods."

"It is," he said, somewhat defensively. "It's not big, but it's sturdy and warm."

"Why do you have a cabin here if you were planning on going back to Kentucky?" She was quiet for a second. "Oh. You weren't going. I get it now. Liar." She opened her door and stepped into the rain, obviously too tired to worry about an umbrella. That was a good thing because he didn't have one.

Ducking her head, she ran for the porch.

"Wait." Angus hustled behind her and up the stairs to the door. "Let me make sure it's clear. I'm sure it is, but I go first." Just in case. He opened the door, and the hair instantly rose on the back of his neck as he sensed a presence that shouldn't be there. "Get to the car, Nari. Now."

"No need." A table light turned on, illuminating Clarence Wolfe in the lone chair by the murder board, his massive body causing it to creak when he shifted his weight. He wore dark boots, dark clothing, and a knife strapped at his side. His face lacked any expression, although his amber eyes glowed with what looked like fury.

Angus frowned. "What the hell are you doing here?" He ushered Nari inside, while Roscoe ran full-on to Wolfe and hit the ex-soldier in the knees before jumping into his lap, his tail wagging wildly.

"Trying to be pissed, which is difficult with a mouth full of fur." Wolfe patted Roscoe and tried to look over the mutt's back. "Get down, boy." His voice gentled and he lifted the dog to the floor. "*You* bought my cabin?"

Nari turned around to face Angus. "This was Wolfe's? The one he bought to stage an Op in?"

Angus nodded. "Yeah." Might as well go with the truth.

Wolfe stood, his body vibrating. "What happened to you guys? You didn't fight each other, did you?"

"Of course not." Nari hurried forward and hugged their mammoth friend. "Long story."

Angus shook his head. "Did you get my text about Dana?"

"Yes, and she's locked down safely with West and Tanaka right now," Wolfe said. "I got to thinking, and I figured you didn't really hightail it out of here. So the question was, where would you go? I figured it was a long shot, but here you are in my cabin. So it looks like the team is back together. Right?" His tone strongly hinted that it must be right.

"Right," Nari said firmly. "Without a doubt. We're in this together."

This was exactly what Angus had wanted to avoid. Damn it.

Chapter Fifteen

Nari finished with the very late dinner dishes as Angus made the bed with her fresh linens. Wolfe had stayed through the steak, salad, and dessert, finally wearing Angus down enough that the stubborn bastard agreed to let the team help with his case. It was obvious Angus had had no intention of really leaving town, and the thought that he'd lied to her hurt. She poured herself a glass of wine and turned, wincing as her hip complained with twinges of pain.

Angus straightened, the firelight flickering over his formidable features. His malachite-colored eyes were nearly iridescent in the soft light. He moved toward her and gently took the wine from her hand. "Hurting?"

"Yes." She looked at the glass. "What are you doing?"

"You have a possible concussion, so no drinking." His smile held more charm than she liked. "This cabin is in the middle of nowhere, and it's rather rustic, but there's one definite plus." He set the glass on the counter and held out his hand.

She took it, electricity flashing along her tired arm.

There was no reason they couldn't try to be friends. "What is it?"

"This way." He drew her toward the heavily barricaded door leading to another porch. He turned her. "See?"

She sighed, pleasure already easing her aches. "You have a hot tub?"

"Yep. First thing I did when I decided to move out here was fill that sucker and make sure it works. It's hot, it's on, and we're both getting in." He released her and walked forward to push the top off the Jacuzzi. "Roscoe?"

The dog padded out, yawning widely.

Angus pointed to the darkness of the forested land beyond the porch. "Scout."

Roscoe sighed. It really seemed he sighed. Then he bounded off the porch and ran into the trees. When he didn't bark, Angus moved back toward her. "I'll grab a drink and two towels and we'll get in."

She hesitated. "I didn't bring a suit."

His throaty chuckle did unmentionable things to her insides. "Baby? You don't wear anything to hot tub in the middle of nowhere."

Baby. He'd called her that before. The soft word sent butterflies whirling through her abdomen. There was too much risk here for both of them. The safety of just one night together had fled and her heart wasn't up for the crushing it would take when he left. "Angus, I am not in the mood."

"Me either. We're going to ease our aches and then go to bed. That's all." He brushed the hair from her shoulder and leaned in to look closely at her pupils. "You're not dilated and you ate a decent dinner, so I don't think the concussion is that bad."

She swallowed. Angus in a sweet mood was too much to handle. "You just want to check out all my bruises, then."

His eyes glowed. "Honey, I've been watching you all night. I know what hurts." He turned her toward the hot tub. "Hang your clothes on the pegs beneath the overhang so they don't get wet. I'll give you a minute." Then he went back inside.

She shivered, and not from the cold. Well, the hot tub would help ease her pain, and it was big enough for both of them to sit in without touching. Plus, it was dark outside. She removed her clothes and hung them on the pegs before easing herself into the heated water.

It felt delicious. Her toes tingled and she wiggled them to get used to the heat. Warmth surrounded her, digging into her aching muscles. The door opened, and she slid to the far side, sitting in a deeper area where the water reached her neck.

Angus walked out, set his glass on the edge, and stripped off his shirt. The wide span of his muscled torso bunched and moved as he did.

Her mouth watered. The light coming from the cabin door lit him from behind and his face remained in shadow. His hands went to the buckle of his belt, and she turned to watch Roscoe sniffing the edge of the porch. Her face warmed and she waited until Angus slid into the hot tub. Water splashed her way and she lifted herself to keep it from her face. Then it dissipated.

He sank down with a groan of pure relief. "Everybody should have a Jacuzzi."

She breathed in deeply and let her body relax. Then she reached for her hair and secured it on top of her head by tying a loose knot. Leaning her head back on the edge, she sighed. "This feels so much better."

"I'm sorry I brought you into this mess," Angus said, shifting his weight and rolling water over her. "I really am."

"It's not your fault." She kept her eyes closed. "Although it's not fair that you get to drink and I don't."

"You have a concussion and I probably don't." He sighed. "Also, it is my fault that you are in danger. I'm the target, and that makes everyone else around me a target. A man tried to kidnap you." His voice lowered and a thread of anger resonated in the dark tone.

She shivered. "I'm aware of that fact." She opened her eyes to stare at him through the night, unable to keep herself from diving into his head a little. "You aren't responsible for everybody around you. Did you ever get counseling after losing your sister?"

His head jerked. "Knock it off, Nari. I don't want a shrink."

That was a no. "I'm not trying to counsel you. Friends talk, too."

"Is that what we are? Friends?" Was that sarcasm? Yep, definitely.

She rolled back her shoulders to let the heated water soothe them, her injured body way too aware of his naked, muscled tightness so close to her. "I don't know what we are, but friends is a good start, don't you think?"

"Sure. Friends is the ending, too." He watched her, his face shrouded by the night. "I am leaving. The second we catch this guy, whoever he is, I'm leaving."

"Back to your solitude and booze, huh?" When he didn't answer, she stretched out her legs, careful to avoid touching him, even though her fingers ached to run over that impressive chest again. "Don't worry, Force. I'm a smart enough woman to know that when a guy tells you he's not a keeper, you should believe him. I believe you."

For the first time his gaze flickered. "I'm sorry."

"No problem." She wasn't asking anyway. "The fact that you feel responsible for your sister has you pushing everyone away. Yet you haven't exactly succeeded, have you? You're attached to the team, and that closeness isn't going away, even if you do." She held up a hand when he straightened. "Don't worry. I'm done analyzing you. *Friend*."

The woman was pissing him off, not analyzing him. Which didn't help a bit, considering she was naked in the water and close enough to grab and kiss. But they'd both been through hell that day. Her body needed to heal and his mind needed to get back on track. Angus settled down in the hot water and kept an eye on Roscoe in case he alerted on any threat. "I'm not completely oblivious to my motivations." He wasn't a moron, for Pete's sake.

"Well, there's that, then," she mumbled.

He wanted to know more about her, too. "You and your bio father don't seem close. What's up with that?"

"I don't really know him," she admitted. "He and my mom divorced when I was a baby, and I grew up with a single mom until my early teens. We lived in a small town and I always wondered why he left us."

Angus rubbed his chest. "I'm sorry."

She shrugged, rippling the water. "I guess a part of me always wanted him to like me, you know? Maybe that's why I took the job with HDD when it was offered—something that seemed to tick him off, actually."

Angus took another sip of his Scotch. "Maybe he just doesn't understand why you took the job when he's obviously been an absent father. There's got to be some guilt on his part for deserting you."

"Look at you, profiling people," she said.

He grinned, feeling closer to her than he had to anybody else in way too long. "We seem to have that in common."

"I know." She rolled her neck. "My mom and my step-dad met, married, and then moved us to Los Angeles, and I loved the city. It was nice to meet other Chinese kids, too."

He wanted to hold her hand, so he tightened his grip on his glass instead.

She straightened. "Different topic. Do you think this new killer is Lassiter or a copycat? Gut response—don't think about it."

"I don't know," he responded instantly, oddly more comfortable talking about psychotic killers than himself. Maybe the lust attacking him would disappear now. "I really don't. Either is possible." He ran through all the details. "He left a note this last time." Angus had already memorized the phrase and now recited it to her.

She moved her arms through the water, sending ripples his way. "It sounds like something Lassiter would've liked, but if somebody is copying him, that makes sense." She repeated the phrase thoughtfully. "*Slivers of time make up each moment, and only the pale horse and his master prevail in the most crucial of breathy gasps.*"

Angus made a mental note to call Jethro in. His friend's retirement would have to wait. "Yep. Classy, isn't it?"

"Well. Pale horse means death, right? The master would be the grim reaper?" She gazed out at the forest.

"The master could be the killer," Angus said. "I started a murder board inside and need to build the profile of this killer. I can do that tomorrow. Then I should rebuild Lassiter's and compare them." His mind clicked facts into place while his body tried to relax in the heat, which was just impossible with Nari so close. One night with her wasn't enough, although he'd memorized every smooth inch and taken each of her soft sighs into his heart to remember later. Yeah, he really was a moron.

She kept low but scooted along the other side of the tub to the steps. "I'm hot and ready to get out. Should we talk about the sleeping arrangements?"

She had her professional voice back and he couldn't blame her. "I'll take the sofa."

"No. We'll share the bed. Give me a break." She climbed out, and he turned his head to give her privacy. Mostly. "We need to be at the top of our game, so let's be adults." Within seconds she had disappeared inside the cabin, with Roscoe on her heels.

He sighed. Why couldn't they just get drunk and fuck?

The forest quieted around him with a sense of foreboding, as if the universe was holding its breath. Now he was getting maudlin. Enough of this shit. He stepped out of the hot tub and replaced the lid, letting the chilly air wash over him. Grabbing a towel, he headed inside, where the lights had been extinguished. The fire had died down, its burning embers barely showing Nari's form in the bed.

He grabbed boxers from his bag and moved into the bathroom to get ready for bed.

Once done, he moved to the bed, then stopped short.

Roscoe lay in the middle, his head on a pillow, snoring softly.

"You have got to be kidding me." Angus yanked bank the covers, needing to use some force with the dog's weight on the blankets. "Get your butt to the sofa or the floor."

Roscoe kept snoring.

Angus sat. "I know that's not how you sound. Move. Now."

The dog opened one eye but didn't move. What a faker.

Nari turned on her side toward the dog. "Let him sleep with us. Please?"

Oh, for Pete's sake. "Fine. But end of the bed. Period." Angus was not going to wake up with a dog in his face. "Move, Roscoe."

The dog whined.

"Oh," Nari crooned, reaching out to pet his head.

If dogs could smile, this one did. He also stretched out all four legs toward Angus, pushing him away.

That was it. "Roscoe? You want to go outside and scout the entire night?" Angus snapped.

The dog sighed and stood, walking on Angus's pillow before settling at the bottom of the bed on Nari's side. He cuddled up, putting his butt toward Angus.

"Were you this nuts before you got blown up?" Angus muttered, flipping the pillow over to the side without paw prints. He honestly couldn't remember. Or maybe his team of misfits had just brought out this side of the canine.

Roscoe farted in response.

Nari giggled, sounding young and light.

Angus smiled, and some of the pressure eased in his

chest. "Because the two of you have bonded so well, he's your constant companion until we find this guy. Period."

"I'd love that," she whispered. "'Night, Angus."

"Good night," he said, listening to the world outside. Nothing seemed out of place, and even though the dog was a lunatic, his instincts were excellent and his training second to none. If a threat was near, Roscoe would hear it long before Angus did.

So he let himself drift off with the fire warming his cabin and the woman and dog sleeping peacefully. The first nightmare landed hard and with no warning: He was back in the morgue with his sister's dead body after Lassiter had kidnapped and killed her, taking her heart. But this time her face had changed to Nari Zhang's.

He woke up, gasping for air and sucking in fur. Instead of being angry that the dog had maneuvered himself between them again, he set a hand on the dog's neck and shared the pillow.

He'd lost to a serial killer before, and he wasn't even sure who was after him this time. How was he going to protect everyone?

Chapter Sixteen

"You can't cook." Angus stared at the fried mess over Nari's shoulder, his voice thoughtful.

She looked at what used to be eggs in the fry pan. "Nope." This time she'd really given it her all.

"Huh." Angus turned and opened the window above the sink to let out some of the smoke. He leaned against the counter, looking broad and dangerous in the morning light. "You really can't cook. Even Roscoe is hiding over by the fireplace instead of begging for a bite."

She set the pan in the sink, staring at him. With his thick, black hair wet from the shower and new scruff covering his stubborn jawline, he looked like sex on a sinful stick. "You sound surprised." Should she be insulted? Nah. She just didn't have the energy.

"I am," he admitted, his dark eyebrows rising. "You're so good at everything."

She warmed from her pinkie toe to her hairline. "That might be the nicest thing you've ever said to me."

He rolled his eyes. "I believe I told you your thigh tasted like heaven the other night."

More heat slid into her face and her abdomen did

that jumpy thing it only did for him. It hadn't been her thigh he'd been talking about. Him in a flirty, playful mood was too much to deal with. Just his scent was speeding up her heart rate. Male and spicy and yeah, sexy. "Regardless, we're going to starve to death if we don't get some takeout."

Several cars rumbled up the road.

"Oh, thank God," Angus mumbled, waving the smoke out the window with a ripped kitchen towel. "Hopefully they brought food."

Nari perked up. "Is Pippa coming?"

"Yeah," Angus said, tossing the towel onto the counter and turning toward the door.

"Do you think she baked something?" Nari whispered, hope filling her. She was starving.

Angus licked his lips. "She bakes and cooks for fun." He shrugged. "I don't get it."

Neither did Nari, but she sure enjoyed it.

Wolfe was the first through the door, with Dana right behind him. The massive soldier balanced three trays of whipped-cream-topped lattes. "I got extra sprinkles for everyone because it's gonna be a long day." He reached the kitchen and set them down on the counter. "What's burning?" His brown eyes scouted the entire area.

"Nari can't cook," Angus said, reaching for a latte and eyeing the mountain of whipped cream.

"Really?" Wolfe's eyebrows rose. "There's something you can't do?" He sounded genuinely surprised.

Nari shook her head. "Knock it off, you guys." She also reached for a latte, though not sure her system could take that much of a sugar jolt. But hurting Wolfe's feelings was off the table, so she'd just sip it slowly. The guy showed love by giving sugar, and so far nobody had been able to ask him to spare the toppings.

Pippa came in next with several heavy-looking bags in her hands. "Was there a fire?" The tall brunette wore spectacular, cream-colored boots over her light jeans.

"What did you bring?" Angus hustled over to help her with the bags.

"Cinnamon rolls, a breakfast quiche that just needs a quick heating in the microwave, a couple of casseroles, and cookies." Pippa angled her head toward the sink. "What's that?"

Angus reached in for a cinnamon roll, humming happily. Actually humming. "Nari burned the eggs," he mumbled around a huge bite.

Pippa's blue eyes widened. "You can't cook? You can do everything."

Nari shoved Angus aside to reach for a cinnamon roll. "Obviously not." It smelled so good, she wanted to go outside and just push the entire thing into her mouth.

Malcolm stomped inside carrying a folding table and a couple of chairs. "Thanks for the help, you guys."

"Oops." Wolfe looked around and then walked over and shoved the sofa to the far wall. "There. I helped." He nodded at the one cushioned chair left. "That's Dana's. In fact, you should sit down, Dana."

The blonde was studying the murder board. "I'm fine," she said absently.

"That's Dana's chair," Wolfe reminded everyone. "She gets the comfortable one. We have folding chairs for everyone else. She's pregnant, you know."

Dana sighed heavily.

Nari smiled around a full mouth of cinnamon roll.

"Pregnant women work in fields all around the world before giving birth, Wolfe."

"Not my woman," the soldier returned easily, stalking out the front door, probably to fetch the rest of the chairs.

Dana turned around and smiled. "Please ignore Neanderthal man. A blow to the head—several, really—might've returned him to the Dark Ages. We're working on it."

Roscoe barked once.

"Oh, you sweetie. I didn't forget you." Pippa dug into one bag and brought out a bag of homemade doggy treats. "I cooked the ones you like best." She took out two and held them for Roscoe, who happily bounded forward.

Wolfe returned, along with Jethro, each hefting a bunch of chairs. "I found a Brit outside," Wolfe said.

Jethro sniffed the air. "Did somebody burn cinnamon rolls?" His accent seemed thicker this morning.

"No. They're good." Nari licked frosting from her finger. "Phenomenal, actually." Who needed to know how to cook with Pippa around? The woman was a miracle. "If you weren't engaged to Malcolm, I think I'd propose," she mumbled.

Pippa laughed and put the casseroles in the avocado-colored fridge. "Where's the rest of the team?"

Wolfe snagged a cinnamon roll. "Raider and Brigid had to report to work at DHS and HDD today but will join us tomorrow. We haven't been able to find Millie Frost, but she was going on a walkabout, or so she told Dana. I didn't call Serena in because she has classes today and I wasn't sure if she was part of the team or not."

The brilliant woman taught game theory at the university and had helped the team with code breaking for a case earlier that summer.

"Let's hold off on Serena," Angus said, taking another roll. "No need to put her in danger right now."

Wolfe nodded. "Also, I talked to Brigid, and she looked over that mail you got from the ex-boyfriend of the first victim. As you noticed, the dog pamphlets didn't go through the mail, but there's nothing there. Just a hint to mess with you."

"Okay," Angus said, standing still as he looked at a picture of a blond woman to the right on the murder board. The one who smiled so brightly at the camera and had Angus's eyes. "I'd rather have a smaller number of targets for this guy." His jaw hardened and his shoulders went back. "Everyone get settled, and I'll be back inside in a moment. Just want to double-check the perimeter." He turned abruptly on his boot and strode outside.

Nari watched him go, her instincts flaring. Roscoe yipped. She faltered and started for the doorway.

"No. Let me." Wolfe stopped her with a hand on her arm. "Finish your breakfast." He grabbed his and Angus's lattes and strode out the door.

Nari's stomach lurched. Everyone had a breaking point. With a serial killer after them, possibly the same one who'd taken his sister, was Angus nearing his?

Angus couldn't breathe. His body flared as if fire ants swarmed beneath his skin, and every joint protested. He hurried into the rain, toward the forest, and let the cool water wash over his face. Navigating a barely there trail, he reached the trunk of a tamarack and leaned against it, partially bending over to gulp in air.

"Panic attacks suck."

Angus jerked and lifted his head to find Wolfe on the trail, lattes in both hands. His eyes were direct and serious.

"Go away, Wolfe. Just give me a minute," Angus gasped.

"Nah." Wolfe loped toward him, handing over a latte. "We need to talk, and you could use some sugar and caffeine. Sit and drink."

Angus's neck prickled. "No. Go inside."

"Sit or I'll put you on your ass." Wolfe smiled, and the sight wasn't friendly. "Sure, it'd be a good fight, but you're injured from the crash yesterday and in the midst of a panic attack. We'd end up on the ground, regardless."

Whatever. Angus dropped to his butt, letting the surrounding fir trees provide protection from the rain. "I would've won," he grumbled, his lungs filling finally.

"Sure." Wolfe sat across the trail against the trunk of a spruce tree, stirring wet pine needles as he did so. He extended his legs and crossed his ankles next to Angus's thigh. "So."

Angus took a deep gulp of the coffee and instantly regretted it. He licked sprinkles from his lips. "I'm fine. Just needed a minute."

"Minutes are all we got." Wolfe drank his coffee.

Wonderful. Clarence Wolfe in a philosophical mood was more than Angus's temper could take. "Okay. You can sit here, but let's enjoy the quiet." Angus was more careful with his next sip.

"My sister died when we were kids. She was a teenager and just a couple of years older than me." Wolfe drank thoughtfully, a muscle ticking in his jaw. "Met some asshole in a chat room, thought he was her age, and met him for a date. He was an adult. Her body was found in our safe little town."

Angus set his head back on the rough bark. "I've read your file, and it's not the same as my situation. Your loss stinks and I'm sorry, but it wasn't your fault." The idea that Wolfe wanted to talk about the past and his feelings only demonstrated how desperate Angus must look right now. His face heated.

"It feels like my fault." Wolfe twisted the coffee cup in his hands, his focus on it now. "I know, logically, that I was a kid younger than she was. That I didn't know about the dangers of the internet, and I really didn't know that she snuck out of our house that night. But still, she was my sister, and a monster took her. Hurt her. Killed her. It'll always *feel* like my fault, no matter what my brain says."

"My sister's death *was* my fault," Angus said quietly. "Without my job, without my obsession with Lassiter, he wouldn't have turned his attention to me and then to my sister. She was innocent, Wolfe. A freaking kindergarten teacher with a fiancé. She just wanted a good life. I got her killed."

Wolfe nodded. "She sounds like somebody who'd want you to hide away from the world and drink yourself to death."

Pinpricks climbed up Angus's throat. "Jesus, Wolfe. Don't give me the what-would-your-dead-sister-want-for-you speech, okay? That's just bullshit. What my sister would've wanted was to teach school, have a couple of kids, and then coach softball. Not to end up with her heart sliced out." He wanted to puke. The sugary drink rolled around in his stomach.

"Nobody wants that, Force," Wolfe said. "Stating the obvious isn't going to get you back on track. If you're running on fear, you'll fuck this up. Considering you're one of the few people I like in this world, I'd hate to have to kill you if Dana is threatened again."

It'd be nice if Wolfe was joking, but he probably wasn't. "You're right," Angus said. "So take Dana and get the hell out of town. Go to an island somewhere until I find this guy and just be safe. In fact, take Mal and Pippa with you."

The quiet ticked around them for a moment.

"Listen." Wolfe sucked down half of his drink. "I can handle you broody, I can handle you drunk, but I can't deal with you being an idiot. If you need to hit somebody, let's do it. I'm happy to take punches from you. But you have to pull your head out of your ass, and it needs to happen now."

Angus took a deep breath. His friend was right, as bothersome as that fact was. "Is this your idea of tough love?"

Wolfe's lips twisted. "Huh? No. Tough love would've been me putting your head through that tree. This is me trying to be understanding and all of that shit."

Against all odds, Angus chuckled. God, he did appreciate his friends. "Okay. I'm focused. I'll be clearheaded by the time we get back in the cabin and I'll profile everyone." Not once had he ever thought Wolfe's would be the voice of reason.

"Good. You might also want to figure out what's up with you and Nari. You're pushing her away so she doesn't get killed, she's avoiding you because she doesn't trust her choices in men, and it's just making everyone else gossipy and curious." Wolfe tipped back his head and finished his drink, leaving whipped cream on his lips.

Angus frowned. "There's nothing up with us." Except a lot of sexual tension and one great night of sex.

"Oh, please. Don't make me try the head-through-the-tree thing." Wolfe lumbered to his feet and held down a hand. "Half of your panic here is the idea that Lassiter or Copycat will go after Nari just because you've been close to her. That might make you avoid your feelings, or it might make you amplify ones you might *not* have. Just figure it out before somebody gets hurt."

Angus accepted the hand and stood eye to eye with the soldier. "I'm not sure I like your philosophical side."

"Dude. I am so done with talking for the week. This was a lot." Wolfe clapped him on the shoulder. "Let's get some work done."

Fat raindrops from tree branches plopped on Angus's head until he exited the forest, where Malcolm was waiting for them. Angus paused, his body chilling at the look on Mal's face. "What's happened?" he asked.

Mal's eyes burned. "We had the news on TV. Apparently joggers beneath Trunky Bridge found a body. Blond female with bright pink streaks in her hair."

Chapter Seventeen

The dead woman could not be Millie. It just couldn't be. Nari scrambled to use every contact she had at HDD to find out more details on the deceased woman, while most of the team did the same. The news report had been brief, and other than the description of streaked blond hair, the joggers hadn't provided any details to the reporter at the scene.

Angus paced outside on the front porch, his phone at his ear.

She thanked her friend and disconnected the call. "The HDD hasn't been called in, so my sources don't know anything."

"I'm waiting for Raider to see if the DHS has anything," Dana said, her phone to her ear. "I'm on hold."

Pippa set down her phone. "Brigid is on it with HDD and her computer, but she thinks Metro caught the case, and they're not sharing. She's trying to track Millie via her phone and GPS and will get right back to us. It's not Millie. It can't be. She took the streaks out of her hair, remember?" She took a deep breath. "Is anybody hungry?"

Nobody answered. Millie easily could've put more

streaks in her hair. Jethro pounded away on his laptop, while Wolfe yelled at somebody in a lab somewhere. He hung up and threw the phone toward the sofa.

"No luck?" Dana murmured.

"No." Wolfe ran a rough hand through his hair. "Anybody? Do we know anything?"

Angus stomped inside, rain dotting his T-shirt. "Tate's not answering his phone, but I got a contact in Metro to affirm that he caught the case. That's all I know. Has Brigid been able to track Millie?"

"Not yet," Malcolm said, sliding his phone back into his pocket. "I've reached out to my contacts at Metro and the case is fresh. They're even trying to keep from sharing with the DHS. Nobody knows anything yet."

The cinnamon roll in Nari's stomach turned to rock. She pressed a hand to her diaphragm. "A lot of women have pink streaks in their hair. We don't even know if this woman is the victim of a homicide." Yet she felt like throwing up anyway.

Angus's phone buzzed and he pressed a button. "Force." He stiffened, his shoulders going back. "Tate. Yeah?" He listened for several moments, not moving. "Affirmative. Thanks." His face lost all expression. "Metro has a female victim with a missing heart who is blond and about five feet tall. They're searching for a note right now."

"Is it Millie?" Nari whispered, her heart aching. She had to figure out how to help everyone in the room. She couldn't fall apart.

Angus shook his head. "They haven't identified her yet. The victim was thrown from the bridge and landed on her face."

"I have Raider and Brigid on speakerphone." Malcolm

straightened, setting his phone on the counter. "Millie is former HDD, so they'd have her prints on file. It should take seconds to determine."

Angus slipped his phone into his pocket. "There is no determination."

Nari frowned. "Why not? What aren't you saying?"

Jethro looked up from his computer. "Why can't they identify her?"

Angus exhaled, looking pissed all of a sudden. "The victim's hands are missing."

Nari gagged and quickly covered the action with a cough. The woman's hands and heart were taken, and she'd been thrown face-first from a bridge. "Either this guy is getting angrier or he wants us to worry while she's identified. If so, then it probably isn't Millie. Right?"

Angus lowered his chin. "Maybe. If it is Millie, he might want to draw out the moment." That fast, Angus was back to being the profiler and not the pissed-off friend. His eyes went cold and flat. He looked at Jethro. "Anything on the last note?"

"Yes." Jethro closed his laptop. "Good thing I brought my own hot spot. The passage is from a seventeenth-century poem by a man named Giuseppe Legonito. He lost his family in a fire and slowly descended into madness. The poem is called *The Fate of the Damned*."

Wolfe grimaced. "That's profound. What was the passage again?"

Angus spoke before Jethro could. "'*Slivers of time make up each moment, and only the pale horse and his master prevail in the most crucial of breathy gasps.*'"

Jethro nodded. "The guy isn't exactly subtle."

Angus dug his fingers into the corners of his eyes. "All

right. Everyone keep working here. I'm going to crash the scene."

"The body won't be there by the time you arrive," Nari said. Why did he have to go out in the storm like that?

"I know, but I want to examine the scene. The more information I have, the better I can profile this asshole," Angus said. He looked at the assembled group. "For now, we go on the presumption that this wasn't Millie, because this guy seems to have a pattern of killing people who look like members of our team. We use every resource we have to find Millie unless we get bad news from the lab."

Nari swallowed. "If that's his pattern, he's hit all the women on the team. Brigid, Dana, Millie, and me." She looked at Pippa. "Both Pippa and Serena have other jobs and don't work for HDD. Do you think he'd find look-alikes for them, too?" She had to keep Angus in his head to keep him in control.

Thunder rolled outside. Angus prowled to the murder board tacked across the wall. "If his intention is to mess with us, it's entirely possible. Although he'll again turn to the real thing soon enough. I've already asked Tate to provide protection for Serena, even though we haven't worked with her for a while." He looked at the picture of his sister and then pivoted toward the door. "Regardless, he's killed at least four women and they deserve justice. I'll be back."

Jethro shoved his laptop into his pack. "I'm with you. We need to talk this out like we did last time. If it is Lassiter, he's had at least five years to plan this. He couldn't go that long without killing."

"No." Angus turned at the door. "So, either he was

killing and we haven't found victims, or there was a reason he couldn't kill during that time frame." He smacked his hand against the wall. "Or the bastard is dead and this is somebody new." He straightened. "If it *is* somebody new, how does he know so much? We need to go back through old files." He scouted the team. "All right. Mal, Dana, Pippa, and Wolfe, you proceed as if this is a new killer. Explore all avenues. Nari, Jethro, and I will proceed as if it was Lassiter because we know that case well."

The group nodded.

Angus angled toward the speakerphone. "Raider and Brigid? Figure out who the hell shot at me yesterday. I don't see a connection to the serial killer, so it might be related to one of our closed cases."

Nari nodded. "That's a good plan." She reached for her raincoat, which was hanging by the door. Her knees wobbled just enough that she had to take her time shrugging into it. Their team leader had intrigued her from the beginning, and Angus had never been more in control than today.

Angus paused. "Where do you think you're going?"

"With you." She patted Roscoe's head and swept by Angus into the stormy day. "We're on the same team, remember?"

Rain beat the area beneath the graffiti-riddled bridge, muddying the sopping wet brown leaves. The crime scene tape remained, but the area had been cleared, and Angus looked up at the distance to the top. It was no wonder the woman's face had been unrecognizable if she'd landed on one of the nearby rocks.

"The area is rather secluded," Jethro said, scanning through the rain while petting Roscoe's wet head. "Although that jogging path is frequently used. This guy doesn't mind taking a chance at being seen, does he?"

"He's overconfident rather than reckless," Angus said. His phone buzzed, and upon seeing it was Tate, he answered. "What do you have?"

Tate cleared his throat. "Wasn't Millie Frost."

Relief nearly dropped him, followed by a strong punch of guilt. Somebody was dead, and that person was as important as his team member. Angus turned toward Nari, who stared at him with wide, dark eyes. *Not Millie*, he mouthed.

She sagged.

"Who was it?" Angus asked.

Papers shuffled across the line as Tate read. "Young runaway from Texas who's been missing for a year. My guess is he found her on the street. The pink streaks in the hair are new, leading us to believe the killer actually sprayed them in, and her face was bashed before she was tossed from the bridge." Tate's voice lowered to a whisper. "HDD called here and I'm getting heat that they're infringing on our case. Did you forget your interviews with them today?"

Angus started. "Shit. Yeah, I did." Damn it. He'd completely forgotten. How could he forget something like that? "I'll make it right."

"See that you do. I'm getting looks here and have to stop talking to you," Tate said. "I'm sending you the sketch of the scene, so you know where the body fell, but don't call me again. If I need your help, I'll reach out to you."

"Wait. Was there a note?" Angus asked.

Tate sighed. "Not this time."

"Damn it, Tate. There had to have been a note. He left one last time." Angus's voice rose, and he quickly quashed all emotion. "Have the coroner check the body carefully."

"No shit." Tate clicked off.

Angus winced. Tate was probably his last friend in Metro, and that was stretching it. He looked around. "Sounds like Metro and the HDD are butting heads, which only helps us for now. They didn't find a note. There has to be a note." The text came in and he scanned the sketch. "According to Metro, the body was over here." Running over to the area indicated on the sketch, he studied the leaves, scattering them.

"The techs would've searched the entire area," Nari said gently.

"There's a note." Angus would bet his life on it. He overturned a rock. Nothing. Going methodically, he turned over each rock in the area, finding nothing but dirt and bugs. "Where is it, damn it?"

Jethro looked up toward the bridge. "I'll scout the bridge." He turned and jogged gracefully up the hill, only breaking stride a couple of times because of his newly healed leg. Roscoe kept pace with him and stopped to shake his fur at the top.

Heat coated Angus's throat and he coughed out the frustration. The rain pounded harder. "Why don't you wait in the car, Nari?"

She tugged the hood of her raincoat over her head. "It's my fault for forgetting my umbrella. I'll go search over by the creek." She turned and slipped on the leaves but kept trudging toward what looked more like a long mud puddle than a creek.

Angus tried to forget that two people he cared about were possibly risking their lives to help him. He studied the area, making sure no cars approached. If anybody came upon them from the woods, Roscoe would catch a scent.

Even so, Jethro and Nari shouldn't be there. He would have expected the woman to think he was nuts, but instead she was going along with his delusion. She deserved so much better than this disaster. She'd been in a fight the day before, was still bruised, and should be resting by a fire with a good book. Instead, she was out in the freezing rain, looking for a clue that probably didn't exist.

He couldn't stop the team from working this case, but he didn't have to let them court danger.

His phone buzzed and he looked down to see a familiar number. "Hi, Serena," he said. "How are you?"

"I'm being tailed by two HDD agents," the professor said, sounding more bemused than angry. "Why? We only worked that one case together and it was months ago. Even if your team is in danger, as these nice agents have informed me, I'm not on your team."

Angus studied the trees up the bank. Surely the techs had canvassed the entire area. "I'm just being overly cautious. The world doesn't have enough geniuses; I'd hate to lose one."

"Sure it does. Anybody with an IQ over one-sixty is a genius," Serena said thoughtfully.

He was too tired to feel amused, but his lips twitched

anyway. "Oh. Of course." Lightning zinged the earth close enough he could smell ozone.

"Where are you?" Serena asked.

"At a crime scene looking for a note that doesn't exist," he said, turning to make sure Nari was all right by the creek.

Serena was quiet for a minute. "In the rain? Nobody would leave a note in the rain, and it's been raining for weeks. Should snow soon. Statistically it should've snowed yesterday, but that's another story, and one you probably don't have time for right now."

"True." He had a flashback to her trying to explain something called methods for entanglement verification to him one time when she'd dropped by the office to meet Brigid, and he shivered. "Thanks, though."

"Anytime. Let me know when I can lose the feds." She hung up, no doubt already on to her next puzzle.

Angus slipped his phone in his pocket. She was right. It didn't make sense to leave a note in the rain. There had to be some sort of clue with the body. "Let's go, gang," he called out. "I want to drop by the morgue."

Nari hunched her shoulders against the rain and picked her way toward him. "We'll need to dry off Roscoe. I'll hurry ahead and get the towel out of the back seat."

Angus turned to examine one more time the place the victim had been. He looked up as Jethro descended the embankment. The bridge caught his attention. Swirls and lines. Gang tags. He recognized a couple, and then the muscles down his back tensed. "Nari." He grasped her arm to turn her toward a concrete piling. "What do you see?"

She turned and squinted, tiling her head. "Is that a dog?"

"Yeah." The outline of a German shepherd was barely discernible, laid over several gang monikers. He moved forward, squinting as the sun went down. "Ah, crap." Lifting his phone, he pressed Redial.

"I told you not to call me," Tate said by way of greeting.

"You're gonna want to get down here." Angus leaned closer to the painted message. "I found the note."

Chapter Eighteen

Dinner had been a quiet affair with the team before everyone left. Exhausted, Nari had gone to bed and snuggled down. The cabin was warm, even a little steamy, with the rain continuing outside. So she'd worn a pink cami with matching shorts. It was more than warm enough, yet she couldn't sleep. Her body hurt, her mind ran too fast, and electricity arced between her and Angus.

They were in bed together. Again. The memories of what Angus could do in bed made her restless. And needy.

Several hours later, after listening interminably to the fire crackle, she couldn't take it anymore. The man in the bed with her was too quiet. "Are you sleeping?" she whispered, turning on her side to face Angus.

"No."

She hadn't thought so. "Are you still trying to figure out what that phrase means?"

"No." He stretched, and the firelight licked along the smooth muscles of his arm. "Jethro will figure it out tomorrow."

She sighed. Jethro hadn't returned to the cabin with

them, saying he had a meeting at the college. "You're not sleeping, which means the case is on your mind. Right?"

"Yeah." He turned to face her, mumbling the quotation they'd found painted inside the dog outline. "*The forest watches, the darkness knows, the time is coming—can you feel the change?*" He levered himself up on one arm. "It sounds kind of dumb, if you want the truth. I'm more interested in the outline of the dog's face and the symbols scratched into the rock beneath it."

Her breath quickened. It was totally inappropriate right now, but with all that powerful muscle so close, she had to force her brain to stay on track. "The symbols might've been left by the gangs."

"Maybe," Angus allowed.

Roscoe snored softly at the edge of the bed.

Angus studied her, his eyes blazing through the soft light. Tension rolled from him, thick with lust. "Um."

"Me too." She met him halfway. When his mouth crashed down on hers the delicious feeling tingled to her toes. She kissed him back, partially pressing herself up against him with her feet trapped on the other side of the dog.

"You sure?" Angus tangled a hand in her hair, his mouth roving wildly over her jaw and down her neck. "This is crazy."

"I know," she mumbled against his mouth, running her hands over his hard chest. Desire swamped her and she tried to free her feet so she could scoot closer. She needed to get closer to him. Now.

Roscoe lifted his head. He barked once—low and dark.

She chuckled. "Ros—"

Angus grabbed her by the arms and pulled her out of the bed, settling her on the floor. Her butt landed first—hard—and the cold wood chilled her thighs. Roscoe leapt off the bed and ran for the front door.

"What is happening?" she gasped, trying to stand.

"Down. Stay down." Angus pulled his gun from beneath the pillow and crouched low, moving toward the front window. The firelight illuminated the scars across his muscled back as he moved silently. "One bark like that means danger. Keep your head down."

Her gun was on the other side of the bed. She kept below the top mattress and crawled around the edge of the bed to the other side, pulling her Glock from her purse. Then she aimed for the back door, her arms on the mattress.

The front window shattered and something rolled across the floor.

"Grenade!" Angus leapt for it, grabbed it, and threw it toward the broken window before Nari could react. An explosion rocked the front porch, and more glass blew inward.

Nari scrambled away from the front door, rushing for the kitchen with Angus and the dog on her heels. Another grenade sailed through the front window.

She ran out the back door and looked around.

"Trail," Angus whispered. "Follow Roscoe." He whistled.

Roscoe bounded into the rainy night, somehow able to see despite the darkness. Nari ran behind him, her bare feet slipping on the wet weeds until they reached the muddy trail. Small rocks bit into her heels, but she kept going. They didn't have a chance against an attacker with grenades.

The cabin exploded and debris blew toward them. Angus tackled her to the ground and she landed hard, the air whooshing from her lungs. Her bare knees and palms scraped against rocks and slid through the mud. Pain throbbed up her wrist to her elbow. Before she could draw a breath, he manacled her around the waist, partially lifted her, and started running again.

They reached a turnoff on the trail, and he followed Roscoe, setting her down next to a tree trunk. "You okay?" He crouched, barely visible in the dark.

She nodded, her heart hammering her rib cage, mud squishing beneath her thighs.

"Nari?" he whispered, his hand cupping the back of her neck.

Oh. He couldn't see her. "Yes," she whispered, shock thickening her voice. "I'm fine."

"Good. Stay here with Roscoe." He began to stand. "Roscoe, guard," he commanded.

"No." She grabbed his wet arm and tried to pull him back down. Her ears rang and her head pounded. "Whoever it is has grenades, Angus. Who knows what else they have."

"I know. Stay here and out of sight. We don't know how many of them there are." He pivoted on his bare foot and instantly disappeared back down the trail; she could just make him out, his figure silhouetted by the fire at the cabin.

Nari shivered and edged partially around the tree, positioning herself on her knees and pointing her gun toward the cabin. Her arms shook from the chilly rain and probably from shock. Her mind was fuzzy and she tried to sharpen her focus, just in case. She wasn't trained as an agent, but she'd learned how to shoot.

The gun felt cold and slippery in her wet hands.

Roscoe stood at her side, his hackles up.

"Go with him," Nari whispered.

The dog didn't twitch. Now he decided to obey commands? Thunder bellowed as if angry with the night, and the fire crackled ominously up ahead, dark smoke spiraling into the sky.

She gulped, trying to see, feeling vulnerable in her thin, wet cotton tank top and shorts. How many attackers were there?

Angus kept to the trees, circling around to the front of the cabin, his gun pointed and his aim steady. The fire burned hot and bright, despite the rain. Another explosion erupted from the front of the engulfed cabin, and he ducked as metal careened over his head.

Damn it. Was that Nari's car? He kept his back to a tree and pivoted around, swiftly maneuvering his feet through the mud. Rocks and sticks cut into his toes, but he ignored them, reaching the front area.

The car was on fire, all four windows blasted out. The smell of gasoline combined with burning wood, choking the oxygen with sinister black smoke. The poison filled his eyes, causing them to tear. He blinked and withdrew more deeply into the trees while moving east, searching for the enemy through the smoke.

If they'd blown up the car, they weren't sure he was in the cabin, and they didn't want him driving to safety.

So he kept silent and moving.

A dark truck blocked the dirt road out of the clearing. Navy blue? He couldn't tell, but it was a Ford, and the windows looked tinted. Where were the occupants?

Shadows flickered from the fire and, high above, lightning flashed.

A figure, tall and broad, came into view near the hood of what used to be Nari's car. There he was. Angus relaxed his grip and moved sideways, crossing one leg over the other repeatedly until he had a decent line of fire. He squeezed the trigger, and the figure dropped.

Then he didn't move. The forest was silent, while the fire roared.

Did the guy have a partner? Angus remained in place, searching for any hint of movement. Nothing. If there was another attacker out there, he or she had training. Like Angus. He counted seconds and then minutes in his head. The fire continued to burn, hot enough that the rain couldn't smother it. The smell of chemicals rode the rain. What accelerant had been used?

"Angus?" Nari whispered.

He jolted and partially turned to find her on the trail, mud covering most of her legs and feet. The rain had drenched her tiny tank top and shorts, clearly revealing her breasts, although she held her gun like she knew what to do with it. "This way," he whispered, motioning her closer.

She jumped and then turned, her eyes wide in the darkness. Then she lowered her hand and picked her way around a series of bushes to reach him. *You okay?* she mouthed, blood on her chin and rain sliding down her face.

He gestured toward the prone figure on the ground. "Roscoe? Scout. Now." He pointed toward the figure.

Roscoe, his paws muddy, put his nose to the ground and moved toward the fire.

Angus kept his gun at the ready, pointed at the prone figure. "Might have a partner," he whispered.

Nari turned, putting her back to him and covering the trail. "Got it."

Now wasn't the time to ask her if she'd shot anybody before. He doubted it. Instead he concentrated on his dog. Roscoe ran in a zigzag pattern, silent, his tail not wagging. He went by the prone figure, sniffed, and then moved on, not alerting but not giving the all clear.

Angus wiped soot out of his eye with his free hand. "The chemicals are strong, as is the smoke. He may not be able to track properly." Was Nari up to this? "Are you okay covering me?" he asked, wishing the team was there.

She looked over her shoulder and gulped. "*Covering* you?"

He tugged her closer, put his mouth to her ear, and clipped command into his voice. "Yes. I have to see who that is on the ground, and there's a chance we have other enemies out there. If anybody fires at me, shoot them." It wasn't a great plan, but it was all they had.

She swallowed and wiped rain from her face. "Okay." Her voice quivered, but she turned and faced the prone body, her gun up and almost steady. "Go. Be careful. Duck if you have to."

He'd never wanted to kiss her more. Instead he bent under a tree branch and crouched low, running past the burning cabin to the body on the ground.

No shots were fired.

He didn't relax. The downed figure was dressed in all black, from head to toe. Angus scouted the area and then ripped off the balaclava covering the man's face. Buzz-cut blond hair, wide features, a couple of scars on his neck. The man had to be in his midthirties and was solidly built.

Angus felt for a pulse. Nothing. He'd aimed for center mass and his bullet had found its target.

Roscoe barked. Once. Sharp.

Bullets pinged the ground next to Angus, and he leapt toward the burning car.

Nari instantly returned fire, shooting toward the blue truck. This close, Angus could make out the color. Navy blue without a front license plate. It was the same truck that had chased him down before. Bullets winged out of the brush near the truck, and Angus crouched behind the burning vehicle. Fire singed him, and he angled himself as far away from the sizzling metal as he could, returning fire.

Another figure dressed in all black leapt toward the navy-blue truck and jumped in the passenger side.

Angus stood. Another explosion rocked the car, blowing him back toward the cabin. He landed on a burning piece of wood and bellowed as pain pierced his rib cage.

The driver of the truck backed up so quickly the vehicle hit a tree.

Angus gasped and rolled over, scrambling to his knees. He aimed at the truck, firing as it turned and sped down the dirt road, while Nari did the same.

It disappeared from view.

She ran the distance between them, skirting burning

metal and wood. "Are you okay?" She grasped his bare shoulder.

He looked down at his rib cage. "Yeah. Just a slight burn." It hurt like a mother. He stood, taking in the ruins. "I don't suppose you grabbed your phone before we ran out the back door?" he gasped, leaning over and trying to find some oxygen.

She slowly shook her head, water sluicing down her front. "No. You?"

"No." He stood and motioned for Roscoe to leave the body alone. "It's gonna be a long walk." He adjusted his boxers and switched his gun to his other hand. "Let's go."

Chapter Nineteen

Dawn arrived, its soft light washing over the wet forest outside with a golden hue. The rain had stopped, started again, and now was taking a well-deserved break. Nari's feet hurt, her head ached, and she kept sneezing as she waited in the back room of a mom-and-pop convenience store they'd stumbled upon nearly an hour before.

The matronly owner handed her hot chocolate, and Nari let the blanket around her shoulders drop just enough to accept the fragrant brew. Then the woman left to go watch the counter.

Nari looked up as Angus entered the room, a blanket secured around his waist and covering his wet boxers. New bruises mottled his ripped abs. "I got through to the HDD, hoping they'll take jurisdiction immediately so we don't have to mess around with locals." As he sat on the other plastic orange chair, she could see that the burn marks down his side were turning an ugly red. "I also updated Brigid and Raider with this new development because they're pursuing whoever shot at me the other day. I'm pretty sure it was the same truck."

Nari sipped the cocoa, humming as the sugary sweetness slid down her throat and warmed her stomach. Even so, she couldn't stop shivering. They could've been killed if Roscoe hadn't barked the warning in time, although she felt like it was the two of them against the world right now, and that thought warmed her even more than the drink. "I'm sorry they blew up your cabin." No way had anything survived that fire, even if the rain had managed to finally douse it.

"It's okay." He rubbed a bruise on his shoulder. "I have copies of all the case files and my clothes are easily replaced."

She rocked back and forth, trying to warm up. "You didn't recognize the guy on the ground?"

Angus shook his head. "No, and the other guy was moving too fast to ID him through the smoke. I just have a hazy picture in my mind. You?"

She took a deeper drink. "The blue truck was between us, so I couldn't tell." Her hands tingled with the need to brush his wet hair from his face and check out the burns on his side, but she forced herself to stay in place. If they hadn't been interrupted, they would've spent another night having multiple orgasms together. Enough was enough. They'd said one night, and she had to keep a clear head, not let her heart get all mushy. "Now doesn't seem like the right time for a romance," she murmured.

His dark eyebrows rose. "I'm not lookin' for romance."

She rolled her eyes. "Shut up. We would've had sex and you know it." The more she was around him, the more she liked him. Or wanted him anyway. Right now, he wasn't exactly likable. Yet the way he'd barreled into the storm to hunt a killer, barely dressed, trying to protect her? Yeah, that was sexy. Worse yet, the image wouldn't leave her mind. She shivered.

"You okay?" His eyes glowed with concern.

"Yeah. Just cold," she lied, cupping the mug with both hands and blowing on the hot liquid.

His gaze dipped to her exposed collarbone. "I'd like to have sex again, don't get me wrong. But I'm all in or all out, and with a killer on us, I have to concentrate and be sane."

Sane. Like he'd go crazy if they dated? She pressed her lips together to keep from smiling at the thought. Did she want to date him? The term was too tame for Angus Force. He chased demons while other demons chased him. She blinked. "I think my concussion is getting to me." She was becoming maudlin. "Do you think you could keep sex casual between us?"

He studied her, his eyes moss green in the morning light. "I don't know."

Her thighs tingled. Was he finally beginning to see that he was part of a team and not just its temporary leader? What exactly did she want? She should figure that out before letting him sink his teeth into her thigh again. "We should figure us out, right?"

"Now that's a question to which I'd appreciate an answer." Quan strode into the room, his black loafers perfectly polished.

Nari's stomach dropped and she drew the blanket closer around herself. "Quan. What are you doing here?"

The administrator walked in behind him, looking casual today in dark jeans and a silk top, with a lovely Hermès scarf knotted at her neck. "We were at an early brunch and received word of the attack." Her shrewd eyes took them both in. "How badly are you hurt? Do we need an ambulance?"

Angus got to his feet. "No. We're okay." He faced his former boss. "I don't know who's after us, but it must have to do with one of our earlier cases." He pinched the top of his nose. "The bomber, I mean. The man who attacked Nari, I believe, is the same one killing women and taking their hearts."

"You have two killers after you?" Quan asked, disapproval in his dark gaze.

It was terribly early in the morning for a business meeting. What was going on between Quan and his boss? Nari set her empty mug on the counter and stood, careful to keep her skimpy clothing covered with the plush blanket. "I'm sorry about that, Quan. I guess all kids rebel a little."

Angus's smile flashed quick and then was gone.

At least somebody appreciated her sarcasm. Yep. The two of them against the world. She was turning into a starry-eyed teenager, but she couldn't drum up the strength to halt herself.

"Nari—" Quan started.

Angus closed in on her, his powerful body providing a shield.

Her temper was rare, but when it appeared she couldn't stop it. "As sorry as I am to have interrupted your *very* early brunch, we felt the correct procedure was to notify HDD of the attack." Why couldn't he at least ask if she was all right? If he disapproved of her staying with

Angus, what was he doing with the administrator so dang early?

Quan gritted his teeth together in a look that made her stomach hurt. "As you know, the HDD is a secretive branch of Homeland Security. We can't have agents making the news. Perhaps you'd be better-suited elsewhere."

Nari's body jolted, but she hid it. Her own father was *firing* her?

"Wait a minute," Angus said, his voice a low growl. "This isn't on her. It's on me."

The administrator held up one manicured hand. "Wait a moment. It's early, and we don't have all the relevant data yet. Let's all take a step back and revisit the situation on Monday in the office." She glanced at a dainty gold wristwatch. "We've sent techs out to the cabin, and you'll both need to be interviewed by investigators. In addition, Mr. Force, I believe you missed your interviews yesterday."

"I know," Angus said, eyeing the woman.

Roscoe tiptoed toward the administrator, and she watched him, standing in place. "I'm not wearing that pattern today," she said, looking more curious than scared of the dangerous animal.

Roscoe reached her and licked her two-inch blue heels.

Nari sighed. "He likes to wear high heels sometimes."

The administrator's eyebrows rose. "He is one interesting German shepherd, but these cost a small fortune, so I'm not letting a dog wear them."

"He just wants to be taller," Angus said, rather defensively. "I hate to ask, but has another body been found today?"

Nari started. He'd been worried about that? So had she.

"We've found one a day, so it stands to reason that there will be."

Quan stepped back. "It isn't our case, but it's my understanding that this killer tortures his victims for some time."

Nari nodded. "Yeah. He's probably been holding the bodies for this grand reveal."

Quan's nostrils flared. "As I've said, that is not our case. The HDD does not work on serial killer cases. I'm ordering the two of you to let the appropriate authorities do their jobs. Now. We will take you to headquarters for your interviews."

"No," Angus said. "We'll meet the investigators at headquarters after we find food, showers, and fresh clothing. Tell them to expect us after lunch."

Nari faltered.

Heavy footsteps sounded and Wolfe poked his head through the doorway. "Somebody need a ride?"

After a shower and a hurried lunch, Nari's body hurt more than ever. She'd downed ibuprofen and was hoping the painkiller would kick in soon. She sat on a sofa in the administrator's office at HDD headquarters. "Thank you," she said, accepting a cup of tea from the woman.

"You're welcome." The administrator sat in a floral chair to the left, a teacup balanced in her slender hands. "Are you sure you don't require medical assistance? You had a concussion and then were almost blown up."

Nari shook her head and had to hide a wince at the ensuing pain. "Thank you, Administrator, but I'm fine."

"Call me Opal," the woman said, gracefully settling

back in her chair. "Would you go over what happened last night for me? I'd like to get the entire picture."

"Sure." Nari took a sip of the delicately flavored tea and then recounted the night's events before asking her own questions. "Do you have an ID on the man Angus shot?"

"Not yet. His prints didn't bring back any information, but his face is being run through facial rec right now. I'll let you know if we figure out who he is." Opal took a sip and looked over at Nari's face. "I've read your file—you are excellent at your job."

For some reason, the compliment raised awareness along Nari's already punished nerve endings. "Thank you."

"As such, it's time you stopped sabotaging your career." Opal's tone was no-nonsense but her eyes kind.

Nari shifted her weight, careful not to spill her tea on her cream-colored slacks. "Is this woman-to-woman advice?" Did she dare ask about Opal and Quan? They might just be colleagues. Or not.

"It could be boss-to-subordinate advice, if you like." There was the woman who'd risen to the top of a dangerous and secretive DHS offshoot. "However, I've always believed in mentoring, and I see a lot of potential in you. Your background in psychology and your business acumen should allow you to rise very high in this organization, or any other, for that matter."

The warning was subtle, but it was definitely there. "Are you warning me off Angus Force?" Nari could play the political game and be coy, but her body had been through a meat grinder, her emotions were raw, and she was just not in the mood.

Opal smiled. "I like the direct approach. Good for you. To answer your question, yes. First you go outside the chain of command and nearly sabotage your career, and now you date a disgraced HDD agent who's a suspect in several murders. You're destroying any chance you have of rising in this organization."

Nari set her tea on the antique sofa table. "I did my job to save a colleague, and you know Angus didn't kill those women." What was Opal's game?

The woman crossed her legs. "Take a step back. Several, really. Look at the situation as if you weren't personally involved." She sipped delicately, the mantle of power seeming natural on her slim shoulders clad in a St. John muted jacket. "Henry Wayne Lassiter brutally murdered Force's sister as the ultimate move in the cat-and-mouse game between them. They shot each other, and Lassiter died. Force moved to the middle of nowhere to fish and kill his liver with alcohol, and then he came back here, still obsessed. He's cracked. Everyone has a breaking point. Can't you see that?"

Nari breathed out. "You think he cracked and turned into a serial killer to keep the game alive?"

Opal's lips turned down. "I don't like it, but yes. Can't you see the possibility?"

"No." Nari would have rubbed her eyes, but she didn't want to smear her mascara.

"Nari," Opal said, almost gently. "You must distance yourself from Angus Force right now. Work hard with your new team and prove that you can rise above your emotional problems with Vaughn. I guarantee you'll see success. And for goodness' sake, separate your professional and personal lives."

Nari studied the woman. It was good advice. "As you have?" she asked quietly.

Opal's smile widened. "You are observant, aren't you? Yes. As I have. For years, I've kept the two parts of my life separate, and yes, I've made mistakes in both. Everyone is human, and most mistakes can be overcome. You have that chance now. And I, now that I'm where I am, can take a risk or two for somebody I think is worth it. You're not there yet, but someday you will be." She leaned forward. "I'm at an age when I'm tired of being alone. Your father is a good man."

Nari had to admire the woman's confidence. "I really do appreciate your advice." It had been a kindness for the woman to take an interest, even if it was because she was dating Nari's father. She stood. "I'm supposed to report to Agent Fields's office to make a statement about the bombing last night."

"Yes. Say hi to Kurt for me." Opal also stood and held out a hand.

Nari took it. "Thank you for everything." She walked toward the door.

Opal's voice stopped her at the doorway. "Nari? I do want to be your mentor, but I'm also your boss. Just in case I wasn't clear, I'm also ordering you to cease all interaction with Angus Force and anybody else who was on his team."

Nari turned. "I see."

Opal was back in full administrator mode. "I do want what's best for you, but it's my job to protect the HDD as an agency. We operate in the shadows and in quiet. If you do anything else to focus scrutiny on the agency, I will terminate your employment. Regardless of my fondness for your father . . . or for you."

Nari straightened. "I understand." She opened the door and walked out into the quiet hallway. She didn't want to cut ties with her friends or with Angus. But Angus hadn't promised her anything, and he still maintained he was leaving town the second he caught the serial killer.

Should she risk everything for a man who hadn't promised her a thing?

Chapter Twenty

Angus pulled at the worn T-shirt he'd borrowed from Wolfe, grateful to at least be wearing clothes. He sat in the interrogation room across from Special Agents Fields and Rutherford. He grinned. "How bad do you two want to go back in time and not show up on my porch in Kentucky?"

"You have no idea," Agent Rutherford muttered, several closed file folders in front of him on the gleaming metal table.

Oh, Angus had some sort of idea. "When do I get my gun back?" Not that he didn't have a few more in a secured locker. A guy had to be prepared.

"Your weapon was used to kill somebody, Mr. Force," Fields said around a cough drop. "It might be a while."

That figured. It was odd to be called "mister" instead of agent. No doubt it was intentional. "He attacked us, as you can tell from my smoldering cabin." Angus crossed his arms and instantly regretted it as pain flashed through his torso from his burns. He kept his expression bland, refusing to show discomfort. "Where's Nari?"

"In another room being interviewed," Rutherford said.

He'd dressed down this Saturday in a logoed golf shirt with perfectly creased slacks. "Run us through what happened."

"Well now, shouldn't we include Metro in on this, considering Tate has covered the cases so far?" Angus asked.

Rutherford rolled his eyes. "Your cabin wasn't in their jurisdiction, and frankly, we don't have time for officers who take photos with their phones and use twenty-year-old fingerprint technology. They can continue with the junkie and vandalism cases. When an HDD agent, even a former one like you, is attacked, we handle it. So, tell us everything about the bombing of your cabin and vehicle."

Fair enough. Angus did so, leaving out the fact that the team had been there earlier in the day and that they were working a case off the books.

Rutherford had his phone recording, but he also took notes on a legal pad. "Why was Agent Zhang at your cabin in the middle of nowhere?"

"None of your business," Angus said easily.

Rutherford kept scribbling. "Are you and Agent Zhang involved in a sexual relationship?"

Ah. That was the tack he'd decided to take. Piss Angus off and see if he'd let something slip? "Again, none of your business." He knew better than to lie to federal investigators, but he didn't have to tell them anything he didn't want to say. "Why? You interested in her?"

Rutherford didn't look up. "The last guy she dated nearly lost his position in the HDD. I don't date nutjobs."

Irritation ticked along Angus's skin. Nicely done. Rutherford had gotten in a hit, but Angus didn't have to let him know it. "You probably couldn't handle her," he agreed, wanting to punch the guy in the nose.

"Can you?" Rutherford looked up, his blue eyes clear.

Angus leaned forward. "Are we really here to talk about my dating life? Tell me you at least have something on the asshole who shot at me and then blew up my cabin. Have you even found Millie Frost yet?" So far Brigid had been unable to track the young tech, so it was doubtful this guy had either.

Fields crunched on the cough drop. By the smell, this one was lemon-flavored. "So you are dating Agent Zhang."

Angus sat back. He started to run through the line of questioning in his mind.

"Okay. Let's go over when you were shot at the other day. Nobody else saw a blue truck or a firefight," Rutherford said.

Angus rolled his eyes. "We didn't engage until we were away from the businesses along the road."

Fields nodded. "That was wise of you. And the grenade and explosion last night at your cabin? Did anybody see the threat? Besides Nari Zhang?"

Angus lowered his chin. "No." He rolled his shoulders. "I've told you everything I know about both scenarios. All I can think is that either I or my team pissed somebody off. We busted a cult a while back and it's entirely possible an old cult member is out for revenge. I don't know. Give me access to my case files and I'll go through them one by one." After he found the serial killer.

"Tell me where you were the night this woman was dumped in the alley." Rutherford took out a picture of the first victim they'd found.

Angus looked down at the dead Chinese graduate student. He shook his head. "This isn't your case."

Fields looked at the picture, his gaze hardening. "No,

but the bodies reflect an obsession with your team, so we called in a couple of favors in order to question you. I suggest you cooperate. Please answer Tom's question."

Heat pricked along Angus's neck, but he forced himself to stay in the moment. "I was at the office when I got the call about the first victim," he said. "I called in West and Wolfe and we headed to the scene."

"Who else was at the office at that time?" Fields asked, not taking notes.

"Roscoe, my dog." Angus forced his temper elsewhere. These questions made sense, even if he didn't like them. "You can interview him if you'd like, but he's a tough one to crack."

"Sarcasm. Nice." Rutherford took out the picture of the redhead draped over the log in the forest, a gaping hole in her chest. This time the cuts were smoother, although the dump area was not Lassiter's style. "Where were you when Sasha McDouglass was dumped in the forest?"

"I was at the office when the call came in. Most of the team had been there but had left." He looked more closely at the young woman. So that was her name. "Who was she?"

"You tell us," Rutherford said, twirling the photo around with one finger.

Angus lifted his head. "What do you mean?"

"She doesn't look familiar?" Fields asked.

Angus studied the photo. "She looks a little like Brigid Banaghan, a former teammate of mine, but that's it."

"All right." Rutherford tapped a finger on the photograph. "You said that most of the team had gone from the office when you received the call about McDouglass. Who was left there with you?"

"Nari." In fact, it was the first time Angus had kissed her. A pit opened up in his gut. They couldn't be going where he thought they were, could they?

Rutherford drew out a picture of the victim found in the laundry room of Angus's former apartment building. "What about this innocent victim? Lizzie Nelson? Where were you when she was dumped, right where you lived?"

Angus looked at the woman, his chest aching. She was so young. So defenseless against a psychopath. "I was sleeping when the call came."

Fields reached into his pocket. "In the apartment complex?"

"No. In my cabin," Force said.

"Alone?" Rutherford asked.

Angus nodded, unable to look away from the gaping hole in the woman's chest. Completely smooth lines this time—much closer to Lassiter's work. "Except for Roscoe."

Fields pulled out another cough drop and slowly unwrapped it. "You still have your cabin in Kentucky?"

"Yes." The burger he'd eaten for lunch rolled around in Angus's stomach.

"Huh. If you still have that cabin, why did you need this one?" Rutherford cocked his head.

Angus grew still. He needed to focus, damn it. "I like cabins." He'd get any of his team still working for the government fired if he admitted they were working these cases together and had needed the cabin to do so. "Real estate is a good investment, you know." Not the truth, but not a lie. He was definitely skirting the edge of a felony, however.

"I have heard there are good returns on real estate." Fields popped the drop into his mouth.

Angus turned on him. "What is up with you and cough drops?"

"I'm on a diet and they're the only treat I get," Fields said, sucking on the drop.

Rutherford sighed. "They still have ten calories a cough drop, you know." He shook his head and opened another file folder, pushing forward a picture of a dead African American woman. "Identify her."

Angus started. "You found another body today." Shit. The victim looked a lot like Serena. Whoever had been watching the team had done so for months. "Are there still HDD operatives on Serena Johnson?"

"Of course," Fields said. "She's safe. Unlike this woman. Her name was Bernadette Wexel."

"Was there a note?" Angus asked, his throat suddenly raw. Another woman. Another death. She looked young and broken in death.

Rutherford leaned toward him. "You know there was, don't you?"

Angus closed his eyes and exhaled slowly. "All right. What did it say?"

"You know. Stop messing around with us," Rutherford snapped. "Stop playing. It's over. You're over. Don't you want to get this all off your chest? Come on. They gave you to us because we know you. You were one of us— don't let me down. Don't let your team down."

Angus stared into the earnest eyes of the HDD agent.

Well, he was going for earnest. "What the fuck are you talking about?"

Rutherford gave up any pretense of brotherhood. "I can help you or I can destroy you and everybody you've touched, including sweet Nari Zhang." He slapped down the five pictures, one at a time, their edges barely touching.

Death and pain and horrible endings.

Rutherford tapped his finger on the first victim, who looked like Nari. "Lori Chen. A bright doctoral student who worked part-time at Miller's Coffee, just down the road from your apartment building. How often do you get coffee there?"

Angus leaned in to study the woman. "Hell if I know." But he did grab a coffee there once in a while, when Wolfe wasn't around to force sugar on him. It made sense that anybody targeting him might've come across her. "That's a coincidence."

"You'd think." Rutherford planted his entire hand over the dead redhead on the log. "Sasha McDouglass. Guess where she worked?"

Angus shook his head. "No clue."

"Squishy's Car Wash. You know. Where you have an account and get your truck washed and detailed regularly. I bet you've talked to her more than once." Triumph filled Rutherford's gaze now.

Angus turned toward Fields. "Are you kidding me?"

Fields just stared at him, his shrewd eyes hard.

Angus sat back. This was actually happening.

Rutherford then slid the picture of the mutilated blonde in front of him. "She lived in your apartment complex and was found dead in your laundry room. Oh, and you don't have an alibi for the time when she was dumped. Oddly enough, the security cameras were all cut by somebody who knew where they were."

Angus cocked his head. "You've lost your mind."

"Have I?" Rutherford pointed to the African American woman. "She's a professor of theology whose family owns the Brickhouse Pub on Eighth Street. She works shifts sometimes to help out. You know the place, no?"

Angus looked more closely at the woman. She did look familiar. "Yes." He often met his team at the bar. It was quiet, with good beer. He pointed to the other victim. The woman with the pink streaks in her hair. "And her?"

"Haven't found the connection yet, but I was hoping you'd just tell us." Rutherford shook his head. "Come on, Force. You're a burnout and an alcoholic. I've seen it before. You were in the game and you caught the bad guy, but you can't let go. You've re-created the case you miss."

Angus shoved his chair back from the table. "I didn't kill these women. Jesus Christ, Rutherford." He wanted to be furious, but instead he felt numb. Stunned into numbness. "I have an alibi for when McDouglass was dumped."

Rutherford smiled, going in for the kill. "Yes. Your lover alibis you. That won't exactly hold up in court and you know it. Also, the second you get wind we're on to you, your cabin blows up? Sounds like a truly excellent way to destroy evidence. What? Did you kill those women in that miserable cabin where their screams would never be heard?"

Angus just stared at him. Oh, he knew the smart thing

to do, but asking for a lawyer felt like defeat. He wouldn't lose to this asshole. "You're grasping for straws with both hands."

"No. We have federal agents serving search warrants on your cabin in Kentucky, Nari Zhang's apartment, and your former apartment here. I have no doubt we'll find the evidence to fry your ass. So make it easy on yourself. Claim insanity or something. Who knows? A jury might have sympathy for an ex-FBI agent who became the monster he'd chased for so long." Rutherford gathered the photographs, sliding them away as quickly as the killer had sliced the life from those women.

Fields sucked on his drop. "How long did you take with each woman? We don't have the autopsies yet, but it looks like the torture took a while."

Angus sat back. "I'm done talking. You idiots need to find a different path." Honestly, the circumstantial evidence against him was a lot worse than he'd thought. A decent prosecutor might even be able to make a case. "You know I didn't do this."

"Wrong." Rutherford sat back.

The door opened and Tate walked in, along with two uniforms. His dark face was unreadable. "Angus Force, I'd like you to accompany me to Metro so we can continue this interview."

Rutherford shoved back from the table. "What the hell? Get out of here."

Tate smiled, showing the predator deep down. "You don't have enough to arrest him, so he's leaving. Force? I need to question you."

Angus sighed. He didn't mind leaving HDD, that was

for sure. There was a better chance he'd get information from Metro, the scrappy underdog here in comparison to the HDD and its resources. "No need to fight over me, gentlemen. I'm happy to accompany you, Tate. Let's go." It was going to be a long-assed day.

Chapter Twenty-One

It had taken all day for Angus to be interviewed by Metro, and Nari yawned widely while waiting in her new rental car to pick him up. It was now almost midnight on Saturday night.

He emerged from the building, so pissed off he looked as if he'd just rammed his head into the car. Opening the door, he slid inside, his muscled bulk shifting the entire vehicle. "Where's Roscoe?"

Nari's temper wasn't far behind his. She pulled away from the curb. "You're welcome for the ride."

"Thank you. Where's my dog?" Angus demanded, his shoulders looking as if they were made of solid rock.

"He's at my apartment, pacing and confused," Nari said, reaching into the back for a fast-food bag. "Figured you'd be hungry. For now, how strong is the case against you? All Agent Fields would tell me was that you might be arrested and I could go to prison as an accomplice after the fact for providing a false alibi, although it isn't false."

Angus rested his head back and his shoulders lowered as he obviously took a moment to try to relax. "Honestly?

I wasn't arrested because they're still trying to build a case, and they don't want me to hire a lawyer. All of the evidence is circumstantial, but it isn't bad as a case. A good prosecutor might be able to make it stick. If they find an ounce of physical evidence, I'm probably screwed." He groaned. "Plus, it's a race right now to see who gets to me first—the HDD or Metro. They both want to arrest me and will the second they have enough evidence."

Nari drove up the interstate. "Do you think the killer intended this consequence? Or is it just that he's after you, after us, and this is a result of the HDD and now Metro both being pissed at you?" At all of them, actually.

"Dunno." Angus bit into a burger, his shoulders too wide for the seat of the compact. "How much trouble are you going to get into for being with me?"

"None." She switched lanes and sped up. Oh, she was probably going to get fired. But for now, they had a serial killer watching them, a bomber/shooter trying to take out Angus and maybe her, and she couldn't think how leaving Angus to fight all this alone would help anything. "Brigid acquired new phones for us and they're in the back seat. We had lunch together while waiting for word on whether or not you were arrested." Thank goodness he hadn't been. Yet.

He glanced into the back seat. "Already programmed?"

"Yeah. Numbers, contacts, everything. She's good at what she does." Nari drove faster and headed for the exit to her apartment.

Angus reached for another burger in the bag. "Did you two have protection?"

"Yeah. There's an HDD detail on her. I refused one, considering I planned to help you." Nari tried for a light tone but definitely failed. No doubt Quan or Opal would find out, and she'd be in for a lecture, a transfer, or termination. Right now, she couldn't worry about it. "If there's another body tonight, will Tate call you?" A new victim had appeared every night, and the idea of another dead young woman made Nari want to throw up.

Angus crumpled up the wrappers and shoved them in the bag. "Considering Tate almost arrested me, I doubt he's willing to share any more information."

Nari rolled her eyes and pressed down her window to punch in the gate key. "How nice it was for HDD and Metro to work together to bring you down. So much for jurisdictional rivalry."

"Oh, they're not working together. It's a fight to the finish," Angus muttered. Anger rode his tone, but he kept it low. "HDD knows me better, so if I had anything to give up, I would've probably done it with them. Then the case is Metro's, so Tate had to be the one to finish the questioning and make the decision on arrest or not. For now. HDD is the one with warrants to search. Did they go through your place?"

"Yeah and they made a mess." She frowned. "You'd think I'd get some professional courtesy." She drove forward and parked near her apartment.

Angus stilled. "Does Roscoe have food?"

"Of course. I bought him food earlier while working on your situation." She slid from the car, anxious to be inside rather than out in the open. Too many people had tried to hurt her lately.

"Good." Angus followed her, a solid form in an uncertain world, instantly changing the feeling of her entire apartment when he walked inside. The cool, calm lines now held a certain tension.

Rosco jumped off the white sofa and came right for Angus with a welcoming bark. Angus caught him in a hug and set him down, vigorously rubbing his fur from head to tail. "I'm okay, boy. There's nothing to worry about." His voice gentled as he reassured his dog.

The moment slammed right into Nari's heart. Angus could be so sweet sometimes.

Then he looked up, his green gaze clear and still sharp with anger. "We need to come up with a good plan for you."

She paused. "Huh?"

He looked at the sofa, which held a Roscoe-size imprint. "We'll stay here tonight, but then you need to leave. Go somewhere safe. I think I can talk Wolfe and Dana into going with you. He's all in on this case, but she's pregnant, and he'll choose her safety every time."

"I'm not leaving." Nari tossed her keys on the entryway table, which was once more in place.

"Yes, you are." His jaw firmed and he looked like an impenetrable stone wall in the center of a peaceful home. "You have to be safe until I catch this guy or guys, and leaving is the best option. You're a target on two fronts, and neither of us can ignore that. Also, every second you spend with me jeopardizes your entire career, and that can't happen." He released his hold on the dog's head. "I'm not asking, Nari. You are leaving."

Her mouth gaped open. "You can't make me," she blurted out. Great. Five minutes with the guy and she resorted to grade-school jargon.

He didn't retreat. "I can and I will make you."

Her head jerked in surprise. "The hell you can. Last guy who tried to manhandle me got punched in the junk. You want to go?"

"Sure." He lifted a shoulder. "However, *this* guy knows what you can do and is prepared for you. Also, I've trained with the best, have about a hundred pounds on you, and am pissed off enough to run through a wall. Feel free to kick me, princess."

A knock on the door prevented her from responding.

She leaned to look through the keyhole and saw Vaughn Ealy on her front porch. Could this night get any worse?

Angus planted his hand on the dog's vibrating head again. "Hello." The guy standing in Nari's entryway was tall and broad, with that look only a cop had. Or a federal agent. He had brown hair, sharp eyes, and seemed familiar with the room.

"Hi," he said, sounding displeased.

Nari sighed and shut the door behind him. "Angus Force, this is Vaughn Ealy."

Thought so. Angus didn't bother extending his hand. "The guy who nearly cost both of you your careers because of his mishandling of his team?"

Nari groaned. "We are not doing this. Why are you at my apartment after midnight, Vaughn?"

"Now, that's a great question," Angus agreed, his skin prickling. The urge to put Nari behind him tightened every one of his muscles, and his left hand curled into a fist as he fought a craving to break the asshole's nose.

Vaughn met Angus's gaze evenly, his expression

showing similar thoughts. He looked down at Nari. "I received word that you refused HDD protection, and then I heard that you bailed out a suspected serial killer. So I'm here, trying to see if you've lost your mind."

Angus paused. She'd made calls inquiring about bailing him out? That was sweet—and stupid.

"He wasn't arrested, so there's no bail situation. In addition, he's not a serial killer." Nari wisely took a step away from Vaughn toward Roscoe, who'd picked up on the tension and was standing at full attention. "My personal life is none of your business."

"Wrong. You work for me, so it is my business. I have cause to fire you," Vaughn snapped.

The threat didn't sit well with Angus. "You know, buddy, I have nothing to lose in beating the shit out of you. How often do you call women names?"

Vaughn rolled his eyes. "That's a line of bullshit. Didn't happen."

Both of Nari's eyebrows rose. "It did happen and you know it. Also, you were wrong about the entire situation, and a young agent could've died. You can try to rewrite the facts, but that's what happened." She spoke clearly and without passion, which really must have ticked Vaughn off.

His lips tightened. "We could argue your faulty memory all night, but that doesn't change the situation. Do you or do you not want to continue your work with the HDD?"

"She does," Angus answered for her. "However, she's going to take leave for a couple of weeks to get her mind back in the game." He held up a hand. "Before you ask, I'm not going with her. I'm staying here to fight the case against me, and after tonight, Nari and I will have no contact with each other." The words were like a punch to the gut, but the woman was too kind, and she was going to ruin her life because of him—if she didn't get killed first. He hadn't protected his sister, but he'd protect Nari whether she appreciated it or not.

Vaughn leaned back. "A temporary leave of absence might be a good idea. When you return your head will be on straight again and we can get work done."

Was it Angus's imagination or did the jerk's gaze drop to Nari's breasts for a minute?

She stood taller, which didn't come close to the height of either man. "I'm done with everybody in this room except for the dog. Vaughn? Go home. I'll report to work on Monday morning as originally planned." She didn't turn around. "Angus? I'll deal with you in a minute."

The tone made his cock hard. Oh, he was a deviant bastard, but Angus didn't care. "Gladly," he drawled.

Vaughn's chest puffed out like a silverback gorilla in a fight for dominance. "Force? How about I give you a ride to wherever you're going tonight?"

"I'm already here," Angus said smoothly. There was no need to let the agent know he was sleeping on the sofa. There also was no need to demand an HDD team on Nari because she was leaving town the next day. "I believe the lady asked you to leave. I'd hate for her to kick your ass."

Scarlet crossed Vaughn's cheekbones.

"Angus," Nari snapped. "Knock it off. Vaughn? Leave." She motioned to the door.

Roscoe growled, finally giving up on obedience.

Vaughn looked at the dangerous Czech German shepherd and then reached for the doorknob behind his back.

"Fine. We can discuss this more on Monday morning. But make the right decision, Nari. I don't want to irritate your daddy by firing you, but I will if need be."

With that last dig, the agent left.

Nari turned to face Angus. "None of that was necessary. Now, you can sleep on my sofa tonight, but tomorrow I think it'd be better if you used Mal and Pippa's guest room until you get your legal situation sorted out and we solve these cases."

"That's fine," he said quietly. "You'll need to decide where you want to go, and I'm happy to pay the travel costs. How about the Maldives?" Those overwater bungalows looked like wonderful places to relax. Then he paused. "No, Wolfe won't want to be out of the country just in case Dana has problems. All right. Hawaii it is. Pick an island and we'll make the travel arrangements tomorrow." His body felt cold at the thought of her out of his life for good, but it was the right thing to do.

She hung her head, as if struggling desperately for patience. "I am not leaving."

"Nari—" He kept his voice as gentle as he could. "I'm not asking or suggesting. You are going, and if I have to hogtie you and hire a private plane with Wolfe as your guard, I'll do it." Fire shot through her dark eyes, only spurring on his unwelcome lust. "Yes, it's kidnapping, but I'm already facing a slew of upcoming charges, so what's one more? Don't fight me on this, baby. You won't win."

Chapter Twenty-Two

Anger shot through her so quickly, Nari's head ached. Even so, the idea that Angus felt responsible for her to the degree that he'd be such a complete ass warmed her girlie parts. She'd have to resolve her issues with that later. For now, she had to face down this stubborn male and win. "I don't work for you, I'm not dating you, and I have not asked for your opinion on my safety or plans." Her jaw hurt from gritting her teeth, so she tried to relax it. "While Neanderthals might interest some women, I am not one of them. I suggest you rejoin this century. Like, now."

"So far, I'm not liking current times," Angus rejoined. He was standing way too close to her with just the dog between them. "I know I'm neither your boss nor your boyfriend, but I got you into this mess and I'm getting you out of it."

"I can take care of myself," she said.

"Didn't say you couldn't."

Roscoe looked from one to the other of them, stood, and walked over to jump back on the sofa. He yawned hugely and put his muzzle on his paws.

She eyed the animal that had just abandoned her to a pissed-off male. "Angus, you're being an ass."

"I'm okay with that." On the side of his face, fresh bruises mixed with slightly older ones. One along the left side of his jaw no doubt corresponded with a bump on the back of her shoulder from when he'd tackled her to the ground as the cabin exploded. When he'd put his body between her and danger, possibly sacrificing himself.

Her breasts tingled. It was late and her defenses were down, while her emotions were up. "Think of another plan because I'm not leaving right now. The team, if we're staying together, needs me. You know that." She was the one who held them together.

"You're more important than any team," he said softly, towering over her without meaning to do so. A dark desperation swirled in his deep, green eyes, drawing her to him more surely than any challenge could.

His sweetness would always be her undoing. Even so, she lifted her chin. "The answer is no."

"There wasn't a question," he said.

That was it. She shoved him, right in the gut. Faster than she could follow, he manacled both of her wrists and turned them, putting her butt to the wall. Gently but firmly. He stepped into her, his spicy male scent washing over her entire body.

"You don't want this," he rumbled, his voice hoarse.

"Maybe you don't," she challenged, her breath quickening. There wasn't anything she wanted more right now than his mouth on her. "What are you afraid of, Angus? Little ole me?" Yeah, she could take him down with one move.

He scoffed. "Right."

Challenge accepted. She lifted her leg and curled it, catching him behind the knee while pushing her whole body forward. At the last second she twisted and sent him down to land on his back on the thick carpet.

He kept her hands, yanking back, and let gravity pull her down.

She landed on him, the breath whooshing out of her lungs from impact with his hard chest. In one smooth motion he rolled them over, pinning her arms above her head.

Her gasp was half cough and half laugh. She tried to pull up her knees to get leverage with her heels.

"Oh no you don't." He flattened his legs over hers, pinning them.

God, he felt good on top of her. Solid and strong. An immovable object in a dark and frightening world. She smiled, not bucking against him. "You can't keep this hold forever." Her legs were immobile and he had her wrists extended above her. She could headbutt him, but they weren't in a real fight, so giving herself another concussion and possibly breaking his nose seemed like overkill. But it was in her arsenal, just in case. "You make one move and you lose your leverage."

For an answer, he secured both of her wrists in one of his large hands. "I made a move. Your turn."

She couldn't. Well, not without hurting both of them. She could call for the dog to help, but she didn't want to confuse or scare Roscoe. "There's not much you can do with that free hand at the moment," she whispered.

His eyelids dropped to half-mast. "Are you about done throwing challenges?"

"Nope." Not until he accepted one. "In fact, I think we should talk about why you—"

His mouth crushed down on hers. Finally. He went deep, his body on hers, his strength all around her. The kiss was raw and heated, filled with anger and loneliness and lust.

Desire plowed through her, shoving out every other emotion. All fear, all anger, all uncertainty disappeared with the force of his mouth on hers. His tongue swept inside her mouth, taking what he wanted. She kissed him back, her hands trapped above her head, adding to the need raging through her.

He released her mouth and then kissed along her jawline, nipping her ear and going lower, suckling her collarbone with his impossibly hot mouth. "How badly are you hurt?"

She ached like crazy. Fighting against the hold on her wrists, she gasped when she couldn't free herself. Warmth flushed through her, pounding down her torso to land between her legs. "I'm not hurt. Bruised, but not broken. Like you." She gasped, widening her legs.

He pressed his erection against her. Electrical sparks flew from her clit through her body, peaking her nipples and seizing her lungs. It wasn't enough. Not early enough. He nipped his way up her neck and finally released her hands to cup her face, leaning back and kissing her again, even deeper than before.

She dug her fingers through his thick hair, holding on and kissing him back. More. She needed so much more.

He leaned back. "You're sure?"

"God, yes." She rubbed against him, needing relief.

"Definitely yes." She ripped his shirt over his head, tossing it toward the sofa, careful of the burn marks on his torso.

He rolled them over, landing her on top of him.

She scrambled up, and he grasped her shirt, holding while she shrugged out of it. Laughing, panting, they disrobed, rolling toward the kitchen. Their mutual frenzy ratcheted up her need even more. When his talented fingers found her core, she groaned, arching against his broad hand.

He rolled again, putting her beneath him. Slowly, he penetrated her.

She gasped at his size, digging her nails into his arms.

He paused. "I'm clean."

"Me too, and on the pill." She gasped, trusting him. Besides, as the shrink for the team, she'd seen his medical records. All of them.

His smile was feral with the oddest hint of sweet. "Good." He shoved all the way inside her with one powerful push.

She blinked, her lungs expelling oxygen, her body on fire. For him. Only for him.

Angus grew still, hunger slashing through him with a power he'd never felt before. He kept his weight off Nari with one elbow and forced himself to let her body become accustomed to him. Her internal walls pulsed around him, hotter than any furnace. He groaned, pressing his forehead to hers, fighting himself. Fighting every instinct he had to move hard and fast—to claim her.

If he even hinted at words like that, she'd probably break his nose.

But it was true. Beyond the moment, past the anger always consuming him, existed a simple truth: He wanted to make this woman his. He abandoned the impossible thought immediately and concentrated on right here and right now. He leaned up, meeting her gaze.

In the midnight hour her eyes glowed a luminous brown, startling with clarity. From the first time she'd met his gaze directly, he'd been struck by the color of her eyes. "You have the most beautiful eyes I've ever seen," he murmured, brushing her hair away from her face.

Her chin lifted. "They're brown. Dark brown."

Not even close. "They're sunlight shining through the edges of molten copper," he murmured, kissing her again, feeling her surprise in the curve of her sweet lips. Her intelligence matched her strength, but it was the kindness in her eyes that glowed and drew people to her.

She sank her nails into his ass and he forgot all about her eyes.

His hands roamed over her silky skin and his lips moved down her jaw to her pert breasts. Her nipples were taupe-colored. He kissed and nuzzled her, nipping one and then the other. Her gasps of pleasure penetrated his brain and he started moving, trying to be gentle.

"More," she said, arching into him, her ankles once again clasping at his back and spurring him on with surprising strength. Then she bit his shoulder, right by his neck, and he was lost.

His control snapped and he captured her hips, partially lifting her off the carpet. Hard and fast, he powered into her, letting his body finally take control. She met each thrust, her small breasts bouncing above a bruise across her rib cage. Even seeing that, he couldn't stop.

Didn't want to.

She threw back her head, elongating her slender neck. He dropped his head, increasing the strength of his thrusts and scraping his teeth along her jugular, careful not to really scratch her.

She moaned his name, running her hands across his chest and up over his shoulders, clutching him closer.

He thrust into her. "Say it again," he ordered, tightening his grip on her.

She opened her eyes, and her pupils were dilated. "Angus," she whispered, the sound pained.

Yeah. He angled his next thrust, making sure to impact her clit.

Her eyes widened and then she arched completely off the carpet, crying out and shutting her eyes. The orgasm visibly swept through her body from her neck down to her core, and then she gripped him so tightly his ears rang. He groaned, barely freeing himself before plunging back into heaven.

She shook with her release, pushing him into his own. He hammered hard several times and then ground against her, shuddering with a release so strong he could barely breathe.

Coming down, he loosened his hold. God, he hadn't bruised her more, had he?

She exhaled, and her body went limp beneath his. Her eyelids remained closed and a contented smile curved her lips. "'Night."

He chuckled against her and then groaned as his dick jumped inside her. "We should probably go to the bed."

"Nope," she mumbled sleepily. "Fine here. 'Night."

He rolled off her and scooted to his knees before

standing, his legs steady. Then he leaned down and lifted her against him.

She cuddled right into his chest, her breathing evening out.

He stared down at her peaceful face. The woman was actually asleep? Huh. He carried her easily to the door to make sure it was locked before walking toward a doorway by the sofa that probably led to a bedroom. Roscoe had turned around and put his face into the back of the sofa, hiding his eyes.

Angus rolled his. "You're a prude," he whispered.

The dog gave one of his fake snores.

Angus chuckled and carried the sleeping woman into a bedroom decorated in light gray with a hint of lavender. Peaceful and controlled, just like Nari. He set her beneath the covers in the ultraorganized room and made use of the attached bathroom before returning to the bed.

A thought occurred to him, and he returned to the living room to dig through her purse for her gun. It wasn't there. Shit. HDD had probably confiscated hers along with his after they'd both shot at the attacker the night before. He didn't want to awaken her to see if she had another weapon. She probably didn't.

He needed to get to his storage unit the next day to arm himself again. Finally giving in to the need for rest, he climbed into bed beside her.

She mumbled and rolled against his good side, pressing her nose to his chest. His heart took the hit and then kept pumping. "You're too much," he whispered, sliding an arm beneath her head so she could get more comfortable against him. "This can't happen for good," he said, knowing he was only talking to himself. Yeah, he liked her. A lot. Then she slid a hand over his stomach, still sleeping, and threw a leg over his knees, as if to keep him close.

He sighed and let himself sink into sleep. Maybe they could have one good night without anybody being shot, blown up, or murdered.

But he doubted it.

Chapter Twenty-Three

Nari sat at her kitchen table finishing off surprisingly good scrambled eggs after having showered and thrown on jeans and a light sweater for the day. Roscoe was flopped across her feet, begging with big brown eyes for another piece of bacon. The TV droned in the background, turned to the news so they could learn whether another body had been found. If not, this was the first morning the killer hadn't left one. She focused on her nearly clean plate. "You can cook. Really cook."

Angus shrugged, standing to put his dish in the sink. "Yeah. I guess. My sister taught me. She was amazing."

Nari sipped her coffee. Should she ignore the opening and keep the morning peaceful? "You don't talk about her. What was she like?" Nope. Curiosity was her bane, as usual.

Angus poured himself another cup and leaned back against the counter, looking delicious with just his jeans on. That bare chest should be admired daily. "She was sweet and smart. It was just the two of us for so long after our folks died. When she was gone the world just got dimmer." He shrugged. "I don't know. It's hard to explain."

Nari took another drink, kind of missing the whipped cream Wolfe always insisted on adding to any caffeinated beverage. "She looked like you. From what I saw of the picture you had." The picture that had now been burned. "I hope you have more photos."

"I usually just use that one for the murder board," he said absently.

She sat up. "You don't have any other pictures of the two of you? Of good times?"

"Somewhere in a box." He downed the entire cup, not meeting her eyes.

She shook her head. "Angus, you have to let go of the anger and try to live again."

"Don't shrink me." He rinsed the cup, seeming miles away.

"Wouldn't ever want to shrink you," she retorted, getting the grin from him she'd hoped to see. Okay. Fair enough. She wasn't his girlfriend or his shrink, so she didn't have the right to get into his head.

He pulled out her spice drawer. "You should probably work on yourself instead of me."

"What?" She stood and carried her dish to the sink.

He pointed. "You're obsessive. These are lined up by color and name, not to mention brand. Talk about a control freak."

She reached around him and slammed the door closed. "I like to be organized. You're the control freak."

"Huh." He looked around the kitchen. "I don't think so."

One of the boxes on the counter buzzed.

Nari winced and grabbed for the box, yanking out the new phone. "This one is mine. The other is yours."

He reached for his box and opened it.

"Hello," Nari said. It was a good thing the phone was the same model as the one she'd lost.

"Hey, Nari, it's Brigid," Brigid whispered tersely. "Are you with Angus?"

Nari went still. "Yes. Why? What's going on?"

Movement sounded, as if Brigid had hunched over. "We've all been called in for questioning, but they're really looking for Angus. I think they found some sort of physical evidence, but we haven't been told what. We're being threatened and all of that. If you're at your apartment, get out of there. Or get him out of there." Her voice rang oddly.

"Where are you?" Nari whispered back.

"In the bathroom at Metro headquarters," Brigid whispered. "Honestly. Tell Angus to get somewhere safe and we'll touch base as soon as we can. We need to find the real killer before they arrest him." She abruptly clicked off.

Nari looked up to find Angus staring at her with an intensity she felt to her toes.

"What's happening?" he asked. "Another murder?"

"No." Nari shook herself. "Brigid said they were all called in and are being questioned about your whereabouts. I think they found more evidence and want you. We have to get out of here." Even so, she opened the dishwasher to pile in the dishes.

Angus strode to the front door and shoved his feet into the boots he'd borrowed from Wolfe. "You can't be with me."

"Sure I can." She was going to help him whether he liked it or not. "Right now, we aren't supposed to know that the police are looking for you, so we're not doing anything wrong."

"No." He ran a bruised hand through his hair. "Damn it. I can't leave you here by yourself. Okay. I'll take you to Wolfe's, and then I'll need to borrow your rental car until I get one of my own."

She ran out of the kitchen and into her bedroom, hurriedly packing a suitcase with everything she'd need for a week or so. She returned, out of breath. "Okay, I'm ready." She hustled toward the door, and Roscoe bounded into step beside her. "They'll look here if they're trying to find you. Let's go."

Angus followed her and made sure the door was locked. "You're not arguing?"

"Nope. Wolfe is being questioned right now, along with everyone else, so if you drop me off at his place, nobody will be there. Also, I imagine the police are watching the homes of everyone on our team." She opened the back door of the car so Roscoe could leap inside and then slide in. She grimaced as Angus motioned for her to scoot over. "Whatever."

"They're looking for me. If I need to outrun them, I don't mind another ticket." He pushed back the driver's seat and started the car. "We probably only have minutes until they get here." He sped out of the parking area. "Tell me there's a back entrance to this complex."

"Yep. Take the next right and then left." She reached back for her seat belt. "Where are we going?"

"I have a storage unit a few hours away and we need to hit that for more supplies." He took a corner slowly.

She secured the belt. "Like clothing?"

"Yes, as well as weapons and the copied case files."

Figured. He couldn't go minutes without his case files. "You know, if the killer isn't Lassiter, it's not our case. Why don't you let Tate and Metro do their jobs and worry about getting yourself out of this mess?" She wouldn't watch his obsession kill him.

"Because the team is the target, regardless of the killer's identity." He spoke almost absently and turned the radio to the news. "Let's keep track in case they find another body."

She looked at her purse on the floor. "Wait. I forgot my new phone."

Angus kept driving. "Sorry, but it's on your counter. Mine is turned off, and I'll toss it in a garbage can on the way—once we're far enough from your place. These phones can be tracked, and right now, I'd like to stay under the radar until we figure out where to go."

She shivered. For years, she'd worked for government agencies. Now she was hiding from them.

Right after a dinner of fast-food sandwiches, Angus knocked on the metal door of the loft, smiling when Jethro opened it.

"Ah, shite," the Brit said as Roscoe pushed past him to start scouting. He sighed. He was dressed in black sweats with a green shirt, and his usual glasses were perched on his straight nose, his brown eyes more resigned than irritated. "Come on in."

"Thanks." Angus gestured Nari ahead of him and then followed, one large duffel over his shoulder and the other in his hand. "Sorry to intrude, but we really didn't have anywhere else to go."

Nari kept moving into the industrial-style loft, walking to the floor-to-ceiling windows gridded with metal. "This place is amazing," she said, turning around and viewing the open design. There was a massive gas fireplace flanked on one side by the living room and on the other by a rec room with a pool table and a bar.

Angus looked to the left, where the cement-block kitchen lay. "You don't—shit."

Roscoe jumped onto the metal dining table, captured a bottle of red wine, and quickly tipped it back. He finished the last gulp and tossed the empty bottle with a shake of his head.

Angus dropped the duffel and snagged the bottle out of the air before it could crash into a wall.

"Nice catch," Jethro said, glaring at the dog. "Get your ass off my table."

Roscoe licked red wine from the fur around his mouth and gracefully jumped down. He did a happy dance and then continued scouting.

"Sorry about that," Angus said, sighing. "I'll pay you back."

Jethro put his hands on his hips, his eyes sparking. "That was a 2014 Opus One Cabernet Sauvignon."

Angus picked up his duffel and carried them both to the sofa. "I'll buy you a six-pack."

Nari turned, looking small and delicious against the tail end of an orange sunset outside the industrial windows. "You were drinking a 2014 Opus One Cab by yourself?" She looked around. "What's going on, Jethro?"

"Nothing." Jethro walked toward the lone set of dishes on the table and carried them to the sink, limping a little.

Guilt swamped Angus. Last time he'd called Jethro in

on a job, the man had almost died. "I'm sorry about this. We'll just stay one night and then get out of your hair."

Jethro pointed to an office alcove beyond the pool table and a monstrous television. "I've been working on the note left for you beneath the bridge, as well as the markings below it."

Angus stiffened. "Tell me."

"No," Jethro said, limping to a silver cabinet at the far end of the kitchen and taking out another bottle of wine. "How does a 2016 Chateau Lafite Rothschild sound?" He deftly opened the bottle.

Nari gasped. "Seriously? That sounds delicious. I had no idea you were a wine connoisseur."

"I'll show you the wine cellar later." Jethro poured three glasses. "We should let her breathe, but what the hell." He handed the glass to Nari.

Angus's gaze narrowed. What the hell? It was red wine. Crushed grapes and sunshine. He accepted the proffered glass and sniffed. Smelled like wine. The red kind.

Nari swirled hers around, sniffed it, and then took a small drink. Her moan went right to Angus's cock, and the pink sliding across her face was the same color she turned while orgasming. Angus took a drink. Yep. Red wine. He walked around the leather sofa and dropped into a guest chair. "Well? If you two are done bonding over crushed grapes, can we get to business?"

Nari frowned and Jethro, the ass, looked amused.

Angus shoved down impatience along with a bunch of other emotions. He was not jealous and he wasn't playing this game.

Nari gave him a look, one he didn't much like, and then skirted his chair to sit on the sofa.

Jethro loped around the other side and sat in a chair much like Angus's, setting the bottle high on a shelf next to the fireplace.

Roscoe whined, his tail wagging on the concrete floor. Then he leaned against the chair, looking up. The furniture was leather and expensive and perfect for the industrial-style apartment. "How about you tell me why you're at my flat after dinner with a duffel full of weapons?" Jethro asked.

Nari started. "Full of weapons? You said one gun and a bunch of file folders." She took another sip of the wine, as if she couldn't help herself.

"I have both," Angus said easily, taking another drink. The stuff wasn't half bad, actually. It'd taste even better on Nari's lips.

Jethro kicked back and flicked a switch near the fireplace. The fire erupted, low with blue hues. "Well?"

Angus gave him the short version of the last couple of days, winding down and finishing his glass. His stomach felt all warm and mellow. Was that what good wine did? No wonder people drank it, although he'd rather have whiskey.

Jethro stood and refilled their glasses, careful to keep the bottle out of Roscoe's reach. "At least he has good taste," the Brit muttered, patting Roscoe's head. He sat back down and looked at them both. "We only worked that one case together months ago, so you think it'll take them time to connect us?"

Angus nodded. "Yeah. They will connect us at some

point, so we'll just stay the night. Then I want to leave Nari with Wolfe and Dana and find a place to figure this case out."

Nari kicked off her boots and crossed her legs on the sofa. "I'm figuring this out as well. Definitely not leaving town." She wobbled a little.

Jethro swirled the wine in his glass, watching the fire play with the tannins. "You're both safe here, if you want to stay." He took a drink, looking as if he was really spending a moment tasting it. "The flat is owned by a dummy corporation, which is owned by a dummy corporation, et cetera and et al. Nobody can trace you here."

Angus sat back, his shoulders relaxing for the first time since the new killer had struck. He should've realized Jethro would be under the radar, considering his ties to M16. He smiled at Nari. "Well, then. For now, we accept your kind invitation." He could keep her safe here until he could talk her into leaving with Wolfe.

Jethro's phone played "God Save the Queen" and he glanced down at the face and sighed. "I have a friend at Metro who works the desk and I've asked for updates. They found another body. Tall, brunette, blue eyes, and they already have an identification." He frowned and read the message again. "Sue Swormton, the owner of the Puff Stadium."

Angus's chest heated. "The Puff Stadium? That's my favorite bakery. I often bought pastries for the office there."

Nari paled. "Pippa is our baker. The killer even knows about her, so he's killed this baker?"

Angus downed the rest of his wine to keep himself from punching the wall.

Nari's hand shook around the glass. "That's every woman connected to the team. He's found a look-alike victim for all of us. Now what?"

Now he had to go after the real thing. Again. For some reason, he'd already tried for Nari. Why?

Chapter Twenty-Four

Nari awoke with a jerk to silence. Real silence. She stretched in the plush bed and rolled over, smashing her face into a mass of fur. She coughed and leaned back. "Roscoe. What are you doing?"

The dog had his head on the adjoining pillow and his butt angled toward her. She petted him. "When did you come in?"

He stretched out his legs, pushing his back into her. Then he rolled over and stood, leaning down to lick her face.

She giggled and pushed him away. "Gross. You have doggy breath. Get off the bed."

With one last swipe at her chin, he jumped over her and landed on the floor. She looked at the unused side of the bed. Angus and Jethro had talked about the case late into the night. Worn out, she'd headed to the guest room. Apparently Angus hadn't joined her. Why would he? Well, they had shared a bed before. And a carpet.

His abandonment shouldn't hurt, yet she rubbed her chest anyway. She was getting in too deep with him.

Morning light streamed through the blinds covering

her window, while a thick, white throw rug blanketed the cement floor. The headboard, side tables, and dresser were all high-end metal and appeared handmade; the adjoining bathroom was, in a word, plush. Dr. Jethro Hanson must've made some serious money after he worked for British Intelligence.

Angus knocked and entered the room. "Wolfe is going to be here in about fifteen minutes with updates from everyone. We figured it'd be best if we only had one liaison to cut down on the chances of anybody finding us, including the killer. Wolfe will know if anybody tries to follow him."

Nari sat up, holding the bedclothes to her T-shirt. She couldn't let go of the feeling of abandonment. "Why didn't you come to bed?" Oh, heck. Why had she asked that stupid question?

He stepped inside and studied her, his eyes a moss green in the early light. Today he'd worn dark jeans and a fresh tee that emphasized every hard muscle in his chest. "You needed sleep, and I was up most of the night going through the old case files."

Her temples ached already. "What are we doing? I mean, seriously. We have wild sex on my floor and then you don't have the emotional balls to just come to bed?"

His chin lifted, making him look oddly dangerous. "What? Am I not adhering to your strict life rules?"

She reared back. The man wanted to fight? "Excuse me?"

"Forget it." He waved a hand. "Just get ready before Wolfe arrives."

"No. Wait a minute here." She jumped from the bed, not caring that she was only wearing an overlarge T-shirt with her legs bare. "*My* life rules? You're the one who's so afraid to show emotion, he's leaving town after making himself a target for a killer." Yeah. She'd figured that one out easily.

"Emotion? Look who's talking." He shook his head, frustration cutting lines into the sides of his mouth. "Every part of your life is in order, except for me. So yeah, you're in for a tumble with me so long as it says safe, but not anything serious."

She couldn't believe they were having this ridiculous confrontation. After everything they'd both been through, he wanted to be an ass? Oh, her emotions felt all over the board, but she didn't care. "Serious? You're the wham-bam-and-see-ya guy."

"Right. Like you're all in if I am. A guy who doesn't fit the mold of what you want. Stop and think, Nari. Who do you see yourself with someday?" When she didn't say anything, triumph filled his gaze. "Yeah. Another government agent, one climbing the ranks, one who's acceptable."

"You need to get hold of your anger issues, jackass," she sputtered, going to him and poking her finger into his hard gut for emphasis. "Everything you do is fueled by anger, and now that you aren't drinking a ton of booze to dull it, it's going to win if you don't do something."

His nostrils flared. "Maybe so. I'm definitely feeling anger right now. But at least I don't have daddy issues and I'm not trying to prove myself constantly to people who don't deserve my loyalty."

She saw red and punched out.

He caught her hand, almost too easily. "Try again, princess." Pivoting, he put her against the bed.

Oh, he was going to get it. She ducked and threw her

shoulder into his gut, twisting to toss him over her head. He flew and landed, grabbing her arm at the last minute to pull her down with him.

She landed on him and he rolled them both over, ducking successive punches.

"Hey." Wolfe poked his head into the bedroom.

Nari paused in the midst of smashing both hands against Angus's ears and looked up, panting wildly. Her mind was fuzzy and her body outrageously turned on. Big-time. "Hey," she whispered.

Angus was on top of her and he peered over his shoulder, his hands on either side of her body. His erection was clearly visible against his zipper. "Hey." His voice was a low rumble.

Wolfe studied them both. "I brought lattes. You guys want to keep fighting each other or do you want to come help us fight a killer?"

Angus pushed himself to his feet and hauled her up with a hand around her biceps. "Good point."

Nari sucked in air, fury and embarrassment heating her entire head. "Yes. Thank you."

Wolfe grinned, his eyes firing. "If you ask me, you two should just fuck and get it over with. Stop this fighting foreplay thing you have going on."

"Nobody asked you," Angus growled.

Wolfe shrugged. "Your loss." He disappeared to the hallway and shut the door.

Nari tried to control her breathing and heartbeat, staring at the metal door. Amusement bubbled through the anger inside her.

Angus coughed and then let it turn into a chuckle. "Guess we've fooled everyone."

She let her body relax, enjoying the moment of secrecy with Angus.

"We just need to get to work," Angus said. "It was a long and frustrating night, and I should've gotten more sleep."

"Me too." She walked toward the bathroom, not knowing what else to say.

"I didn't hurt you, did I?" he asked.

She rolled her eyes. "Of course not." The guy had taken special care to avoid her bruises and had even pulled her to land on him rather than the floor. Angus Force would break his own arm before he hurt a woman. "Let me get ready really quickly and then I'll be out." She didn't wait for his response before shutting the door and leaning against it. What the heck was wrong with her?

Angus stared at the murder board he'd set up on one brick wall in Jethro's office area. He had freaking lost his damn mind with Nari. What was wrong with him?

Jethro had placed a lid on the pool table earlier, and they'd spread out all the case files with barstools surrounding it.

Wolfe sat on one, happily gulping down more sugar than a human body could probably process in one day. He sat up when Nari entered the room. "Yours is on the table with the pink sprinkles. I figured you'd want some pink today."

Angus gestured toward a plate of pastries. "Apparently Pippa spent all night baking."

How did Nari look so amazing after just a few minutes

of getting ready? She'd put her silky hair in a ponytail and wore dark jeans and a light-yellow silk shirt that somehow didn't have one wrinkle. Her eyes were a clear, deep, brown today, reminding him of the final moment as the sun disappears behind a mountain and the darkness rushes in.

Jesus. He really had lost his mind.

Nari took a deep breath and reached for her latte, looking up as Jethro and Roscoe entered the apartment after obviously having gone for a morning walk. "Morning."

"Good morning." Jethro shrugged out of a leather jacket. "There's tea in the kitchen if you'd rather have that."

Wolfe chuckled. "She'd much rather have the latte. I got her favorite. It's caramel with two extra pumps, whipped cream, and sprinkles."

Nari sighed quietly.

Angus grinned, letting in a little humor. "So. Let's get started. Wolfe? How would you like to go on vacation with Dana and Nari?"

Nari stiffened.

Wolfe shook his head. "Can't leave town. The HDD and Metro were as direct about that point as anything. They want us all near until they nail your ass for murder."

So much for that plan. Angus took a drink of his latte and braced himself for the jolt of sugar. It was shocking his team didn't weigh five hundred pounds each after working with Wolfe for over a year. Of course, they got shot at a lot, and that probably burned many calories. "What do you have, Wolfe?"

Wolfe sobered. "I agree with just having one liaison to keep us off the radar for now. Metro was rather, I guess you could say *insistent* that we don't work either case.

The HDD piped in with the old interference-with-a-federal-case language, which is a felony, as you know. So we have to be careful." The soldier's eyes glittered.

Angus nodded. "Agreed. Did the teams meet earlier?"

"We did." Wolfe eyed the pastry dish. "I brought all the research we compiled, along with dog food for Roscoe and this stuff for you all."

Nari pulled out a barstool and sat, while Jethro moved toward the kitchen.

Wolfe angled his head to view the Brit. "I didn't forget you. I have a chai tea for you. It's the one with green sprinkles."

Jethro turned around, his eyebrows arched. "There normally aren't whipped cream and sprinkles on chai tea."

"I got it specially made for you." Wolfe tilted his head toward the cup holder, his smile genuine. "You're one of us now, dude. Especially after you and I bonded blowing up the drug cartel holdings in Mexico. Besides, if we get caught with this current case, you'll be charged just like we will."

"Wonderful," Jethro muttered, stalking toward the sugary treat. He was moving better this morning. In fact, he looked like the M16 agent he'd once been.

Nari cupped her drink. "Please tell me that Brigid has found Millie."

"Yep. Get this: She's at a wellness spa resort in Thailand. I talked to her myself and basically told her to stay there for a while. Turns out that was already her plan." Wolfe reached down to pet Roscoe's head.

Some of the tightness in Angus's chest relaxed. Millie was safe. That was one thing off his mind. He scrubbed both hands down his face and moved toward the table, pulling out a barstool and sitting. "Okay. Let's cross that one off the list and move on to who wants me or us dead."

Wolfe flipped through a stack of files and handed out purple ones. "Pippa color coded everything. That woman is a master at organization." He paused. "Not as good as you, Nari, but close."

Instead of smiling, Nari just took her file folder.

Angus winced. He shouldn't have said what he had in the bedroom. "Being organized is a good thing."

Jethro finally took a seat, still eyeing his chai tea. He set it down next to his file folder. "I imagine there are several people who want you dead, my friend."

Sad but true. Angus flipped open his folder and studied a list of enemies still living after the cases of the past year.

Wolfe leaned forward. "The team started with recent cases and went backward, including your time in the FBI. Brigid had to hack some files, so we need to destroy a lot of this after we're finished." He pointed to a picture on the front page. "This is Barry Barnes, one of the cult members we busted. He made several threats about the team before he was put away for a short stint. Got out of jail just three weeks ago, and he has a sketchy past. Brigid is trying to track him down now."

Angus studied the innocuous-looking man. About forty years old, blue eyes, saggy jaw. The guy had a gut. "I don't see him as the man who got away the other night, but maybe he got in shape while in prison." He looked up. "Any ID on the guy I killed?"

Wolfe shook his head. "Nothing that we found, and Brigid doesn't think the HDD has identified him either. But their system is harder to hack, even though she's on the inside. She's working on it."

Thank God for their talented hacker. They went through the entire file, and by the end of it, even Angus was surprised by how many people might want him in the ground. Huh. He sighed. "All right, let's move on to the current case." He opened a file folder on the six recent victims.

It was time to find this guy. He rolled his neck and slid back into his role as a profiler of evil.

Chapter Twenty-Five

Nari tried to even out the sugar rush from the latte with a cheese-and-bacon protein roll baked by Pippa. It was shocking how many people wanted Angus and the rest of their team dead. She took a deep breath and opened her file folder to see what had been compiled on the serial killer. She whistled. "Wow. Brigid really hacked everybody this time, didn't she?"

Wolfe nodded. "Yeah, we all called in any favor we could find. The newest victim is on the second page."

Nari turned to see a brunette who looked defenseless in death, and tears pricked the backs of her eyes. The poor woman. Nari had never gone to the bakery, but she'd enjoyed the goodies Angus had brought to the office on more than one occasion.

Angus read the papers without saying a word, but tension radiated from his hard body. She wanted to reach out to him and offer some kind of comfort, but they weren't exactly getting along just then.

Angus flipped the page and stared at the picture. "She didn't stand a chance."

Nari studied the heartbreaking picture. "He's being

more subtle, finding a baker. Pippa doesn't work as a baker, and most folks outside our team don't even know she exists. So, how does the killer?"

Angus nodded. "I was thinking the same thing. How does the killer know Pippa bakes?"

Nari shook her head. "Not many people are close enough to any of us to know that." Pippa wasn't even on the team, although she lived with Malcolm and was part of the little family they'd all formed. Nari looked up. Angus had been the best profiler in the FBI before he'd left the agency. "What's this guy's next move? I mean, who?"

Angus's jaw was hard as he flipped through the records. "Let's work through it with the notes we've found. Normally, if I had to guess right now, I'd say he'd want to go in opposite order from these kills, mainly because you and I are spending so much time together. He'd save you for last. Except that's not what he's done. He's tried to take you already."

Nari shivered. "Why?"

"I don't know. There's something we're missing." Angus looked at Wolfe. "When you report back, let Malcolm and Pippa know that, if this guy hadn't tried for Nari, I'd think Pippa would be the first target." He took a drink of his latte. "Although, the guy might take any opportunity, so everyone needs to be alert and guarded."

"What about the men?" Nari asked quietly. "Maybe he's going after the entire team."

"It's a possibility," Angus said, his green eyes glimmering with intelligence. "But there's a sexual component to all these killings, and I think this guy gets off on harming women." He turned the page. "Let's go through the notes and I'll develop a profile."

Wolfe looked at Jethro. "You helped catch Lassiter, right? What are your degrees in?" He munched on a cinnamon roll.

Jethro reached for another sheet in his file folder. "Philosophy, with emphases in rational choice, game, moral theory, ethics, and decision theories," he said absently, reading along.

"As well as psychology and criminology," Angus added.

"Huh." Wolfe licked frosting from his fingers. "Somebody is trying to explain away evil."

Jethro jolted and then returned to reading.

Nari eyed a blueberry muffin. Sometimes Wolfe was so insightful it was scary. Or impressive. Maybe both.

Jethro cleared his throat. "There weren't notes with the first two victims, and we've tracked down the origin of the note with the third victim." He turned toward Wolfe. "The passage was from a poem called *The Fate of the Damned* by Giuseppe Legonito. The poet lost his family in a fire and went crazy all by himself."

Wolfe sat back. "Well, that fits Angus."

Angus winced. "Thanks, Wolfe."

"Sure." Wolfe set down his folder. "What was the saying you found on the bridge?"

Angus spoke instantly, not looking at the papers. "'The forest watches, the darkness knows, the time is coming—can you feel the change?'"

Jethro tapped a Cross pen on his paper. "The passage is from an eighteenth-century poem by Aiden Donnelly, who studied under Robert Burns for a while and was also Scottish. He, too, went crazy. This poem, like the other, is about death."

Angus sat back. "That doesn't help me."

"No, but this might." Jethro pushed a picture of the graffiti beneath the bridge toward Angus.

Nari leaned closer. She'd seen the graffiti, but the photo made the symbols easier to discern. She squinted. "Wait a minute."

Jethro nodded. "Yeah. It's Latin for Vosegus, who was a Celtic god of hunting and forestation."

Angus exhaled. "Lassiter was big on the Celtic gods."

"I remember," Jethro said somberly. "Of course, anybody studying the case would know that if they had access to all the case files, which we're assuming."

Angus didn't respond to that thinly veiled question. Instead he turned the page. "Did anybody get their hands on the note found with the fourth body?"

"No." Wolfe leaned back in his chair. "No other notes have been entered into any computer system. Metro might be worried we can hack their system, or they're trying to keep information from the HDD so they can solve the case, or maybe they're just being cautious. Is there any chance your friend will slip us info?"

"Tate?" Angus snorted. "Not a chance. Even if he doesn't think I'm guilty, he won't risk his job. I wouldn't blame him."

Nari flattened her hand on the table. "Special Agents Fields or Rutherford might be able to get us any notes." She focused on Angus. "You're going to need a lawyer."

Angus tapped his fingers on the table. "I know. Does anybody know of a good one?"

Nari thought through her friends. "I know a couple, but you're going to want a defense attorney, and one of the best. I'd have to ask around. I'm surprised you agreed to hire a lawyer."

He leaned forward. "If I get charged, I'll have a right to see the evidence against me. Those notes would count."

"Yeah, but you also won't be able to hide out from the police," Nari said quietly. She hadn't liked that idea anyway.

Angus looked at Jethro. "I need a phone. Can I borrow yours?"

"Oh." Wolfe reached into the pack he'd set by his feet. "I forgot. Brigid secured several burners for the two of you." He tossed a couple across the table. "Just in case."

"Thanks," Angus said.

Nari reached for the burner, feeling guilty at even needing one.

Angus caught her expression. "Listen. Whoever is after us might be able to track us via GPS, so we shouldn't have our phones with us. You're not doing anything wrong."

She held the small device in her hand, her anxiety up. It was time to get back to a routine she could live with, and that started with returning to work the next day. Maybe she could even get some information on those other three notes so they could finally put this case to bed. "We're doing a lot wrong," she muttered.

Wolfe looked at them and then at Jethro. "I need a break. How about we grab lunch and catch up? It's been a while since I saved your ass in Mexico and you still owe me a couple of meals."

Jethro slid off his stool. "I can't argue with that. Of course, you did get me shot first." He grabbed his jacket by the door. "We'll bring you two something back. Any allergies?"

"No," Angus said, while Nari just stared at them, her face heating up.

She cleared her throat. "You don't have to leave us. We're fine."

Roscoe bounded off the sofa and stood by the door expectantly. Even the dog wanted to be away from them? Nari frowned at the disloyal pooch, who gave her the soft, puppy eye look. She softened. Had the tension been that thick during the meeting?

"'Bye," Wolfe said, quickly escaping with Jethro and Roscoe right behind him. As soon as the trio left, the entire apartment quieted.

Angus set his burner on the table. "So."

"So." She twirled hers around and tried not to look at him. "You had no right to try to force me to take a vacation with Wolfe and Dana." Her shoulders went back and she braced for an argument.

"You're right. I'm sorry," Angus said.

Her head jerked so fast her neck hurt. "What?" She stared at his rugged face.

He shrugged. "You were right. This guy is after you as well as me, and you have every right to hunt him down. Getting you out of town would make things easier for me, not for you. It was selfish and I'm sorry."

She wobbled, almost falling off her stool.

He rolled his eyes. "Give me a break. I've apologized before."

"Ha." She looked into the empty kitchen, sorry nobody else was around to witness this. "You have not."

He reached for a muffin and carefully unwrapped it,

his hands large and capable, bringing back memories she needed to banish if she was going to concentrate. Those long fingers had stroked her to orgasm too easily.

She cleared her throat. "Do you want a psychologist's insight before you create your profile?"

"Sure." His voice only held a hint of sarcasm.

She bit back a sharp retort. "Why do you dislike shrinks so much?" She'd asked him before, but he'd always refused to answer. Well, mostly.

He bit into the muffin and chewed thoughtfully. "When I was chasing Lassiter, my boss at the FBI thought I was getting obsessed and ordered me to see the agency shrink. He was a smart guy and we ended up collaborating more than working on my brain. Nelson was his name, and he was supposedly an expert in abnormal psychology."

"And?" Nari prodded.

Angus took a deep breath, looking at the half-eaten muffin. "He analyzed all the data and concluded that Lassiter was obsessed with me and playing an intellectual game. That he wanted me to stay in the game, so I was essentially safe from attack. It sounds weird, but it made sense at the time."

"But every game has an end," Nari said.

Angus nodded. "Yeah, and I was supposed to be the end. Not my sister. I trusted the shrink's analysis over my own instincts because I agreed that I'd become obsessed. Driven. I should've locked my sister down. I didn't, Lassiter took her and he killed her."

Nari held back her questions and thought it through. So that was why he was so insistent upon her leaving town. He felt that he'd failed to save his sister and he was driven to save the women on his team. "Would she have allowed it?"

"Huh?" He looked away from the muffin and up at her. "What do you mean?"

"Think about it, Angus. You chased this guy for over a year. Do you really think your sister would've just disappeared for that entire time without any sort of end date? Was she the type of woman who'd do that?" Curiosity as well as confidence prodded Nari on, and she kept her voice gentle.

Angus cocked his head. "Well, no. She was as stubborn as you are." He pursed his lips. "Hmmm."

"Based on the psychologist's recommendation, I would've thought she was safe, too." Nari tried to sound logical, not as if she was offering comfort, even though that was exactly what she wanted to do.

Angus's eyebrows rose. "Oh, I had a detail on her at all times. Lassiter got past them."

Nari couldn't help it any longer. She reached out and put her hand over his warm one. "You did everything you could." Was there a way past his anger?

He flipped his hand over to capture hers, his hold firm. "There's always more, but that's looking back. I know you're trying to ease me right now, but I need to keep angry to keep my edge." He looked through the file folder again, still holding her hand.

"Okay," she murmured.

He looked at the murder board and his shoulders settled. Had his mind been drawing conclusions from the connections he'd made on that board all night? "Because, even though nobody else believes this, I'm telling you that it's Lassiter. I've created profiles in my head, whether

I've wanted to or not, but none of that matters. I know it's him. Staring at this murder board just confirms everything I know in my gut. I'm done trying to find another avenue just to make sure I don't miss anything. The instincts I ignored before are wide awake."

Nari swallowed, her mind spinning. "Are you sure?"

Angus took a moment, obviously thinking it through. His chest settled, and a strong light glowed in his green eyes. "Yes. I'm sure. He's alive and he's killing again."

"Okay," she said quietly.

He started. "What do you mean, okay?"

She blinked, even though the argument that had ended with them rolling on the floor was still at the forefront of her mind. "If you say it's Lassiter, it's Lassiter."

He frowned. "Right now, I need your analytical brain."

She shook her head. "Listen. I believe you for many reasons, and the fact that you're able to provide multiple orgasms is not one of them." Her hands flattened on the table. "You're being intellectually honest and you're working from the facts."

He frowned. "Okay?"

She nodded. "This isn't a situation of an instinctual fixed action pattern, Angus. This is instinct, or gut feeling, based on learning served by memory and intelligence. You know Lassiter. You've studied him. If you think this is him, your neurons are firing the way they should. You're no doubt correct."

He grinned. "God, you're sexy when you go all psychobabble on me."

She returned his smile. "That's a first. You would've never said that a year ago."

"Damn straight. I probably turned that corner during the multiple orgasms phase of our relationship."

She lost the smile. "So. Lassiter, huh?"

"Yes," Angus said, the humor on his face sliding away to show fury. "He has to move on to the actual team now, Nari. He won't be able to stop himself."

Chapter Twenty-Six

After inhaling a delicious burger Wolfe brought back for him, Angus finally felt reenergized. He stood and paced in front of the murder board, his mind reeling as he let himself pursue the case as he'd wanted. "First thing we need to determine is what happened to Lassiter's body. Why did the FBI think he was dead when he wasn't?" He reached for his creased and coffee-stained manila file folder.

Nari poked her head out of the bedroom, a phone to her ear. "What kind of retainer can you afford for an attorney? That'll narrow my search."

"Doesn't matter. Just find me the best," Angus said absently. "One who's free tomorrow, actually." He looked at Jethro and Wolfe, who sat on barstools once again while Nari disappeared back into the room. "Since I've been on this case, I've tried to track what could have happened to Lassiter. Back then, I found his hidey-hole, I shot him, and he shot me."

Jethro nodded. "You were taken to the hospital and had the bullets removed. What happened to Lassiter?"

Angus didn't need his notes for this. He'd memorized

everything. "He was alive at the scene and died on the way to the hospital. The autopsy was performed by Dr. Andrew Palletino, who was one of the best. Nothing in the records indicated any sort of coercion or malfeasance."

Jethro drank a beer out of the bottle. "You said 'was.'"

"Yeah. He died of a heart attack about three years ago," Angus said. "Was in his seventies, overweight, and smoked, believe it or not." He reached for his own bottle, ignoring the disgruntled look from his dog. "Lassiter's body was sent to Town House Mortuary, cremated, and then released to the woman who'd served as his nanny. She's dead as well, of natural causes as far as I could tell."

"What about the paramedics? The ones in the ambulance?" Wolfe asked, twirling his beer bottle in his hands.

"I checked them both out, interviewed them under the auspices of an HDD case, and they seemed fine. Also had Brigid run their financials and nothing popped on either one," Angus said.

"Why don't I take another run at them?" Wolfe asked, flashing his teeth. "The problem had to have happened in that ambulance, and I'm not constrained by a badge any longer."

Like Wolfe had ever been constrained. "Okay, but when the ambulance arrived at County, a Dr. Shelman verified time of death. I've interviewed her as well and she seemed solid." Angus shoved a hand through his hair, trying to find an angle he hadn't already pursued. "I can't explain any of it, but I know Lassiter is alive."

"Okay," Wolfe said easily, finishing his beer.

Angus turned, looking at the ex-soldier. "That's it? Just okay? You trust me?"

"Sure. If you say Lassiter is alive, I believe it. I always

have," Wolfe said, bending to the right and plucking another beer bottle out of a bag.

Angus didn't know what to say, so he took another big gulp of the microbrew. Responsibility landed harder than ever on his shoulders. His team trusted him, so he had to be smart. To be right about this. "Take a run at the paramedics. Jethro, how about you go at the doctor? I've had Brigid track her as well, and no red flags, except the woman works way too hard."

"Is she pretty?" the Brit asked.

Angus shrugged. "Only if you like them tall, leggy, and smart."

"I do." Jethro smiled. "Finally, an assignment that won't get me shot."

"Maybe," Wolfe said. "You never know. If the leggy doctor is the bad guy, she might shoot you in the face. Just sayin'." He pushed his beer away from the edge of the table as Roscoe had tiptoed closer. "Nice try, puppy." He patted Roscoe's dejected head. "Don't feel bad. Next time I come, I'll bring your buddy Kat to see you."

Angus concentrated on protecting his team. "I would've thought Pippa would be the first target, but Lassiter has gone after Nari. Now he might go in random order, just to mess with us. Or there's a clue in the notes we haven't found yet." He made a mental reminder to demand all notes the next day at Metro. "How's Dana? Being scared like this probably isn't good for a pregnant woman."

Wolfe nodded. "She's writing an in-depth piece on all this and expects interviews from all of us once we catch this guy. Doesn't seem scared, but she never does. Although she might be getting a little tired of me telling her to sit down. Isn't sitting down supposed to be healthy?"

Angus shook his head. "I don't know anything about pregnant women. Sorry."

Wolfe finished his second beer. "Speaking of which, I need to get home and check on her. Sometimes she forgets to eat when she's working, and although I'm sure Pippa has been cooking, she's not pushy like I am." He looked around the spacious apartment. "This is a great place, Professor. It's even in the middle of an industrial complex, so there aren't other people living around here. Nicely done."

"Thanks," Jethro said.

Wolfe grinned. "Where's the control room for all those cameras you have mounted around the place?"

Jethro returned the smile. "I don't know what you're talking about. Any cameras are probably owned by the businesses that keep warehouses here by the railroad tracks."

"I counted seven," Wolfe said cheerfully. "If I had more time, I'd find your hideaway."

"I counted nine," Angus said, turning back to his board. "There are two on the west side that you can only see if the sun hits them just right."

Jethro might've sworn something uncomplimentary under his breath.

Nari stayed in the bedroom to make her calls while the guys worked by the murder board. She finished the arrangements with the attorney, inwardly wincing at the exorbitant retainer. They might have to rob a bank just to get the guy in the same room as Angus. She glanced at her watch and hurriedly sent a video call.

"Hello," her mother answered, squinting while pushing buttons on her phone. "Nari? Is that you?"

Of course it was her. They chatted every Sunday. "Hi Mom."

"Oh, hi, sweetie." Her mother set down the phone, facing her. "I found a new holder for the phone. Isn't it convenient? The Dixon boy next door brought it over when he saw me trying to put the phone on the porch to talk to my friend, Diedre. He's such a nice boy. Teenagers are better than ever these days if you ask me."

Nari didn't have anywhere to put her burner phone, so she sat on the bed and held it. "You look well."

Her mom's hair was long and straight, pure black and beautiful. Her eyes were brown and soft. "Thank you. So do you." She reached for something on the table and brought back glasses to perch on her nose. "I need readers now. Can you believe it?" She studied Nari. "Is that a bruise on your chin?"

Darn it. Nari had thought she'd covered it. "Just a little one from training. You know." Lying was wrong, but worrying her mother was worse. "Have you been training at all?"

"Of course. I knocked your Uncle Boahi on his butt twice yesterday. Ticked him off, too." She smiled. "He's dating a girl I don't like. I guess at forty she's a woman, but she giggles like a twit."

Then the woman didn't have a chance. Nari finally relaxed, crossing her legs on the bed. "Where's Dad?"

"Oh." Her mom leaned toward the camera. "He's out

putting food on the grass for the darn squirrels. The man was tired of them eating the food out of the bird feeders, so he bought squirrel food off that eBay. Squirrel food." She leaned even closer, her eyes the only thing visible as she whispered, "It's just seeds and more seeds, Nari. The man paid a hundred dollars for seeds." She chuckled, the sound light. "Men."

Nari laughed. That sounded just like her dad. He'd loved her as his own from the second he married her mom. Why she was trying to impress the man who'd abandoned her, who'd only been a father via check, was something she should figure out. Angus had been right about that. "I bet the squirrels are happy."

Her mom leaned back, showing her entire face again. "They are, because they're still eating out of the bird feeder." She looked beyond the phone and then returned. "So. Are you still spending time with that big lion man?"

"Wolfe. His name is Wolfe, and he has a fiancée I very much like," Nari said, shaking her head.

"Oh yes. Wolfe. Good name. Not as good as Force, though. Angus Force is a name I like." Her mom smiled. "How are things with Angus?"

Nari sighed. Nothing got by her mother. "I don't know. We're working on several cases and he's completely focused. So am I. Also, I know he doesn't want a relationship, so I should work on a friendship."

"Oh, for goodness' sake. Men don't know what they want." Her mother whipped off the glasses. "Just last week a very nice couple came into the store, and he was looking for the perfect oval-shaped diamond to put on her hand. She couldn't stop glancing over at this lovely square emerald surrounded by diamonds."

Nari grinned. "What happened?"

"I suggested she try on the emerald ring and she reluctantly agreed. The girl absolutely lit up when I slid it on her finger." Her mother smiled.

Nari held her breath. "Please tell me the young man caught on." Her mother had been known to smack a customer or two with a wooden spoon back in the day. That was illegal these days.

Her mom nodded. "I had to give him the 'mom' look, but it worked. They paid cash, too." She sighed happily. "Oh. Before I forget, have you stopped wearing your fitness tracker? I'm just killing you on steps."

Nari winced. "I've been a little busy, Mom."

Her mom sniffed. "It's no fun winning the spa weekend bet if you don't at least try. Promise me you'll get in steps this week."

Nari sighed. "I promise. I'll give you a run for your spa money." Man, she could use a spa day right now. "Speaking of which. Why don't you get an updated tracker for your wrist and stop wearing the one in your bra? It takes forever to sync."

"I own a jewelry store, dear. Give me a break," her mom said. Then she blushed. "Frank. How'd it go with the squirrels?"

"Perfect." Her dad kissed the top of her mom's head and then leaned in until only his nose was visible on the screen. "Nari? That you?"

Nari coughed back a laugh. "Hi, Dad. I can't see your face."

Her mom moved over and then started. "Oh. That's Mrs. Edleton at the door, dropping off the leaflets for church. Nari, talk to your dad for a moment." She stood up and moved away.

Nari's dad sat and squinted into the camera. "Is that a bruise on your chin?"

She sighed. "Yes. Training. What's new with you?" Her heart warmed at the sight of his blondish gray hair and deep blue eyes. His face was red from sunburn and his whiskers about a day old. He looked healthy.

"Well, citrine is the new diamond these days. Don't know why. One of those movie stars must've worn it, so now everyone wants citrine bracelets. I've been designing a lot." He leaned in, his mouth getting bigger. "Also, I bought some damn seeds off the internet to feed the squirrels and the animals don't want them. Don't tell your mother. She thinks I was brilliant to find the squirrel food. Darn stuff is just seeds. Stupid internet."

"I won't say a word," Nari promised, her heart turning over.

Her dad leaned back. "I kind of heard you talking to your mother, and if this lion fella doesn't like you, then he's a moron."

She sighed. "I think she was talking about Wolfe at that point, and he's engaged. Angus Force is the one she wants me to date."

"Who do *you* want to date?" her dad asked, rubbing his beard.

"I'm not sure," she said, not wanting to go into it with her father. "It's complicated."

He smiled then, his eyes warm. "Only if you make it complicated, pumpkin. Sometimes life just is. If you want the guy, get the guy. Unless he's a moron. If he's a moron,

then kick him to the curb. Life is way too short for morons."
His eyes twinkled with humor. "Plus, nobody is good
enough for my little girl anyway."

"I'll try to remember that," she said softly.

"Good. Plus, did your mom tell you we're coming to
visit? Next week." He smiled, no longer looking charming.
"I can't wait to meet this guy."

Chapter Twenty-Seven

Angus sat in the interrogation room next to his attorney, whom he'd had to pay ten grand just to shake hands with. "You'd better be worth the money," he muttered.

The door opened and Tate Bianchi walked inside with a female detective who was nearly as tall as he. She was built like a model and had brown hair, brown eyes, and a stubborn chin. The woman also moved like she could fight.

Tate studied his lawyer. "Scott? How the hell does an ex-government employee afford you?"

Interesting. Angus watched the interaction, letting his skills as a profiler loose.

The lawyer stood and held out a hand. "It's good to see you, Tate." They shook hands as Tate obviously readjusted his approach to the meeting.

Tate motioned to his partner. "This is Detective Buckle and we're working the case together."

Scott smiled, all charm. "Scott Terentson from Terentson and Terentson." He shook Buckle's hand and waited for her to sit before reclaiming his seat.

Angus watched the lawyer out of his peripheral vision.

He had sandy blond hair, intense blue eyes, and a decent physique. However, so far, Buckle didn't seem impressed. "So, Tate. I guess you can complete our interview now," Angus said. "Does that mean you think I'm guilty?"

"I just want to find the truth," Tate said evenly.

Buckle focused on Angus. "Lassiter is dead. You understand that, right?"

Angus liked that. Big-time. "As much as I appreciate your direct approach, Lassiter is not dead. I'm sure of it."

Tate reared back, his nearly black eyes glinting. "How are you sure of it? Has somebody contacted you pretending to be Lassiter?"

"No." Angus met his gaze evenly. "I'm sure of it because I was the best FBI profiler they've ever had and I know these current kills were made by Lassiter. The question isn't who's doing this. The question is how the hell Lassiter is still alive."

Tate shook his head. "You really do sound crazy, Force. I've reviewed everything about the night Lassiter died and I've interviewed everyone involved."

"On his days off," Buckle said softly, no expression in her sharp eyes.

Angus sat back. Apparently he owed his old friend one. "You didn't find any clue that he was alive?"

"No," Tate said quietly.

That didn't change the situation. "Lassiter is a genius with an IQ of about one-eighty," Angus said. "That makes him unique among all humans. No doubt, he's smart enough to fake his death to avoid prison. Think about it. It took me almost a year to hunt him down in the first place, and nobody else even came close to finding him."

Scott leaned forward. "As such, my client wants to assist the police. He's a valuable source."

Buckle smiled, showing a slightly crooked bottom tooth that mellowed her somehow. "He's not a source because he's a suspect. Our prime suspect, actually." She leaned toward Angus, her eyes softening. "How about you tell us the truth and we all go on from there? You were once a good guy, and the fact that you've killed has to be wearing on you. Please let me help you."

Angus almost smiled. She was good. He turned to Tate. "You going to be bad cop?"

Tate just stared at him.

Scott sighed. "All right. I can see we're not going to get along, and truth be told, that saddens me." He twisted his wrist to read his Rolex. "I have lunch with the mayor, so let's go ahead and hurry this along. Please provide me with all the evidence against my client.'"

Tate's eyebrows rose. "We haven't charged your client, thus you're not entitled to any evidence, Counselor. Somehow, I think you know that."

Angus fought the urge to yank the case file out of Tate's hands. "Fine. Just read me the notes left with the last three victims. I can help you decipher them."

Buckle leaned back and lost the charming smile. "What do we get?"

"What do you want?" Angus shot back.

"We want you to take a lie detector test," Buckle said evenly. "With our tech."

Scott held up a hand. "No. Lie detector tests are unreliable and not admissible in court. He refuses."

"I accept," Angus said. "You show me the notes and I'll take a lie detector test anytime and anyplace."

Scott turned toward him. "That is against advice of counsel."

"Understood," Angus said, not looking away from Detective Buckle. "Do we have a deal?"

"Yes," Tate said, opening his file folder. "There was no note with the fourth victim. Or if there was one, we still haven't found it. Here's a copy of the note left with the fifth victim. The original is being tested at the lab right now."

Angus took the copy of the piece of paper.

Scott leaned over and read out loud. "*There once was a starry night upon which the darkness of lovers fell.*'" He frowned. "What the hell does that mean?"

Angus shook his head, memorizing the script. "The notes are usually from an old poem or text, and the identity of the author is often more important than the actual words." He handed the copy back to Tate. "And the last victim?"

Tate studied him for a moment and then handed over another copied note.

Angus flushed hot and then ice cold as he read it.

Dearest Angus,

This last week has been a bitter disappointment, truth be told. An opening move in any game should be as bold as the master's. I'm afraid that each one of these offerings, all six of them, were merely false starts. Oh, their screams were music to my soul, and I made sure each of them said your name several times. I would never, truly never, forget to include you, my friend. Yet I am sure you are as disappointed as I. This week should've held more meaning for both of us.

But, as you know, plans were made to be altered. I hope to find more meaning with originals rather than inelegant copies. I shall see you soon.

> *Your friend,*
> *Henry*

PS On first glance, the game can only be played according to the limitations on each piece, unless you're the master of the game.

Angus needed to throw up. He swallowed, keeping his expression as stoic as possible. Finally, proof that he'd been right. He should feel vindicated, but all he felt was exhausted. The bastard was alive and Angus had known it the entire time. "Well. I guess this answers all questions." He shoved the copy back to Tate.

Detective Buckle snorted. "Right. My guess is that you wrote this to throw us off. Or maybe there are two personalities in that alcoholic head of yours? It'd be a damn good defense tactic."

"Excuse me?" Angus said, focusing on the woman.

She smiled. "Yeah. Hotshot FBI agent takes down a monster, can't live with the dead haunting him, and reinvents the monster with a second personality. Is that what happened? Is that your defense?" She leaned toward him again, bringing the oddest scent of lilies. "Come on, Force. Tell us what happened."

Scott pushed away from the table. "This interview is finished. Do not harass my client again." He waited until Angus stood and then preceded him out the door.

Angus's head swam as he strode out of the building, ignoring the stares of other cops. "What do you think?"

"My opinion?" Scott asked, walking gracefully down the steps to the sidewalk. "They're going to arrest you within the week."

Nari dressed in a navy-blue skirt suit for her first day with her new team. Her shoes were Louboutin, her shirt Gucci, and her attitude one of confidence as she strode into the new office. Three men had gathered around the table right inside the door, and Vaughn looked up from a series of maps. "You came. I thought you were leaving town."

"No." She didn't offer an explanation.

"Well." Vaughn stood while the other three men just stared. "In order to be on this team, you can't be hanging out with suspected serial killers. Is that understood?"

How rude to bring that up in front of people she hadn't even met. She was supposed to be their sounding board, someone they could discuss their cases with, but Vaughn was doing a good job of making her work impossible. She searched for the right answer to his jackass of a question. There wasn't one. She turned toward the three other men, putting her back to Vaughn. "I'm Nari Zhang." She held out a hand to the first one, who was around thirty with brown hair and eyes.

He stood and accepted her hand, shaking lightly. "Hank Bistle. It's nice to meet you."

She did the same with the others, finding more puzzlement than judgment in their eyes. When she was finished she turned back to Vaughn. "Is this the entire team?"

"No. We have two more out on assignment," he said,

displeasure in his eyes. "The administrator and your father sent them out, but they'll be back soon."

Oh, he just had to mention that Quan was their boss. Irritation caught in her throat, but she spoke through it. "I see. Well, I look forward to meeting them." She turned and smiled at the other men. "I'll go organize my office and get settled in. If anybody wants to talk or bounce ideas off me, I'll be there." Then she walked calmly and confidently out of the main room and down the hallway to her office, where she exhaled, strode around her desk, and flopped into her chair. This was a disaster.

Vaughn followed her. "What the hell was that?"

She sat up. "What do you mean?"

He shut the door and leaned back against it, crossing his arms. "You are not in charge here, and you do not leave a room unless I give you permission to do so."

She rolled her eyes. "Are you kidding me? If you don't want me here, Vaughn, then grow a pair and tell the administrator."

He reared up, his neck elongating. "Excuse me?"

She swallowed. Should she step out of her shoes? The idiot looked like he was about to charge. "You heard me. You're the lead on this team and you have a say in who's on it. If you really don't want me here, tell the administrator. She'd probably understand and just transfer me." In fact, why hadn't Vaughn done that? "Unless you want me here?"

"I don't want you here," he said, his jaw tight.

She frowned. Had he just looked away for the briefest of seconds? She tilted her head to study him and he stared right back, not blinking. Another sign of deception. Then she glared. "Wait a minute. Did you request me for this team?" she asked.

"Of course not." He shook his head and wiped his mouth.

Ha. Another sign somebody was lying. "Are you kidding me? You were so hurt that I dumped you that you requested me for your team? Why? Just to make me miserable?" Which she would not let him do. "Good luck, buddy. That was a waste of your time."

His face flushed and his arms uncrossed. "Fine. Yes, I did request you for this team, and yes, I'm going to teach you a lesson."

"I believe I taught *you* a lesson before," she mused, firing up.

His nostrils flared. "Oh, we're just getting started. You almost ruined both of our careers and one of us has to leave the HDD. I vote for you."

Her jaw almost dropped open. "You want me on your team to force me out?

"Yes. Want to bet I can do it?" Vaughn asked, his smile actually ugly.

A knock on the door had him moving to the side and opening it.

Bistle smiled and poked his head in. "The rest of the team is here and I'm sure they want to meet Nari." He looked her over.

Was he making sure she was all right? Apparently Vaughn didn't have the respect of his team that he imagined. He wasn't nearly the leader Angus was, and that was a shame for the team. Nari smiled and stood. "Thank you for getting me." Then she walked by Vaughn and kept walking as Bistle motioned her down the hallway.

Once in the main room, she nodded at two newcomers. "Hello. I'm Nari and I don't work with this team." Without waiting for a response, she kept walking right out the door and turned left, heading down to Quan's office. The receptionist looked up and Nari ignored her, opening Quan's door and walking inside. "I can't believe you'd put me back on the same team as that megalomaniac," she said instantly, halting at the sight of him sitting at the table with the administrator, both drinking coffee.

"Nari." Quan set down his cup. "What are you doing?"

Opal's hair was up in an intricate bun. "More importantly, what are you talking about?" she asked.

Yeah, that's what Nari had figured. She rounded on Quan. "You're a smart man and you know the only reason an asshat like Vaughn would want me back on his team after I dumped his butt is to make my life miserable." The hurt behind her anger wanted to be let loose and she held on tight.

Quan stood. "We will discuss this at another time."

She settled. "No. We will not. You suck as a father and you suck even bigger as a boss." She dug into her purse and withdrew her weapon and badge. "I quit. Asshole." Then she turned on her very nice shoe and walked out the door, her head held high.

Chapter Twenty-Eight

Angus sat in the passenger seat of his attorney's Jaguar, wishing he were behind the wheel. "Why didn't they arrest me today?"

Scott wove in and out of traffic. "They're not done building their case, and you promised to take a lie detector test. Against my advice, by the way." His hands were competent and the look he gave Angus one of resigned irritation. "In my experience the clients who actually listen to me don't end up behind bars for the rest of their lives. That's something for you to think about."

"I won't fail the lie detector test because I'll tell the truth," Angus said, watching the buildings speed by outside.

Scott took another fast turn. "I've had honest clients fail before; the test is only as good as the person administering it. You're obsessed with this case, and that kind of emotion might screw you in a test."

Angus shook his head. "I'm not worried about that."

Scott took a sharp right next to a brick building across from a vacant field. He drove around back, where Nari's rental car awaited. Angus had borrowed it after dropping her off safely at the HDD office. He'd waited until she'd walked inside before leaving.

"What do you think about setting up an insanity defense?" Scott asked, turning off the engine and turning to look at Angus.

Angus paused in the act of opening his door. "Are you nuts?"

"The question is, are you nuts?" Scott returned, his gaze somber. "If we need a defense, that'd be a hell of a one considering your record with the FBI. I could make you look like a freaking hero if need be."

Angus dropped his chin. "I'm really starting not to like you."

"I get that a lot," Scott said.

Angus's door was wrenched open, and the barrel of a gun pressed inside. He grabbed for it, and the shooter fired several times. One bullet ripped along Angus's arm and pain shot up to his shoulder.

Scott bellowed.

Angus grabbed the shooter's wrist and pulled, pushing his way outside and shoving while holding on to the gun. The guy punched him in the ear and he saw stars. He grappled with the shooter, fighting for the gun. The attacker grunted and hit his rib cage, where his burns were healing, and he coughed, nearly doubling over in pain. Even so, he kneed the asshole in the groin.

The guy was about twenty with green eyes, a blond buzz cut, and a nose that had been broken more than once. He bent over, crying out, and loosened his hold on the weapon.

Angus grabbed it free, lifted it, and shot the man several times.

Movement at the side of the car caught his eye and he turned in time to see a wide-eyed, blond woman swing a shovel at his head. His temple exploded and he went down into instant darkness.

Then, nothing. He had no idea how long he was out. He came to with a jolt, his head on fire. "What? Where?" he mumbled, feeling for the massive lump already forming on his temple. "God." Blinking, he forced his eyes to focus as his memory returned and he found himself half-sitting in the passenger seat, his door still open. "Scott?" He turned to find the attorney slumped over the steering wheel, bleeding profusely. Was he even alive?

Angus fumbled for the guy's phone on the dash. The blood all over his hand made it slippery, but he managed to punch out 911.

"Nine-one-one, what is your emergency?" a young female voice said.

"I have shots fired and need an ambulance," he said tersely, his head swimming, as he gave the address. Nausea rolled up in him, and he dropped the phone, turning to puke outside his open door. Then he gasped, sucked in air, and turned to help Scott. "Where are you hit?" He felt around Scott's forearm and found two holes. What about the head? "Hold on, buddy. I hear sirens." They were faint, but getting louder.

Angus might've passed out again, and when he came to, EMTs were rushing around and Scott was already loaded into an ambulance. "I'm okay," he said to the man checking his pulse.

"No, you're not," the guy said. "We need to get you to a hospital. There's a second ambulance that'll be here in just a couple of minutes."

"No." Angus tried to stand. "I'm fine. I'll be okay."

The EMT stood back to get out of the way. "Sir? There's been a shooting here and you have to stay."

Who had hit him in the temple? Who were those kids? "Listen. I have to go."

"Not a chance," said a low voice.

Angus turned to see Tate standing at the rear of the Jag, his bald head gleaming. "Hey. Is Scott alive?"

"Barely," Tate said, his gaze dropping to the ground. "Step this way, Angus. Now."

Angus caught the glint of the attacker's gun by his foot. He walked toward Tate and away from the gun. "I'm not armed." Which turned out to be unfortunate. He let Tate secure the weapon while he leaned against the vehicle to regain his equilibrium. "There was one shooter and one young woman with a head-splitting shovel." He hadn't recognized either one of them.

Tate handed the weapon over to a tech. "You'll have to come down to the station with me and make a statement. Unless you need a doctor?"

"No. Let's get this over with," Angus said, wiping his bloody hands on his jeans. "You'll need to get the CCTV from the building to identify them."

Tate smiled, and it definitely lacked humor. "This office is owned by one of the best criminal defense attorneys in DC, and it's across the road from a field he also owns. Do you really think there's any CCTV to be found? No cameras, no proof." He leaned in. "Although you're incredibly observant, Angus Force. Something tells me you already knew that fact."

"Wait a minute. Why would I shoot my own lawyer?" Angus asked, blood dripping into his eye.

Tate shrugged. "Insanity defense?"

Ah, hell. Angus thought through his options, although his brain was fuzzy. "Fine. I do require medical attention." At the very least he could get his injuries on record. He stumbled toward the oncoming ambulance. Pain swamped him. Maybe he really did need a doctor.

Nari tripped walking into Jethro's apartment. "Thanks for picking me up." She blinked several times to become accustomed to the darkened apartment.

"No problem," Jethro said, flipping on the lights. "I take it you didn't win at poker?"

"No. Pippa cleaned us all out." Maybe Nari had drunk too many margaritas, but it was worth it. For one night she'd just had fun with her friends and forgotten all about work, serial killers, and Angus Force. Speaking of whom . . . She tilted her head and heard the guest shower running. A naked Angus Force.

Roscoe padded out of the guest bedroom, his ears perked up.

Jethro sighed. "It sounds like Angus just got home. Where was he today? Do you know?"

Nari shook her head. "No. I left him a message that I was going home with Brigid and Raider after work and I haven't heard from him. You two weren't together?"

"No. I had class all day." Jethro looked at the dog. "You need to go out, buddy?"

Roscoe kept walking, stopped for Nari to pet his head, and then continued through the door.

Jethro chuckled. "Don't engage the dead bolt. The door locks automatically and I'll use the keypad to get back in." He left to chase the dog and shut the door. The sound of locks engaging clicked through the quiet.

Nari paused and then headed into her bedroom, turning toward the bathroom. She hiccupped. Why were she and Angus dancing around each other? They could have a relationship for now. Right? Shutting the bedroom door, she dropped her jacket on the floor and then kicked off both shoes before walking into the steam-filled bathroom.

A pair of gray sweats and a ripped blue T-shirt were on the floor. She paused. Those weren't Angus's clothes. "Angus?" she whispered.

"What?" he asked, sounding growly inside the shower.

Relief had her laughing out loud. "Just making sure," she muttered, unbuttoning her blouse and throwing it toward the door. Then she shoved off her skirt and panties. Oh. Her bra. She reached behind herself to release it and struggled, finally remembering that it clasped in front. She clicked it open.

Then she padded across the thick bath mat to the walk-in shower tiled in natural, dark stone. She walked around the corner to discover Angus with one hand on the rock, his head down, hot water sluicing over his broad back. "Hello," she said, humming at the sight of his spectac-ular butt.

He turned his head and his dark hair swept forward, flinging water. "What are you doing in here?"

She slid her hand down his skin, rippling over an old knife wound. "I thought you might be lonely." The man truly did have a tough-guy, badass, strong body.

He turned around.

She gasped and stepped back. A dark bruise rose over

a lump on his temple, a few new bruises marred his right arm, and a bandage was wrapped around his other arm above the elbow. "What happened to you?"

"You don't want to know." His gaze raked her, glittering with angry lust. "This isn't a good idea. Trust me."

That was just it. She did trust him. "I do," she said, moving forward to slide her hands up the hard planes of his chest. "What happened to you?"

"I don't want to talk about it tonight." His look at her aching breasts aroused an almost physical burn. "I'll tell you everything tomorrow, but I'm all talked out tonight." Reaching forward, he tangled one of his hands in her hair. "You're so pretty, Nari."

Angus was freaking beautiful in a way she'd never be able to define. The wounded passion in his eyes called to her more strongly than any siren ever could. She leaned in and kissed his chest, right between his pecs.

He inhaled sharply, the hand in her hair twisting and pulling back her head. The erotic pain shot from her head down her torso to zing around and land hard in her abdomen. He pulled more, and she dug her nails into his pecs to keep her balance.

Then he kissed her. Powerful, intense, and desperately hard. Electricity coursed the length of her body, tingling to her toes. The scorching kiss stole her breath, and his body pressing against hers destroyed her mind. He slid his tongue inside her mouth, exploring her, devastating her with his fully unleashed demand.

And a demand it was. Angus Force wasn't holding anything back this time. He was all male, all demanding, all hers.

He grasped one of her hips and lifted her against the

wall, stepping between her legs while kissing her the entire time. She shuddered, held aloft, and pressed her thighs against his hips. He was so intelligent and driven that sometimes she forgot the sheer strength in the man.

She held on and returned his kiss, tasting whiskey and mint. He'd been drinking, too? Questions tried to filter into her mind, but then he pressed between her legs and she was lost. Slowly, he penetrated her, his mouth working hers the entire time.

He didn't relent.

An inch at a time, he impaled her against the wall. It was the most erotic feeling she'd ever experienced. The stone was chilly against her back, and Angus was hotter than sin against her front. She shivered from the delicious contradiction. "Angus," she whispered against his mouth.

For an answer he released her lips and clamped his hand on her hips, holding her in place. Then he pulled out and pushed back in, a lock of his wet hair falling onto his bruised temple. In the steamy light, bruised and battered, he looked like a conqueror of days gone by. Strong and wounded. His green eyes burned her with an intensity she'd never forget.

In that moment he was everything.

Chapter Twenty-Nine

She felt like heaven around him. After a truly shitty day Angus was more than ready to lose himself in Nari. She leaned forward and bit his neck, urging him faster. He held her hips tight, pulling her into him, powering inside her in an attempt to stay there forever.

Her heat gripped him and he groaned. God, she was tight and slick, as if she wanted him as much as he wanted her, which was fucking impossible.

Her head was back on the dark stone, with her silky hair trailing down and framing her lovely face. Her pink lips were slightly open and her cheeks flushed a dusky rose. If there was perfection in this crappy world, it was Nari Zhang. She was taking all of him, her eyes darker than a midnight sky, but full of stars.

"Angus," she whispered, his name so sweet on her lips.

Something split wide inside him, opening him in a way he didn't want. To her. Only to her. But it was too late to stop. Electricity burned down his spine, sparking his balls.

He thrust harder, letting her drop down against him so he could strike her clit.

She cried out and arched against him, her nails scoring his chest. Her eyelids closed and her thighs clamped on to his hips with the force of her climax. Waves rippled along his cock inside her and he thrust harder, panting with his need to reach the finish line.

She sighed and he let himself go, pinning her to the wall as his body shuddered with his own release. He gasped for air, careful to keep from dropping her.

He leaned back. "Are you okay?"

Her smile was sweet and more than a little satisfied, although her eyes stayed closed. "Yes. 'Night."

He smiled. For the first time that entire horrendous day, he smiled. "Nari? You can't go to sleep in the shower, sweetheart."

"Tired." Her eyelids slowly opened, looking heavy. "Just a little nap?" Her smile was cute. Just plain and simply cute.

"No." He set her down gently and then turned her beneath the still-warm spray. "Here. I'll wash your hair." He'd wanted to run his hands through her hair for months, and no doubt Jethro had good shampoo. So Angus took care of her.

From head to toe he cleaned her, paying special attention to his favorite spots. In no time at all he was aroused again, and she was moaning at his touch. He took her again and then started over with the shower. By the time they had finished, the water had finally cooled.

He turned off the water and dried her with a soft towel, then chuckled as she tried to close her eyes and snuggle against him. "Fine," he whispered, picking her up and taking her into the bedroom. He had no clue where her clothes were, so he yanked one of his clean T-shirts out of his duffel and pulled it gently over her head.

Then he put her in bed, skipped his boxers, and climbed in beside her.

She cuddled against him immediately, her butt to his thighs. He liked that about her. A lot. In fact, there wasn't much he didn't like about her. Her yawn moved her entire body. "Oh. I forgot to tell you. I quit my job today."

He stared into the darkness. "That's big news. Why?"

As she told the story, he went from being curious to relieved to pissed off to impressed by her. "Wow." He ran a hand down her arm. "I'm sorry." He couldn't imagine a father betraying his own daughter like that.

She shrugged. "Me too. I guess after I talked to my dad in California—the man I really feel is my father—I lost interest in trying to know this guy, who was just a sperm donor, really. Oh. By the way. My parents are coming into town in a week to visit, and my dad really wants to meet you."

Angus grinned. He hadn't done the meeting-the-dad thing in years. "Doesn't he design jewelry?"

"Yeah. He's really creative." She yawned again. "Before that he was a marine."

Angus's eyes opened wider. "Interesting."

She chuckled. "Yeah."

"So. We're doing this." He felt too mellow to worry about it.

"Yeah," she said softly. "You have the balls for it?"

He kissed the back of her head. "Yep." He should be worrying or pushing her away, but he was done with all that. "No guarantees."

She snorted. "Totally agree. We go slow and see if we

even like each other. But we stop dancing around and pushing each other away. Just think of the energy we'll save."

The way she looked at life intrigued him. Though he didn't have happily ever after to give anyone, not when he was going up against a genius sociopath once again, he'd give her what he had right now. The idea that she'd quit her job actually eased his mind a little bit. It'd be easier to keep her safe if she worked the case from Jethro's well-secured apartment.

She pushed wet hair off her shoulders. "Now's the time you tell me why you have a lump the size of Texas on your temple and were wearing somebody else's clothes before getting into the shower."

He paused. Oh, he'd dated before, but he'd always had to keep his work confidential. "How good a friend are you with Scott Terentson?" She had been the one to find the lawyer.

"Don't really know him," she mumbled. "He just came highly recommended."

Well, that was something. "I got him shot today." Angus gave her the full story, not liking the way her body tensed more with each sentence. "I checked in with the hospital after the cops were done with me, and he survived surgery but is still unconscious. He's in ICU. It's touch and go right now." Guilt burned hot inside Angus.

Nari slipped her hand beneath his, where it rested on her bare thigh. "It wasn't your fault. I take it the police took your clothing?"

"Yeah." In fact, they were exploring the theory that he'd shot Scott for some reason, although they needed more proof before obtaining an arrest warrant. At least that was the official line. Angus didn't think Tate really believed he was a killer. Well, probably.

Nari sighed. "This just keeps getting worse."

The woman had no idea.

The murder board was illuminated by the morning light trying to filter through the clouds as Nari paced in front of it. She gingerly ate a leftover muffin from the day before, staring at the line of events depicted on it. It was interesting that Lassiter had not given away his identity at first; undoubtedly he'd been messing with Angus's head. The psycho really did think this was a game. A game of chess against Angus Force.

The door opened and Angus brought in Roscoe. "It's cloudy, but it finally stopped raining," he said, hanging his leather jacket near the door.

He looked at the neatly organized file folders on the table and then the perfectly aligned murder board. "Ah. Okay."

She tried not to blush. Organizing materials helped her to relax. "There's coffee in the kitchen."

"Bless you," Angus said, turning immediately toward the stainless-steel coffeepot. He poured a generous mug. "Did Jethro head to work?"

"No." Jethro strode out of his bedroom, dressed in dark slacks and a button-down shirt. "I don't have classes on Tuesday, so I thought I'd take the day to assist you with the Lassiter case. What's on the agenda?"

Nari looked at the murder board. "I'm going to come up with an exact timeline based on all the notes of Lassiter's crimes from the beginning to right now." She still wasn't clear on everything and maybe putting the timeline on paper would show some sort of additional pattern they'd missed. "I assume we're proceeding as if it's Lassiter for sure?" If Angus said it was Lassiter, she believed him.

"Oh, that newest note was definitely from Lassiter," Angus said, looking dangerously sharp in the morning light.

"Okay," she said, checking his stance for stress. Yep. Definitely stressed, but apparently in control. Man, he was tough.

Angus took a deep drink of coffee. The lump on his temple had decreased dramatically, leaving a tough-guy purple bruise. "Also, I talked to Wolfe while walking Roscoe, and they're tied up securing the cul-de-sac with a gate and some other warning systems. So they're out of commission for the day."

Jethro moved to the kitchen and made himself tea. "I can play wingman. What's the plan?"

"Well, if Nari is coming up with the timeline, how about you and I take another run at interviewing the paramedics and the doctor who all pronounced Lassiter dead? There must have been a crack in that system." Angus looked at Nari, his gaze direct. "I'll leave Roscoe with you, and with the security measures in place, you'll be fine. But I need you to stay here. Please."

The "please" sounded like it hurt, but at least he was making an effort. She rolled her eyes. "I'm not going anywhere today." The need to organize the timeline would drive her all day.

He apparently decided to ignore the eye roll because he approached the table and took two of his file folders. Then he moved toward her, an unreadable glint in his eyes.

She froze, not sure why.

"'Bye. I'll check in." Then, right in front of Jethro and Roscoe, he kissed her full on the mouth.

Warmth spread through her, making her whole body tingle. She couldn't think of an appropriate response, so she just enjoyed the feeling and tried not to pay attention to Jethro's reaction. Her brain kicked back in once Angus had opened the door. "Wait a minute. Somebody keeps trying to kill you. Shouldn't you lie low for a while?"

He paused, looking over his shoulder. "I'm armed, and I'm sure Jethro is as well. I'd rather the next attempt happened away from you anyway." He disappeared into the hallway.

Jethro hesitated, his dark-blond hair still wet from his shower. "I'll cover his back." He looked like he wanted to say something else, but then shrugged his shoulders. "Engage the dead bolt as soon as we go. I'll call when we're headed up so you can unlock it for us. Thanks." Then he was gone.

Nari looked at Roscoe, who'd sat on his hindquarters to watch the proceedings. "I guess it's you and me, boy."

He panted and went into the kitchen, where Angus had left a bowl full of dog food and some water. Roscoe sighed and looked over his furry body toward her.

She grinned. "You'd much rather eat that than anything I could cook for you, although I will refill your water." His happily wagging tail spurred her on, and she lifted her burner phone to her ear to call Pippa.

"Hello," Pippa said, the quiet sound of her typing coming over the line.

"Hi. Am I interrupting?" Nari asked, leaning down to grab the water dish.

The typing stopped. "No. I was just finishing up some financial records for a couple of clients. What's going on?" Pippa asked.

Nari took a deep breath. She'd wanted to keep her emotions to herself to figure things out, but her mind wasn't working fast enough. It was time to confide in a friend, and Pippa had great insights. "Angus and I slept together."

"It's about time," Pippa said, laughing. "All right. Tell me everything."

Chapter Thirty

"Thank goodness Brigid is so good at her job," Jethro said mildly, sitting in the driver's seat of his car and staring out the window at a nice single-family home in a large subdivision in Virginia.

That was the truth. Angus looked through the file folder, although he'd already memorized most of the contents. Okay. All of the contents. "I don't have a badge and you're a college professor, so there's a chance this guy won't talk to us. Last time I met with him, I was casual, so maybe he won't mind some more questions." He scouted the peaceful neighborhood with its small, manicured lawns and now empty flower beds, not seeing a threat.

Jethro did the same. "How did the two attackers find you and your lawyer yesterday, do you surmise?"

"Dunno," Angus said, looking again at the white-painted house with dark-blue shutters. "They caught my tail at the police station, that's for sure. How they knew to find me there, I don't know. Could be luck, but something tells me it's more." He hadn't figured it out yet, and frustration tasted like sour candy in his mouth. "Somebody knows too much about us."

"You think somebody in Metro or the HDD is involved?" Jethro asked.

Angus prodded the lump on his head. "I don't know. Lassiter is a serial killer who works alone, but he did have a lot of money, so maybe he bribed somebody for information? But who? If not, how?"

"So long as they're not here looking to shoot me," Jethro muttered, stepping out of his vehicle.

Angus followed suit. "It's not like you'd catch any attention with a Bentley Continental Flying Spur," he returned, carefully shutting the door of the ridiculously expensive black automobile.

Jethro shut his door and peered across the quiet street. "I like fast cars, and this one has a twin-turbocharged, twelve-cylinder engine that produces six hundred sixteen horsepower and will take me to sixty mph in four-point-three seconds."

Someday Angus was going to ask exactly who Jethro was running from, but today wasn't the day. "I thought you British tough guys drove Aston Martins," he said, loping across the street to the sidewalk and toward the cheerful blue door. "Bond would kick your ass."

"Not in an Aston Martin," Jethro returned, striding up the four clay-colored steps to the front door, where he knocked.

The door opened and Angus smiled. "Hi, Jeremy. You probably don't remember, but I'm—"

"Angus Force," the young man said, his sandy blond hair tousled, as if he'd just gotten out of bed. He'd thrown on faded-green sweats and a worn Georgetown sweatshirt. "Dude, I already told you everything I know. Why are you on my front porch? In fact, how did you even find me? I moved three years ago."

"I have good sources," Angus admitted. "This is my colleague, Jethro, and he has a couple of new angles on the case. Do you mind if we just ask you a couple of questions?" He didn't like playing good cop, but this guy didn't have to talk to them at all.

Jeremy sighed and pulled the door open. "Come on inside." He gestured them into a living room covered with fast-food wrappers, red cups, and old newspapers. Definitely a bachelor pad. A beer pong table was set up just beyond the sofa. He looked around. "I had a party Saturday night and am still hung over, so try to keep your voices low, would you?" Shoving papers off his sofa, he dropped onto it, emitting a soft sigh. "Beer is bad. Really bad. Although not as bad as Jäger." He shuddered.

"Amen to that, bloke," Jethro said, lifting a pizza box from a chair and sitting. "Would you please run me through what you remember about the day Henry Wayne Lassiter died in your ambulance?"

Jeremy scrubbed both hands down his whiskered face. "Why do serial killers always have three names?"

"It's one of the great mysteries of life," Angus said, sitting on the other chair and ignoring the laundry littering the floor. "Did he say anything to you before he died?"

"He'd been shot in the face, the chest, and the leg," Jeremy said. "People don't usually talk while bleeding from multiple wounds." He looked around and grabbed an open Pepsi, then peered inside. Shrugging, he took a deep drink. "He died right before we got to the hospital."

Jethro nodded. "I'm aware. Then you transferred to Dr. Shelman and she called time of death?"

"Yep. She's a hot one, isn't she? I saw her last week when we caught a pileup on North Fifth Bridge. All business and bossy, she is." He grinned. "One of these days she's going to say yes when I ask her out."

Not if he didn't learn to clean up his place and stop playing beer pong on Saturday nights. "Good luck with that," Angus said. "Is your partner still living over on Green Street?"

The amusement fled Jeremy's olive-colored eyes. "No. I figured you knew. Janice died almost six months ago. Traffic accident after work." He rubbed his hands down his sweats, his pain nearly palpable as he looked around the room. "The place didn't look like this when she stayed over." He shrugged and rubbed his gut.

Alertness danced down Angus's back. He'd met with Janice about eight months ago. Was her death a coincidence? "What happened in the accident?" he asked.

"She got hit by a truck. Hit-and-run," Jeremy said. "Never found the guy."

"I'm sorry for your loss," Jethro said quietly.

Jeremy shrugged. "What are you gonna do?" He shook himself. "Why is all this being brought up again? And don't you guys all coordinate?"

Angus sat up, his body going on full alert. "What do you mean?"

"I already told all this to the other detective yesterday. He said it was the last time you guys would bug me." Jeremy drank more of the old Pepsi.

Angus shared a look with Jethro. "Tall guy, big shoulders, African American? Works for Metro PD?" Maybe Tate really was on his side here.

"No. White guy, big shoulders, pretty tall," Jeremy said. "Works for the FBI. He had brown hair and a mustache with a beard, and his suit was expensive-looking. Like seriously expensive." He rubbed his chin again. "Even his shoes were something. Italian and shiny."

"How dark was his hair?" Angus asked. The description kind of fit Special Agent Rutherford from the HDD, but he had blond hair.

"Pretty dark," Jeremy said.

"What did you tell him?" Angus leaned forward, adrenaline shooting through his veins. "Start at the beginning and tell us everything."

Angus drummed his fingers on his jeans-clad thigh as Jethro broke numerous speed limits to reach the hospital.

Jethro parked at the end of the parking area, away from other vehicles. "You know, it's entirely possible it was somebody from the FBI who interviewed Jeremy yesterday."

Angus nodded. "I'm aware." He twisted his phone in his other hand, waiting for Brigid to send the accident report concerning the paramedic who'd died months ago. She'd seemed like a nice woman—bubbly and earnest.

Jethro cut the engine. "Take a minute here, mate. Lassiter is a killer and he enjoys getting close and personal, right? So, there can't be any connection between him and the paramedic's death. It doesn't make sense. If he wanted her dead because she knew something that you didn't pull out of her before, he wouldn't cause an accident, would he?"

Angus slipped his phone in his pocket. "He'd much rather kidnap and torture her, I know." Yet it might have been even more important to keep her quiet. Six months ago Lassiter hadn't wanted to make his presence known. "He'd have the patience to just arrange an accident if he had a bigger plan in mind." One that started with the killing of victims who looked like the members of Angus's team. "We need to talk to the doctor."

"The long-legged one." Jethro stepped out of his car and scouted the area. "Don't see any guns pointed at us. It's probably safe for now." Sarcasm uttered in a British accent still sounded classy.

Angus stood and shut his door. "We have to find the person who keeps trying to kill me."

Jethro looked at him over the car. "You make it sound like a nuisance case. Somebody wants you dead, mate."

"It *is* a nuisance," Angus muttered, shoving his hands in his jacket pockets and striding across the long expanse of parking area toward the emergency door entrance. "I can't be chasing Lassiter and have somebody keep trying to shoot me or blow up my homes." They had to figure out who the team had pissed off the most, so he could concentrate on the more important case, damn it. He entered the doorway and walked to the receptionist, a sixtysomething woman with long, gray hair styled in one of those fancy braids. "Hello," he said, wishing for his badge.

"Hi." She looked up behind thick glasses and smiled. "How can I help you?"

He put on his most charming smile. "We're looking

for Dr. Emily Shelman. Do you know how we could find her in this big hospital?"

The woman reached for her telephone. "Can I tell her who's looking for her?"

"Of course." Angus kept his casual smile in place. "Please tell her that Angus Force, from the FBI, and Jethro Hanson, from British Intelligence, just have a couple of quick questions for her about a patient. Nothing scary."

The woman's eyes widened. "Oh, my." She twittered and looked toward the mostly vacant waiting room. "I feel like I'm in a James Bond movie."

"Wouldn't that be fun?" Jethro asked, the accent in full force.

She blushed a beet red. "Oh, that's perfect." She dialed and spoke for several seconds to somebody named Nancy. Then she frowned and hung up the phone. "Well, this is odd."

Oh, shit. Angus took a step toward her. "What's odd?"

"Dr. Shelman has been off work since Friday morning and she didn't show up for her shift this morning. Nancy is quite worried. They've called the doctor's apartment several times but haven't heard anything." Before the woman finished speaking, Angus was already halfway out the door.

He sped into a full-out run for the car with Jethro on his heels. "We have to get to her place. Now." Angus pushed his bulk inside the car and flipped through the file folder for an address. He knew how to get there but couldn't remember the apartment number. Then he barked out the address while Jethro sped out of the lot.

Jethro wove in and out of traffic, pushing the pedal and

breaking the law. Finally they screeched to a stop in front of a modest brick apartment building.

Angus was out of the car before the engine had silenced, running up two flights of stairs to door number six. The memory of the tall blonde with the intelligent eyes flashed across his mind, spurring him on. He knocked on the door while trying to peer through a break in the curtains on the front window. The room beyond was dark.

He tried the knob.

Locked.

"Hold on, Jethro." Angus turned around and back-kicked the door. It flew open with a crash and collided with the wall on the other side. Angus drew his weapon from beneath his jacket and went in low, while Jethro went high.

Silence. The cold and dusty kind.

He flipped on a light with his elbow and motioned Jethro to the left, toward a living room and an open doorway. Jethro nodded, his movements silent and his gun out.

Angus continued along the wall toward the open kitchen, where he turned right down another hallway to search a master bedroom and bathroom. He returned to the living room. "Clear."

Jethro emerged from the other doorway. "Office and guest bathroom are clear."

Angus looked over the kitchen counter to see a clean floor. There were two dishes in the sink: a plate and a coffee mug.

Jethro studied the room. "Nothing is out of place and I don't see any sign of a struggle."

Angus forced his breathing to remain calm so he could think. "The receptionist said that the doctor had taken the weekend off. Maybe she stayed away longer." He wasn't sure if he was trying to convince Jethro or himself. "We need to search the place. Look for any sort of travel plans and a contact list, if she has one." These days, everybody kept lists in their phones. He reached for his and texted Brigid to start a search for the doctor.

"I don't have gloves," Jethro said, looking at him. "Do you?"

"No," Angus said, eyeing the coat closet near the door. "Maybe she has some mittens we can borrow."

Jethro sighed. "Wonderful."

Sirens echoed in the distance.

Somebody had heard them force entry and had called the police. Angus headed toward the door. "New plan. Let's get the hell out of here."

Chapter Thirty-One

Morning brought fresh rain. After organizing the timeline the day before, Nari felt nicely relaxed as she sipped her first cup of coffee of the day. Angus and Jethro had been gone most of the day before, but once Angus had returned to the apartment, he'd spent the night showing her his own attention to detail. She smiled as she sipped, her heart feeling all warm and gushy.

She had to knock that off because this was casual for now. Even so, a night with the hard body of Angus Force should be celebrated at least a little.

Roscoe whined over by Jethro's bedroom door.

Nari glanced at the clock. It was after nine, and Jethro didn't seem to be a guy who slept in. Didn't he have classes today anyway? She wandered over and peeked into the room, drawing back at seeing the neatly made bed. "Angus?"

"What?" He emerged from their bedroom, finger combing his wet hair.

"Jethro didn't come back last night." The professor had said he was meeting friends for a late dinner but would return early to prepare for classes. She frowned and tried not to overreact. "Didn't he say he'd be back?"

Angus reached for his phone on the table. "Yeah." He dialed and waited before he spoke. "Jet? Give me a call." Then he hung up.

Nari bit her lip. "He's an adult, and ordinarily I wouldn't worry, but somebody has been killing people around us lately." She paced over to the murder board and then back, looking at her color-coded files. "Why wouldn't he answer his phone?"

Angus dialed another line. "Brigid? Do a GPS search on Jethro's phone, would you?" He winced. "I know you're at work at HDD. Sorry about this. Please do it, though." He hung up. "I'm probably going to get her fired."

Nari looked at her coffee, which was no longer appetizing. "He has to be okay. Right?"

Angus didn't answer. "He can take care of himself." He looked around, as if trying to solve a mystery. "I didn't realize he hadn't come back."

Heat slipped into Nari's face. They had been rather preoccupied getting naked together.

Angus's burner phone beeped and he pressed the Speaker button. "Hey, Bridge. Where's the Brit?"

"His phone tracks to his apartment building," Brigid said, just as the front door opened and Jethro walked in. "I have to go back to work." She clicked off.

Angus took a menacing step toward Jethro. "Where the fuck have you been?"

Jethro shrugged out of his leather jacket and tossed mail onto the counter, both of his eyebrows rising. "Gee,

Dad. I'm sorry I missed curfew." He looked at Nari, his gaze full of questions.

Oh, she wasn't in the mood. "You said you'd be home after meeting friends for dinner and you didn't come back. At the very least you could've called. People have been shooting at us lately, you know." She tapped her foot on the concrete.

His lip ticked up, but he wisely refrained from calling her his mom. "Dinner went well, I got on with a visiting professor, and we went to her place for a nightcap." He did look relaxed this morning and, with his hair rumpled, more like a James Bond than ever. "I stayed for breakfast." He paused. "Do I need to add any more details?"

"No," Angus bit out. "We get the picture."

"Excellent," Jethro said, patting Roscoe on the head and walking toward his bedroom. "Now, if you'll excuse me, I need to shower and get to class by one this afternoon." He whistled a jaunty tune and disappeared into the bedroom.

"What an ass," Angus muttered, then turned to stare at the murder board.

Nari laughed. "Well, I guess he's all grown up now." Angus's responding smile warmed her heart. Shared moments like that made her like him even more. "I have to go to HDD and do an exit interview as well as fill out some HR forms. Do you need the rental car?"

He studied her. "Yes. I'll drop you off at HDD and then pick you up afterward. You'll be safe at the agency so long as you remain there. Promise me?"

"Sure," she said. "It should only take a few hours,

from what I understand." She needed to keep her COBRA insurance.

Angus dialed a number and left the phone on speaker.

"What?" Brigid's Irish accent emerged with her exasperation.

Angus grimaced. "Sorry to keep bugging you, but do you have any leads on the missing doctor?"

"No," Brigid said. "I have a computer running a search, but I'm up to my Gaelic ears on three other cases, being monitored by the administrator, and I'd prefer Opal Clemonte didn't fire me on my first week in the new computer headquarters. I will call you if I get a hit on your doctor." She clicked off again, and somehow it was louder this time.

Nari sipped her coffee. "We have to stop relying on Brigid so much. Her plate is too full right now."

"Agreed," Angus said, rubbing the back of his corded neck. "I don't have another computer expert, though."

The man didn't have a team at all, but why bring that up? More importantly, she would not ask what his plans were after this case had concluded. Why breach the tenuous peace they'd found between them?

His phone buzzed and he clicked the Speaker button. "Force."

"Hey, Angus, it's Raider," Raider said. "I'm at work right now, at the DHS, and I've gotten called into my boss's office. The Metro PD is trying to find you and you're not answering your cell phone. Thought I'd pass on the message."

Nari chewed on the inside of her lip, a bad habit she'd had in college but had thought she'd conquered. Metro couldn't find Angus because he'd left his phone at her apartment and was using a burner.

Angus sighed. "Thanks, Raid. I'll call Tate." He disengaged the call and then quickly dialed another number.

"Tate Bianchi," Tate answered absently.

"Hi Tate, it's Angus," Angus said calmly. "I heard through the grapevine that you're looking for me."

Silence pounded for the briefest of moments. "Angus? Where are you?" the detective asked, papers shuffling in the background.

Angus paused and then looked at the phone. "I'm at a friend's place, hanging out. What do you need?"

"I need you to come down to the station and talk to me," Tate said evenly. "Like right now. In fact, because your truck was crashed, I'm happy to send a car to pick you up. How does that sound?"

Nari shuffled her feet. Were they going to arrest him? She wasn't sure who to call as a lawyer now.

Angus lifted his gaze to her face, no expression in his eyes. "I don't need a ride. I'll see you in an hour." Then he ended the call. "I might need another lawyer."

Angus sat once again in the interrogation room of Metro PD, facing Tate and Detective Buckle. He wondered what Buckle's first name was. Probably something tough like Margaret or Bernadette. Maybe Hayden. Yeah. She looked like a Hayden Buckle. Tough and savvy.

"Angus?" Tate asked. "Did I lose you?"

Angus sighed. "No. I'm just getting bored. We've gone over all this before and my timeline and alibis haven't changed." The empty seat next to him served as a reminder that he'd gotten Scott shot. The lawyer was still in the Intensive Care Unit and hadn't awakened after his surgery. "Maybe we should wait until my attorney is up to working again."

"We don't have that kind of time," Buckle said, her eyes sparking. "Speaking of lawyers, it turns out the gun that shot Scott has your fingerprints on it."

Angus nodded. "No shit. I mean, no kidding. Pardon my language." He was close to losing it and needed to get a grip. "I grabbed the weapon out of the shooter's hand and then shot him with it, so no doubt my fingerprints are on it."

"Only yours," Tate said helpfully.

Angus lifted a shoulder. "The guy was wearing gloves. I already told you that." He looked back at Buckle. "Did you check the clip and bullets?"

"Yep. No fingerprints on those at all," she said.

Angus leaned forward. "There you have it, then. If I was dumb enough to leave my prints on the gun, do you really think I was smart enough to wipe the clip and bullets? No. Somebody else had that gun and I think you know it."

Buckle leaned forward, mimicking his movement. "I think you're smart enough to mess with us in that kind of way. Wipe some of the gun and not the rest. Right?"

Sure, he was smart enough. "I didn't shoot Scott," he said. Again.

"Is this the guy who did?" Tate flipped over a picture, showing a blond man with green eyes. He wore a blood-stained sweatshirt and was pale in death.

Angus pulled the picture closer. "Yeah. That's him."

His shoulders stiffened. "I shot him a few times with his gun. Where did you find him?"

"Ballistics confirms that the same bullets killed him as the ones that were taken out of your lawyer," Detective Buckle said. "Why did you shoot this guy?"

Angus stilled. "I told you. He shot Scott and tried to shoot me. Who is he?"

"You tell us," Tate said, working well with his partner. "Who is he?"

Angus barely kept from sighing. Was he this much of a pain in the ass when he interrogated a suspect? "I hereby identify this man as the guy who shot Scott and tried to shoot me. I don't know his name. We didn't exactly talk." He angled his head to see the now-closed file folder. "Was the blonde with him? Did you find her?"

"Ah. The blond girl who knocked you out?" Detective Buckle asked, just enough derision in her tone to be annoying.

"Yes. The one with a big-assed shovel," Angus agreed. He studied the two detectives. They were good, and he was running out of time. "How about this: Let's play a game where you tell me something and then I give you information in return? Okay? Either you two start ponying up or I'm leaving. Walking right out of here." Unless they arrested him, which was definitely an option.

"What do you want to know?" Detective Buckle asked, her voice pure reasonableness now.

Angus took a deep breath. "Who's the dead guy?"

"His name is Willie Treeland, and he has a record that spans the gamut from assault to grand theft. How'd you get hooked up with him?" Tate asked.

"Why would he try to kill me?" Angus asked. Or, more

importantly, "Who would hire him to shoot Scott and then me?"

"You tell us," Buckle said. Again.

Angus stared down at the dead young man. "I don't know. My team was trying to run a background search on all our old cases, but we were disbanded, as you know. My guess is that it has something to do with one of them." He looked up. "Where did you find this guy, and where is the blonde?" The woman had looked young—maybe twenty years old.

"No blonde," Dr. Buckle said.

Angus sat back and rolled his aching shoulders. "Well, I gave you her description. She was with this guy and she swung a shovel. My guess is that she was just along for the ride."

"Why?" Tate asked.

"Because she didn't kill me after she knocked me out," Angus said quietly. "I think she tried to save her boyfriend, and wherever you found him, she'll be nearby." It was fairly simple and they knew it. "So. You have me for another hour and then I need to pick up a friend at work."

"Nari Zhang?" Tate asked.

Angus didn't flinch. "My friends are none of your business. Now. Where did you find Willie Treeland?"

Tate studied him, his dark eyes inscrutable. "He was found dead in his truck a block from a hospital parking lot. North Ridge Hospital, which is the closest to where the shooting occurred."

Angus leaned forward. "I assume you pulled the CCTV?"

"Yeah. A block away; there wasn't any sign of the truck," Detective Buckle said, her unpainted nails tapping on the table. "So, once again, no video of what happened that day. I find that to be an interesting coincidence, don't you, Tate?"

"I surely do," Tate said. "It's almost as if a trained agent made certain this happened. A frightened young blonde wouldn't have thought of it, agreed?"

Buckle nodded. "Totally agree."

The two were good—really good. They worked well together. "You know, if I ever get a team back together, I'd be interested in the two of you," Angus said slowly. Wait a minute. A team back together? Where the hell had that thought come from?

Buckle's laugh wasn't filled with mirth. "Darlin'? The only team you're going to put together is one in prison. But thanks for the offer."

Chapter Thirty-Two

Nari signed yet another piece of paper guaranteeing her silence on anything and anybody having to do with the HDD. All she wanted was insurance coverage, darn it. The HR office was surprisingly cheerful, with several bright posters framed on each wall. She sighed and read over another document.

"Nari?" Opal Clemonte said, poking her head in the door.

Nari stood. "Administrator. Hello."

"Hi." Opal smiled. "How about I conduct your exit interview over brunch? I'm starving."

Nari faltered. No doubt the woman wanted to talk about Quan, but she couldn't exactly refuse the head of the HDD. "I'd enjoy that."

Opal nodded at the HR assistant sitting across the table from Nari. "I assume she's finished?"

"Yes, ma'am," the young woman said instantly, gathering the papers together.

Well, Nari was finished now, apparently. She leaned toward the nice brunette. "Do you need me to come back later to sign anything?"

"No." The woman shook her head. "We're fine. Honest."

Nari smiled and walked toward the doorway. Was everyone afraid of the administrator? Sure, she had an imposing job, but she seemed nice enough. "Are we eating in your office?"

"No. Let's get away from the office and go to the club. I'll bring a detail because there's a question regarding your safety right now." Opal led the way, dressed today in cream-colored, linen pants and a matching jacket with a silky, lavender-colored shirt. Her boots were a cream leather with two-inch heels.

Nari stared at the boots. They were spectacular. Was there a polite way to ask where she'd bought them? She hustled to keep up and took her phone out of her purse to text Angus about her brunch plans. Though she'd promised not to leave the office, being with the HDD administrator and a protection detail should be enough to keep her safe. They exited the building, where a car was already by the curb with one of the security agents waiting to open the door.

"Thank you, George," Opal said, settling into the back seat next to Nari. Once the door had closed, she turned to face her. "You could have my job someday, you know. You have the background and the strength for it."

The woman was still trying to mentor her? Nari grew warm. "I quit yesterday, remember?"

Opal sighed. "You quit because your father put you in an untenable position, and that hurt your feelings." She patted Nari's hand, a diamond-and-sapphire ring shining brightly on her finger. "I don't blame you, but you shouldn't destroy your entire career because of hurt feelings." She clasped her hands in her lap.

Nari swallowed. The woman definitely had a point. "I appreciate your taking an interest."

Opal chuckled. "I like you. I also like your father, although he acted like a moron in this case. I don't think he wanted to hurt you, but he's been confused why you chose the HDD. The guilt he feels about your childhood has blinded him." She shook her head. "Men, even the smart ones, can be such dumbasses sometimes."

Hearing the elegant woman use the word "dumbass" made Nari laugh out loud. Wasn't that almost the same thing her mother had said the other day? She covered her mouth and calmed herself. "I totally agree."

"I know." Opal peered out the window at the traffic. "But we need to set the boundaries of how much harm they can do. I don't want to overstep, but are you still seeing Angus Force?"

Nari paused. Was HDD trying to get to her through Opal? Wait a minute. Opal *was* HDD. "I believe he's innocent."

"That's irrelevant," Opal said quietly. "That doesn't mean he won't demolish both your career and your heart." The car rolled to a stop in front of a building composed of white brick and long columns. She waited until the door opened before stepping out.

Nari followed. Her career and her heart? Yeah. Angus could probably affect both, but she trusted him. Didn't she? Frowning, she walked up the stairs and into a restaurant with old-world charm. Dark wood, fine bottles of wine in a cabinet, and burgundy-colored carpets.

Opal smiled at the host. "I have a reservation for Clemonte."

"Of course." The young man lifted two thick menus. "Follow me, please."

The conversations in the room were muted. Nari recognized three US senators, several lobbyists, and the White House chief of staff. The maître d' passed them all for a spacious table in a private room toward the back.

"This is lovely," Opal said, sliding along the plush bench.

Nari sat across from her and accepted a menu, waiting until the host had left before speaking. The woman had clout to score a private dining room for two people. "Are you questioning me about Angus for the HDD?"

Opal's laugh was contagious. "No. If I wanted you questioned, I'd haul you into an interrogation room, not take you to a delicious brunch."

Well, that was fair. Nari read the menu. The second Opal put down her menu, a waitress appeared. They both ordered and then waited for mimosas to be delivered.

"Cheers," Opal said, holding up her glass.

Nari clinked and then took a sip. Excellent. "I doubt you usually conduct exit interviews."

"No," Opal agreed, her beautiful eyes shining. "Only when somebody's father goofs up their team placement out of confusion because men are dumb sometimes. You know, I do try to be involved during those situations."

Nari laughed. The woman did have a good sense of humor. "So what's happened?"

"Well, you quit. I yelled at your father for a good amount of time and then we made up."

"I've never seen anybody yell at my father. How did that go?" Nari asked, taking another sip.

"It was probably easier to take since we're dating each other," Opal said.

Nari set down her glass. "I wondered if we were going to discuss that matter."

"There's nothing for us to discuss." Opal partially turned to look beyond Nari. She frowned. "What in the world?"

The door opened and a man moved inside, even his face covered in a black mask. He moved gracefully and held a weapon.

Nari reacted instantly. She charged.

Angus shifted on the seat. Nari should be about finished with brunch and he was done with this interview. "Either arrest me or I'm out of here." Hopefully they wouldn't call his bluff.

A knock sounded on the door, and Tate stood to open it, leaning down so a uniformed cop could say something in his ear. His broad back visibly tightened and he turned, his eyes burning. "We apparently have another victim. She's already been identified as Dr. Emily Shelman. Does that name ring a bell?"

Angus straightened. "Yes, but I think you already know that. She's the doctor who called time of death on Henry Wayne Lassiter six years ago. Where did you find her?"

A muscle ticked down the long cord of Tate's neck. "She was found in your HDD office by a janitor sent in to clean."

The news was like a punch to the gut. Angus swallowed. "Was there a note?"

Tate looked at Buckle. "I want to view the scene."

Buckle nodded toward Angus. "What do you want to do with him?"

Angus stood. "Either take me to the scene or I'm going there on my own. Come on, Tate. You know I didn't do this, and I can help analyze the scene and the note. I can compare it to all the others for you."

Tate's expression didn't so much as flicker. "All right."

Buckle straightened. "Hey. We don't want him with us."

Tate shrugged. "He's going either way, and I'd rather keep an eye on him. We could place him under arrest, but he'd be out in hours, and then we'd have to hand the case over to the prosecuting attorney's office—if the HDD didn't try to steal the entire case before we could. I'm not done yet."

Angus walked toward the door. "Stop talking about me like I'm not here." How annoying. He sent a quick text to Nari, letting her know he might be late and to please hang out at HDD headquarters after brunch with the administrator. Maybe she could spend some time with Brigid. He sent a second text making the suggestion while following Tate out to his unmarked car. It certainly wasn't the Bentley Angus had spent time in the day before.

The drive was made in silence and Angus studied the two detectives in the front seat. They worked well together, but there were no signs of affection or even friendship. It was a new partnership. "How long have you two worked together?" he asked, testing his theory.

"Three weeks," Buckle said, peering out the passenger side window. "Why?"

"Just curious." She'd answered one question, so he went for broke. "What's your first name, anyway?"

Tate cut him a look in the rearview mirror.

Angus shrugged and grinned. "We've spent a lot of time together and I've been wondering."

Buckle partially turned around to look at him. "What did you guess?"

"Something strong and old-fashioned. Margaret or maybe Hayden." He tilted his head. "Or Joan. Yeah. Joan would be a good name for you." His guessing game was pissing Tate off. Interesting.

"Hmmm," Buckle said, turning back around.

Of course, Buckle was a good name, too. Angus looked out the window as they drove toward the mainly deserted parking area of his former office building. "Did the janitor say how the killer got inside?"

"No," Buckle said. "However, the uniform who called it in didn't see any sign of forced entry."

That didn't mean anything. That crappy old office would be easy to breach; it wasn't as if HDD had sprung for security cameras. Not even in the elevator. Angus tried to settle his bulk in the back seat, but his knees were still shoved up. Not that he complained. Buckle would probably push her seat back even farther.

They drove across the parking lot, and he surveyed the dismal park to the left of the seventies-style building. For a short time the place had meant something to him. They'd put away some dangerous criminals from this building, and it was a slap in the balls for Lassiter to drop a body there.

Crime scene tape cordoned off the building and several patrol cars were parked with their lights swirling. Techs searched the parking lot on the other side, and one guy was visible in the park.

"You stay with us," Tate said.

"Right." Angus exited the vehicle and looked around. The entire area felt deserted. He turned and ducked under the crime scene tape before walking into the building he'd entered thousands of times. "The elevator is a little sketchy," he warned them.

Buckle rolled her eyes, but when the cab jerked and hitched on descent, she planted a hand against the wall. Once they finally hit the bottom and bounced, she was the first out of the elevator. Her sigh of relief was palpable.

Angus looked at the techs fingerprinting the entire room. "He wouldn't have left any evidence. You know that, Tate." Angus partially turned to face somebody he'd thought was a friend. "You also know that the feds are going to take this case if you don't solve it, and quick. I can help you."

Buckle brushed by him, careful where she stepped. "Don't a lot of killers try to insert themselves into investigations of their crimes?"

"Yes," Angus answered before Tate could.

"This way," a uniformed officer said, gesturing them toward what used to be the computer room.

Angus hid his relief that the victim hadn't been left in his office, where he'd spent many a night. He strode across the bullpen and looked into the computer room, where the doctor had been dumped on the eastern counter, her feet bound and her heart missing. Her eyes were closed and her blond hair hung off the side of the counter, almost to the floor.

"Jesus," Tate said, taking in the scene.

A tech handed over a note already secured in a plastic bag.

Tate turned and held it up so they both could read it.

Dearest Angus,

This one was so much more satisfying, and I can only surmise it's because we're both engaged again. How I have missed you. From what I've been able to glean, you've missed me as well. To think that you were wallowing away with alcohol in the middle of Kentucky without me. I can't tell you what that means to me. Who would've thought that we'd both survive the night we shot to kill? It's kismet, my very good friend. Until next time.

> *Yours,*
> *Henry*

PS The night grows tired, the energy unleashed upon this moment in time that cannot last. A vision of the abyss, drawing me in, only her face halting the time that must occur in the game of the gods.

Tate crossed his arms. "How does this killer know you were drinking yourself to death in Kentucky?"

"That's a damn good question," Angus said. He had to go with trust here. "I think somebody in either the FBI or the HDD has helped Lassiter somehow."

Tate rolled his eyes. "Sorry, buddy. I don't see that."

Buckle excused herself to take a phone call and immediately returned. "Angus Force? You're under arrest for the murder of Dr. Emily Shelman. Turn around and place your hands at your back."

Tate frowned. "What are you doing?"

"We have the results from the security tapes that were taken from the doctor's apartment building." Buckle smiled. "Guess who broke down her door yesterday?"

Angus sighed. Well, shit.

Chapter Thirty-Three

A bullet winged by Nari's head and she ducked, plowing into the man dressed all in black. "Run, Opal!" She knocked the man into the door, and he aimed an elbow down on her shoulder, grabbing on and dragging her toward the door.

Pain ripped down to her ribs and she shot up, hitting his chin with the top of her head. Then she grabbed for the gun. He fired several times, and crystal shattered. He fired again, and Opal screamed before the window was blown out. Nari swung wildly, hitting him in the wrist.

The gun flew across the room and smashed into the wall. He tried to snag her again, lifting her off the ground.

"Get out of here," Nari ordered Opal, kicking him in the knee so he'd drop her. She landed hard and kept her body between the attacker and the administrator. "You have to go. Now."

The man grabbed Nari's neck and lifted her, throwing her hard to the floor. Pain burst through her shoulder. Then he reached for her. "You're coming with me," he rasped, his voice hoarse. It was the same man who'd tried to take her before—she could tell by his size and the way he moved.

Opal rushed by her, swinging the crystal vase from the table. Blood poured from her arm, soaking her cream jacket. "You shot me, you asshole," she hissed, hitting him in the side.

The man swiped the vase out of her hand and swung for her head.

Opal ducked and punched him in the groin. At the same moment Nari kicked his knee from flat on her back, turning him toward the wall. Then she jumped up and kicked him beneath the chin. His head flew back and he fell against the wall.

"Help!" Nari screamed as loudly as she could. Where was the security detail?

The man turned toward the window and Nari rushed in front of him to stop him.

Opal clutched her arm and dropped to her knees. "Nari?" Her voice sounded faint and her eyes widened in alarm. Then she pitched sideways.

Nari hesitated.

The man grabbed her again and pulled her toward the window. Nari executed a side kick and then broke his hold by twisting and letting gravity pull her down.

"We're not done," he rasped.

Running footsteps sounded along the hallway. The attacker swore and ran past her, diving through the broken window.

Nari rushed toward Opal and dropped to her knees, yanking off her jacket. "Hold on." She pressed her jacket to the wound and the fabric was instantly soaked. "You're losing too much blood."

The door burst open and two men she didn't recognize stood there. "Get an ambulance. Immediately," she ordered, reaching under her shirt and ripping off her bra. She took the material and wound it around the top of Opal's arm, trying to stem the blood.

Opal was deathly pale but held perfectly still. "Call DHS," she whispered. "My phone is in my purse—speed dial number nine. Code word Rough Rock."

Oh, yeah. Nari leapt for Opal's purse and pulled out the phone, her hands slippery with blood. She speed-dialed nine, and somebody picked up without saying anything. "Rough Rock," she said, urgently.

"Received," a male voice responded, clicking off.

"You'll be okay," Nari said, panic sweeping her at the amount of blood coating the floor. Had the shooter hit an artery? No. The woman wouldn't still be conscious in that case. "Just hold on."

Sirens sounded, and suddenly the entire building was overrun with armed agents in suits. Opal faded in and out, coming to with her lips turning an alarming blue. "Status?" she asked one of the three agents flanking them as the paramedics arrived.

One man, bigger than the other two, stepped forward. His voice was low and his eyes alert. "The security detail is down, ma'am. They're out but not dead, and we'll transport them to the hospital right after you. We're quietly shutting down the area to find the shooter and confiscating all CCTV in the area. We will find this man, ma'am. You have my word."

Nari felt sick. She gulped down bile as her adrenaline ebbed.

Opal nodded. "We have to put a lid on this."

"Yes, ma'am. No worries there." The agent motioned behind Nari, and the paramedics rolled in the stretcher.

"Can I go with her?" Nari asked, removing her hands from the bloody bra to let the paramedics take over.

Opal groaned when they lifted her onto the gurney. "Yes. Please accompany me," she gasped, blood dotting her lip, her smile wan. "This was a heck of an exit interview."

"I know." Nari scooted out of the way and allowed the head agent to help her up.

"Are you all right?" he asked, releasing her arm.

She nodded. "I'm fine." Then she gave a quick description of the shooter, although he'd worn a mask. "I think it was the same guy who attacked me at my home, but I can't guarantee it. He was the same size and moved similarly." When Opal held out a hand Nari took it and ran along the hallway to the back of the ambulance beside the stretcher.

"Nari?" Opal whispered once the doors had been shut.

Nari leaned down, putting her ear to Opal's mouth. "Yes?"

"When you can do so discreetly please call your father and let him know what has happened," Opal whispered.

Nari nodded, tears pricking the backs of her eyes. "I'm so sorry about this." She leaned back and held Opal's hand while the EMT went to work on the wound. "It's my fault." Who would've thought the guy who'd attacked her would be so brazen as to try to take her while she was with the HDD administrator? Maybe he didn't even know who Opal was. But Lassiter would know. Had it been he?

Opal faded, her eyelids closing.

Nari tightened her grip. "Opal? Hold on. Please."

Angus stormed out of the police headquarters, more pissed off than he'd ever been before. Night had started to fall, and with the darkness came the rain. Hard, cold, biting rain. "Why couldn't I get hold of Nari?" He'd been lucky Tate had allowed him a second call, and that Raider had picked up.

"Get in the vehicle." Raider Tanaka waited by his Jeep at the curb, arms crossed and black eyes searching. Apparently he didn't mind getting wet; his thick, black hair looked drenched. "I've scouted the area and haven't detected any threats to you." He motioned Angus into the vehicle. "Let's move, though."

Angus opened the passenger side door and jumped inside, dropping the bag holding his belongings. His temper wanted to be let loose, but he held back. Not only was there another dead woman, but now he'd wasted almost an entire day being charged, arrested, and then bailed out.

Raider slid behind the wheel.

"Thank you," Angus said. "I can't imagine what kind of favors you had to call in to get me out today."

Raider drove away from the curb. "The entire team called in favors. We even contacted Millie at some spa to have her contact a couple of her friends for help. The end result is the same—you're out for now. Any word on your lawyer?"

"No," Angus said. "And I haven't been able to call anybody else. Who picked up Nari?" He wanted her safe and locked down until he got out of this mess.

Raider drove through traffic, his hands capable on the wheel. "I need you to take a couple of deep breaths. Nari is fine. Now breathe."

Angus stilled. All the thoughts rioting through his brain stopped cold. "Where is Nari?"

Raider took a sharp left, keeping an eye on the rearview mirror. "She's visiting Opal Clemonte in the hospital."

"What happened to the administrator?" Angus asked, watching the traffic stream by outside and looking for any threats.

"She was shot by a man who was trying to kidnap Nari. This happened in a public place—well, in a private club, actually." Raider switched lanes, glancing at his side mirror.

Angus grabbed his arm, fire lancing through him. "The same guy who tried to take her before? Was it Lassiter?"

"She fought back and the administrator was shot," Raider said evenly. "Nari is fine right now. She's at the hospital, surrounded by a multitude of armed HDD agents."

"Take me to the hospital," Angus said, his heart speeding up as adrenaline flooded his system.

Raider nodded. "That's where I'm driving." He switched lanes again. "She's at the one on the east side, not the one where your lawyer is."

Angus ran his hand down his worn jeans. Even people

on his periphery were getting hurt now. "I don't think Lassiter has ever shot anybody before."

Raider glanced at him before retuning his focus to the road. "No, but most people don't fight as well as Nari. He might've used a gun with his hostages before; it would make sense, he managed to take so many. But this would be a first, right? Going into a place with so many other people was an incredible risk."

Angus tried to work with the profile in his head and not freak out that Lassiter had been so close to Nari. Again. "Yeah. For him to take a risk like that, he's upping the stakes." Even so, it was out of character for the pro-lific serial killer. "We have the team pretty much locked down—perhaps that was his only option?"

Raider took another left to the small hospital on the other side of the city. "We're not going to get in to see her, you know."

Angus paused. "You can't be here with me."

Raider snorted. "I bailed you out, Force. That's on record, and if DHS wants to fire me because of our asso-ciation, it's going to happen whether or not I walk into the hospital with you." He jumped out of his Jeep.

Angus stepped into the rain, hit again by the loyalty of his team. What would his life be like if he left town and never worked with any of them again? He owed them all, and not only for recent events. Knowing them and leading them had probably saved his sanity as well as his life. "Are you happy with DHS?"

"It's only been a few days." Raider ducked his head against the rain and hurried toward the entrance. "But I miss the team already, if that's what you mean. We were odd, but we got things done." He reached an overhang and paused, shaking out his hair. "Brigid really misses everyone. She doesn't like the new computer room or the other techs, and they don't allow dogs or kittens in the offices."

Brigid had enjoyed working with Roscoe snoozing on her feet and Kat curled up on her keyboard. "I wish I could think of something," Angus said, eyeing the several agents milling around the waiting room.

Raider opened the door. "Well, if these agents beat the shit out of us, we can sue and maybe retire on a beach somewhere."

Angus walked inside as if he owned the place. All heads turned to him, and he ignored the stares, striding toward the receptionist, who was watching them all with wide blue eyes. She had to be around twenty years old and she kept fiddling with her pen. "Can I help you?" she whispered.

"Yes. I'd like to see Nari Zhang and Opal Clemonte," he said, smiling at her.

Her gaze lifted to his left. "Um, I—"

"No way are you getting past me, Force," Vaughn Ealy said, extricating himself from the pack of agents and leading with his chest. "This is your fault and we all know it. I suggest, strongly, that you get the hell out of here while you can still walk."

Angus turned. "Listen, you piece of shit. You've caused more problems for Nari and the administrator than any shooter ever could. Tell me, do any of your buddies here know about your plan to get your ex on your team just to mess with her head?"

Vaughn barreled toward him.

Angus braced himself, more than ready for a fight. Itching for one, actually. Vaughn hit him first, and Angus turned, throwing him into a wall. Then Vaughn turned and charged again.

Chapter Thirty-Four

Nari sat on the hard orange chair next to the hospital bed while Opal slept quietly after surgery, the beeps of the machines oddly comforting. The administrator lay in the bed, one arm out and connected to a saline solution. Bandages covered the upper part of her other arm. Even in a hospital bed, she had presence.

"Hello? Opal?" Nari's father hurried into the room, his suit jacket over one arm. Panic sizzled in his dark eyes. "Opal?"

Nari relaxed back into the chair. She'd called Quan; he'd been on assignment in Texas. He'd asked her to stay with Opal until he could arrive from the airport. "She came through surgery fine, and they gave her a healthy dose of painkillers. She was shot in the arm and the surgeons had to extract the bullet."

Quan moved closer to the bed, looking down. He reached out and patted Opal's hand. "She's going to be all right?"

"Yes," Nari said. "The bullet nicked an artery, but we got the bleeding under control and the surgery was smooth." She was so tired it was difficult to keep her eyes open, but she tried, so she could give Quan all the details. "Opal should be released tomorrow, and if she's feeling all right, she can return to work whenever she wants. The bullet didn't do much damage."

Quan whirled on her, his black eyes sparking. "Didn't do much damage? Are you kidding? The administrator of a secretive governmental branch was shot in a private club. The damage might be irreparable."

Nari stiffened, waking right up. "We called it in, and the HDD descended. The word is out that a public official, one who works in Homeland Security in computer research, was shot by an angry ex-lover. The cover story is good, and all the local news outlets have already run with it." It was both impressive and frightening how quickly HDD had put out the false story.

"You had better hope so," Quan snapped. "I haven't worked my entire life to build this career only to have you ruin it by sleeping around with the wrong men."

Oh, he did not. Nari rose, standing nearly eye to eye with him. "Wait a minute, Father. You're the one who doesn't seem to be able to keep it in his pants."

Quan's nostrils flared. "My choices don't adversely impact other people."

The hurt, after all this time, was surprising. She took the emotional blow and settled herself. "Really? What about forcing me to work with a jerk who just wanted to get me out of the HDD? Or is that what you want, too? I'd say that was an adverse result." Didn't she mean anything to him? "By the way, the shooter was after me when Opal got injured. Any concern, father of the year?"

He inhaled sharply, faltering for the first time ever. "I'm glad you are unharmed."

"Do you even care about her?" Nari gestured to the woman on the bed. "Or is she all about your career, too?"

"I'd like to know the answer to that question as well," Opal said sleepily.

"Opal." Nari's father moved to her and took her hand, concern darkening his features. "I'm so sorry you were harmed. How are you feeling?"

Nari focused on the woman in the bed. "Hi, Opal. The doctor said you did great in surgery and that they took out the bullet. Your arm will be fine, even though you have some stitches and might need to take it easy for a little while."

"I don't take it easy." Opal smiled, looking from Nari to Quan and back. "It seems I missed something here. Quan? Are you being a dick to your daughter?"

Nari coughed out a laugh. "Yes."

Quan shook his head. "It's Angus Force's fault you're in this bed, Opal."

Opal rolled her eyes. "It's the fault of the crazy bastard who charged into our nice lunch and shot me. Did you even ask how she's doing?"

Quan looked at Nari, thoughts scattering across his face. "No. I'm sorry. How are you?"

Nari's mouth nearly dropped open. Maybe Opal was a good influence on her emotionally distant father. Did she care any longer? She wasn't sure. "I'm fine. Opal was pretty tough, hitting the guy with a vase." Even though Nari had told the administrator to run, she'd stayed and fought after being shot.

Opal cleared her throat. "I'm getting drowsy again. Before I fall asleep, I want to make you the offer I'd planned to at lunch, Nari."

Nari paused. "What offer?"

Opal coughed. "You quit because your feelings were hurt, but you're good at your job. I'm creating a position for a psychologist who will answer to the chief of staff regarding the mental health of the agents under me. All of them. I want to concentrate on their overall well-being. In addition, this person will be consulted on a myriad of cases. You have all the attributes I want in the ideal candidate." She trailed off toward the end. "Think about it, and we'll talk when I can keep my eyes open." She fell asleep.

Nari gaped. That sounded like a dream job. Her dream job. Well, she'd still be with the HDD and under Quan on the organizational chart, and she wouldn't get to work with Angus or Roscoe. But those days were gone.

Quan released Opal's hand. "You're my daughter and I do care about you, but you're a liability. Do not take this job."

A shadow crossed the doorway. "You are such a dick," Angus Force said, storming inside. His shirt and several of his belt loops were torn, and blood dripped from a cut on his bottom lip. His knuckles also looked swollen. He took one look at Nari. "You okay?"

She settled. For the first time that day the world centered itself. Tears pricked the backs of her eyes. "Yes." Then she barreled into his warm body, burying her face in his hard chest.

Angus took the impact of her small body, tucking an arm around her. He glared at Quan. "Could you be any more of an asshole?"

Quan glared right back. "My daughter wouldn't be in this situation if it weren't for you."

Yeah, that was probably true. It didn't give the jackass the right to hurt her feelings like this. Angus held her more tightly and smoothed her hair away from her face. "Is the administrator all right?" he whispered, running his gaze over Nari's face to make sure she was healthy and in one piece.

Nari nodded. "Bullet to the upper arm, easily extracted, should go home tomorrow." Her voice was thick with emotion and her dark eyes looked tired. "Why are you all bloody?"

He smiled and held back a wince as his lip protested. "Vaughn and a couple of his buddies tried to stop me from getting to you."

Her face turned pink. "You went through a bunch of HDD agents to get to me?" Her voice hushed, and she looked at him the way nobody in his entire life had looked at him. As if he could do anything. As if he was her hero. His body heated, and he wanted more than anything to hold that look forever. To actually be a hero, which he'd never come close to.

"Yeah," he whispered, cupping her still-bruised jaw. "Vaughn is getting stitches right now. I could go hit him again if you want."

Her smile was like the sunset between darkened rain clouds. Bright and real. True. "That's okay. I trust that you did a good job the first time."

"I helped," Raider groused from the doorway, wiping blood from his cheekbone.

"Raider!" Nari cried, turning and giving the big agent a hug. "I've missed you."

Raider hugged her back, his angled face softening. "I've missed you, too. It's only been a week and it's not the same."

Angus tugged her back to him and put an arm over her shoulder. "We'll figure something out."

Nari faltered. "I'm sorry I wasn't there when Raider had you bailed out. I helped from here on my phone, but I couldn't leave Opal until she was out of surgery." She turned pale and bit her lip.

Angus slid his finger along her lip, getting her attention. "I know. You did everything I needed you to do." How much pressure had Quan put on her to be the perfect HDD employee? She was apologizing for something that didn't require an apology. He leaned down and kissed her nose. "Thank you for your help."

She blinked, her pupils dilating.

Jesus. Didn't anybody ever thank her? She was so damn good at everything that she made her job seem effortless and even fun. Probably because she did have fun. But that didn't mean she should be taken for granted, and Angus had done that very thing for a year. He sighed. "How about I take you somewhere safe and make a bubble bath for you?"

"Now wait a minute here," Quan said, stepping closer. "Your dalliance with my daughter almost got her and the leader of the HDD killed. It's over. It's time for you to leave."

Nari looked up at Angus. "Did he actually just say dalliance?"

Angus tried not to laugh. "Yeah."

Raider looked down the hallway. "Um, gang? I have a cadre of HDD agents headed this way, and while a couple of them didn't seem to mind your beating up Vaughn, they're not going to like your being in the administrator's room."

Angus caressed Nari's arm, then took her hand. "Let's get out of here." He started walking toward Raider, who'd already edged into the hallway.

"Nari? I'm telling you not to leave here. Listen to me," Quan said, a bark of command in his voice.

Nari looked over her shoulder, holding tight to Angus's hand. "I'm glad she's going to be okay, Quan. Have a nice night." Then she walked out into the hallway. "I'm starving. Have you eaten?"

"No." Angus nodded at the agents watching them leave, and a couple nodded back. "We can grab something on the way home. I've had a rough enough day without you trying to cook something." Her answering laugh was a balm to something inside him that he hadn't realized needed soothing.

He opened the outside door. The rain slashed at them, and he took off his jacket and set it over her shoulders.

She sighed and leaned into him, tripping over her feet. Just how exhausted was she? "Before I forget, the guy spoke to me, and his voice was all raspy. I don't know if he was faking it or if it was real. Did Lassiter have a raspy voice?"

"Yes. Very," Angus said, fury rising in him faster than a tornado. For a second he'd forgotten that Lassiter had had his hands on Nari. Not once, but twice. The bastard really wanted her, but it wasn't going to happen. Angus didn't care what he had to do or who he had to go through, but Nari would be safe.

No matter what.

They reached the Jeep and Angus sat in the back with Nari, holding her close. She didn't even pretend not to want to snuggle into him, and it felt good. Right.

As Raider started the car, his phone buzzed. He pushed a button. "Brigid? You're on speakerphone."

"Hi. I just wanted to let you guys know that Angus's arrest has hit the news. Pictures, profiles, and everything else. The anchors are making a big deal about the hero FBI agent going bad." She sighed. "I'm sorry, but I figured you should know."

Nari sat up, her body stiffening.

"No," Angus said, drawing her near again. "Tomorrow. We'll deal with the shitstorm tomorrow. For tonight we're going to be grateful we're alive and free."

For now. It was all he had, and he was going to hold on with both hands.

Chapter Thirty-Five

Nari would never forget the look in Angus's eyes when he'd barged into the hospital room looking for her. Only her. He'd fought an entire squad of HDD agents to get to her, as if she mattered more than anybody else. Her heart warmed as much as her body as she let the hot, bubbly water cocoon her. Apparently when Angus Force promised a bubble bath, he delivered.

He walked back into the bathroom and topped off the wineglass sitting on the edge of the tub. "I saw the new bruises when I undressed you."

She had almost attacked him at the time, but the bubble bath had been drawn, and he'd been insistent. "Yeah. I fight better than this guy, but he's no slouch. He brought a gun this time." She was pretty sure it had been Lassiter, but she didn't want to ruin the peaceful moment by saying his name again. Not here and not now.

Angus sat with his own glass of wine, right outside the tub. "I don't know where Jethro gets this stuff, but it's pretty good."

Amusement tickled through her. "That's a Sine Qua

Non 'Pearl Clutcher' Chardonnay from 2012. I'm surprised Jethro let us have it."

Angus winced, looking at his glass. "I found it in the wine cellar. Figured he wouldn't mind."

She laughed out loud, stirring the bubbles. Then she sobered, sighing as her muscles soaked in the heat. "I don't want to spoil the mood, but my brain is going nuts."

He looked down at his ripped shirt and pulled it over his head, showcasing that broad, strong chest. "Okay."

Now her body went nuts. She shook her head to clear her mind. "I'm not a profiler and don't know Lassiter like you do, but it's odd he's coming after me first, considering I'm the closest one to you."

Angus nodded, his torso still looking relaxed—and sexy. "I agree. He likes to draw out the suspense and would want to save you for last. Plus, the risks he has taken in getting to you are extreme. Before, he liked to work under cover of darkness."

"What does that mean?" she asked, spreading her fingers through the warm water.

Angus took another drink of the expensive wine. "All I can figure is that he's working under some sort of time constraint that we don't know about. I've run it through my mind and just don't see what it is." He was quiet for a moment. "Or he may be misdirecting us."

Nari blew a bubble away from her mouth and sank deeper into the tub. "Misdirecting us?"

"Yeah. We're concentrating on you, while he's stalking another target. Oh, he would've taken you earlier if he could have, but now we're convinced he's after you. He might be preparing to take Pippa. Or Brigid, who's working out of the house and still living in Raider's apartment until their house is built."

"You think Brigid is the most vulnerable?" Nari asked, making a mental note to call her friend. She might need to talk.

"Now that you quit your outside job, Brigid is the most accessible, although she's at HDD all day," Angus said. "But Raider is with her to and from work, as well as at home, and he can fight. Plus, she has been training and is a good shot."

Nari took a big sip of her wine before broaching the next subject. "I'm tired of waiting for him to make a move."

"Ditto," Angus said absently.

"I think we should break up." She looked at a bruise on his jaw.

His chuckle wasn't what she expected. "No."

Her gaze flew up to his face. "No? You can't say no. It's not up to you."

"We just decided to actually date, even though we didn't exactly say the words, and you want to break up? Of course I can say no. Especially when the reason you want to break up is asinine." His tone remained slightly amused, but with a thread of steel beneath it.

Sometimes the guy was a freaking mind reader. "Just hear me out."

"Sure." He took another drink, and his muscled throat was too sexy as he swallowed. "Go for it."

She took a deep breath. "Obviously, Lassiter will try for me if he gets the chance."

"Yep," Angus said congenially.

"So, let's break up, I go back to work at the HDD and

we create a trap." Her stomach ached at the thought, but at least they'd control the situation, which would be something new.

Angus finished his glass of wine. "A trap with you as bait."

She swallowed. "Yes. It's not ideal, and it's terrifying, but if we set the trap right, we'd finally have him."

"He's a genius. You don't think he'd see a trap a mile away?" Angus asked, sounding merely curious.

"No. Well, maybe. But if he's investigated me at all and found out about my problems with Vaughn and the HDD, he'd think I was a hothead." She partially sat up, warming to the subject. "So my dumping you and returning to work with the new job Opal offered me, maybe even taking a couple of risks, wouldn't be out of character. I could look like I was being very careful, but still give him some type of opening. Especially if I moved back to my apartment, which would be a great place to lay a trap."

Angus thought about it, looking at his empty glass. "Well, it's a good plan. Sure. Let's do it."

She sat farther up, surprise and anticipation lighting her. "Really?"

He turned his gaze to her, the green of his eyes the hard edge of a mysterious forest. "No, not really." He swept out his hand. "Have you lost your fucking mind?"

She sank back down into the bubbles. "For a second there I thought you were going to be reasonable."

"Jesus Christ, Nari. Don't you know me at all?" He set the glass down as if afraid he might snap it in two. "Even if you dumped me, even if you returned to work at HDD, even if you went back and decided to date that moronic and now bruised Vaughn Ealy, I wouldn't leave you alone for a second until we caught Lassiter. Use you for bait?" He stood, looking broad and dangerous in the soft bathroom light. "Not in a million years." He leaned down and plucked her right out of the tub.

She yelped, plastering bubbles all over his bare chest. "What are you doing?"

"Taking you to bed." Then he kissed her.

Hard.

Urgency drove Angus as he tossed her nude and soapy butt on the bed, following her down. The idea that she wanted to use herself as bait with the most dangerous serial killer in the world right now had Angus almost frantic to claim her. His hands cupped her soapy breasts and his head naturally dipped to her core.

He found her and sucked her clit into his mouth.

She gasped and stiffened, her nails digging into the bedspread. She tasted like sweetness with a hint of rose-scented bubbles, and he went at her, not giving her a chance to think. He settled in, sliding his hands down her body and popping bubbles to cup her smooth ass and lift her to his mouth.

She moaned, her head thrashing on the comforter.

He didn't go slow or draw it out. Instead, he licked her clit and pressed a finger inside her wet heat. She detonated seconds later, crying out, her body undulating with the force of her orgasm. He let her come down and then placed one kiss on her clit before licking his way up her body and sucking a pert nipple into his mouth.

Her hands were frantic in his hair, clutching and

pulling. Erotic pain shot down his spine. He nipped her other nipple, and her body trembled. "Angus," she whispered, pulling hard enough on his hair that he had to look up at her flushed face. "Now," she said, pulling harder.

He slid up her body, kissing her jawline and positioning himself at her entrance. This was different. She was different, or maybe he was. This was more.

He pressed inside her, feeling like he was coming home. She held her breath and caressed his arms, down and then back up, spreading her legs wider. The second he was all the way in, he gripped her tight and thrust hard. Then he moved inside her with deep, slow strokes, prolonging the agony for both of them.

She was here, she was his, and no way was he letting anything happen to her. He was so deep inside her that the pleasure was indescribable. He pounded harder, and the sound of flesh against flesh filled the silent night. Then he stopped.

Her eyelids flew open. "What are you doing?" she gasped.

"Getting your attention." He might die if he didn't start moving, but this was important.

"You've got it," she said, scratching his buttocks with her nails.

He leaned down and kissed her as her internal walls caressed his dick with an insistent pull he wouldn't be able to ignore for long. "You are not using yourself as bait." In this most primitive of moments, the woman was going to listen to him. "Tell me you get me."

"I'm trying, really hard, to get you." She moaned, rubbing her breasts against his chest.

"Try harder," he suggested, his voice so hoarse he wasn't sure the words were clear.

Her eyes opened then, dark pools of feminine knowledge. Meeting his gaze, she tightened her grip on his cock, squeezing with internal muscles he hadn't known existed.

His eyes almost rolled back in his head. Oh, she was dangerous. He kissed her deep, claiming her in a way he'd never be able to put into words. Then he grasped her hands and pushed them above her head, holding her in place. Tremors took her, nearly killing him, and soft gasps escaped from her pretty mouth.

She liked it when he trapped her hands. Interesting.

Yet he needed more. So much more. He stared into her eyes, looking for the answers to everything. Why was it this one woman who drove him crazy?

"I'm not letting you sacrifice yourself, Nari." He said the words with conviction and started to move again, letting the pleasure blind him. He'd thought to fuck the fear and desperation out of both of them, but those thoughts disappeared faster than the bubbles had.

Instead he could only feel her. See her. Want her.

He thrust harder and faster, letting himself be taken over for the first time. His hands were firm on hers, and she curled her fingers through his, effectively splintering something inside him and putting the pieces back together around her.

She cried out and her fingers tightened as her body shook beneath his. The orgasm was powerful around him, and he powered into her harder, deeper, hotter until the zaps of fire licked down his spine and exploded in his balls. He dropped his head to her neck and let the passion have him.

Coming down, he struggled for breath above her. Gently, he moved his mouth along her neck to kiss her sweet mouth, releasing her hands as he did so. "In case you wondered, the answer to you using yourself as bait is a negative."

Chapter Thirty-Six

It felt good to have the team back together. Nari chewed happily on one of Pippa's perfect croissants at her cheerful kitchen table while the rest of the gang read through case files around her. "I still think I should be the bait," she said, reaching for her mimosa.

"No," Angus said absently from his position on the sofa.

Brigid looked up from across the table. "Hey. I thought I should be bait because I'm probably the easiest to get to."

Angus nodded, again not looking up from his file folder. "Good analysis. I figured the same thing."

Raider's head shot up from the adjoining chair. "You think Brigid should be bait for a serial killer?"

"Hell no," Angus said, finally lifting his gaze. "Not in a million. After you do a quick dive to investigate the HDD agents we've worked with to see if there's anybody who had a chance to leak information to Lassiter, I think you should take a leave of absence or something and put yourself completely under the radar. Even though HDD is secure, you have to go to and from, and it's not worth the risk." He bumped knuckles with Raider.

Nari snuck Roscoe a piece of a bacon roll as Kat licked her ear from his perch on her shoulder. She patted his head. "I missed you too, sweetie." He meowed softly.

Wolfe came in from the other room. "Kat's in a good mood lately because it's cold outside and I have to wear jackets. Still fits in the side pockets and roots around for old Goldfish Crackers from last year."

Jethro finished typing on his laptop next to Brigid. "I'm ready to discuss the quoted passages in the newest notes."

Nari sipped her mimosa. "They sounded similar to the other ones."

The Brit pushed back his chair from the table. "They're different. All of Lassiter's previous passages, even the ones from years ago, dealt with death in one form or another. Self-delusional narcissistic mentions of death, dying, and being the bringer of the end."

"What a nutjob," Dana muttered, next to Angus on the sofa.

Malcolm leaned against the counter and kept filching cookies as Pippa set them to cool on a mat. "What's different about these?"

Jethro's brows lowered. "The first is from a text written by a wronged lover—guy by the name of Georges Rermante. '*There once was a starry night upon which the darkness of lovers fell*.'" Jethro shook his head. "There isn't much about him except that he was torn between duty and love, and he chose duty at the end because of betrayal."

Angus shook his head. "Why can't Lassiter just come out and say what he wants to say?"

Jethro shrugged. "The next is from a poem by a master in chess in the nineteen hundreds. '*On first glance, the game can only be played according to the limitations on each piece, unless you're the master of the game.*'"

Nari accepted a warm cookie from Pippa. "Sounds like he's the master and it's the same narcissistic theme."

"At first glance," Jethro agreed. "But when you delve into the life of the chess master, a guy by the name of Norm Litehnshaw, you see more. He fell in love with his brother's wife and turned quite mad. Oh, he was probably nuts in the first place, but she became all he thought about, and he lost the ability to play chess. He lost everything until he killed her."

Nari swallowed. "Then what?"

"Then he returned to chess, won for a while, and finally was killed by his brother as revenge." Jethro looked up from his computer.

Angus's green gaze flicked to Nari. "So the logical conclusion is that Lassiter is in love with Nari and has to kill her to continue the game?"

Jethro shrugged. "I just find the data. You analyze it."

Angus frowned. "It doesn't feel right. Or at least not complete."

"Maybe he's in love with you, Angus," Pippa said, tossing hand mitts to the counter. "Maybe he can't concentrate because he's obsessed with you and knows that if he gets Nari, you'll come to him."

Dana frowned from the other chair by the sofa. "So you think the person trying to shoot Angus is Lassiter?"

Angus shook his head. "Lassiter would never work

with a partner, and the night of the bombing there were two of them. Same with the first time that navy-blue truck chased me down and shot at me. I don't know who that was, but it definitely wasn't Lassiter."

It was impressive how quickly Angus could put himself in the mind of a killer. Impressive and a little daunting. Nari smiled and he smiled back, relieving her. Okay. He was all right.

Angus cleared his throat. "He failed twice to get Nari, and he's going to become desperate. He's already killed the doctor who pronounced him dead, so anybody he's ever been associated with is in danger. We have to find him now, and the key to that is to find where he's been since I shot him six years ago."

Brigid opened her laptop, her curly, red hair falling over her shoulders. "So far, nothing. I've looked everywhere. It's like he just disappeared. I even searched hospitals and rehab places during that time period, figuring he would've needed a while to recuperate after being shot several times. Not only is there no record of him, there's no record of anybody having that kind of injuries that I haven't been able to track down and verify."

Nari patted her hand. Brigid was the best; if anybody could find the information, it'd be her.

Angus looked at Jethro. "How about the last note? The one found with the deceased doctor?"

Jethro typed in a couple of commands. "'*The night grows tired, the energy unleashed upon this moment in time that cannot last. A vision of the abyss, drawing me in, only her face halting the time that must occur in the game of the gods.*'"

"What the hell does that mean?" Wolfe grumbled.

Jethro dug his fingers into the back of his neck. "It's a passage from a set of ramblings by a patient in the Canterbury Mental Hospital in the early nineteen hundreds. His name was Morgan Trowcrow, he was in his early thirties, and he'd murdered his mother before going on to kill seven more women who looked like her."

"So, his mom stopped the time that had to occur? Until he killed her?" Raider asked.

Jethro lifted a shoulder. "He wrote the passage several years after being admitted, and supposedly he was in love with one of the nurses, who he tried to kill several times. There were notes in a doctor's journal that the nurse might be the woman to whom he referred, and it's possible she symbolized the institution that kept him from killing." He looked at Angus. "Or not. Who knows?"

Malcolm leaned against the counter, stress lines by the sides of his mouth. "How the hell does this help us catch this wacko? I say we just hunt him down and end him."

Wolfe nodded. "I like that plan."

"So do I," Angus mused. "Brigid? Any luck with facial rec and CCTVs around town?"

"No. I haven't spotted him once," Brigid said. "He's good at hiding, and he manages to blend in when he needs to. I'll keep looking, though."

Dana reached for a homemade bagel from the tray on the coffee table. "I've been trying to track down financial records but haven't found anything. Lassiter obviously had a lot of money stashed away or he wouldn't have been able to survive these last few years. So far, nothing. He really is smart."

Angus nodded. "Madness and genius are often flip

sides of the same coin." He focused on Raider. "Any news on who has been trying to kill me?"

Malcolm stepped forward. "We've narrowed it down to a couple of the cult members we busted a year ago; we can't find one of them. He disappeared off the grid when he was released from prison, so we're calling in more favors to locate him. He's our best bet right now."

"Sounds good," Angus said. "Is there any connection between him and the guy who shot my lawyer?"

"Not yet," Brigid answered. "I haven't found anything. Also, the dead guy who bombed your cabin? There's nothing in our records, and HDD has reached out to Interpol, but nothing so far. I'll keep on it."

Nari ate another croissant. Why not? They were stuck in the middle of no-answer-land. Carbs didn't count there. "We need a plan."

Angus nodded. "I'd make myself bait, but I don't think those passages from Lassiter refer to me."

Nari perked up.

"No," Angus said before she could offer. "Using you for bait is a nonstarter." He shook his head. "The only option is to continue to track him down via medical, financial, or physical evidence from cameras. At some point, probably soon, we will get a line on him. Then we're at go."

Seeing Angus in full control streamed awareness through her body, and she ducked her head to sip her mimosa, memories of the night before ticking through her mind like an old film.

"Roscoe," Angus warned.

Nari looked up to see the dog edging her way, his brown gaze on her drink. "None for you, puppy," she said softly, reaching out to pat his head. "The wine you had the other night is going to have to do it."

"The very good wine," Jethro interjected with a look at the dog.

Kat dug his claws into Nari's shoulder for balance and leaned over to swat the dog on the ear.

Nari winced. "Kat. Take it easy." She gingerly lifted the kitten to the floor, where he could play with Roscoe. She wanted to relax, but they had too much to do. "What's the next step in the case against you, Angus?"

He watched the dog and kitten goof off. "I should probably find another lawyer, considering mine is in a coma." Worry fanned out from his eyes, where guilt glowed. "Although I agreed to a lie detector test, I think I should wait until I have an attorney. I'll put in a call to Scott's partner tomorrow."

Nari nodded, her heart hurting for him. And for Scott. The lawyer had to wake up, and not just to provide a witness account that Angus hadn't shot him. Apparently he was a good guy, according to everyone who knew him. "He's strong, from what I understand. He'll be okay, Angus." Nari's phone buzzed and she lifted it. "Hello."

"Hi, Nari. It's Opal." The woman sounded much stronger today.

Nari smiled. "How are you doing?"

"Good, if they'd hurry up and release me. Apparently paperwork trumps all else, even when one has been shot in the line. Well, kind of in the line of duty." Opal chuckled. "I just wanted to make sure you understood that the job offer I made while passing out was intended. You're made for this position."

But she'd be working for Quan again. "I appreciate the offer and will definitely think about it. Please stay healthy."

"I'll try. Call me in a couple of days." Opal clicked off.

"What offer?" Dana asked.

Nari told her the details.

"Sounds perfect for you," Wolfe said.

A year ago it would have been. Now, Nari wasn't sure. Her gaze moved toward Angus, who hadn't said anything. Come to think of it, he hadn't said much the night before when she'd told him about the offer. What did that mean?

Chapter Thirty-Seven

Another quiet morning failed to bring peace. Angus drank orange juice and looked out the industrial windows as Nari slept in the other room. The day before with the team had felt right, but now he was on his own again. Oh, they were there for backup, but their time of working for the HDD in their dismal offices was over.

A year ago he would've been shocked at how much that bothered him. After a spectacular dinner of chicken Parmesan cooked by Wolfe, of all people, he and Nari had returned and spent the night rolling around and destroying Jethro's guest room. The mattress might never be the same. He grinned.

The door opened and Jethro jogged in with Roscoe panting behind. "We went for a nice run. I have to shower and get to class, but I thought we could go over all the notes from Lassiter again tonight. I feel like we're missing something."

"Agreed," Angus said, scrubbing both hands down his face. "There's a clue in there, a kernel of truth that I just haven't caught." It was driving him crazy.

Jethro disappeared into his room while Roscoe padded to his water bowl and went to town.

Angus's laptop dinged and he lumbered over, bare-chested but wearing old jeans. He turned on the screen and opened a browser for his email. Hopefully Brigid had found something for him.

A picture appeared, upside down. He frowned and clicked twice to turn it, taking a step back. "Shit." The blonde from the other day, the one who'd hit him with a shovel, lay on weeds surrounded by trees. She was naked with burn marks across her pale skin, her feet were tied, her hands were palms up, and her chest gaped wide open, shards of ribs poking out. Her heart was gone. A shovel lay next to her, covered in blood.

He grew still, anger billowing inside him. Then he scrolled down.

Dearest Angus,

I hope you do not mind that I took care of this little problem for you. She was much harder to find than one would've thought, thus making this side errand for my friend much more pleasurable for me. To be truthful, she was a fighter. Young, but with a lot of spirit. You know how much I like spirit. Her heart even tasted like it had more energy. Someday I hope we can enjoy such a meal together, but I know that is unlikely. For now, I shall take care of all the problems plaguing you, my very good friend. It is the least I can do.

Yours,
Henry

Angus launched himself into motion, grabbing his phone and dialing quickly.

"Tate Bianchi," Tate answered.

"It's Angus. I'm sending you an email I just received with a picture of a new victim. She's the woman who hit me in the head trying to save the guy who shot my lawyer. The shovel is right next to her." He leaned over and typed quickly, forwarding the email. "I know this looks bad for me, but you have to find her. She's in the forest somewhere. Also, there's a letter from Lassiter—it's coming with the picture, and there's no quotation at the end. I don't know what that means."

Tate's voice became muffled, no doubt because his phone was resting on his neck. "Just a second." He waited and then swore. "Where is she?"

"I don't know. Get it to a tech or a lab or something and find her." Angus next forwarded the email to Brigid, asking her to try to trace the IP address. "This is the first time Lassiter has reached out via email, so we might be able to trace him. He's off his game and he's getting desperate. This might be a chance, Tate. Don't screw it up."

Typing came over the line. "I've sent it on. For now, you know I have to bring you in. This looks bad, but my gut is on your side. Come in and talk to me about this."

Angus swallowed. "Find me and I'll come in." He clicked off and then destroyed the burner phone. If he was in interrogation all day, he wouldn't be ready to go the second Brigid traced the IP address.

His email dinged again.

Dearest Angus,

   *I hit Send too quickly. Doesn't that happen to
everybody? Anyway, I wanted to say how much
I've enjoyed being back in your life again. I have
no doubt you've missed me as much as I you.
For now, I'm going to leave you another present.
In a time of life and of love, only maternal energy
prolongs the journey.*

                    Yours,
                    Henry

"Jethro?" Angus bellowed. "Get out here."

Jethro loped out, freshly showered and dressed in slacks and a button-down shirt with his backpack over one arm. "What are you yelling about?"

Angus rattled off the last line. "Do you recognize it?"

Jethro paused and reached for a bottle of water to put in his pack. "Yes. It's a phrase from a short story written by Frederick Litmuslion about fifty years ago. He lost his mother at a young age and it affected the rest of his life, to the point that he murdered four women who were nothing but kind to him."

Angus stilled. "What do you mean?"

Jethro shrugged. "They were motherly figures, powerful women who were in charge, and he slaughtered them mercilessly. Why?"

"It's definitely Lassiter." Angus went through the last week. "Shit." He dialed HDD and was told that the administrator was on leave. "Nari?" He ran into the bedroom. "Call Quan. I need to know where Opal is."

Nari sat up, blinking sleepily. She reached for her phone and dialed. "Quan? Where are you?"

Angus grabbed the phone. "Quan? Are you with the administrator? Where are you? She's in danger."

The next moment Opal came on the line. "Nari? Hello?"

"Ma'am, this is Angus Force, and you're in danger. Do you have a detail with you?" he asked.

Opal chuckled. "I'm always in danger, young man. I can assure you that Quan and I are more than safe at my place. You attended the holiday party here, remember? The security is superb." She chuckled again. "Um, have to go. 'Bye." She hung up.

"Shit." Angus looked at Nari. "Stay here with Roscoe. I'll call it in to HDD, but I need to get to Opal. She's Lassiter's next target." The bastard somehow knew where she was. He ran out of the room, dialing HDD for backup.

"You need me?" Jethro asked.

"No," Angus said tersely. "All of HDD will descend there before I can even have Brigid trace her location. Protect Nari." He yanked on a shirt and ran out the door, grabbing his jacket and weapon on the way. He had to get to the woman before Lassiter did. The head of HDD was in danger from a serial killer because of her connection to him.

This was all his fault.

He'd made the drive in less than an hour.

Angus kept his back to the perfectly manicured hedges, his gun out and his aim steady. The administrator was correct that her security was excellent. It was just unfortunate that it had been turned off—or cut. He had easily scaled the gate and now ran up the long drive toward the luxurious house. Where was everybody?

The place should be crawling with HDD agents. Yet only silence, thick and heavy, surrounded the place, along with the rain. He blinked water out of his eyes and kept running, reaching the side of the house. If Lassiter was around, it'd be better to go in the back.

Angus crouched low and ran along the side of the home, ducking beneath the various windows. It was a gorgeous, Victorian-style house, white with a wide porch in back. He stepped gingerly onto the porch and angled to the first sliding glass door to peer inside. The room appeared to be a guest room, with floral patterns, and appeared untouched. When he looked through the next slider he saw a prone figure on the ground, facedown.

Rain pummeled him, and he had to wipe his eyes to see better. Was that Quan? Angus could make out dark hair. He forced himself to breathe evenly while reaching for the handle. The door, high quality and heavy, slid open easily.

Keeping low, he pushed inside and shut out the rain. The room appeared to be a kitchen nook, with a round table and high chairs, flanked by twin hutches holding pale pink and blue dishes. He listened and could only hear the rain. So he moved forward, dropped to his haunches, and leaned over to see better in the semidarkness of the cloudy day. It was Quan; his eyes were closed and blood flowed from his forehead.

Angus felt for a pulse. It was steady and weak. The man was alive.

Where the hell was HDD? The agents should already be there.

Angus reached for his phone to call for an ambulance. Dead. He shook it. Jammed? Had somebody jammed all electronics? That would explain the malfunctioning gate.

He shoved his phone back in place and leaned over in case Quan could hear him. "I'll be back. Just hold on. Also, sorry I suspected you of being tied to Lassiter." He stood and walked silently out of the breakfast nook, through a sparkling-clean kitchen to a living room that looked out to the rainy porch.

Silence ticked around him, heavy with warning. He followed a hallway to the left and cleared a spacious office, two bedrooms, and a bathroom. Nothing.

Yet instinct propelled him to stay silent and not call out for Opal. He turned back the other way and cleared another bathroom, an exercise room, and a laundry. That left the closed French doors of what must be the master bedroom. He took a deep breath, hoping against hope that he wouldn't find Opal Clemonte dead in there.

Then he opened the door and walked inside. The bedroom was wide, with white furniture and a king-size bed covered with a purple bedspread. Perfectly made. His shoulders relaxed and he cleared the closet and bathroom before walking back out. All right. Was there a panic room? If so, how the hell would he find it? For now, he had to get Quan medical attention.

He returned to the living room, where Opal now stood near the fireplace, a gun in her hand and a bandage around her injured arm. She was facing out the windows, tracking something with her eyes. "Are you okay?" he asked, keeping his voice low and looking for the threat.

"No." She turned to face him. Fire lanced from her eyes and she looked every inch the powerful operative she was, even in her light-green linen pants and matching sweater.

He shook his head. "Where's the threat?" he whispered, edging toward the sliding glass door.

"Right here." She lifted her gun and pointed it at his head.

He paused. "What the hell are you doing?"

Reaching for the bookcase behind herself, she tossed a pair of handcuffs at him. "In front is fine."

He caught the cuffs, his head spinning. "I'm not the threat, Administrator. What happened to Quan?"

She smiled then, and the world ground to a stop. Holy shit. Quan hadn't been the threat, but his lover had? Could Angus raise his gun fast enough?

"You won't make it, and believe me, you don't want to die yet," she said quietly, no emotion in her eyes. "The game is just getting interesting. I need you alive for now."

The game? Lassiter's last few quoted poems ran through Angus's head. This was crazy. Insane, actually. "It's your face haunting Lassiter?" Angus shook his head, trying to angle his body between the woman and the breakfast nook.

"I have a clear line on Quan's head right now," Opal said easily. "You take one more step and I'm blowing out his brains. What there is of them, that is."

Angus stopped moving. "That last email. The one about maternal energy that brought me right here. That was from you."

"Of course. Email is such a tacky way to correspond, but you were using a burner phone, so I didn't have the number. More importantly, the blonde with the shovel hasn't been found yet, so the note next to her body is useless right now. I was under a bit of a time crunch here, Angus." She glanced down at her watch. "Cuff yourself or I shoot your girlfriend's father. Now."

Angus stared at her. If he leapt at her, she'd get a shot off first.

"Oh. Drop your gun." She settled her stance and aimed at Quan's head.

Angus set his gun on the arm of the sofa and quickly cuffed his wrists together. He could fight with his hands bound if necessary, but he had to get her away from Quan. "You're gonna have to catch me up here, Administrator. You're working with Lassiter?"

"I'd say *working with* is a misnomer," she said.

None of this was making a damn lick of sense. Angus saw that Quan was beginning to stir. He had to distract her. "What's your plan now?"

Her smile revealed the megalomania that lurked deep within her ambition. "Now? Oh, now we're going to go visit an old friend of yours."

Chapter Thirty-Eight

Nari finished some instant oatmeal she'd found in the back of Jethro's cupboard while Roscoe slept near her barstool. She glanced at her watch again. Angus had been gone for nearly an hour and there had been no word so far. Was Opal safe? Was Quan safe? She set her spoon down in the empty bowl and swallowed rapidly.

There had to be something she could do.

Jethro had gone to work, saying he only had one class and would be back. With Roscoe at her feet and the door double-locked, she was safe but useless. There had to be a way to help. She looked at her watch again.

Time was moving too slowly.

Her phone tinkled a cheery tune and she picked it up. "Hi, Mom." It'd be good to hear her mother's voice.

"Hi, sweetie. Where are you?" Her mom sounded upbeat.

"I'm at a friend's house," Nari said, pushing away the bowl.

Her mom was quiet for a moment. "Well, okay. The car at the airport was nice, but I figured you'd be here when we arrived."

Nari jerked fully alert. "Arrived? Where are you?"

"At your apartment, of course. It's a good thing I still had that spare key from when I visited in the spring." Her mom sounded matter-of-fact. "Are you coming home soon?"

"Mom? Where's Dad?" Nari asked, running to the door, panic heating her lungs until it hurt to gasp a breath.

"He's planning to beat that Angus Force to death. We couldn't believe it when we received your email about him being a killer. I even watched a news report on him on the plane ride here." Her mom clicked her tongue.

"Mom? Where's Dad?" Nari insisted.

Her mother sighed. "There's not a thing in your fridge, so your dad took that nice rental car to the store. You remember the one where they make the homemade pasta that we found last time? Well, he's there, and I'm planning to cook—"

"Mom? Get out of there. Get out of my apartment and run to the neighbor's. Right now." Nari yanked open the door and ran outside into the hallway.

"What? Why—" Her mom screamed, and the sounds of a struggle came over the line.

"Mom!" Nari yelled, taking the cement stairs two at a time.

The scuffle continued, and then silence. The phone went dead. "Mom!" Nari yelled again, running outside into the rain and straight for her rental car. Nothing. Nobody was there. She quickly dialed Brigid while jumping in the car.

"You've got Brigid," Brigid answered.

"Bridge? Send the police to my apartment right now. As fast as you can," Nari directed, starting the engine and gunning the car out of the narrow alley by the industrial building. "I think Lassiter has my mom." Tears choked her throat and she drove faster, trying to see through the rain and her tears.

Rapid typing came over the line. "I just sent the local police and transmitted an alert to HDD agents," Brigid said urgently. "They're on the way. Tell me where you are."

"I'm on my way there. Just a second." Nari sped up, zooming through the industrial park. She put Brigid on hold and punched in Angus's burner-phone number. It went to the automated voice mail. "It's Nari. Call me. Lassiter has my mom." She hung up and returned to Brigid. "I'm back." She swerved through the gates onto a busy street, ignoring the angry honking from other drivers.

"I sent out a call to the team, and Wolfe and Raider are headed your way. Malcolm is locking down the cul-de-sac. I'll stay here at the computers," Brigid said, her Irish brogue thick with emotion. "She'll be okay, Nari. We'll get there."

Nari couldn't breathe. She swung around a white SUV and punched the gas pedal to the floor, flipping on the windshield wipers as she did so. Her mom had to be okay. "He must've sent them an email from me with tickets. Even had a rental car waiting," she gasped.

Brigid kept quiet. "Metro is two minutes away from your apartment. Just hold on."

Nari drove faster, weaving through traffic, nearly jumping the curb twice. She sped away from the commercial area, winding by the trees that marked a nicer suburban area. The world flew by outside her car. Her hands shook, but she kept going as fast as possible.

A van shot out of a side street, clipping the back of her car. She screamed as the car spun wildly around and plunged into a tree. The airbag shot out, smashing into her face. It slowly deflated, tossing powder in the air as it did so.

"Nari!" Brigid yelled over the phone.

The world buzzed. Nari shook her head and tried to clear her vision. Had she just hit somebody? She fumbled for the phone. Something wet trickled down the side of her face.

Her door was ripped open and rough hands yanked her out. She tried to protest, lifting her arms, but the man didn't relent. Her head swam. Nausea attacked her, and she finally focused on the face of the man pulling her.

"Lassiter," she mumbled, right before he placed a rag over her nose and mouth.

Then there was only darkness.

"Nari. Wake up." A gentle nudge prodded Nari's shoulder.

She groaned and opened her eyelids, instantly regretting it as pain exploded down her face. Coughing, she shut her eyes until she could slowly open them without crying. Where was she? What had happened?

"Nari?"

"Mom?" Nari partially turned as memories slammed into her faster than the van had earlier. She sat up and instantly swayed, becoming dizzy. "Ugh." She blinked several times and tried to focus her eyes.

A soft hand smoothed back her hair. "Take a minute. You're okay."

Her mom's voice calmed her a little. She opened her eyes to see her mom sitting next to her, eyes wide with concern. "There you go."

The floor was hard underneath softness. Nari looked down to see a royal-blue rug with gold trim. They were in a small, barred cell across from what looked like a morgue table. Her body went cold. "Where are we?"

Her mom sat with her legs extended on the carpet. "In a basement. I woke up here with you." She rubbed a bruise along her jawline. "The guy took me by surprise. You?"

Nari nodded. "I think he rammed my car." The memory of Lassiter pulling her out of the car shot through her, followed by a strong dose of panic. "We have to get out of here." She stood and studied the cell. Two sides looked like solid cement, while two had long, steel bars set into the concrete floor. Going to the door, she pulled on it, but it was locked securely.

Two royal-blue, high-back, baroque-style chairs were placed facing the cell on the left side, while straight ahead was the makeshift morgue, complete with surgical implements on a counter. The cement floor was stained a dark red, especially around a drain near the table.

The oatmeal in Nari's stomach lurched around and she swallowed rapidly. They had to get free. Her gaze shifted back to the chairs. Why were there two chairs? That was odd.

A door beyond one of the cement walls opened and closed, and a man turned the corner. "Well, hello."

Nari put herself between her mother and the cell bars, staring at Henry Wayne Lassiter. He wore black slacks and a dark sweater, and a scar marred the right side of his jaw, as if he'd had several surgeries. His dark-blond hair swept back from his face, thick and wavy, as if he was the protagonist in a 1980s romcom. His blue eyes were razor sharp and lacked any semblance of humanity. Even so, intelligence shone bright.

From her research on him, he was a classic narcissist and sociopath with psychopathic tendencies. There was no reasoning with him or getting him to see her or her mother as human beings. He didn't experience empathy.

He was motivated only by self-interest and his own feeling of superiority. "You can't kill us," she said quietly.

He smiled and walked to the nearest chair, limping slightly with his left leg. "I do like it when they beg." His voice was scarily raspy.

"I'm not begging," Nari said, fighting to keep her voice from trembling. "I'm saying that if you kill us, Angus will leave town. He'll bury himself in the middle of nowhere with a mountain of whiskey and not look back. The game will be over, and nobody will challenge you like that again. Ever."

"That's not what happened when I killed his sweet sister," Lassiter said, settling back in the chair as if chatting with a friend.

Nari smiled, but her lips wobbled, so she stopped. "True, but times have changed. He wouldn't be able to take two deaths like that."

Lassiter slowly shook his head. "I know my friend better than you do. He was obsessed with finding me before, and once I cut you up, piece by piece, he'll have no choice but to continue the game."

Nari's mother made a distressed sound behind her,

and Nari straightened. "He won't continue any sort of game with you. I promise."

Lassiter flattened his hand over his thigh and rubbed it. "Angus will be so proud of how I've overcome all those bullets."

Proud? The nutjob wanted Angus to be proud? "He'd admire you more if you let us go," Nari said. "In fact, it'd make him wonder more about you. About figuring you out, because that'd be a shock to him."

Lassiter smiled. "You're a smart one. Figures. My Angus would only like an intelligent woman." He sighed. "Well, friendships are two-way streets, no? I should have my needs met, too. If I eat the heart of the woman he loves, I'll always have a part of him, too."

Nari's mom gagged.

"While that's interesting logic," Nari said, "I think you should intrigue him instead. Throw him a curveball. Let us go and make him worry about why." She was grasping at straws, but it was all she had right now. The stun guns mounted on the wall behind the two chairs promised there wouldn't be any sort of a fair fight here.

"I do like your line of thinking, but I don't have the time required to play a long game with you. The rest of the team will have to do, and it'll be lovely watching them witness Angus's descent into that dark place only I have been able to take him." Lassiter pressed his fingers together, watching his narrow hands. "It has to be you, Nari. Your mama is just a bonus." His smile revealed a flash of the evil inside him.

How was she going to get her mother out of this? Nari looked around the room. How many women had he butchered here? "Why are you under a time constraint?"

"It's a long story." He picked off a piece of lint from his pants leg.

There was only one solution. Nari took a deep breath. "Let my mom go. Seeing her fear and stress after you kill me will only torture Angus more."

"No." Her mom pushed her to the side. "Take me. Let her go."

Lassiter's blue gaze narrowed. "So that's what a mother's love really looks like." He tilted his head to the side. "I wonder if I'll feel such sweet warmth when I eat your heart."

Nari scrambled for a way to turn his attention. "It's my heart you want. Taking two of us at a time breaks your pattern. It's not what you want and it'll lead to bad luck. Very bad luck."

He laughed. "I like how your mind works. To be honest, I've never eaten a brain. Yours might be interesting."

She stepped away from the bars. Once he went for a stun gun, she was out of options. "You have changed your routine, haven't you? Why?" she asked.

He lifted his chin. "I was in rehab for a long time, and then I took counseling from a friend in this game. Well, somewhat."

The door out of sight opened loudly. Who was coming? Nari stiffened, trying to see.

Lassiter turned, the smile sliding from a face that most women would consider good-looking if they couldn't see beneath to the monster. "What in the world have you done?"

Angus came into view, his wrists handcuffed together.

"Angus," Nari breathed, rushing to the bars. She grabbed them. What was going on?

Opal walked behind him, her gun pressed to his back. Was this some type of rescue plan? What was happening? Nari stared at the woman, who was staring at Lassiter.

The two chairs. Wait a minute. Oh, crap.

Chapter Thirty-Nine

The second Angus saw Nari's terrified eyes, he settled. Everything inside him went calm and cold. He tilted his head to stare at Lassiter. "Looks like the bullet to the face did some damage."

Delight filtered across Lassiter's face. "Angus, my friend. It's nice to have you in my space, but this is much too early." He cranked his head to look beyond Angus. "Opal? The game is over. I have Nari in my cage."

Opal pushed the gun barrel harder against Angus's spine. "She's still alive with a beating heart, so I'd say we're at a tie."

Nari stumbled back from the bars, her face going pale. "Opal?"

Angus scanned the entire area with his peripheral vision. Opal had refused to talk on the way here, promising that all his questions would be answered when the time was right. Not that he hadn't figured a lot of it out already. "Here's what I think." He kept his focus on Lassiter to hold his attention.

Lassiter rubbed a scar on the lower half of his jaw as he stood and turned to face them. "This is quite inappropriate, Opal. You've pushed our game, but not me. He can't be here right now. I'm not done." The guy sounded like an impetuous child.

"I can't very well set him free now," Opal drawled.

In a split second Angus decided Opal didn't exist. "Henry? How long have you and Opal been working together?"

Henry smiled, his face clearing. "For about seven years. I take care of problems for her and she does the same for me. She's smart. You know I like them smart, my friend."

Anger spiraled through Angus, and his laugh felt strained. "Yes, I do. So. That at least explains how your death was faked and you disappeared for rehab. If anybody could make that happen, it'd be the head of the HDD."

"Yes." Lassiter rubbed his thigh, where Angus remembered shooting him. "Unfortunately, rehab took longer than I would've hoped. The second I could, I returned here for our game. It was some time after you began looking for me, however. It's nice that we're on the same wavelength."

Angus shook his head. "So you knew so much about our team because our boss was working with you. I thought it was Quan."

Opal shoved Angus harder. "Quan's a moron. It's because of me that you're alive, Henry," she spat. "You owe me. But the second you were well enough, you wanted to play with him and put my entire career in jeopardy."

Oh, this was so fucking weird. Angus continued to ignore her, focusing on Lassiter instead. "I was alerted by Miles Brown, an elderly clerk, that there was a problem with your file, but he had a stroke before I could talk to him."

Lassiter inclined his head. "Well, I owe Opal for that. It always comes down to billing and medical records, right? Apparently there was one medical bill still left in that file that Opal hadn't caught. Miles was no doubt closing out all his records before retiring, and he must've caught a hint. Opal took care of him, though."

Angus almost shut his eyes, but he had to stay in the moment. He'd grieve for Miles and face his guilt later. The administrator had somehow gotten to the clerk. Strokes were easy to fake. "Henry? What about the female paramedic who pronounced you dead?"

"Opal again," Lassiter admitted. "She's good at making accidents look real. Well, the whole HDD is, actually." He sighed, as if giving up a secret. "By the time I was well enough to come home, she'd compiled dossiers on everybody in your life. It was like the best birthday present ever." His gaze finally rose so that he looked over Angus's shoulder at Opal. "Well, that and the ultimate game, which I didn't know we were playing for a while."

The ultimate game? What? For him? Angus dropped his chin to regain Henry's attention. "She was trying to kill me, and you were trying to get to Nari? Was it all some narcissistic game between you two? Whoever got there first won?" It made an odd and sick kind of sense. "She shot at me, bombed my house, and hired that blond moron who ended up shooting my lawyer."

"I did, but not because of a game," Opal said, kicking him in the back of the shin. "I worked hard to reach my position, and if you were just dead, Henry could concentrate his work elsewhere and return our relationship to status quo. You're very difficult to kill, you know." She leaned to the side. "And Henry, don't think for a second that I forgive you for shooting me."

Lassiter blanched. "I didn't think you'd fight to save Nari at the club. Shooting you was an accident. You know it was," he said. "I thought to impress you by taking the girl while you were there. But she can fight."

Was he somehow dependent upon Opal's approval? Did the woman understand that? Being nice wasn't helping. "Yeah, Nari kicked your ass twice," Angus said.

Lassiter's nostrils flared and his face turned a motley red. "She did not. Either way, I guess you get to watch her die. You know how long I can make death take. Just think of the things you'll get to watch me do."

Angus tensed.

"No," Opal said, punctuating the word with the barrel pressed to his spine. "Be a good boy, Angus." She angled to the side again, and her rose perfume filled the air.

Nari coughed. "Why did you date my father?"

Opal sighed. "He's second in command, and I needed some hold on him. Sex is an easy weapon, dear." She chuckled. "So, Henry? You'll finish your work here and then leave HDD agents alone? Find another game to play?"

Lassiter nodded. "Yes. I can live with that."

Opal laughed, the sound rough. "Excellent." She pushed Angus.

Nari stepped up to the bars again. "How long have you been batshit crazy?"

Angus subtly shook his head. There was no guarantee Opal wouldn't just shoot Nari and declare herself the victor over Henry. They were both unstable and psychopathic.

He had to diffuse the woman now. "Opal? I called in the entire HDD to your house when you sent that email. Yet nobody was there."

"Yes, well, I *am* the boss. I called in and told everybody to stand down and that you had been taken in by the FBI. I'll have to figure something out about that when they find your body. I guess the bad guy somehow fooled me." She hummed. "I'll work on that."

Lassiter puffed up. "He doesn't die until I'm done with the two women."

"This is your domain," Opal said. "Please wait until I've left the premises, however."

At least Angus had taken her attention away from Nari. For now.

"All right," Opal said. "Nari and Nari's mom, both step to the back of the cell and sit down so Angus can join you. If either of you makes a move, I'll shoot him." The gun looked at home in her hand. "I'm tempted to do so anyway."

Lassiter turned and looked at Nari. He licked his lips. "I'll get my lab ready."

Nari wrapped her arms around Angus's waist, her heart thundering in her chest. He was there and solid, and she clung to him for a moment inside the cell.

"Are you all right?" he asked, kissing her forehead, his cuffed hands between them.

"Yes." She stepped back. "This is my mom, Louise."
Angus nodded. "Hi."
Her mom's face was pale but stoic. "Hello."

Angus looked over his shoulder to where Lassiter was bustling around his lab, humming happily. Opal had gone elsewhere to take care of some phone calls, after making Lassiter promise not to start until she'd said goodbye and left to avoid the screaming. "We're at the end of a long driveway and nobody will hear us. Chances are this place is soundproofed, too."

Nari's knees wobbled. "Did you see the stun guns?"

Angus nodded. "Yeah. He can't stun all three of us at once, but he doesn't have to open the doors, either." His gaze darted around.

Nari couldn't breathe. "How long do you think we have?"

He dropped another kiss to her cheek. "Don't worry. We'll figure something out."

There wasn't anything to figure out. Nari swallowed. "No matter what happens—"

"No," he said. "Don't even think it."

Nari looked around. She'd already tried with Lassiter, and Opal didn't seem to care. There was no way to reason with them and there was no way out. "There's only one solution," she whispered.

"What?" Her mom reached down to hold her hand. "What can we do?"

Nari gulped in air and lifted her face to Angus. "You're gonna have to kill me."

He cocked his head. "Excuse me?"

She breathed in. "If you do, you win the game. It'll freak Lassiter out and maybe he'll open the door."

"Or he'll just shoot me and then torture your mom," Angus hissed.

That was a risk they'd have to take. "We don't have another option." She grabbed his arm. "Listen. You know this guy better than anybody else. You're smarter than he is and you already caught him once. We can't get out with force, and nobody's coming to rescue us. It's on you, Angus. You're going to have to make it look real." She hated to put that on him, but they were running out of time. Lassiter was lining up his instruments as well as several cigarettes and a blowtorch. She shivered.

"Damn it," Angus muttered, his head hanging and his eyelids closing. He inhaled and then slowly exhaled, the muscles in his arms vibrating. Finally he looked up and nodded. "All right. But don't really die on me." Without warning, he flipped her around and lifted her by the neck with his hands, turning to face Lassiter. The metal of the cuffs dug into her skin. "Henry? I don't think the game is going to end the way you think it will."

Lassiter paused in sharpening a knife. He turned his head and his eyes blazed blue. "What are you doing?" He tossed the knife on the table and strode toward them, tripping in his haste, but quickly regaining his balance.

"She's mine," Angus said, tightening his grip.

Nari panicked and grabbed at his hands. Her legs hung free so she could kick back, but she forced herself to dangle.

Lassiter smiled. "You wouldn't kill her. Give me a break."

Angus tightened his hold even more, and Nari coughed, her breath cut off. She struggled, her legs slipping uselessly against his.

"No," her mom cried, grabbing at Angus's arm.

Angus dropped Nari and she landed on her feet, wobbling. He roared out and swung, hitting her mom in the face with an elbow. Her mom crashed into the bars and went down.

Nari turned toward her, and Angus grabbed her again, lifting her up easily. God, he was strong. Tears flowed down her face; she couldn't see her mom.

Lassiter laughed, but the humor didn't reach his eyes. He wrung his hands. "You won't kill her."

"She's mine," Angus growled, his voice feral. "I won't let you touch her. Hurt her. No. If she's going to die, it's going to be on my terms." He shook her, his grip unbreakable. She clawed his hands, and darkness edged in from the outskirts of her vision.

"No!" Lassiter cried, running past the chairs for one of the Tasers. He rushed forward and pushed the button.

Nari's mom jumped up, right in front of them, and took the shock from the Taser. She screamed and her body convulsed. Then she fell.

"Mom," Nari whispered, beginning to lose consciousness.

Lassiter howled and fumbled with the lock, opening the door and rushing in headlong, spittle flying from his mouth. Angus dropped Nari to her feet and kicked Lassiter in his bad leg. The man hissed and flew sideways. Grunting, Angus rushed him and manacled him in a headlock.

Lassiter punched Angus in the eye and flipped backward.

Nari wobbled, trying to get breath back into her lungs. Unconsciousness still lingered right at the edges, and she had to suck in air to stay on her feet. Her ears rang, and tears still poured down her face.

Lassiter pulled a knife from a sheath at his ankle and stabbed at Angus, who jumped back, his hands still cuffed. The two men circled each other, panting and dodging. Lassiter struck, and Angus blocked with his arm, letting the knife slash down his forearm to protect his face. Blood flew across the room.

Everything came into focus.

A door opened. "Henry? Do you want dinner first?" Opal came around the corner. Her eyes widened and she reached to the back of her waist.

Nari screamed and ran full bore at the woman, her head down.

Opal drew and fired. The bullet whizzed by Nari right before she slammed into Opal with enough force to crash them both into the metal door.

Angus hissed in pain behind her.

Nari punched Opal in the face, breaking her nose. Opal slammed both elbows onto Nari's shoulders, and pain ripped down to her tailbone. Nari grabbed Opal around the neck and then twisted her, putting her in a stranglehold. The woman clawed her nails down Nari's arm, ripping the skin open. Nari tightened her hold, ignoring the pain. Opal started flopping like a landed trout, sputtering, and then she went limp. Out cold.

Nari released her, kicking her away.

Pain lanced through her entire body, but she forced herself to stand and stagger to help Angus. She turned the corner just in time to see Angus, on top of Lassiter, plunge the knife through the serial killer's neck, impaling the monster to the carpet. Blood coated the blade and his cuffed hands.

"Angus," Nari whispered, stumbling toward him. Blood covered the right side of his chest, and she couldn't tell where he'd been hit.

"Nari." He fell to the side, right near her unconscious mother.

Nari made it to them, falling to her knees and touching both of them.

Angus coughed. "I need a fucking vacation. I mean, I really do." His eyelids closed.

Her mom stirred and rolled over. She shook her head and then put a hand to her temple. "Phone. We need a phone."

Nari tried to force herself to stand, but the room swirled around. Just then, the door crashed open, and Wolfe ran in with his gun out and Raider right behind him. "We need an ambulance," she whispered, trying not to pass out.

Her dad ran in after them, also armed. He reached them, skidding to his knees. "My girls." He hugged Nari close and then kissed her mom. "Louise, my love. Are you okay?"

Her mom nodded and leaned into her husband's arms. "How did you find us?"

He kissed her temple. "That walking thing you wear in your bra to count your steps. They tracked the GPS."

"Oh." Her mom's eyebrows rose. "I forgot all about that."

So much for the wrist tracker Nari wanted to buy for her. She struggled to stay conscious and looked at Wolfe and Raider. Their tall forms morphed and darkness edged through her vision. "Opal is in league with Lassiter. She's the mastermind." Nari leaned down, making sure Angus was still breathing. "Angus? I love you," she whispered.

Then she passed out.

Chapter Forty

The last face Angus wanted to see upon waking up in the hospital was Special Agent Tom Rutherford's. Angus blinked, his arm feeling as if it was caught in a vise. Rutherford ate from a bag of popcorn, leaning against the counter, with Special Agent Fields and Detective Tate Bianchi next to him. Angus coughed. "What are you guys? The three wise men?"

Tate snorted. "How are you feeling?"

"Like I got shot. Again." Angus looked around the hospital room. "Where's Nari?" He began to sit up.

Tate waved him back down. "She's getting checked out in another room, but she's fine. Wolfe and Raider are with her now."

Angus winced. "How bad is her neck?"

Rutherford shook his head. "She's fine. Just bruised." He crumpled up the empty bag and tossed it into the trash. "Her mom is fine, too. The doctors are monitoring her heart rate after the electrical blast, but she's bossing them all around. Seems like a nice lady."

Had Rutherford mellowed? "Am I dead?" Angus asked.

"No." Fields pulled out a notebook. "However, considering the head of HDD turned out to be a major wack job, we need to get your statement now rather than later. We've already gotten statements from Nari and her mom. Your turn."

"Wait a minute," Angus said, pushing a button near the bed to sit all the way up. He looked at the IV stuck in his arm. "Anybody want to catch me up on myself? Just for a second?"

Tate rolled his dark eyes. "You're fine. The bullet went right through your shoulder; they just had to stitch you up."

Rutherford smiled, his blond hair perfectly in place. "You might need some rehab, but don't be a wuss. You're fine, and you caught a serial killer. Dana Mulberry has already written a story, and you're once again a hero. Yay, you."

Angus blinked, trying to keep up and not go right back to sleep. "What about Opal?"

"Oh, she's in custody," Fields said, tapping his pen against the paper. "She'll be charged and dropped into a hole somewhere far from the HDD. Go ahead and tell us everything so it can be redacted pretty damn quick."

Angus sighed and ran through everything that had happened. "How's Nari's father?"

"He seems like a great guy," Tate said. "He's hovering over her mom and Nari. Guy used to be a marine."

Angus blinked. "I meant Quan Zhang, who's the second to Opal at the HDD." He narrowed his gaze at the two agents. "Did you two know that Nari's biological father was second in command?"

"Yep," Fields said. "They have the same name, dude."

Had Special Agent Fields just called him "dude"? Angus gave him a look. "I'm aware of that, but the names of the higher-ups aren't actually on our paychecks, are they? We're a secret agency for a reason." Somehow, it was reassuring that Fields and Rutherford had known of Nari's connection to the leadership in HDD. Not that he was starting to like these guys. Not at all.

Tate cleared his throat. "Your agency is weird. Who doesn't know the names of their bosses?"

Fields shrugged. "Force's team has never quite been on the inside, and I guess the administrator had a lot to do with that."

"Plus, you're a bunch of screwups," Rutherford said helpfully. "Now finish with your statement, would you?"

Angus did so, trying to ignore the pain in his arm. Wait a minute. "Did you jackwads tell them to hold off with the pain meds until after I gave my statement?"

"Of course," Rutherford said. "If you'd hurry it up, I'll call in the nurse."

Angus glared at him and then finished his statement, answering questions from all three men until he'd repeated himself about three times. "I'm done. If you want to talk to me again, find my lawyer. Well, find *a* lawyer."

Tate brightened. "Hey. I forgot to tell you. Scott came out of the coma and verified your story. Although I guess it's all verified now anyway."

Angus settled. "Scott is okay?" The weight of the guilt

he'd felt over getting his lawyer shot had been stifling. It started to lift.

"Yeah. He will be, although it might be a long run of recuperation. He's back, though, and he said to tell you that you'd be receiving a bill." Tate winced. "I'm glad I won't see that number."

That was a worry for another day.

"Goodbye," Angus said pointedly. "Please find Nari and send her in." He needed to make sure she was all right. The feeling of his hands on her neck would give him nightmares for years, but she'd been correct. The move had made Lassiter open the door.

The three men took their leave, and soon another walked inside.

Angus partially sat up. "Deputy Administrator Zhang. How are you?"

A bandage covered part of Zhang's forehead and he walked as if his bones hurt. "I am well. How are you?"

Angus could use a big old dose of painkiller. "I'm fine. Bullet just went right on through." What were the correct words of sympathy for somebody whose girlfriend had turned out to be a psychotic killer who had just been using him? "Nari was really brave and put Opal down, if I remember right."

Zhang shuffled his feet. "I was wrong about you, and I apologize."

"You were wrong about Nari," Angus countered evenly. "She's the one deserving of an apology. For a lot of things."

Zhang sighed and looked down. "I know. You're right." He breathed in and then met Angus's gaze. "I don't know who will be made administrator, but I'd like to reinstate your team, if you'd like to remain employed and working together."

Hope filled Angus, along with the persistent pain in his arm. "With full pay for the time we've been off?"

"Yes. Of course." Zhang touched the bandage on his head and then put his shoulders back, looking more in control than he had when he'd walked inside. "Please take a couple of days, talk to the team, and then let me know. Good job today." He turned on a polished loafer and exited the room.

Angus sat back. If Nari didn't show up soon, he was going looking for her. Where the hell was she?

Nari hugged her mom as she rested on the bed, ordering the doctors around. "Let them do their jobs," Nari whispered.

Her dad, his blond hair wavy, sat next to her, patting her hand. "Let her boss everybody. It makes her happy."

Nari chuckled. "That was so brave, the way you jumped in front of the Taser, Mom."

Her mom grinned. "It was the only way your crazy plan of Angus strangling you was going to work." She coughed and then laughed. "I was terrified, but I acted well. When Angus threw his arm, I acted like he'd hit me."

Nari sighed. "He didn't connect?"

"Of course not. I can fake a hit." She pushed Nari in the arm. "The nurse just told us that he was out of surgery. You should go reassure that boy that he didn't hurt you. Well, maybe play it a little soft so he stays mellow, but you know what I mean." She leaned toward her husband. "Nari used the L word. The real L word."

"Wait a minute. I haven't met this guy yet," her dad protested, his blue eyes gleaming.

Nari sighed. "I'll be back." She hugged her dad and exited the room, almost running into Quan. "Hi."

"Hi," he said, leading her around the corner. "I want a moment to speak with you before I go home. I'm sorry for, well, everything." He awkwardly patted her shoulder.

Her eyebrows rose. "All right."

He stepped back. "I'm not a demonstrative man and I don't know how to be parental."

She looked at the bruise on his head. "Do you not want me around because you sucked as a dad?"

His smile was a surprise. "Yes. Well, it wasn't that I didn't want you around. I just couldn't figure out why you'd want to be around me, so I figured it wasn't a good thing."

She shook her head. "Working for a super-secret governmental agency makes everyone paranoid. Maybe I just wanted to get to know you." She could finally see the flawed human being in the father she'd never known. Nari looked back at her mom's room. "Besides, don't worry about it. I have the best parents in the world."

He nodded. "That's what I thought. But I would like to know you and maybe be friends?"

That was odd, but what the heck. "I'd like that." She needed to see Angus, and now.

"Good. I told Agent Force that he could put his team back together, and if he does, you have the choice of working with that team or taking the job Opal offered

you. It was actually my idea—that job, I mean. It's needed."
He shuffled his feet.

The team was back in action. Nari nearly hopped. "I'll think about it. Thanks." She'd consider everything later. "I have to go now."

He nodded. "We'll talk soon."

She turned and walked as sedately as she could toward the room where Angus was supposed to be. Upon arriving, she had to make her way through the entire team. Wolfe had somehow gotten the kitten inside, and the animal was perched on Angus's chest, purring contentedly.

Angus lay in the bed, looking dangerous and irritated, hooked up to an IV. "Where the hell is Nari?" he snapped.

"I'm here," she said soothingly, moving around Wolfe's solid bulk to reach the head of the bed. "How's the shoulder?"

"Fine." He looked her over, his eyes flaring at the marks on her neck. "Jesus. Did I do that?"

She touched her bruised skin. "Considering we're both alive right now, I'll take a couple of bruises." She smiled at Pippa and Malcolm, who'd moved out of the way so she could stand by Angus. "Did you tell everyone the team can go back to work?"

"Yes," Brigid said, holding Raider's hand and positively beaming. "Yay. Back to work. Do we get a new office?"

"One with windows would be nice," Dana said, snuggling into Wolfe's side. "I'll text Millie to tell her to get back home."

Angus cleared his throat. "Nari told me she loved me.'"

Nari started, looking down at his handsome face. "What are you doing?"

He shrugged. "Like they're not a bunch of gossips. Plus, we're family. I figured it out—why we all drive each other crazy. We're family, and we share stuff like that with family."

Was he drugged? She looked at the IV.

He chuckled. "No, I still haven't gotten pain meds, which I wouldn't mind, if anybody sees a nurse." He grabbed her hand, holding tight, his eyes so green it almost hurt to look at them. "I love you, Nari Zhang. When I first met you, right now, and forever. No matter what, you're everything to me."

Whoa. Nari's knees went weak. She swallowed. "I, ah, love you too." Heat filled her face.

He pulled back the covers and yanked her into the bed, throwing the blankets over her. "I'm not the type to play around or date or seek. I know what I want and it's you. No taking it slow. People keep shooting at us; we need to enjoy every damn minute we have together."

Nari sat next to him and snuggled into his unbandaged side. "When you start talking you sure do it with a vengeance," she said, smiling at Pippa's teary expression.

"I know. Marry me?" Angus said.

She stilled. He hadn't been kidding. He was all or nothing. "Yes," she said.

The group around them, their assembled and chosen family, all burst into pleased applause. Kat meowed, bit Angus's chin, and then went back to sleep.

Angus sighed. "We might as well go all in and buy one of the lots in the cul-de-sac. What do you think?"

She put her hand over his chest and kissed his whiskered chin. "I think yes. I love you, Angus Force." In fact, she always had.

Epilogue

Angus Force walked along the trail from the lake in Kentucky, a full bucket of fish in his left hand. Roscoe scouted ahead, chased a rabbit, and then ran back to pant around Angus's feet. He'd had a beer while on the lake— just one—and the dog was still irritated he hadn't shared.

They reached the outside of the cabin and Roscoe stopped, his ears perking up.

Angus grinned. "I know. We're not alone."

Nari walked out onto the porch, a glass of wine in her hand. She waved. "Did you get dinner this time, or is it frozen pizza again?"

He took a moment to drink her in. Dark hair, even darker eyes, and a smile only for him. "We caught dinner." Though he'd be the one cooking it. The woman had almost burned down his cabin the night before boiling water. Sure, it might've been his fault for distracting her and getting her naked, but still. She was a menace in the kitchen.

Roscoe ran down the trail to her, licking her legs. She dropped to her haunches and hugged him around the neck, her hands rubbing his furry body.

Lucky dog.

Angus walked forward, his arm feeling better after the two weeks at the cabin. The bruises had faded from Nari's neck, and all their many other injuries had healed.

She stood and smiled, her eyes alight with happiness. "This was a good idea. Taking a month off and relaxing."

The month's vacation was a good idea for the entire team before they returned to work for the HDD, which everyone had decided to do. He leaned down and took her mouth, tasting chocolate and wine. "I figured you'd like Kentucky," he said, kissing her again.

"I do." She looked at the bucket. "I am not cleaning those."

"I know." He set it down and pulled her closer for an even deeper kiss. "This is our last night before chaos descends. Maybe we should just make a run for it now."

"Nope." She kept her arms around his waist and leaned back. "This is the perfect place for a retreat. Raider and Malcolm managed to rent really nice RVs, and Wolfe somehow got his hands on a motor home. Millie said she'd be fine in a tent, and Jethro is still insisting on staying at the motel in town, although I think we can change his mind."

"And Serena?" Angus asked, knowing full well that Nari and Pippa were starting to matchmake with poor Jethro.

Nari shrugged. "I think she's bunking with Millie, but we'll see. You never know."

Right. Well, so long as he was bunking with Nari, he didn't care. "This isn't really the type of team that likes retreats." They weren't in to bonding or anything. "Please tell me you don't have activities planned."

"Just fun stuff like making s'mores and fishing," she promised. "And Pippa is going to teach me to cook."

"No. Not in my cabin," he protested. "I love this place."

She slapped him in the stomach. "Funny. Very funny. Oh, and my parents are going to pop in the second week. My dad still wants to arm wrestle you."

Angus sighed. How had he gone from being all alone with his dog to having this many people in his life? People he'd do anything for. The anger that had ridden him for so long was gone. He shook his head. "I don't know. Maybe you should try to convince me some more."

She smiled, tucking her hand in his. "Now that's a good idea. Let's go inside."

He forgot all about his fish and walked into the cabin with her.

Once there, she turned toward him. "I love you, you know."

He did, and he savored the warmth of that love every day. "I love you more." It was the truth. It had to be. Then he kissed her and took full advantage of their last night of peace together for a couple of weeks.

His family was on the way.

Please read on for an excerpt from the next book in Rebecca Zanetti's Dark Protectors series.

REBEL'S KARMA

Chapter One

The smell of the earth, deep and true, centered her in the hastily created tunnel. It probably said something about Karma that she preferred darkness, muddy walls, and being underground to any other circumstances. Battery-operated lanterns had been dropped haphazardly along the trail, their artificial light dancing across the packed dirt walls and highlighting minerals she couldn't name as she descended quickly, the swish of her skirt the only sound.

She bent her head, trying to stay in the moment and not panic at the job to come. One she was no more prepared for than she had been for mating a Kurjan general nearly two centuries ago. Or was it closer to three?

Taking a deep breath, she turned the corner and faced the cell. The cell that had been dug just the day before, in case it was needed.

It was.

She swallowed.

The male sprawled across the ground, so large he could probably spread his arms and reach the cement blocks on one side and the steel bars on the other. If he'd been conscious. Bruises mottled his face and neck, while a wound bled freely beneath his jaw. The red ran past his ear to pool on the dirt beneath him.

She couldn't breathe.

It really was *him*. Even with bruises, blood, and dirt covering his face, she recognized him from more than three years ago. He'd tried to pull her into a helicopter with him after he'd attacked the Kurjan stronghold. He was bad, he was the enemy, and yet . . . he'd saved several kidnapped human females from the Kurjans.

Had he thought he was saving her? Or had he hurt those human females? Were they now in worse danger than they'd faced when captives of the Kurjan nation?

She waited patiently, as she'd been taught. The guard would get to her when he had time. The medical supplies in her pack became heavy, so she set them down, stepping closer to the bars to study the male.

Benjamin Horatio Lawrence Reese. He was a vampire-demon hybrid, large even for his kind. At about six-foot-seven, or maybe -eight, he was as tall as many Kurjans. The wideness of his torso tapered down at his waist, then was matched by the length of his legs. His boots had to be a size eighteen, and his hands were big enough to cause colossal damage. Oh, she'd been hit before, but one punch from him and she'd be dead.

He could never know how much she already knew about him. How she'd been training for this day for years—since he'd tried to take her from another Kurjan holding. Her home.

The air changed, and she stiffened as the guard made his way down the tunnel, his white hair glowing as he came closer. He was a Cyst: one of the elite soldiers and spiritual leaders of the Kurjan nation. A single line of white hair bisected his pale scalp, leading down to a long braid. His eyes were a deep purple tinged with red, and he spared her not a glance as he unlocked the cell and then stepped back.

She took a deep breath and entered, wincing as the coppery smell of blood assaulted her nostrils. Then she dropped to her knees and reached inside the pack for the materials that would clot the bleeding wound. How badly injured the hybrid must've been after the skirmish to still be bleeding.

The second she touched his head, his eyes opened.

He was fully alert in a second, his deep eyes an unreal, metallic color. "Karma," he murmured.

She drew back. He remembered her name? Nobody remembered her name.

"Do you need blood?" she whispered, leaning closer, even as the guard locked the cell door and disappeared down the hallway, leaving her with the enemy. Right now she was useless to the Kurjans, so if the prisoner killed her, they'd find a plan B.

"No." Benjamin sat up, looked around, and put his back to the cement brick wall. He took up all the available space in the cell with his impressive size.

She shook her head, her lips trembling. "You must be badly injured or you would not have been captured. You need blood."

"I let them take me. I've been searching for you for years."

God. The Kurjans had been correct. He really had been looking for her. "The baby? Rose?" Karma held her breath. When Benjamin's people had attacked the Kurjan holding, she'd gone with her instincts of the moment and forced him to take a toddler who had been kidnapped by the Kurjans—and she'd paid for that decision. "Is Rose well?"

Benjamin nodded. "Rose is fine. She's at Realm headquarters with a nice family."

Relief and fear were an odd combination in Karma's blood. "Realm Headquarters?" The Realm was the enemy of the Kurjans. Its people were evil, or so she'd been taught. She'd always wondered, because lies were everywhere. She held out medical supplies, although the wound beneath his jaw was already closing as he sent healing cells where they were necessary.

"I don't need those," he murmured, studying her with an intensity that shot tremors through her abdomen.

"I don't understand why you'd come looking for me," she said, sitting back and keeping her knees covered with her dress. It had been the plan, but she hadn't believed it. The Kurjan leaders had noted that this male kept showing up in different attacks, and he took ridiculous risks for a soldier with his experience. They'd known he was coming. Why would this male put himself in danger for her? "You let them take you hostage?"

"Yes." Benjamin's voice was low and rough, with a hint of what must be demon ancestry.

She rested her hands on the thin material over her knees. "I don't understand."

A bone snapped loudly into place somewhere in his body, but he didn't even flinch. "Let's start here. I'm Benny Reese." He held out a hand the size of a frying pan, as if they were meeting at a village game instead of in a cell.

She hesitated and then slid hers against his. "Karma."

His hold and shake were gentle, and he released her before the mating allergy could hurt either of them. She'd been mated centuries ago to a Kurjan, and no other male could touch her for long without both of them developing terrible rashes.

"What's your last name?" he asked. Another bone popped into place.

She jerked at the sound. "I do not have a last name."

"Oh." He looked beyond her at the steel bars securing the cell. "I was out for a while. Where are we?"

"We are at a temporary holding area before you are transported to a more secure location." She coughed. "For questioning."

His smile nearly knocked her over. Even the slight tipping of his lips turned his rugged face from dangerously hard to nearly boyish with charm. Amusement, real and true, glimmered in his metallic eyes for a moment. "Darlin', I've been tortured before. You don't need to worry yourself about that."

She had bigger things to worry about than the life of this massive hybrid. She allowed herself one moment to stare into his unusual eyes. Oh, many immortals had metallic silver eyes, gold eyes, even copper or purple. But his were a combination of all metallic colors, mingling into a hard-edged glint, even with the humor lurking there. In another time, she might've thought him beautiful. She'd learned long ago that beauty masked the darkest of evils.

Vampires were bad, demons were bad, and this male was a hybrid of both. When he decided to kill her—and he would at some point—she wouldn't stand much chance of surviving. Yet she still couldn't comprehend why he'd come for her. "Why are you here?"

"For you. To rescue you because I couldn't last time." He stretched out his arms and healed a broken finger in his left hand.

His words didn't make any sense. "Why?" Surely his ego wasn't such that he'd spent three years chasing her down, risking his life just because she'd rejected his help last time. She wasn't worth that.

He sighed. "I'd hoped to ease you into the truth, but here it is." He held up his right hand, showing a demon marking with a jagged R in the center. The R was a crest representing his surname: Reese. Demons mated with a branding and a bite, while the marking was transferred from the demon to the mate during sex.

Her mouth dropped open and she hurried to shut it. "You're mated?" Why did that thought nauseate her? How odd.

"No. The brand appeared when I touched you three years ago." His chin lowered, and he studied her, towering over her even as he sat. "When you shoved me away and refused to get into that helicopter with me."

She snorted and then quickly recovered. "Impossible. I'm already mated." Well, she had been mated a couple of centuries ago, although her Kurjan mate had died shortly thereafter. Sometimes she forgot what he had looked like, and that was fine with her. "Your brand appeared for someone else."

"No." Benjamin looked down at the dark marking. "The mark hasn't faded, and it's pulsing like a live wire now that you're near."

Oh, Lord. Her research on Benjamin stated he might be insane. She sighed. Dangerous and unstable? There was no way she could succeed in this mission. "Benjamin—"

"Benny. Might as well get cozy with me now." His smile held charm and determination that warmed her in an unexpected way.

For the second time in her life, she let her instincts take over. "Just leave. Take an opening and find freedom," she whispered tersely, her stomach cramping. "Forget about me."

"Not a chance." His gaze ran over her face like a physical touch.

Movement sounded down the tunnel, and she stiffened.

Benjamin tensed and set his jaw. "Get ready, darlin'. We're about to escape this place."

Connect with  U s

Visit us online at
KensingtonBooks.com
to read more from your favorite authors, see books
by series, view reading group guides, and more.

 Join us on social media

for sneak peeks, chances to win books and prize packs,
and to share your thoughts with other readers.

facebook.com/kensingtonpublishing
twitter.com/kensingtonbooks

Tell us what you think!

To share your thoughts, submit a review,
or sign up for our eNewsletters, please visit:
KensingtonBooks.com/TellUs.

Books by Bestselling Author
Fern Michaels

___The Jury	0-8217-7878-1	$6.99US/$9.99CAN
___Sweet Revenge	0-8217-7879-X	$6.99US/$9.99CAN
___Lethal Justice	0-8217-7880-3	$6.99US/$9.99CAN
___Free Fall	0-8217-7881-1	$6.99US/$9.99CAN
___Fool Me Once	0-8217-8071-9	$7.99US/$10.99CAN
___Vegas Rich	0-8217-8112-X	$7.99US/$10.99CAN
___Hide and Seek	1-4201-0184-6	$6.99US/$9.99CAN
___Hokus Pokus	1-4201-0185-4	$6.99US/$9.99CAN
___Fast Track	1-4201-0186-2	$6.99US/$9.99CAN
___Collateral Damage	1-4201-0187-0	$6.99US/$9.99CAN
___Final Justice	1-4201-0188-9	$6.99US/$9.99CAN
___Up Close and Personal	0-8217-7956-7	$7.99US/$9.99CAN
___Under the Radar	1-4201-0683-X	$6.99US/$9.99CAN
___Razor Sharp	1-4201-0684-8	$7.99US/$10.99CAN
___Yesterday	1-4201-1494-8	$5.99US/$6.99CAN
___Vanishing Act	1-4201-0685-6	$7.99US/$10.99CAN
___Sara's Song	1-4201-1493-X	$5.99US/$6.99CAN
___Deadly Deals	1-4201-0686-4	$7.99US/$10.99CAN
___Game Over	1-4201-0687-2	$7.99US/$10.99CAN
___Sins of Omission	1-4201-1153-1	$7.99US/$10.99CAN
___Sins of the Flesh	1-4201-1154-X	$7.99US/$10.99CAN
___Cross Roads	1-4201-1192-2	$7.99US/$10.99CAN

Romantic Suspense from
Lisa Jackson